OFF AND RUNNING

OFF AND RUNNING

A Novel By

PHILIP REED

BRASH
BOOKS

Text copyright 2015 Philip Reed

ISBN: 1941298710
ISBN 13: 9781941298718

Published by Brash Books, LLC
12120 State Line #253
Leawood, Kansas 66209

www.brash-books.com

For my father, Tom, who always inspires me.

PROLOGUE

Jack cut the headlights on his old Nissan Pathfinder and backed into the spot among the trees where he had chosen to hide. He killed the engine and settled in, watching the big house across the road, perched on a rocky knob overlooking the cove and the ocean beyond.

It was almost five o'clock, and Jack saw the nursing staff was changing shifts. Lights turned on and off in the house. Cars pulled in and out of the driveway. Through a front window he saw Garrett, the great man's son, leaning over his desk. He was reading something as he absentmindedly smoothed his thick, graying hair. Seeing Garrett again, after all this time, made Jack's stomach churn.

The leather seats creaked as Jack reached into the duffel bag on the seat beside him and took out the little five-shot Smith & Wesson. The cop who sold it to him, back when he was a police reporter on the *Arizona Sun*, said he bobbed off the hammer so it could slide into your pocket nice and easy, without catching on your clothes. Reaching into another pocket, he checked to make sure he had the key he would use to enter the house. That is, of course, if they hadn't changed the locks since he left.

Jack made sure the dome light was turned off, and then he eased open the car door and stepped out. It was dark now, and a cold wind kicked up and rustled the leaves around him. The long drive up here from Los Angeles had left him stiff, and his ears felt plugged. He waited until his head cleared and he found he could hear the surf booming out beyond the cove.

For a long moment Jack stood there, balanced on a point in time, a sharp and significant point from which he knew he could still return to all the things he had ever loved in his life. But then the moment passed. He slid the gun into his pocket and started off through the trees, heading for the big house.

PART ONE

THE HOLLYWOOD HILLS

ONE

They were cruising up the canyon into the Hollywood Hills in Carolyn's green '65 Mustang with the radio blasting and the top down. The smell of dust and afternoon heat was in Jack's nostrils, and the promise of a new writing job was lifting his spirits.

Carolyn, his literary agent, had phoned him a few days before and asked, "How do you feel about Walt Stuckey?"

"Loved his show," Jack said, trying to guess where this was going. "But I don't know much about Stuckey himself."

"No one does. That's the thing. But he wants to write his bio now, so maybe you can write it for him."

"Me?"

"Yeah. I pitched you to him. How you'd been a reporter, a playwright, and a TV writer. So you understand show business. Not only that, but you're both from New Jersey. So you can both"—she broke into a very poor Jersey accent—"talk to each odder in dems and dose, ya know?" She dropped the imitation. "It could be a perfect match. So if he likes you, you'll write his bio. What do you think?"

Jack thought it was worth a shot. And besides that, he really needed a paying gig. So now, here they were, bombing along in Carolyn's convertible and listening to news reports of how in a couple of months, when the calendar flipped over to the year 2000, the Y2K bug was going to bring down civilization. *Just let me get this book written first,* Jack thought as they pulled up in front of the gates to Stuckey's house. *All I want is my fifteen minutes of fame.*

They climbed out of the Mustang and walked to a gate from which they looked down on a house shrouded in trees. In the silence of the canyon, Jack heard the gurgle of a stream somewhere. Carolyn pressed a doorbell. Below, in the house, they saw a face look up at them through the front door window. *Bzzzzt!* The gate swung open, and they clomped down redwood steps. The front door opened, and an old man stepped into view.

"How are ya, Carolyn?" the man said, shaking her hand. "Thanks for comin'."

In those few words Jack heard the Joizie accent and knew he was talking to the famous Walt Stuckey, one of the greatest entertainers of the century. Sure, the face had changed, the frizzy hair had fallen out, the eyes were milky and slung in droopy bags, age spots unkindly decorated his face. But the voice was the same—the voice that had spoken to him so long ago.

"This is Jack Dillon, the writer I was telling you about," Carolyn said.

Walt cupped his ear. "I'm deaf as a post. Your name again?"

"Jack Dillon."

"Jack." He raised a finger, committing the name to memory. "I got a lousy head for names." He turned and walked into the house, waving them to follow as he repeated, "Jack, Jack, Jack... Okay. Got it." He suddenly turned, craning to look up at Jack. "Christ, you're tall. How the hell tall are you, anyway?"

"Six two."

"Six two! What a wonderful sound that has to it. Six *anything*, I'd take." He began walking again then stopped. Jack almost ran into him. He jabbed a finger in Jack's gut. "Football?"

"Track. And I teach in a dojo."

"Joe who?"

"Dojo. I teach karate."

"Karate? Watch out for you!" He made a few quick chops accompanied by yips and cries of vaguely Asian origin. Kinda silly, really, but Jack couldn't help laughing. *Some guys can make anything funny*, Jack thought. Besides, it was so strange to be here with the real Walt Stuckey. He had an odd, unreal feeling, as if he was hearing him on TV, or that he himself had wandered into a TV skit.

Jack remembered how *The Walt Stuckey Hour* had come on at ten o'clock on Sunday nights and had run from 1967 to its abrupt and mysterious cancelation in 1973. Walt Stuckey was the man with the watery eyes and the frizzy hair that he scratched in a constant state of confusion. He was the pie-in-the-face butt of every joke. And while America watched and laughed—and talked about the show the next day—no one really noticed Walt Stuckey. They were watching the eye-popping guest stars with gaping cleavage and purring voices, the wisecracking comedians with the steady stream of one-liners, the jugglers and gymnasts and knife throwers.

The show came on too late for Jack to watch, but his parents tuned in every week. And as they settled in front of their ancient TV set, Jack snuck out of his bed and lay at the top of the stairs. He could hear Walt introducing the acts for that week's show, capping the lineup with his trademark slogan: "Get ready, folks, 'cause we're *off and running!*"

During those moments, Jack heard something so rare in his house—the sound of his father's laughter. Jack's father was a huge frightening man whose mouth was set in a permanent frown of disapproval. He was a tool and die maker who went off each day to a job he hated. Yet he laughed whenever Stuckey fell for the guest stars' jokes and had his toupee yanked away by a fishing hook or his tie scissored off.

Walt led them to a couch surrounding a big glass coffee table. On the walls were beautiful paintings, and somehow Jack knew they were originals. Walt bent to sit, got halfway down, then just let go, landing on the cushions with a loud *oooof*, saying, "Down to China!" Walt paused as he looked closely at Jack then turned away.

"Carolyn, Jack, you have to excuse me. Just before you got here I looked at my calendar and…well, I'm such a goddamn idiot. I don't know why I do these things." They waited. "I musta forgot you were coming or—anyway, I been having trouble with my teeth, and I made this dentist appointment. Gotta leave here in ten minutes if you can believe that nonsense. What an idiot I am sometimes." He clapped his hands. "But maybe we can get to know each other in the time we have."

"Sure," Carolyn said, hunching forward eagerly, ready for the pitch. She was a big woman, with big hair and a generous smile. She ran her agency out of her West LA apartment, and she didn't exactly represent name writers. But she was fiercely loyal to her clients and felt they were always on the verge of breaking through. She shared the excitement of their dreams of success and also the crushing disappointment of their rejections. And she had saved Jack's butt more than once by landing him quickie writing jobs as the wolves circled his door.

"Walt, as I mentioned on the phone, Jack's the perfect writer for this project. He's a veteran journalist—so he can do all the interviewing and research required. He was an investigative reporter in Arizona, and he even went undercover in the casinos of Las Vegas. Then his career segued into TV where he wrote for television and film. Not only that, but like you, he's from New Jersey, so he can understand the influences that must have—"

Walt held up his hand, cutting off the sales pitch. "Okay, Carolyn. Okay. Thank you." He turned to Jack. "Have you written anything I've ever heard of?"

Tough question. But six years in Hollywood had taught Jack a lot about self-promotion. It wasn't the facts, it was how you presented them. Besides, he felt oddly relaxed sitting here with this forgotten TV legend.

"I wrote one of the first episodes of *True Blues*."

"That cop show on CBS?" Walt seemed impressed. "How'd you get that gig?"

"The executive producer read a play I'd written. He liked it and—"

"So whyn't they put you on staff?"

"They were creating a new show and moved me across the lot. *Real Cops*—great show, but they didn't give it a chance to find an audience. The network yanked it after nine episodes."

Walt nodded sympathetically. "They're gutless wonders up there in the Black Tower."

Jack laughed, thinking of the black high-rise where the network execs had their offices looming over the writers' bungalows on the studio lot in Burbank.

"Oh, so you know about the Black Tower?" Walt said.

"What TV writer doesn't?"

Walt scratched his baldpate where the trademark frizzy hair used to be. The voice, the gestures, the everyman attitude, were wonderfully familiar to Jack. And it seemed so improbable that he would be here, alone in this huge house with this TV legend. He had somehow thought that Walt Stuckey had died unnoticed, disappearing along with all the other good things from his childhood.

The phone rang, echoing through the house, and Walt reached for a portable receiver on the coffee table. He looked at the caller ID number and frowned.

"It's my son," he said. "Excuse me just a minute." He clicked the phone on. "Garrett, I've got some people here, so I'm gonna have to—"

Jack heard an insistent voice coming through the earpiece.

"I know, Garrett. I know. Who? Oh it's—it's that writer I was telling you about. Okay. Call you back."

Walt disconnected and seemed confused for a moment. "My son Garrett, he's after me to do this show—kind of a father-and-son reunion thing. He pitched it to the network and—I don't know. Anyway, where was I?"

Walt rubbed his head again, looking old and lost.

"Your autobiography," Carolyn prompted.

"Right," Walt said, refocusing. "I feel I got *something* to say. I don't know what. I'm not a writer. Never was. But if I could just find the right writer and tell my stories, maybe something would fit together, and there'd be a book. But maybe no one even wants to hear about Walt Stuckey anymore."

"What are you talking about?" Jack said, surprised at his own words. "Everyone loved your show. I know I did. I don't see how a book about you can miss."

Walt's face began to change. The features that had drooped and fallen with age rearranged themselves into a smile, and Jack was suddenly looking at a much younger man.

"You tellin' me you watched my show?"

"Hell yeah."

"Naw, you're too young. That was back in '67—over thirty years ago."

"I was almost six when it first aired. I used to watch it with my parents."

Actually, Jack thought, *I didn't watch it. I listened to it.* Remembering this, he traveled back in time to the old house. He could feel the hardwood boards cool on his cheek as he lay there, listening to the magic of television, broadcast from Manhattan, the buildings of which were just visible over the hilltops east of his New Jersey town.

The old man's milky eyes cleared, and they drilled suspiciously into Jack, looking for the opportunist, someone who saw the pile of cash and was ready to say anything to dig out his gold.

"Jack, tell me something, wouldja? Seriously now. The stakes are high. We might even get a shot with this father-and-son show, and that means I'd be in the public eye for the first time in decades. I want to get reintroduced to America. So I'm gonna ask you flat out: Are you the guy to write my book?"

Jack mulled the question, thinking of the money he needed, and Sarah's impatience with his writing career. Maybe this could be his meal ticket. But he hated himself for thinking like that—like some Hollywood hack. So he let all the conflicting thoughts dissolve and spoke when he felt sincere again.

"Walt, I gotta be honest, 'cause it's always easier to do that up front."

Walt nodded.

Jack continued. "A lot depends on what your idea of good writing is. If you think good writing is using lots of fancy words from a thesaurus, or making analogies and all that, then I'm not the guy for you. But if you want someone who can tell an honest story in simple words anyone can understand then, yeah, I'm your man. Besides, you're never gonna find a bigger fan of your show."

Jack sensed his words were hitting home. But then Walt's eyes clouded again. And age returned to his face.

"Ah, who the hell knows? I've got these stories—just memories really. I worked with the greatest entertainers of my time. But maybe no one gives a damn anymore."

"Would you cut that out? I was telling you how my parents watched the show, right? Well my dad was a huge fan and—" Jack paused, ready to tell Walt about his dad, downstairs, laughing. Maybe he could make Walt see how he had given rare moments of laughter to a man who basically thought that life was nothing more than a fistfight in a dark alley.

But before Jack could continue, Walt slapped his thighs signaling the end of the meeting with a loud, "Okay!" He heaved himself to his feet.

Carolyn intervened. "Jack brought some samples of his writing. Can we leave them with you?"

"Sure, sure."

Carolyn set a folder of articles on the glass coffee table. Walt didn't even look at them. He was brooding again, walking them out of the house, mumbling, "I don't know what's wrong with me, setting up a dentist appointment. Maybe I have that disease where you lose your memory. I always forget what you call that."

"Alzheimer's," Jack said then laughed. "I guess I walked into that one."

Walt laughed too. They were almost to the door when Walt said, "So what exit did you take?"

Jack smiled. It was a test. People from New Jersey always asked what exit you took off the New Jersey Turnpike.

"Sixty-eight onto Route 46 to Ridgefield Park."

"Next to Hackensack?"

"Yeah. That's the place."

Walt nodded, satisfied. He seemed to connect something in his mind, and smiled. "I can hear your accent when you say 'yeah.' You go, *yih*."

"Hey, what can I say? New Jersey born and raised."

"That's a good thing," Walt said. Then he seemed to drift away into the past. He spoke in an odd, disconnected tone of voice. "Ya know, you remind me of a guy who used to work for me. His name was Jack too."

"A good guy, I hope."

"Yeah, he was the best." Walt seemed to suddenly snap back to the present. "See ya later, Jack."

"I hope so."

And Walt Stuckey closed the door.

They piled back into Carolyn's Mustang and headed down the winding canyon road. Jack thought how odd it was that Walt had let them come, even though he had a dentist appointment. Then, suddenly, it hit him that the whole thing had been a ruse, just a way to take a quick look at a writer, a hack who might be able to breathe life into his past without wasting a whole hell of a lot of time. And then Jack's negative side took over, and the voices in his head began the familiar predictions of rejection and failure. He began thinking he'd never hear from Walt Stuckey again, that it was just another near miss like the others he'd had since moving to LA. Another brush with fame, then back into obscurity and isolation. Maybe the Y2K bug and the end of society would be a blessing in disguise.

That night after dinner, while Chloe did her homework at the kitchen table, Jack told Sarah about the meeting. He tried to describe how disorienting it felt to be in Walt Stuckey's presence, hearing that voice again, seeing the face so aged and yet recognizable.

Sarah looked up from a sink full of dishes. "So. Did you get the job?"

"Don't know yet."

"When will you know?"

"Carolyn's gonna call tomorrow. But I'm just saying, whatever happens, it was great to meet him, you know? It was like a piece of history. Can you understand that?"

She turned back to the dishes, and her distain hung in the air like a bad smell. He knew now they could get into a fight if he wanted to. He would say something sarcastic, and then they would argue about money and his career—or lack of it, as she would be quick to point out. And then there would be the yelling and the door slamming, and he would go to sleep on the couch in his office all pissed off and misunderstood.

He couldn't remember if they had fought that night. But he did remember that Carolyn called first thing the next day. It confirmed one of Jack's rules of show business: if *they* call you, it's good news; if you have to call *them*, you're chopped liver, as Walt might say.

"Walt liked you," Carolyn said over the phone.

"Yeah?" Jack was noncommittal, thinking it might be the good news before getting a kiss-off. What she said next he could still recall word for word.

"He's going to pay you ten grand to write a book proposal. That's an outline and four sample chapters. You get five grand up front, five when it's finished. When the book is sold, you'll split everything sixty/forty."

When the book is sold. *When*, not *if*. Jack loved the sound of that.

TWO

As the Walt Stuckey biography took shape, Sarah's attitude toward Jack's writing began to improve. She gradually warmed to his stories about Walt, laughing and later urging him to retell the stories for their friends. Once, he overheard her on the phone saying to a friend, "Did I tell you Jack is writing a book with Walt Stuckey? Yes, *that* Walt Stuckey. Isn't that a hoot? Jack's up at his house all the time. They're, like, buds."

In their weekly get-togethers sitting around the glass coffee table in Walt's house, Walt never asked Jack anything about his life. Occasionally Jack would volunteer a detail or two in reference to something they were discussing—he said he had a daughter and that he had been a police reporter in Phoenix and later an investigative reporter. Walt listened without response, as if forcing himself not to react. Jack wondered if Walt had learned not to encourage hangers-on who might glom onto him and later pressure him for a job or to borrow money.

One day, something happened that showed Jack how right he had been.

From time to time, the ringing phone interrupted their interviews. Jack switched off his tape recorder and waited while Walt took calls from a variety of people. Often, it was his son Garrett, a wannabe producer, calling to discuss the father-and-son comeback show he was pitching to the networks for them to cohost. But today, each time Walt spoke into the receiver, he looked puzzled and hung up. Finally, in frustration, Walt thrust the receiver at Jack. "See if you can understand what the hell this is all about!"

Jack listened and found it was a recorded operator's voice asking him to accept a collect call from a woman named Sandy Blades. Jack accepted the charges and a desperate woman's voice came on the line. "You have to help me. I—I used to work for Mr. Stuckey—clean his house—and I'm in jail now, in Salinas. I need money for my bail because—"

"What are you in for?" Jack asked. In the background he could hear echoing shouts, cell doors slamming.

"I didn't do nothin' wrong. Okay? They said I took some jewelry but—"

"Who?"

"The lady I work for. I clean houses, okay? But I didn't take nothin'. But Mr. Stuckey has to loan me five hundred dollars for bail…"

Jack relayed all this to Walt, who became enraged.

"Who is it?"

"Sandy Blades. You know her?"

Walt grabbed the receiver away from Jack and screamed into the phone, "Now you listen! I don't know you! I won't help you! And don't call again!" He slammed the phone down. Seconds later, it began ringing again. He looked at the phone as the ringing echoed through the rooms of the hillside house.

"*Those people*," he said, pointing at the phone. Then he looked up. On his face was a mixture of anger and loneliness. "At any one time, I have five people like that after me."

For two months Jack read every newsclip about Walt Stuckey he could find. He watched a collection of old tapes of the show and did hours of interviews with Walt. Then, one day, it felt like it was time to start writing. Besides that, Walt seemed eager to read some actual pages of the book. And yet, Jack sensed Walt was also nervous that what he read wouldn't be any good. This would invalidate the bond that they had shared in interviewing. *Pressure's on,* Jack thought. *Any idiot can ask questions.* It was time to prove himself as a writer.

Autumn was here now, and during the night, the first rain of the season hit LA. The steady downpour rinsed the coating of dust off the cars and the houses and even the leaves of the trees, the water flowing in dirty torrents into the gutters and from there into the sewers and out to the ocean. That morning arrived bringing with it cool, brilliant sunlight. The world was sparkling clean again. Jack went to the office in his apartment with the sunlight streaming through the window. The apartment was quiet since Sarah was at her job as a paralegal, and Chloe was at school. He sat at his desk and took out a lined yellow legal pad. He took a deep breath and focused on blocking all the negative voices that so often plagued his work. And he plunged in.

Jack opened the book with a simple, funny story that represented the theme of the book: Walt as an everyman. At the pinnacle of the show's success, Walt arrived at the stage door to the studio in Manhattan where the show was taped, only to be denied entrance. The guard, it seemed, watched the show all the time but never paid attention to Walt Stuckey. He couldn't believe that the Walt Stuckey on TV was this ordinary man demanding entrance to the best show in America. Of course Jack elaborated a bit and invented pieces of dialogue to tie the whole thing together.

As Jack wrote, he found the right words jumping into his mind. His pen moved across the legal pad under its own energy. Transitions were smooth as silk, jokes fresh and punchy. And throughout it all, he heard Walt's droll, understated voice, his self-deprecating take on his life, his successes, and the golden age of television. The voice was so distinct you could practically hear the Joizie accent.

A week later Jack arrived at Walt's house carrying the first sixty pages of the book in a manila envelope. It had a nice bulk to it. As they settled at the coffee table, Walt spied the envelope.

"Got somethin' for me?"

"Yeah, the first four chapters."

The envelope changed hands.

"Mmmmm. Thick." Walt hefted the envelope, feeling the weight, just as Jack had. "Okay. Good." Then he turned his eyes on Jack. "How do you feel about it?"

"It seemed to write itself. I haven't had that feeling in a while." Jack couldn't help smiling. "For a writer, there's no better feeling."

Walt nodded. "I hear ya, Jack. I hear ya." Then, almost shyly, he added, "I'm heading up north tonight." Walt spent his weekends at his Pajaro Beach house on the Monterey Peninsula. "I'll take it with me and read it there. I'll show it to my lady friend—I call her Lady Mary. Christ, she's tough. But if she likes it too, hey, we're golden."

Four days later, the night before Thanksgiving, Jack returned from the park with Chloe. The message light on his answering machine was flashing. He pressed play.

"Jack? Walt Stuckey. I read the stuff you gave me."

Jack held his breath.

"It's good. Damn good. I like it. Christ, it even passed the Mary test. Lady Mary thought it was a real kick in the pants!" The old man paused, then with real feeling he belted out his tagline: "We're off and running, kid." *Click.*

Jack saved that recording and played it for Sarah when she came home. They had a very happy Thanksgiving. Three weeks later Carolyn sold the autobiography, titled *Off and Running*, to Epic Press, for a $50,000 advance. It was less than Walt Stuckey had wanted. It was a whole lot more than Jack had dared hope for.

THREE

Jack arrived at Walt's one day in early December during a heavy rain. Sitting around the coffee table, they could see streams of water flowing down the windows. Outside, across the canyon, the brook that cut through the property had swelled to a torrent.

Now that they had a publisher, Walt had become especially talkative. Jack sensed that the reality of the book—of Walt's life story—was growing in the old man's mind. In fact, it was a vision that they shared. Although it wasn't printed and had no cover illustration, it was real to them both. As it developed and grew in their imagination, Walt opened up more and more. And on that day, Walt began sharing stories Jack knew would probably never make it into the book. Walt even told a bizarre story about how he always felt he was "too small," because once when he was bedding a starlet, she yawned as he entered her and said, "Is it in yet?"

They both laughed at that, and Walt said, "Sure, I guess you could say I'm famous. But I've had this feeling all my life that nothing I do is good enough. And now, like a jerk, I've passed this complex on to my kids."

"Who are you talking about?"

"Garrett, my oldest son."

"The others are from your second marriage?"

"No. Garrett and Suzie are from my first. Teddy and Pete are from my second. Anyway, Garrett's the oldest. A few years ago, him and his wife, Diane, had a little baby named Ben. I just adore him. Lemme tell you, being a grandfather is the best thing ever invented. Anyway, I felt it was fitting that Garrett would be my successor. I've partnered with him on some projects and…well, I made him executor of my estate."

Jack saw the pain on Walt's face and waited, knowing this would be difficult.

"I—I don't know how the hell you're gonna handle this in the book, Jack. It's very painful for me. But I'll just say it, and you can massage it later."

Walt looked away. "Maybe I'm misjudging Garrett, but I doubt it. I've always had a knack for judging people. Like the way I booked the acts for the show. If I liked 'em, I booked 'em. And my audiences liked 'em too. It's like the way dogs are—they take one sniff of you and lick your hand or take a chunk out of your leg."

Jack laughed. "And we all know dogs are never wrong."

"When I'm in Pajaro Beach, Garrett comes down all the time from his place in San Francisco, and he's always pushing this show idea. I mean, he doesn't have the experience to be a producer. He's—he's hardly got any experience at all. Except for that goofy sitcom he was on that lasted a whole half of a season before the network yanked it. And I got him that job!"

Walt stopped, breathing hard, his face twisted in a knot of emotion. In the silence Jack listened to the drumming of the rain on the roof and drifted away into his own world for a moment, thinking of his daughter, Chloe, and the powerful mixture of emotions he had for her. How could he love his daughter so much but so often be at odds with Sarah?

"I always wanted to work with Garrett," Walt continued. "Other entertainers worked with their kids and did all right. But Garrett and me, we're always at each other. Don't get me wrong. I love spending time with my grandson. But with Garrett there, and the friction between us—well, I just can't figure out what the hell the problem is."

"You think the father-and-son comeback show has a shot?" Jack asked.

"They've been talking about that thing for years, and now that our book is coming out, Garrett's hot to move on it. But the network won't do it without me being involved. And just the thought of working with Garrett scares the holy crap out of me."

For a moment, Jack thought this might be the time to ask Walt why the network abruptly canceled his show back in the seventies. It was the one topic they hadn't yet covered. Every time they got close to the subject, Walt veered away. This time was no different. Walt began rambling about his conflicted feelings for his son, and his various obsessions and complexes. As Jack listened to this increasingly candid outpouring, he thought he might have crossed the line from biographer to headshrinker. But later, as he got ready to leave, standing by the coffee table, with the rain beating on the windows, he realized he had crossed a different line—from biographer to friend.

"I gotta tell you somethin', Jack." Walt wagged his finger at him, the way he did to emphasize a point. "Around you, I never go dry."

"You've got a million stories," Jack said, shifting his weight.

"It's not that," Walt said firmly. "I've been interviewed a lot. And I never felt I had much to say. But around you, I never go dry."

Jack nodded, paused, and thought that maybe this was the time to share his feelings about his own father, how they were never close at all, but how Walt's show had made his father laugh, had opened him up—opened up a man who was emotionally dead to his family. The only other time Jack saw his father show emotion was when he married Sarah at a guest ranch, high in the mountains of Arizona. During the wedding vows, Jack happened to look over at his father and saw tears dripping off the end of his nose. A year later, his father's two-pack-a-day, unfiltered-Camels habit caught up with him. Six months after that, his father was dead.

"Walt, ya know, I got something I been meaning to tell you," Jack began. "Writing this book's really important to me, 'cause, you see, my dad was—"

"Okay!" Walt clapped his hands, ending their conversation. Jack didn't have a chance to finish what he was going to say. *Maybe,* Jack thought, *Walt isn't interested at all in me and my life and my feelings.* He was just using him as sounding board, someone he could confess to as a way to purge his conscience.

As they walked to the door, Walt said, "Listen, Jack, I want you to see my place up in Pajaro Beach. And I want you to meet Mary. Lady Mary. She's really something. And she likes me. An old goat like me! She's gotta be in the book. Why don't you and your frau pick a weekend, get a sitter, and come up? On me. I'll pay for everything."

"I'd like that, Walt," Jack said. "I'd really like that."

Jack said good-bye and left, feeling surprised by the sudden invitation. As he closed the gate behind him at the top of the stairs, he looked back down at the house and saw Walt's old face looking up at him, his features melting behind the rain running down the window.

When Jack told Sarah the great entertainer had invited them to his Pajaro Beach house, she went into a flurry of planning. A sitter was booked within hours, time off was requested from her legal firm, and she began laying out her clothes for the trip. But Jack had mixed emotions about the whole thing. Sure, it made sense that he see Walt's getaway house and meet Lady Mary. But he realized that, like Walt, he had been more comfortable with a strictly professional relationship. As a newspaperman, he had been trained to seek objectivity, not familiarity. This was new ground for him.

FOUR

Jack arrived at Walt's Hollywood Hills house a week later for their standing meeting with these conflicting thoughts still circling in his mind. He pressed the bell by the gate, and his hand hovered over the knob, waiting to be buzzed in. But the only noise he heard was the rush of the rain-swollen creek behind Walt's house. He pressed the buzzer over and over with increasing concern. Finally, he moved along the edge of the waist-high fence until he could look down the hill and in through a living-room window. The house looked empty. But that didn't make sense, because Walt's little white sports car, the 1987 Mercedes-Benz SL500, was still in the carport.

Maybe he's on the phone, Jack thought. He took out his cell phone, flipped it open, and dialed Walt's number. Reception was spotty here in the canyon, but he did get a signal. Moments later, he heard the phone inside the house begin to ring and ring and ring. He clicked off the phone and stuffed it back in his pocket.

Jack climbed over the fence and walked down the redwood stairs, thinking that at any moment, Walt would just appear in the window and wave him in, apologizing for the delay and explaining it away somehow.

But the house remained silent.

Looking through the small panes of the front door, Jack could see the kitchen and part of the hallway that led toward Walt's bedroom. He crouched in front of the door and pushed open the mail slot.

"Walt!" he shouted through the slot. "Hey, Walt! It's Jack!"

He pressed his ear to the open mail slot and felt a cool rush of air from inside the still house. He squinted to look through the mail slot and found he could now see all the way down the hallway. And that's when he saw just the bare foot and ankle of a person protruding from the bathroom.

"Oh, Jesus," Jack heard himself say. He stood up and ran along the side of the house, trying to find a window to get a better look through. His mind was spinning, running through all the possibilities. Maybe someone had broken in? But the house seemed undisturbed. Maybe Walt had a heart attack? But why was he lying in the hallway?

When Jack finished circling the house, he looked once more at the ancient front door. He could probably smash his way in. Maybe Walt was still alive and needed his help. Yeah, he should get in there as soon as he could. He backed up and got ready to kick the door just above the latch. But something stopped him. Instead, he reached once more for his phone. He called Walt's housekeeper, Maria, who lived five minutes away and kept a key for emergencies.

And then he dialed 911.

———————

A pair of cops arrived just before the housekeeper.

"Are you family?" the first cop asked, looking Jack over as they hurried down the walk to the front door.

"No. I'm—I'm—" He couldn't think how to explain it. "Look, I'm working with Walt Stuckey on a project. I came here for a meeting and…"

They were at the front door now. Jack stooped and looked through the mail slot. "You can see him in there. You've got to help him."

The younger cop crouched and looked through the slot.

"Who did you say it is?" The second cop was older, with a generous paunch and graying hair. "Who'd you say is in there?"

"Walt Stuckey."

"Walt Stuckey? He's the guy in there?"

"Yeah," Jack said.

"Son of a gun," the older cop said.

"Aren't you going to break the door down?" Jack asked.

"Why? What's going on?" the young cop said, straightening up and looking at Jack suspiciously.

"Walt Stuckey," the older cop said, shaking his head. "I loved his show."

"You've got to get in there," Jack said. "You've got to help him."

The housekeeper's car pulled into the driveway, and they all turned.

"Here's the key," Jack said. "Maria! Hurry!"

The young cop put his hand out, blocking Jack. "Sir, when we gain entry, we need you to stay outside. We'll let you know as soon as—"

But Maria opened the door now, and Jack dodged around the cops. He ran down the hallway and knelt next to Walt. The old man was naked, lying face down, half in the bathroom, half in the hallway.

"Walt," Jack said. "Oh, Jesus! What happened, Walt?"

He touched Walt's shoulder, and it was cold. But not dead cold. Just cold.

He's alive! Jack thought. *Alive!*

An iron hand yanked Jack up onto his feet and propelled him away from Walt. It was the young cop, muscling him backward. "I told you to stay outside!"

Paramedics were pushing past them now. Jack dug his heels in and put on the brakes in the kitchen, shoving back against the cop, who felt his strength and decided to back off.

"Okay," Jack said. "I'll stay here."

"Okay," the cop said and turned away.

Jack looked back down the hallway as the paramedics began their dance, the dance he had seen so many times on the streets covering stories as a police reporter. Starting IVs, taking vital signs, putting a blanket over Walt's nakedness, positioning him next to the gurney.

That's when Jack first heard the phrase mumbled by the paramedic: possible stroke.

A stroke, Jack thought wildly. *Okay, so that's not so bad. People recover from strokes. So there's still a chance.* Still a chance his friend would live.

Yes, seeing Walt like that, naked and so vulnerable, made Jack realize he had feelings for Walt that went way beyond just a money-making writing project. Even if Walt had closed himself off from other people because of his broken marriages and past relationships, Jack knew they actually shared something real. And they were creating a damn good book together. And stroke or no stroke, Jack would see that their book was published.

FIVE

"Why can't I see Walt?" Jack asked as he stood at the nurses' station at the Cedars-Sinai Medical Center two days later.

"Gosh, Jack, I know you're eager to see my father," Garrett Stuckey said, "but it's just too early."

"Is he still unconscious?" Jack asked looking past Garrett and into the room across the hallway. He could see Walt, in one of those horrible hospital gowns that button down the back, lying in the bed. His eyes looked glazed, and his mouth was open as he seemed to be staring up at the television on the wall.

"I just want him to know I haven't forgotten about him," Jack pressed. Actually, he wanted to see for himself what kind of shape Walt was in. Two days of calling Garrett had yielded little beyond empty phrases about his father's condition and vague references to the book. Jack kept asking to visit Walt in the hospital, but Garrett insisted his father wasn't up to it. Finally, Jack drove to the hospital uninvited but was stopped by Garrett outside Walt's room.

As the executor of Walt's estate, Garrett had immediately flown to Los Angeles to supervise his father's care and manage Walt's fortune, which Jack had learned was about $37 million. Now he seemed to be standing guard outside Walt's room, limiting access to his father as Walt's other children arrived from across the country to check the status of their trust funds and see if they were soon going to collect their inheritances.

———

Meeting Garrett face-to-face, Jack saw no trace of Walt's looks in his son and heard nothing of the Joizie accent in his speech. Garrett was about forty, medium height, stocky, and athletically built. He seemed big and Waspy where his father was small and ethnic. But the most startling difference between father and son was their hair. Instead of Walt's frizzy—now bald—head, Garrett had thick, straight black hair, graying slightly, which he drew attention to by incessantly tossing it back with a nervous tic. When Garrett shook Jack's hand his grip was weak and uninterested, and he seemed more concerned with riding herd on the nursing staff and his siblings than talking with his father's biographer.

Jack had spent the past two sleepless nights desperately hoping he could finish the book and collect his share of the $50,000 advance. Working on Walt's book showed Jack his talents really were, as his agent, Carolyn, said, "Perfectly suited for writing star bios." So Jack was determined to keep this project alive so he could write more biographies later. And if he had to eat a little shit to do it, he was prepared to develop a taste for the stuff. He'd show Sarah that he could make it as a writer and provide a stable home for Chloe.

"I tell you what, Jack," Garrett said, maneuvering so he blocked Jack's view of Walt. "Let's head down to the restaurant, get a bite. I know there are a few things we have to discuss."

"Okay," Jack said. They headed for the elevator. But Jack glanced back once more and saw Walt looking toward him. For a split second their eyes connected, and Jack thought he saw a spark of recognition and a flicker of change to his expression.

"I'm starving," Garrett said as they walked. "I've just been so darned busy taking care of Dad. The nurses had Dad's diet all screwed up, so I had to go over the whole darn thing with them again. Gosh, I mean, how hard is it to understand a simple set of directions? I mean, jeez—"

On the elevator, while Garrett rambled on about the incompetent hospital staff and the horrible traffic in West LA, Jack reviewed a speech he had composed to convince Garrett he had enough material to finish the book. They arrived at the restaurant, and the hostess guided them to a table among doctors and the families of well-heeled patients.

"Ironically," Garrett said, sitting down at the table, "my dad's never been healthier. Heart's fine, lungs're good, and they even think his mental faculties are all there. He just can't talk."

"But that'll come back," Jack said hopefully.

"Hard to say. With a good speech therapist? With the right diet? Maybe. But it'll take time."

Time, Jack thought, *is something I don't have a lot of.*

Soon a mousy waitress arrived, and Jack ordered his favorite, a Reuben with fries. Garrett kept the waitress standing by their table as he grilled her about how the food was prepared—as if there was some chef back there eager to please him. *It's just a damn hospital restaurant*, Jack thought, impatiently waiting to discuss the book.

Finally Garrett said, "Okay, give me the Caesar salad. But no eggs. Okay? And I want lo-cal dressing on the side." When the waitress left, Garrett said, "After what happened to my dad, I'm really cutting back on the fat. Strokes run in our family."

Jack sensed that Garrett was the type of guy who wanted to run the conversation. But he couldn't wait any longer. He had carefully rehearsed an introduction into the subject, something along the lines of, "As you can imagine, I'm anxious to continue work on this project, and I feel confident I've got more than enough material to finish writing the book."

Jack wasn't really confident at all, of course, given the vibe he was getting from Garrett and the negative things that Walt had said about his son. But he felt that, between the tapes and the press clippings, he could piece together a decent book and get his part of the advance.

But once he started talking, the speech that Jack heard coming out of his mouth was very different. "Garrett, look, your father and I made a good start on the book, and I think you oughta let me finish it. I know it wouldn't be as good as if Walt was alive—I mean *healthy*—" (Shit! Why'd he say that?) "—but I can finish it, and I can make it good."

Jack plowed on, outlining what he could do with the book and how great it would be until Garrett finally raised a hand to stop the outpouring. With silence restored, Garrett took a deep breath and was about to speak when the waitress set their food in front of them and turned to go.

"Miss!" Garrett snarled, staring at his plate in horror.

"Yes?"

"What is this?" He pointed at his salad.

"Caesar salad."

"Caesar salad with what?"

"Lo-cal dressing."

The color of Garrett's face matched the contents of the ketchup bottle Jack had upturned over his fries.

"And where did I say I would like you to put my dressing?"

Jack wondered if the waitress was, like him, thinking of the same convenient location.

"Oh! On the side!" The waitress realized her mistake and, apologizing, took the salad away.

"Jesus Christ. *These people.*" Garrett rubbed his face.

They sat in silence, Jack's Reuben sandwich cooling in front of him, until a new salad arrived with a tidy little cup of dressing on the side. It looked as watery as skim milk. They dug in, Garrett attacking his salad with a predatory gusto. He even wolfed down all the crackers in the little basket and littered the tabletop with crumbs and wrappers.

Their talk drifted aimlessly. Jack waited for the conversation to turn back to the book. Finally, he cut Garrett off in midsentence.

"We were talking about the book—"

Garrett looked up at him, startled, then annoyed. "Yes, Jack. I remember what we were talking about."

Jack rushed on. "Look, I've got to know what's going to happen with it, because I've got a couple of other projects I'm juggling now." *Projects like staring at my dreaded spec script*, Jack thought. But it didn't hurt to bluff a little. "Walt's book is my first priority, so I want to stick with it. But I've got to know where it stands. As I said, it would be best if I just kept writing based on the material I have—"

"Jack, I understand you're in a difficult position. It's just that—"

"Our agent talked to the publisher, and they still want the book. I don't see any reason why it needs to be canceled or postponed."

"You don't? My father just had a massive stroke, and you don't see why it has to be postponed? I think my father's recovery is far more important than—"

"Look, I'll write the material I've covered in the interviews. When Walt's better I'll show him—"

"Whoa, Jack. Whoa, boy. Whoa, whoa, whoa." Garrett waited for silence as if he were presiding at a board of directors' meeting. He took a deep breath, his furrowed brow indicating he was about to say something profound. He opened his mouth—and the waitress interrupted again.

"Did either of you gentlemen happen to save room for dessert?"

Garrett looked up at the waitress, who had spoiled his big moment. "Decaf coffee. Sweet'N Low. And *non*fat milk," he growled.

She turned to Jack.

"Coffee with cream, please." He hoped it was heavy cream, thick and fatty. He'd always felt that the packages that said *fat-free* or *salt-free* should also say *taste-free.*

As the waitress disappeared, Garrett said, "Naturally, my father spoke to me about the book several times. He seemed pleased with the progress you were making. I read it too—the stuff you sent. Short chapters. Punchy. Captured the basic facts about his career. I have a few niggles, though, little things here and there…"

"Okay," was all Jack said, because he sensed he was being set up for a sucker punch.

"There's one thing that troubles me." Garrett left him hanging while he thoughtfully dug something out of a back tooth. "The way my father *sounds* in the—the stuff you wrote…"

"I took it right off the tape," Jack said quickly.

"I don't doubt it. But you left in all the cussing."

"Actually, I didn't leave it *all* in."

"You know what I mean. My point is, he comes across too harsh. People won't like that."

"Walt liked it."

"But he's not always right. What I'm trying to explain to you is—"

"Garrett, it's an *auto*biography—*auto*. That means Walt gets to decide how he wants to sound in his own book."

Garrett stared at Jack a moment before continuing. "Jack, this would be a whole lot easier if you didn't take things so personally, okay? I've done some writing too, you know, and I know what it's like to have your words changed. But I'm just talking about a 'damn' here and a 'hell' there. That's not going to ruin your precious style, will it?"

Jack realized he was breathing hard. He wondered how much of his anger showed on his face. Probably quite a lot, he realized. *Come on, Jack. You said you'd eat shit to get this project in print. Dig in, boy.* He took a few deep breaths and slowly felt his control returning.

Jack forced a smile and kept his tone even. "Garrett, I spent years working for newspapers where editors completely rewrote my stories. And sometimes the result was better. Sometimes it wasn't. I'm not going to cry when you cut my *precious* words. If you like the tone of the first chapters—great. All the other questions we'll take on a case-by-case basis."

"Fine. That's all I'm suggesting," Garrett said. "Now, in terms of a course of action, I'll take over my father's role. You create the material, I review it *before* it goes to the publisher. If you think you can work that way, then let's continue." Garrett thought of something and threw out one more bone. "Oh. And I'm aware that my father owed you a check. If you decide to continue, I'll see that you get paid. So are those conditions acceptable?"

"Fair enough," Jack said, thinking, *I sure hope Walt recovers and kicks your sorry ass off this project.*

Jack stood up, leaving his coffee untouched. "I'm at a meter, so I gotta get going." He reached for his wallet, but Garrett waved the gesture away. They shook hands, and Jack started across the restaurant, already relieved as hell to be on his way out the door.

Garrett's voice stopped him. "Jack? Next time we get together, I expect you to bring all the tapes you made of your interviews with my dad."

"No problem," Jack said lightly, pasting a smile on his face as he made a mental note to himself: *make backup copies of all the tapes.*

PART TWO
THE MONTEREY PENINSULA

SIX

The next week, Garrett told Jack to come up to the Pajaro Beach house, where Walt was recovering. Jack would have a chance to finally see Walt's beach house, interview Walt's girlfriend, Lady Mary, and say hello to Walt, who was still not talking. And, Garrett casually mentioned, they would begin to work on the book and review the niggles he had here and there in the first half of the book.

Early the next morning, Jack said good-bye to Sarah, left a note for Chloe, who was still asleep, and started driving to Pajaro Beach from LA, a six-hour drive. He followed a complicated set of directions, winding his way along narrow roads, passing under windblown cypress trees, and feeling the ocean nearby. He arrived at dusk. The mansion—which Walt referred to as the "beach house"—appeared ahead of him, perched on the rocks above a cove. He pulled into the drive and stepped out of the Pathfinder. It was February by now and the ocean wind was cold on his face. He looked up at the house, thinking, *Man, what a spread.* Connected to the three-story clapboard house was a large garage, apparently converted into an office, with picture windows looking out on the ocean. Jack could see Garrett inside, seated behind a desk, reading something.

He went around to a side door and knocked. Garrett waved him in. As he entered, Garrett held up a sheaf of papers. "Good stuff, Jack!" He waved the pages again. "The new chapters you sent. Very powerful."

Jack had sent him several chapters that dealt with Walt's drinking problem that developed after the show was suddenly canceled. In his typical fashion, Walt took all the blame for his problem, and Jack wrote it that way—sure that Garrett would hate it. But now this.

"You think it works then?" Jack felt himself being drawn in, even though warning signals went off in his head. *Careful, careful.*

"Works? It's the best damn chapter in the book. This is real writing."

"Yeah?"

Garrett imitated Jack's Joizie accent. "*Yih.* The writin' is real good."

"Thanks, Garrett."

"Of course I have a few niggles here and there"—Jack was really starting to hate that word—"things I think would make it really jump off the page. But my first take on it is very positive."

A guy sitting at a nearby desk rose. He had been so still Jack hadn't noticed him.

Garrett said, "Jack Dillon, meet the faithful Ernie."

Ernie stood and approached Jack like a dog waiting to be kicked. He was stocky, powerful, with a lined face and a suspiciously full head of brown hair, probably a rug. For some reason Jack thought *ex-military* and imagined him in a dingy white T-shirt doing calisthenics and following orders mindlessly. He had that look of blind obedience to any orders from an authority. For years, Walt was in charge. Now, Garrett was the boss, and Ernie looked ready to do anything he asked.

"Ernie's been with my dad for years. He came on board as Dad's bodyguard and driver. But now he does a little bit of everything. He keeps this place running. Right, Ernie, old boy?"

"I do my best." Ernie smiled, shaking Jack's hand, his grip like a vise.

"Good to meet you, Ernie. Walt mentioned your name a couple of times."

"He did?" he asked with a puppy dog look of gratitude on his face.

"Yeah. Along with the garbage man and the plumber." Garrett laughed boisterously. "I'm sorry, Ernie. Jack, I give this fellow such a hard time. But he can take it. Right, Ernie?" He clapped Ernie on the shoulder.

The phone rang and as Ernie reached for it, Garrett hissed, "The third ring, dammit! I told you—the third ring."

Jack somehow thought this was a joke and looked to Garrett for an explanation. Garrett shrugged and defensively explained, "Never answer the phone on the first ring. You know how these show-business types are. You don't want to sound desperate."

"Show business? Is this about that father-and-son show Walt and you were pitching?"

Garrett left the question unanswered, listening as Ernie finally answered the phone. "Stuckey Productions. Garrett Stuckey's office."

Jack looked at Garrett and saw he was hanging on Ernie's words and expression for any clue about what the caller wanted. Ernie cupped the phone and said, "It's Mike Schmidt."

"Schmidt?" Garrett asked hopefully.

"From the Chevrolet dealership. He wants to get your Suburban in for an oil change."

"Oh for God's sake," Garrett said, disappointed.

"What should I tell him?"

"I don't care. You handle it."

Ernie returned to the call, arranging a service visit. It was on the tip of Jack's tongue to press the point and get an answer about the father-and-son show. But judging from Garrett's reaction, he already had an answer. Garrett returned to reading the manuscript and spoke without looking at Jack. When Ernie finally hung up, he said, "Ernie, why don't you go home early today? I think we can take things from here."

A clock on the wall showed it was a few minutes before five. This was going home early?

"Good to meet you, Jack."

"See ya around, Ernie." The exchange made Jack feel like part of the help, which, he realized, was fairly accurate.

Ernie hoisted a scratched, faded black plastic briefcase onto the desk. Snapping it open he tossed in a battered thermos and an uneaten banana, snapped it shut, and with a mumbled farewell, disappeared.

"Good old Ernie," Garrett said. "My father has such fondness for the little people of the world. His great failing."

"His *failing*? It was what made people love him." Jack wondered why he was defending Walt. He had his own ass to worry about. "How long's Ernie worked here?"

"No one really knows. He seemed to appear one day and attach himself to that desk over there."

"Walt told me how Ernie pulled him out of the ocean that day he got hit by a wave down on the rocks. You gotta love a guy who does that for you."

Garrett was reading the manuscript again. Head down, he muttered, "Yeah, well, maybe Walt loves him. But some things are going to change around here."

Jack craned his neck to see what section of the manuscript Garrett was on. He watched as Garrett reached for a pencil and drew a line through a sentence. Jack turned away and concentrated on his breathing. Looking around, he found his eye drawn to a doorway leading into the main house. He felt the silence and mystery of the distant empty rooms.

"How's Walt?"

"Huh?" Garrett looked up. "No change."

"Has he started talking yet?"

"He says one word over and over again: no. 'No, no, no, no, no.'"

"So he can talk?"

"If you call that talking."

"What's the speech therapist say?"

"It's a start. You never know."

Garrett saw Jack was looking toward the main house. "Want to say hi to Dad?"

"Sure."

They rose. Garrett carefully placed the manuscript in a drawer and locked it. Jack followed him into the house. As he stepped through the doorway, a wonderful smell filled his nose. He found himself in a large kitchen, where a chunky blond woman was leaning over a bubbling pot on a large stove. She heard them and turned.

"Jack, meet Hilda, best cook on the peninsula."

She laughed, her blue eyes twinkling.

"Jack's writing a book about Dad."

"Hello, Jack," Hilda extended a hand, then pulled it back. "Wet. I been wrestlin' with da bird." She indicated a chicken prostrate on the chopping block.

"Not only is her cooking healthy, but it actually tastes great." Garrett dipped a finger in the pot and licked it.

"Garrett! I swear ta God!" Hilda raised a wooden spoon, ready to whack him.

He backed off, laughing. "Come on, Jack."

A kid came running down the hallway and rammed his head into Garrett's belly.

"Whoa! Whoa!" Garrett said, lifting up the little squirt. "Ben, can you say hello to Mr. Dillon? He's a writer."

Jack sensed Garrett was playing the part of a TV dad for his benefit, almost as if Jack was writing a book about him and he wanted to come off looking like a bighearted guy. But Jack went along with it, smiling and shaking Ben's little hand when he extended it.

Ben looked away shyly, then whispered something in Garrett's ear. Garrett's face clouded, and he bellowed, "Diane! Diane!"

A door opened, and a woman appeared along with the sound of a TV newscast. She was carrying a copy of *People* magazine and seemed somehow both nervous and annoyed at being interrupted. She was small and birdlike, carefully made up and expensively dressed.

"Oh, uh, Jack, this is my wife, Diane. This is Jack. He's the guy writing Dad's book. Excuse me, Jack." He took Diane's arm and moved her back into the room she'd come from. "Ben told me you said he couldn't—" The door closed.

Jack looked down at Ben. Ben looked up at Jack.

"Hi, slugger," Jack said.

Ben stuck out his lower lip.

"You mad at me or somethin'?"

"Yeah."

"What'd I do?"

"I don't know."

"Wanna fight?" Jack asked him.

Ben smiled. Then he exploded into action. He began punching and kicking Jack's knee for all he was worth.

"Ow, ow!" Jack pretended he was mortally wounded. He really hammed it up, and Ben loved it, laughing and giggling. Finally Jack stopped him and crouched in front of him. "Look, if you ever have to punch someone, make a fist like this." He showed him how to keep his thumb on the outside of his fingers. "Otherwise you might break your hand. Now punch my hand. Go ahead."

Ben swung, laughing, his little fist smacking into Jack's open hand. They played around for a few minutes, tussling. Then Jack felt the door open and looked up to find Garrett and Diane had emerged from their conference. They frowned down at him.

"Just giving Ben a few pointers. Self-defense, you know…" Jack could feel their disapproval. "See ya later, Ben. Go easy on your dad now, okay?"

They moved deeper into the house. Jack noticed large oil paintings on the wall. More originals. The furnishings were lavish but outdated, from the seventies, no doubt. The shag carpet tickled Jack's ankles. Huge picture windows looked out on the water, lights sparkling across the bay.

As they continued forward, Jack heard the sound of a sports commentator and a cheering crowd. They turned into a side room, dark except for a TV showing a basketball game. Watching the screen, his face lit by the flicker of the television, was Walt, sitting in a wheelchair, his lap covered by a shawl. A young woman in a nurse's uniform sat on the couch nearby.

"Dad!" Garrett said in an abnormally loud voice. "Look who came to see you."

Walt turned his head slowly and spotted Jack. His face lit up. "How ya doin', Jack? I thought of somethin' you might want to work into the book. You know, I was telling you how we used to book the acts for the show—"

Jack was stunned. It was almost like hearing a voice from the dead. He felt prickles rising on the back of his neck.

Walt seemed surprised too, surprised and pleased to feel words coming out of his mouth. He paused and took a deep breath. The nurse moved forward, kneeling beside him. She softly said, "Yes, Mr. Stuckey? Tell us about the show."

Walt breathed deeply; he looked up at Jack. "I had a method of dealing with the talent that was unorthodox. But it worked for me. See, what I'd do is—is—" He took a deep breath and opened his mouth. He took another breath and tried to speak. Nothing came out.

The nurse turned to Garrett. "Did you hear that? He was talking! He was really talking!" She turned back to Walt. "You can do it, can't you? You can talk."

"I've heard him say things like that before," Garrett said quickly. "Go on, Dad, show them how you talk."

Walt frowned at his son. "No," he said. "No. No, no, no."

"There you go," Garrett said. "He's talking. Come, Dad, talk some more."

"No, no, no."

Jack noticed that each *no* had a slightly different inflection, as if he thought he was really saying something.

"No, no, no, no. NO!" Walt was getting frustrated.

The nurse stood and faced Garrett. "That's the most I've heard him say. He'll say a word here and there. And he says, 'No, no, no.' But this is incredible. I think he must want to talk to— I'm sorry, what's your name?"

"Jack."

"He wants to talk to Jack."

"What're you? A speech therapist?" Garrett said. "You're a nurse. So nurse him. Look he hasn't even eaten his yogurt, for Christ's sake. That's your job. Do your job."

The nurse realized that she had apparently stepped out of her place. She clammed up, stung by the response, and looked away. But Garrett was worked up now and wouldn't stop.

"I've heard him say lots of things. Right, Dad?" He crouched in front of Walt and took his hands, clapping them together and singing. "Yes, we have no bananas! We have no bananas today!"

Walt joined in happily, like a child. "Yes, we have no bananas! We have no bananas today!"

"See? He talks. He sings. He wets. He's a life-size Walt Stuckey doll." Garrett looked around at them, his face blue in the TV light.

Walt continued singing, "Yes, we have no bananas! We have no bananas today!"

The nurse took Walt's hands and held them still. "It's okay, honey," she said.

"You wanted to hear him talk. Let him talk. Let him sing." Garrett turned to Jack, calming down a little and maybe even realizing he had overdone it. "You see, sometimes stroke victims can sing when they can't talk. Doctors don't understand it, but it has to do with different signals coming from different speech centers in the brain."

The nurse began spooning yogurt into Walt's mouth. Walt made a face, and it dribbled down his chin. "No, no, no, NO."

"Come on, Mr. Stuckey. It's yogurt. It's good for you." She began pushing it in. He kept spitting it out.

"Jack, let's go get some dinner. Bye, Dad."

Garrett walked out of the room. Jack hung back. He looked at the nurse. Tears were trickling down her cheeks.

"I never did get your name."

"Doreen."

"Hey, Doreen."

She nodded, sniffing, unable to speak.

"It sucks, doesn't it? Seeing him treated like this."

She nodded, looked in Garrett's direction, and said, "Asshole." Then: "I never knew Walt before, but since I started working here, I went back and watched some of the shows."

Jack waited.

"He was sooo funny. And he seemed like such a nice man."

Her words were simple, but they touched Jack.

"I only met him recently," Jack said. "But you're right. He was a very nice man. Complicated. But he had a good heart. That's why his fans loved him."

"I've worked with a lot of stroke victims," Doreen said, her voice shaking. "And I can feel them in there, in the dark. And I know how frightening it is. I feel so bad for him."

Jack crouched in front of Walt and looked in his eyes. It was like looking at a prisoner through steel bars. And then he realized how much he missed being with his friend.

"Walt, hey, I wrote some new chapters that you're really gonna like. I got in all that stuff you told me to about how you booked the Beatles on their first trip here." Walt seemed to smile. "And the publisher said they're going to release the book in the fall. We're off and running, buddy."

"Jack, let's move it. I'm starving." Garrett was at the doorway, scowling at him.

"Just bringing him up to date on his book."

"What's the point?"

Jack rose and moved toward Garrett, walking silently on the thick carpet. He felt light on his feet, ready for something, although he didn't know what. He realized he had a lot of pent-up anger inside him so he tried to breathe easy, from his diaphragm. But the anger was down really deep, and he couldn't get at it.

Garrett watched Jack advance. He backed away, saying, "I figured we could head into town for a quick bite. What kind of food do you like?"

"Steak," Jack growled.

"Steak? Well, I'll see what I can do."

They walked back down the hallway, leaving Walt in the room alone with the television and Doreen and the past.

———

"You can sleep down there," Garrett said when they returned from dinner, gesturing at a boathouse, built among the rocks just above the water's edge.

Jack got his duffel bag out of the car and headed off in the darkness, thinking Garrett would show him to the boathouse, maybe help him get settled. Wrong. Garrett was heading for the house, walking unsteadily after three Michelob Lights.

"See you in the morning." Garrett banged the door shut before Jack could answer.

Surf boomed in the distance, outside the cove. Closer, Jack heard the water lapping at the shore. He moved down through the trees, along a path twisting between boulders showing pale in the starlight. It reminded him of Boy Scout camp, walking back to his cabin in the Maine woods after ghost stories around a campfire, feeling the sudden cold gathering around him, the fear of the unknown in the dark forest. He hadn't thought of that for years.

The boathouse was a long narrow shingled building, with double doors at one end. Inside, Jack groped for a light switch. A single bulb sparked to life, hanging above a boat overturned on sawhorses. In the back was a wooden workbench, the surface littered with tools, as if someone just walked away from a project and never returned. Along one wall was a cot, neatly made, with an extra blanket at the foot. Jack imagined Garrett barking at the maid. "Go down to the boathouse and make up the bed. A fellow will be sleeping down there tonight."

Jack threw his duffel bag on the bed and pulled off his boots. Across from his bed was a small woodburning stove with a stack of firewood beside it. Minutes later, he had a fire crackling in the stove. He turned out the light and left the stove door open and watched the flames burn down to coals, throbbing in the darkness.

At dinner Garrett had said he had arranged for Jack to interview Mary at lunch the next day. "I don't know what the hell you'll get out of meeting her." Garrett yawned. "But Mary has to be mentioned in the book, so you might as well get it out of the way."

Lying in bed, feeling the warmth of the fire on his face, Jack turned on his tape recorder. He rewound the tape to the section where Walt talked about how he met Mary. A quick review wouldn't hurt. He had intended to make copies of the tape back in LA but ran out of time. And he hadn't thought Garrett would be so insistent about getting the tapes under his control. Jack knew he would have to stall Garrett long enough to get copies made in the village tomorrow.

He pressed the play button on his recorder. In the stillness, Jack heard Walt's voice.

"I met Mary about four years after my divorce. It was my third divorce—and I swore I'd never tie the knot again. Christ, I was lonely. I don't know what else to say. I was lonely and…and lost, really. The kids were gone, I had a beautiful house—hell, I had houses all over the world—and I had money. But I had no one to share it all with. I needed a woman to share my life with me. I wanted someone to talk to, to laugh with and—to share my bed. I needed that too, believe me. I was horny as an old goat."

Jack loved the way Walt spoke, his succinct style, his occasional use of unexpected words, and of course the familiar Joizie accent.

"But I was so goddamned suspicious. I'd had three marriages already, and each one was nothing but pain. Pain, Jack! It seemed that the only reason women were after me was because they thought I could do something for them, get them into show business. Or they wanted my money. I didn't want that kind of a woman again. I would rather be alone than go through that again."

Jack turned off the tape and lay there in the dark, thinking back over the past few months. He loved sitting around the coffee table in Walt's Hollywood Hills house talking about the show, bringing the memories alive in Walt's mind again. He remembered how he had begun writing the first chapters and found the words coming faster than he could get them on the page. He'd always remember the day Walt called him and said he liked the chapters. "We're off and running, kid!" He had been on top of the world after that call. Now Walt was silent, and Jack was alone again.

He turned the tape recorder back on, and Walt's voice filled the room.

"I started spending more and more of my time up in Pajaro Beach. But my house up there was like a tomb—just me and Ernie. Good old Ernie. Well, for breakfast, I'd go to this coffee shop, one of those joints where the locals hang out, ya know? I spent so much time there, I got to the point I could recognize just about everyone who came in.

"Every morning, in would come these four ladies. And one of them caught my eye. Jack, I was smitten. I don't know what the hell it was about her, but I had the most God-awful schoolboy crush on her." Laughter from both of them. "But I didn't know how the hell I could ever meet her."

"Didn't she recognize you?" Jack heard himself asking on the tape.

"I wore a hat and glasses—which I never wore on the show. Besides, this was twenty years after the show. So one morning all the other ladies are in there, but not this lady I'd taken a fancy to. Well, they all left, and then along comes Mary. I hadn't met her yet, but I'd heard the other ladies call her that. Well, Mary's all in a dither. Her car has broken down, and she had to walk to the restaurant, hoping they waited for her or some such nonsense like that.

"Anyway, here's my chance, Jack. I stand and go to this lady, my heart beating like a maniac, and I say, 'I'm going in that direction, I could give you a ride.' Well, she looks at me, and I think she is thinking, 'Who's this pervert?' So I say something asinine like, 'I assure you, my intentions are honorable.' She looks at me and says, 'Walt Stuckey, I loved your show, and you can take me anywhere you want to.' Oh God! I was so relieved—and so happy. I was just like a kid again!

"I drove her to work that day and picked her up that night. And ever since then we've had the time of our lives, traveling all over the world, staying the best hotels. But, it's the damnedest thing, she won't quit her job."

"What's she do?"

"She used to be a nurse. But then she became an executive secretary at a hospital on the peninsula. I told her, 'What the hell do you need to work for? I'll give you anything you want.' She says, 'You want me to stop working, marry me.' I tell her, 'You know I won't do that.' And she says, 'Then it's none of your damn business.'"

Jack clicked off the tape recorder and lay there in the darkness. When he had called Sarah earlier that night, he told her the book was back on track. But lying here in the darkness, he wasn't so sure. He thought of Walt as he had seen him in that room, watching TV, being spoon-fed like a baby. He thought of Garrett, riding herd on the help, drawing red pencil lines through sentences in the manuscript Jack had written with Walt. And he felt very angry about the way things had turned out.

Jack dozed for a while. When he woke up, the coals in the stove were dead, the room cold, and a new thought was in his head: *Is Mary as angry as I am?*

SEVEN

J ack was in the office going over the manuscript with Garrett when he looked out the window and saw an old diesel Mercedes wagon pull into the driveway. A woman stepped out, wearing a leather jacket over a simple white top with tight black pleated pants. She was in her late thirties, thick blond hair, tall, long-legged, and fit. And Jack noticed she had, well, an outstanding figure. *She's the kind of woman who would look great sitting on a horse*, Jack thought, and realized that Walt had already given her the right nickname: Lady Mary.

She walked around to the side of the office and tapped on the glass door. Garrett looked up. He glanced at his watch, annoyed, even though he was the one who had set up the meeting.

"Ernie." Garrett jerked his thumb at the door.

"Oh." Ernie leaped out of his chair and opened the door for Mary.

"Interrupting anything?" she said as she came in.

"Just slogging through this chapter." Garrett sighed.

"You must be Jack." Mary's voice was soft and intimate. A slight lisp whispered at the edge of some of her words. And the imperfection made Jack like her that much more.

Jack stood up and took her hand. "Hey. Walt talked a lot about you. I just wish we could meet under happier circumstances."

"Yes, well." Sadness in her eyes—but there was acceptance, too. "Walt had so many things he wanted to show you, Jack. Pajaro Beach was his real home. He used to tell me all the things you two would do—"

Garrett cleared his throat loudly, head still down in the manuscript.

Mary got the hint. "I'll let you two finish," Mary said. "I'll go in to say hello to Walt."

She was moving toward the house when Garrett called after her, "If he's asleep, don't wake him!" He turned back to Jack and pointed at the manuscript. "Sorry, Jack, this part just doesn't work for me. I mean, obviously you've written it to be funny, but—"

Jack stood up. "I've got to get my tape recorder before I head out." He pulled the door shut behind him and walked down to the boathouse.

Garrett's voice came from behind. "And bring up those interview tapes you made with my dad!"

Jack gave no indication he had heard.

When he got back up to the house, Mary stood beside the Mercedes waiting for him.

"Garrett said you were going to bring him something."

"Ah, let him wait."

Mary laughed, mischief in her voice. "So we're off then?"

"Yeah, let's split."

Climbing into the Mercedes, Jack saw Garrett look up from the manuscript and scowl. Jack waved to him. Ernie waved back.

———

"You on your lunch hour?" Jack asked as they drove to lunch. "I heard you work in a hospital."

"Lunch hour? Oh, Garrett didn't tell you? Of course he didn't. Why would he?"

"What happened?"

"After the stroke," she began, "I told Garrett I wanted to take care of Walt. We weren't married but—well, we've been together for five years. I felt I would be the best person to take care of him.

I trained as a nurse years ago, and I know all the doctors on the peninsula. Plus, I could find a good speech therapist. I hired one to try to get rid of this lisp."

"Your what?"

"My lisp. Didn't you notice?"

"No."

She looked at him, wondering if he was fibbing to save her feelings, which he was. Finally she just said, "Thank you," and smiled. He noticed her mouth was full and her smile was crooked.

The winding road followed the coast. Jack divided his attention between Mary and the views of the coastline, waves exploding on jagged rocks, foaming, and returning to the ocean.

"So I told Garrett I wanted to take care of Walt. He said nothing. I told him I was quitting my job, where I've worked for fifteen years for a boss whom I absolutely adore. Garrett said nothing."

"I'm gettin' a bad feeling about this."

"Wait till you hear. I gave notice and left my job, and *then* Garrett announced that he was moving here with his family to take care of Walt himself."

"What an asshole."

She nodded. "Garrett pretends to be giving Walt the best care in the world. But you see, he's got Walt right where he wants him. He's Garrett's prisoner."

"But Walt's got other kids. They must have some say in all this."

"Garrett's the executor of Walt's fortune. They're scared to cross Garrett, because he'll cut them off."

Mary turned inland and downshifted as they climbed a steep hill running up to a cliff above the bay. She worked the shifter with confidence. They didn't speak again until she pulled into the restaurant and they stepped out of the car. Sycamores rose high above, framing a rambling adobe restaurant overlooking the ocean.

"This is where Walt and I had our first date," Mary said.

They sat at a table in the restaurant overlooking a garden, a lawn, and then the rocky cove. There was a heavenly smell of baked bread in the air. The waiter set down a basket of sourdough rolls and asked what they wanted to drink. Mary ordered a glass of white wine. Jack asked for a Sierra Nevada on tap.

"You know, I'll try one of those too," Mary told the waiter. "I'm sick of wine."

"It's damn good beer," Jack said. Then, when the waiter left: "Maybe there's something I can do about Garrett."

"What?"

"I'm not like Walt's kids. He's never going to leave me any money. So I can burn my bridges."

She broke open a roll, releasing a puff of steam. "But, see, if you cross Garrett, he'll sabotage the book."

"I thought of that." Jack sank his teeth into a warm, moist piece of bread. "But we're in this state of mutual dependence." He chewed slowly on the bread, drawing out his dramatic pause. It was a real relief to be here with Mary, away from the big cold house with all the fear inside. "Garrett could fire me and kill the book. But then he'd lose the money. And we both know he's so tight he squeaks."

"True. But his ego is so frail that he'd sacrifice the book to keep Walt from getting any attention. He'd do that, Jack. He's that low. I mean, he's ruined my life."

Her eyes got shiny and she looked away.

Jack watched her and nodded. "You know, I'm pissed 'cause this screwed up my big break. But for you it's much worse. It's got to be a real bummer what happened."

"Major bummer. I mean, I know it's hard for you to understand this, at your age—how old are you, anyway?"

"Thirty-five next month."

"I'll be forty soon." She made a face. "Two months ago, we were traveling all over, meeting people, having the time of our lives. The whole world was open in front of me. I thought I was set. Now I've lost my best friend. I'm getting old, losing my looks…It's a big scary world out there. Where do I fit now? What have I got anyone is going to want?"

After a moment, Jack said softly, "I don't mean to say anything inappropriate, but you ain't exactly losing your looks."

She laughed, sniffed back her tears, and spontaneously reached over and squeezed his hand.

The waiter brought their beers in tall frosty glasses. Jack sat back and took a long pull and could feel it go all the way down. He thought of something and leaned forward again. "Last night, Ernie gets a call and Garrett thinks it's about that father-and-son show they were talking with the studio about. Sounded to me like things are heating up—Garrett's waiting for the network to make a decision."

"Yes, before the stroke, Walt told me they were interested, particularly when they heard Walt had a tell-all bio coming out. No doubt Garrett will try to worm his way into the producer's slot."

"Exactly. But I'd say it looks like Garrett needs the book. And Garrett needs me."

Mary was about to speak when the waiter appeared. Mary ordered the grilled mahi-mahi. Jack went for the Mexican platter.

As the waiter left, Mary said, "Everything you say *sounds* good. But I've known Garrett a long time. We can laugh about him being an asshole, but Jack, he's a deeply disturbed person. He's—he's sick, really."

"What are you saying?"

"He's clever in a twisted way." She turned the beer glass in her fingers. Jack noticed she had beautiful hands, smooth with long slender fingers. "And some of the things he's done to the staff makes me feel like he's just plain sadistic."

"Yeah, Walt told me stories of things he'd do when he was a kid—the way he treated his sister and his stepbrothers."

"So I think Garrett is manipulative enough to get what he wants and cut you out of everything."

"So could I. For example, we're going over the manuscript now. Garrett calls his notes 'niggles.'" Jack put the word in quotation marks with his fingers. "It's up to me to change the 'niggles' in the computer and print out a new manuscript before it is sent to the publisher. But somehow, I doubt that that will happen."

He was expecting a laugh. Instead she frowned.

"He'd go into a murderous rage."

"Ya think?"

"Yes. I mean that literally—he's violent."

"How do you know?"

"Last week, Hilda, the cook, came back from shopping and parked in the driveway to unload the groceries. Garrett came out and happened to look into one of the bags and saw she got *whole* milk."

"So?"

"Just think of the fat."

"Oh yeah," Jack said, getting it. "He's got that thing about low-fat stuff."

"So Garrett said, 'Who's this for?' And Hilda said, 'Your father.' So Garrett said, 'My father's on a fat-free diet!' And she got so nervous, she said, 'But he looks like he was in Auschwitz.' Whoa. Garrett went off—big-time. 'I didn't order this!' he kept yelling. And she became so afraid that—that he would do something to her. So she ran inside."

Mary began laughing. "And Ernie went nuts too. It was like they were feeding on each other. I mean, Ernie's strange, okay? He's like this attack dog for whoever is in charge. So Garrett's outside tearing open the bags and throwing food all over the place. And when he tried to come in, Hilda locked the door. This made him madder, so he tried another door. And Hilda and the nurse ran from door to door, locking them, while he screamed at them from outside."

Jack watched Mary's face as she laughed. Something was coming from inside her, a vindictiveness he hadn't seen at first. She wasn't quite as aloof as she tried to pretend. And why should she be? Her life traveling the globe with Walt had come to a crashing halt. And she was left out in the cold.

"Later Hilda told me what frightened her was the look on Garrett's face. His face was a hideous red, and his eyes were bugging out. It was like, if he got inside, he would have killed both her and the nurse both." She wasn't laughing anymore. She leaned forward and spoke softly. "I think he's capable of it. I really do."

While the waiter set salads in front of them, Jack thought of the scene: Garrett's face like a balloon filled with hot blood, ready to explode. When the waiter left and they were alone again, he spoke softly.

"I just had a crazy idea. Garrett told me that heart trouble runs in the family. That's why he's on this stupid low-fat diet. I'm just goofing around now."

"Sure. I understand. What's your idea?"

"Maybe we could get Garrett so worked up he'd have a heart attack."

"Things like that have gone through my mind," she said, picking up a fork. "I mean, a simple traffic accident would solve our problems."

They ate in silence for a moment, both pursuing the same thought.

"Really, the best thing you can do now is finish the book. Walt loved what you wrote. When he flew up here Friday nights, he'd always have the new chapter. He'd make me read it to him while we were driving home. It was enormously satisfying to him—he felt his image was intact. But soon Walt will die, and my darling will go to heaven and be at peace."

"While we're left here to beat our heads against the wall," Jack said, thinking of his recent years in Hollywood, his sputtering marriage, how everything had come up short.

Jack's bitterness startled Mary, but she nodded sympatheti-cally. "Your book will come out. And it will be successful. I've read it. It's damn good."

Jack took a deep breath and reached for his tape recorder. Time to get back to work. He pressed record and set it close to her.

"Let's go back in time now," he said, imitating Walt Stuckey's introductions on the old TV show. "Back to a simpler time, a happier time."

She was laughing at his imitation. "That's good."

"Back to a time before Garrett." Then in his own voice: "Tell me about your relationship with Walt."

She dabbed her lips with the napkin. "I'll tell you anything you want to know. But I guarantee you, it'll never make it into the book."

"Why? Walt told me he wanted a section of it to be about your relationship."

"Garrett will get out his razor knife and cut it right off the page."

Hamming it up now, Jack said, "Just let him try. Remember, I still control the book."

She looked at him for a moment before answering. When she did, her voice was weak and distant. "I certainly hope so."

EIGHT

Time got away from them. One beer led to another. The next thing Jack knew, it was three thirty. He thought about phoning, but screw it, what was wrong with doing a longer interview if it was for the good of the book?

When Jack got back to the house, Garrett was in the office, bent over the manuscript. Without looking up, Garrett said, "Have a nice lunch?"

"Yes, thanks." Jack was thrown off by Garrett's attitude. He had expected him to be suspicious of the way Jack had conspired with the enemy. He was smart enough to see that Jack and Mary hit it off, and he probably knew they had trashed him big-time. Now this pleasant, relaxed tone. Why?

They worked on the book all afternoon and through the following day. The next morning they were still in the office, reviewing the final chapters that Jack had written. Ernie was sitting nearby at his desk, as if chained there. Jack never saw him even get up. He wondered if there was a little pot for him to pee in hidden under the desk.

The door opened. They looked up and saw the nurse, Doreen, wheeling Walt through the office on his way outside for some fresh air. Walt was wearing an old cowboy hat to keep the sun off his baldpate.

In his overly loud voice, the voice he always used when talking to his father, Garrett said, "Hi, Dad!" as he covered up the manuscript with some other papers on his desk. "How ya feelin' today, cowboy?" Garrett answered his own question, saying, "Shucks, Garrett boy, I'm feelin' fit as a fiddle ta-day."

Ernie guffawed, enjoying the horseplay.

Walt slowly raised his head and looked up at Garrett, then turned to take in Jack. Deep in the sad eyes there was a spark of recognition, a surprise that jarred him back into the real world. He smiled, nodded, and said, "Jack, I been meaning to tell you about—"

Doreen looked startled. She shot a look at Garrett but said nothing.

Walt began humming and rocking, trying to form words.

Doreen crouched next to Walt in the wheelchair and gently said, "Look, Mr. Stuckey, they're working on your book."

Behind Walt, Garrett was shaking his head, gesturing to Doreen.

"Don't mention the book!" he whispered to her.

"What?"

"The *book*. It might confuse him."

Doreen looked at Garrett with an are-you-for-real expression. Then, seeing the color in Garrett's face rising like a geyser of blood, she quickly wheeled Walt out of the room. They moved down the path toward the ocean.

"Stupid bitch," Garrett hissed as the door closed.

"What's wrong with mentioning the book?" Jack kept his voice even.

"Not you too!" Garrett said, turning on Jack.

"Hey, it's Walt's book."

"In case you can't tell"—Garrett spit the words like nails— "my father's in a delicate mental condition. Any mention of the past could completely throw him off."

"Is that what the doctor said?"

"No, I'm making this all up. Of course it's what the doctor said!" Garrett's eyes were popping, his face ready to explode.

Jack thought back to his lunch with Mary. How much could Garrett's heart take? He pictured Garrett falling to the floor, thrashing in pain. The paramedics might have trouble finding the house. No one's fault—just one of those unfortunate things that happen sometimes. He sure hoped Ernie didn't know CPR.

Jack continued. "Since it's Walt's life story, it seems kind of stupid to keep it a secret from him."

"Stupid? Let me try to explain something to you. He's trying to sort out reality from unreality now. The past from the present—"

"I get all that. But how is the mention of something that was definitely a part of his life going to upset him? I mean, what you're saying is you might as well not mention anything that ever happened to him."

"What I'm saying is, that *bitch* ought to know better than to stick her fat ass into my family's business."

"Jesus, Garrett, it was an innocent remark."

"Is that what you think?"

"Yeah."

"*Yih?*" Garrett imitated Jack's Jersey accent. "Well, here's what I think. Dad has ideas about what his career and all that was all about. And then there's reality. Okay?"

"I'm not with you."

"Sure, people loved him. But not for the reasons he thinks. So I'm the one who's going to clean up the book. Okay?"

"In an autobiography, I think a person has the right to explain who they think they are. That's what the book's about. And I don't think that will upset Walt at all. In fact, it could help him."

"Oh really. And exactly what are you basing this on?"

"My gut."

"Your gut?" He stood up and began charging back and forth. "Okay, so as long as you approve of making gut decisions, then I'll act on it too."

He stomped over to the window, looking at Doreen and Walt down on the pathway to the ocean.

"Ernie, go tell Doreen to get up here. And I want you to stay with Dad."

Ernie hurried outside, relieved to be out of the line of fire.

Jack watched Ernie moving away from the house and began to get a sick feeling.

"What are you going to do?"

"Act on my common sense, as you suggested."

"Garrett, if you're pissed at me that's one thing. For Christ's sake, don't take it out on her."

"She can be replaced. But you—oh, you're some hot-shit Hollywood writer."

"I never said that. I'm just saying she didn't do anything that—"

Doreen opened the door and stepped inside. Her face was white. "Ernie said you wanted to—"

Garrett breathed deeply, his eyes raking her, seeing the way she cowered in front of him. "You're fired. Get out of here."

"What?"

"Are you deaf *and* stupid? I said you're fired."

"Garrett, don't do this," Jack said.

"Leave your key on my desk and get the hell out of here."

Doreen stammered. "Mr. Stuckey, please. I—I really think this is unfair to—"

"You should have thought of that before you made so many fucking mistakes with my father."

"What did I do?"

"Look, Garrett, this is my fault," Jack said. "I shouldn't have said anything. If you want an apology from me—"

Garrett turned on him. "This has nothing to do with you!" Spit flew from his lips, his teeth exposed, his eyes wild with rage.

Garrett headed for the hallway to the house. Doreen caught him by the arm. "Mr. Stuckey—"

He stopped, looking at her hand.

"I have a little boy. He's only five, and he has this condition where I have to buy—"

"Let go of me."

"The treatments are very expensive, and if I lose my job—".

"Excuse me, Doreen. Garrett," Jack said. "I'm not going to let you do this."

Garrett spun and stabbed a finger at Jack. "Watch it, pal. I'll pull the plug on your book."

"Please," Doreen said. "For my son."

"What makes you think I give a damn about your son? Or your pathetic life? Put your key on my desk and get off my property."

Garrett disappeared into the house. Doreen slowly turned to Jack.

"I'm sorry. I tried to stop him but—"

"Great job. Thanks a lot." She looked at Jack, and her sarcasm changed to despair. "Oh, what's the point? What's the point of anything?" She threw the key on the floor and walked out the door.

Jack stood alone in the room, listening to Doreen's old car accelerating away. Ernie had gone inside with Garrett. And the house was suddenly quiet. Jack noticed he could hear the waves crashing on the rocks down at the cove.

Checking once more to make sure there were no sounds of approaching footsteps, Jack stooped, picked up the key, and pocketed it.

NINE

It was almost midnight, and Jack was in the boathouse reading and feeling like hell about what happened when he heard *tap, tap, tap* on the door.

He had been looking at scrapbooks from the early sixties—his eyes were on the yellowed press clippings of *The Walt Stuckey Comedy Hour,* but his mind was churning with what happened that day. Wind moaned through the trees outside. A buoy clanged somewhere out on the dark waters. The fire in his stove shot sparks out onto the planks of the boathouse floor. He was tired, and his nerves were like broken glass.

Tap, tap, tap.

There it was again, so faint Jack thought it was a branch on the window. He waited.

Tap, tap, tap.

He moved through the gloom of the boathouse in his bare feet, jeans, and a T-shirt. He opened the door.

"I had an idea," Mary said, standing there, arms folded across her chest, wearing a big woolly sweater over a white turtleneck. Her thick blond hair was tangled by the night wind. Cold wind swirled into the room.

"An idea?"

"About what we could do about all this."

He stood aside, and she stepped inside. He closed the door.

"So you heard what happened?"

"Doreen called me."

"What a jerk I was, showing off—"

"Jack don't—"

"—trying to be a hero, standing up to Garrett."

"It wasn't your fault."

"Yeah, right. It's always my fault. Ask my wife." He felt stupid saying that, so he laughed.

Mary saw Jack's books on his bed spread open under the light. "You're writing."

"Just reading. But I can't concentrate. Tell me your idea."

She half turned and nodded in the direction she came. "I just live around the edge of the cove there. There's a path through the woods. I was in bed, trying to sleep, but I kept thinking of Doreen. And then I thought of you alone over here. And then I had this thought. I—I didn't know how else to tell you."

She stood in the middle of the boathouse looking around.

"I've never been in here. I see it from the house all the time, but I've never been in here." She looked at the boat and the sails and the oars stowed in the rafters and the cans of cheerful paint. "It reminds me of summer…" she said, smiling sadly. "Summer… and being young."

"I like it here. Beats the hell out of staying up in the death house." He didn't know what made him say that.

Moving together toward the stove now, she said, "It's awful in that house. All the people tippy-toeing around, afraid to set Garrett off. And little by little, Walt's slipping away. Slipping away…"

She warmed her hands at the fire.

"Tea?" He indicated a pot of water on top of the stove. "It's all I've got. Well…" He laughed. "I can drop a little brandy in it too. A depth charge."

She laughed. "I'd almost forgotten about those. It's been a while since my drinking days."

He poured a mug of tea and added a glug of brandy from the pint bottle. She took the mug and warmed her hands on it, inhaling the alcohol in the steam. They stood beside each other, and he noticed Mary came up to his shoulder. Suddenly, he thought about what it would feel like to hold her. She looked so good in that woolly sweater. It had been a long time since he held a woman—really held a woman. Sarah cut him off when his career started to fade, and she never really warmed up again.

"Don't have any chairs," he said, indicating for her to sit on the cot. He sat beside her, and they were awkward, alone like this in the middle of the night.

Mary set her tea down and peeled off the bulky sweater, leaving it behind her on the bed. Jack saw her shape in the white turtleneck tucked into faded jeans. And he saw how young and smooth her face looked in this light. She had been in bed, trying to sleep, she said. But she had lipstick on, Jack noticed. And a little mascara.

Her voice was dreamy as she said, "I've been thinking a lot about our lunch. You don't know how good it feels to talk to you about all this."

He knew what she meant. He had so many things he wanted to tell her—about his marriage, about his love for Chloe, about the anger he felt about the direction his life and his writing career was going. But he didn't want to scare her, come off like a psycho or something, so he just nodded and waited for whatever would come next.

"So what's your great idea?"

She looked in the fire as if for an answer, then turned to him and said, "We're going to heal Walt."

"Heal him?"

"Yes, and when Walt's better, he'll throw Garrett out of the house. He'll write him right out of his fucking will."

"I love the sound of that. But how're we going to do it?"

"I called the speech therapist who examined Walt. She said a stroke victim will often make enormous progress if there's some reason to recover."

"Like…"

"Like some job, something left undone, something that needs to be finished."

"The book."

"Exactly. The book has to be finished."

The fire had burned down to coals. The room was dark. Jack took the last swallow from his mug and found that it was mostly brandy. The liquor was doing its job. He felt strong, warm in his center, like he still had a chance to make something good happen. He waited for Mary to continue, knowing it would all be good news.

"We need to find a way to get to Walt on our own. It won't be hard, because Walt is awake all night. That's why he sleeps all day—because he understands what's happening around him, and he can't stand it. But at night Garrett isn't there. So he lies awake. Now, if we could just find a way to get to him—"

She stopped talking because Jack was moving beside her, reaching into his pocket and taking out something. It was a brass key, the key Doreen had thrown on the floor that afternoon as she walked out the door.

TEN

Walt's house loomed ahead of them, huge and dark and silent.

Mary was leading, feeling her way along the path under the cypress and pines while Jack trailed, holding the manuscript. She stopped suddenly, and he bumped into her. Her hand found his, and they continued, connected now.

They stopped and looked up at the big house. There was an enormous central area—with a dining room and living room— that separated the two wings. One wing housed Garrett and his family, the other was where Walt's bedroom was. It had once been a study, but they'd recently added a wheelchair ramp and an outside door. Just off the living room was a small room where they knew the night nurse was either dozing, reading, or maybe watching TV.

Mary turned to Jack, still holding his hand, the wind moving her hair.

"When we get inside, close the door to the hallway." He could smell the brandy on her breath. He leaned forward to catch her words, one of his hands on her arm, steadying them. "And before you turn on any lights, make sure the shades are pulled."

They crept up the wheelchair ramp and came to the rear door. He eased the key into the lock, feeling it slide over the tumblers. This entrance wasn't used much, so he was afraid the lock would be rusty. He pulled in on the door handle to take pressure off the dead bolt and turned...turned...turned...

Click! The bolt shot back. Not loud. But not exactly an innocent night noise either.

They froze, looking through the glass, expecting to see the nurse poke her head out of the room down the hallway. Jack waited, holding his breath, and he became aware once again of the sound of the surf and the wind. It was a restless night. The kind of night that made even a sturdy house give off ticks and groans that couldn't easily be explained.

But the nurse didn't appear. No lights snapped on suddenly. There was no reason not to slide the door open and...

They stepped through the door, and Jack pulled it shut after them. They were inside now, inside Walt's bedroom. If Garrett caught them in here, Jack knew it would be adios to the book and his dreams of finally being a published writer.

The thick carpets sucked all the noise out of the air around them. A faint whisper came from the central heating system. Other than that, the house was enveloped in a suffocating silence.

Jack moved across Walt's room to the door to the hallway. He paused and listened, hearing the faint sound of late-night television. The nurse had her portable TV set on—white noise that would blot out any sounds they made, he hoped. He closed the door to the hallway.

Turning, Jack surveyed the room in the faint glow of a nightlight. Walt was lying in a hospital bed with the back raised at an angle, his arms outside the covers. His breathing was hoarse in the stillness. A bureau along the wall was stacked with pill bottles and medical equipment.

Jack crossed the room and slowly pulled the shades. He turned on the small tensor light beside the bed and saw that Walt was indeed awake. His sad eyes, the only link to the prisoner inside, followed them around the room. Watching them, his hands began fluttering excitedly, trying to convey his feelings. He motioned Mary to his side. She took his hand, bent over, and kissed him. Walt sighed and said, "Lady Mary."

"Yes, Walt, Lady Mary has come to rescue you. With Jack too."

"How ya doin', Walt?"

Walt laughed. When he smiled, the skin on his old face was baby smooth. He laughed again and said, "How the hell do you two think you're gonna—"

They waited for more, so glad to hear his familiar voice.

Walt took a deep breath and said, "No." He started frowning. "No, no, no."

Watching his face turn from laughter to frustration, Jack realized the words were getting stuck somewhere between his brain and his mouth. The words Walt heard so clearly in his mind were lost in the dark corridors of his consciousness, speaking to a dead audience. *The greatest entertainer of his time has no comeback line*, Jack thought.

Mary felt Walt's anger and patted his hand.

"Walt, honey, you don't have to talk."

"No," he said. "No, no, no. NO!"

They looked at each other in alarm. Jack watched the door, thinking it might open at any second to reveal the nurse. Or worse yet, Garrett.

Mary bent over Walt, talking to him softly, alternating soothing words with light kisses on his lips. Jack saw that her body was pressed to his, her chest to his, and oddly, he found himself wondering if a stroke victim was still capable of getting aroused. He knew this was an inappropriate thought, but felt all bets were off that night. So he stood there by the door like a sentry, watching Lady Mary kiss Walt and hoping for Walt's sake that something was stirring under the covers.

Walt stopped trying to talk and lay back, his forehead smooth, his features relaxed, and his eyes bright. He breathed out a long sigh and yielded to the sheer pleasure of Mary's affections.

Mary turned to Jack, speaking softly. "Walt, you remember the wonderful book you were writing with Jack? Well, it's time to get back to work on it." She paused, and they both watched his face for a reaction. They saw the words going in and connecting to something. But he remained silent, waiting for more.

"Jack brought some new chapters with him," Mary continued. "He's going to read them to you and see what you think. How's that sound?"

Walt nodded.

"Jack, you want to set it up?"

Walt turned, his face expectant. Jack left his post at the door and pulled up a chair beside the bed. He knew that Mary was doing her best to treat Walt as if he were in perfectly good mental health. He would do the same.

"Walt, this new chapter isn't about the show at all. I thought it might be time for a break from talking about television and celebrities. Remember that great story you told me about that old Mercedes you bought? I thought that would be a good way to segue into a chapter about your classic car collecting and some of your other hobbies."

Jack looked for a reaction. A look of burning anticipation showed in the old man's eyes, and Jack imagined it was the way he reacted before the stroke when he flew up from LA, clutching a new chapter, and asked Mary to read it aloud. In the silence, he imagined Walt saying, "Sounds dandy, Jack. Fire away."

Mary sat on the edge of the bed, holding Walt's hand. They were like children ready for a bedtime story. Jack found his place in the manuscript, cleared his throat, and began.

Maybe it was because my old man could never afford a car when I was a kid growing up in Hoboken. Maybe it was because I had some sort of undiagnosed condition where I couldn't resist anything made of chrome and glass. Whatever the reason, I spent every minute away from the show trying to figure out how to get my hands on any car that caught my eye. The one I wanted in the worst way

*was a 1960 300 SL Mercedes Gullwing, the kind where the
doors open up like a bird in flight.*

*I located a 300 SL up in New England, owned by an
old German who'd brought the car over himself from the
Fatherland. It wasn't a stock model. It had been built
for testing by Mercedes. And it had something no other
model had: a switch under the dashboard that fired up
the supercharger.*

*I can still remember standing next to the Gullwing in
the German's barn.*

*"Flip za switch," the German told me, "unt za car
turns into a freakin' rocket."*

I had to have that car.

Jack stopped reading and looked at Walt. His eyes had closed
as he listened to the words, his own words. But as silence settled
on the room, his eyes snapped open again. Jack imagined him
saying, "Why hell'd you stop reading? Go on! Go on!"

*After a lengthy negotiation, I finally bought the Gullwing
and drove it back to New York. The only problem was,
there was nowhere it could stretch its legs. I drove the
damn thing around Manhattan doing no more than
twenty-five miles an hour for two years. I was too busy
to get away. Then, finally, I saw a two-day window of
free time. I threw some clothes in the car and headed
for upstate New York. My idea was to drive to Montreal
and back.*

*I'm about halfway there, it's about midnight, and I'm
still doing the speed limit. Out of nowhere this brand new
Corvette blew by me doing about 120 miles an hour. Well,
I couldn't let that pass. I'd waited long enough. I planted
my foot on the gas pedal.*

Ninety, one hundred miles an hour, no problem. But the Corvette is still way out in front. I hit about 115, and the thing flattened out. The well was dry.

Jack looked over and saw that Walt's eyes had opened. He was straining forward, his lips moving, trying to form words. Jack began reading again.

Then I remembered. The supercharger! This was the time to use the supercharger! I'd never used it before, and I didn't know what would happen. My hand trembling, I reached under the dash and flipped the switch. VA-ROOM! That old Kraut was right. Za car took off like a freakin' rocket. The Corvette never saw me coming. And I was about thirty miles down the road, still accelerating, when I threw a rod, and the engine blew up. The thing was totaled, but I didn't care. It had all been worth it just to feel that supercharger kick in.

Mary began laughing. Then Walt began laughing and nodding, tears showing in his eyes as he said, "Za supercharger, yah," and laughed some more.

Their laughter must have hidden the sound of the door opening because, the next thing they knew, the nurse appeared frowning beside them, saying, "What's going on here?"

Mary turned to her, very smooth, as if she had nothing to hide, and said, "Oh, Leslie, it's you. Come in, come in."

"How did you get in here?"

Leslie had teased-out hair and violently long red fingernails. Her body was lean and muscled under loose scrubs, and the strap of a black bra showed on one shoulder. She made Jack think of a nurse in a porno movie, ready to rip off the scrubs and do it with a big, hairy, fake-looking doctor.

"Have a seat," Mary said, moving behind her to shut the door.

"I asked how you got in here."

"Walt gave me a key long ago."

"Garrett had all the locks changed."

"Leslie, have you met Jack Dillon? He's writing Walt's book."

"Good to meet you, Leslie." Jack copied Mary's tone, acting as if nothing strange was happening.

"No one's supposed to be in here."

"Of course not. But you know about Walt and me?"

"But Garrett told me you weren't—"

"Leslie, are you Garrett's slave? Or are you trying to help this patient?"

"I'm trying to keep my job, lady."

Jack decided to take a new approach. "Mary, I think we better tell her, don't you?"

"I guess so."

"Garrett told me he was losing faith in the staff, the nursing staff, because Walt's not making any progress."

"It's not our job to rehabilitate him. We're just supposed to—"

"You know how Garrett is. He feels you aren't creating an atmosphere conducive to his father's recovery. So our idea was, we'd come in here, read him the book, remind him of who he is, with the idea that it might bring him back. And he's responding, isn't he, Mary?"

"Oh yes. It's so great."

"No," Walt suddenly piped up, his face working with difficulty. "No, no, no."

Leslie stepped toward Walt possessively. "It's too cold in here. And look—" She roughly pulled up the covers, shoving Walt's arms underneath. He fought her saying, "No, NO! NO!"

Jack continued, hoping to regain control. "We know Garrett will be pleased with the change in his father's condition, and this will reflect well on you and the staff. But of course, we couldn't exactly ask you to condone this approach. So we better not say anything to Garrett."

"What's condone mean?" she asked, resenting the fact that Jack was speaking above her head.

"Well, I just meant we couldn't ask you to go along with this."

"You're damn right I won't go along with this. And when Garrett hears about this—"

"Garrett isn't going to hear about this," Mary said firmly.

"No? Everything you say is bullshit. First thing in the morning, I'm gonna report this whole—"

"Listen, Miss Bitch," Mary said, using a tone that surprised Jack. He'd never heard her speak this way before and, hearing it now, he realized there was something deep in her personality he didn't know about, a time or place or situation that had hardened her. But he knew this wasn't the time to wonder what it meant, so he watched silently, hoping she knew what she was doing.

Mary stepped toward Leslie, her finger stabbing the air.

"Leslie, so help me, you say one word to Garrett about this, and his wife is going to hear all about your *paid* apartment and the way Garrett drops in for you to give him a little afternoon delight. And that's the end of your job here and the end of any work you get from the nursing agency."

"Garrett does *not* pay for my apartment."

Jack couldn't help noticing she denied the lesser of the two charges. But he thought that Leslie might be ready to back down.

"Leslie, Garrett's wife will buy our story, and she'll come after you. Now, you can play along with us, or you can get your ass fired. What's it gonna be?"

Mary paused, her eyes burning into Leslie's eyes, breathing hard, letting her threat sink in. Time to soften it now so Leslie's pride would let her accept it. Mary put her arm around her shoulders.

"All we're asking is for you not to mention this to Garrett. Just pretend you never walked in on this."

"But if he finds out…"

Mary laughed pleasantly. She dropped the harsh tone just as quickly as it erupted. "You can handle Garrett. And when he sees the progress his father's making, he'll give you all the credit."

"And you deserve it," Jack said.

"Because you made the right decision here."

Leslie folded her arms across her chest. "I don't know...I don't like this one bit."

"The medical field is filled with tough decisions, Leslie. We know you'll do the right thing," Mary said.

They turned and headed for the back door. Jack made the mistake of looking back into the room, back at Walt, who was half-raised on one elbow, reaching out to them, a look of terror on his baby-smooth old face. *He looks like a child,* Jack thought, *like the first day I left Chloe at the sitter's.* She had screamed and kicked and tried to get back into her father's arms. Where she knew she was safe, where she could feel his love.

It was the same for Walt now. The only two people who loved him were leaving, and in the nightmare of his confused mind, he had no idea when they would ever come back.

When they got back to the boathouse, Jack opened the door for Mary, but she hesitated, standing there in the darkness, the sound of the surf outside the cove. She said, "I'm so sorry, Jack. I think I just ruined your book."

"I don't think she'll do anything. You really tore her a new one."

"I don't know. I'm afraid she's going to tell Garrett just for spite."

The energy was gone between them. They stood there, awkward, wanting to say something that would salvage it all.

"I'm so sorry, Jack," she said, looking down and using her little voice once again, the one with the disarming lisp and the bright easy laugh. But it suddenly sounded off key to Jack as he thought of all he had to lose.

"Are you really sorry?"

She looked up, surprised. "Of course I am."

"It was your idea to go up there. And you didn't seem all that surprised when Leslie came busting in."

"Jack, what are you saying?"

"I don't know exactly. I thought we were on the same side but now—"

Her eyes searched his face. "Please. It's late. Let's talk tomorrow. Things will seem better then."

"I guess they'd have to," he said. "Because right now they seem pretty damn awful."

She nodded and reached out and touched his arm. Then she was moving away from him, the darkness swallowing her. A moment later, after she had disappeared, he heard her voice on the wind, saying, "Good night, Jack."

ELEVEN

Jack got, at the most, about one fitful hour of sleep. Stumbling toward the house in the bright stillness of morning, he felt like he'd been bashed between the eyes with a ball peen hammer. He threw down two cups of coffee, bracing himself for Garrett's wrath. But Garrett's manner was unchanged. Maybe Leslie hadn't spilled the beans after all.

"Shall we hit it?" Garrett asked. They settled at the big conference table in the office, the white block of manuscript pages in front of them.

"Where were we? Oh yes. Now, I've got a little niggle with this section."

Jack gritted his teeth at his use of that word. He waited for Garrett to explain his point.

"You open this chapter by saying that the show was *live*, so it was like a stage play seen by millions of Americans. But then you bring in examples that were in taped acts. That goes against the theme of the chapter—the theme you set up."

Jack skimmed the opening, the words unsteady in his vision. Man, his brain was like a lump of clay. "I hate it when you're right," he said at last.

Garrett grunted a laugh. "Just doing my job."

"Here's a fix," Jack paused, looking at the pages. "I'll remove the sentence about the show being live. Just open by saying that things always seemed to go wrong and then use a few examples."

"But you're quoting my dad, so it needs to be accurate." Garrett reread the sentence. "Did he really say this?"

"Sure he did. Why?"

"It doesn't sound like him."

"It's on the tape."

"Better check it."

Jack made a note to do so.

"Now," Garrett added sharply. "Check it now."

Jack looked at him.

"I mean right fucking now."

Jack looked at Garrett and saw that horrible look in his eyes, the almost sleepy look of pleasure that preceded his tirades, as if he were letting go of all sanity before he slipped into a trance of rage. And Jack suddenly realized that this had all been an elaborate setup.

"And while you're at it, Jackie boy, get the rest of the tapes." He stood and picked up Jack's coffee mug. "I'll get you a refill." He disappeared into the house.

Jack sat there wondering what to do. He looked around and found Ernie sneering at him, his eyes narrowing, giving him a flat, animal look of cruelty and stupidity. Jack had the sudden distant memory of kids ganging up on him on the playground. Separately they were cowards; together they were a pack of wolves.

"Get him the tapes, Jack. He already asked you for them three times."

"Sure," Jack said, standing. "I'll just go ahead and grab those all-important tapes."

Jack opened the back door and headed for the boathouse. Okay, he'd get the damn tapes. He'd transcribed them all anyway. But part of him didn't want to give them up. He liked the idea of having an actual recording of him, Jack Dillon, interviewing this entertainment legend. He wanted history to know—as if it cared—that he had had a relationship with this comic genius who had entertained millions. He wanted the record to show that he had shared moments and memories with Walt. Yes, moments and memories that brought back emotions.

In the gloom of the boathouse he laid out the eight ninety-minute tapes that constituted his relationship with Walt. Looking at them, he remembered how they sat around the coffee table in Walt's house, delving into the past, the names of movie stars in the air, the rain pouring down outside, a feeling of intimacy and trust between them. Now Garrett would eavesdrop, listen with a cynical ear, maybe use the tapes to rewrite the manuscript.

After he started working with Garrett, he had intended to make copies of the tapes in case he had to hand them over. But when he found out how much that would cost, he postponed the idea until he got the second half of his advance. He just didn't think things would unravel this quickly. But now this. Garrett was trying to sever all connections between Jack and Walt. He wanted to make Jack a nonentity again, stamping out his existence in Walt's world and banishing him to the realm of all the little, insignificant people who had passed silently through their household.

Jack felt sick to his stomach. He was tired and churned up and didn't know what to do. How few could he give Garrett and get away with it? Four, five?

Back in the office he found Garrett seated at the desk. No coffee refill was in sight. Ernie stood to one side of Garrett's desk, arms folded across his chest, poised and ready.

Jack put four tapes in front of Garrett.

"That's all?"

"I've got a few more at home. Forgot to bring them."

Garrett nodded. "Okay, Jackie. Okay. Whatever you say." He took the tapes and put them in the desk drawer. He locked the drawer.

Bad sign, Jack thought.

"I thought you wanted to listen to them."

"I'll do that later," Garrett said, rising slowly, the sleepy look in his eyes burning off and the rage gathering. His face was turning red, filling with color like the top of a thermometer left in the blazing sun.

"Tell me something, *Jack*." Garrett spit out his name with disgust.

Here it comes, he thought. Leslie blew the whistle on them. But Garrett didn't want to confront Jack until he controlled the tapes. Very slick. He had underestimated Garrett.

In the stillness Jack flashed on what Mary had said last night. *I'm so sorry, Jack. I ruined your book.*

"Can you explain something to me, Jackie boy?"

"I'll give it my best shot."

"What the *fuck* gives you the right?"

"I'm not with you, Garrett."

"Who the *fuck* do you think you are?"

"Want to see my ID?"

"You know what I'm talking about. You think you can play God. So you and that bitch go into my father's room. *My father!*" Spit flew from Garrett's lips, and his eyes bugged. "Just what the hell did you expect to accomplish?"

"Something you'd never understand."

"Try me."

"We wanted to help him. *Help*—get it?"

"Help him? How?"

"For starters, we thought we'd treat him like a human being."

"Meaning?"

Easy, Jack, he said to himself. *Don't unload yet. Maybe you can pull this out.*

"I'm waiting for an explanation, Jack." Garrett's head was cocked, neck exposed, revealing patches of mottled skin.

"Look, I know I shouldn't have done it, okay. I apologize. I'll wear a dunce cap all day. But can we just skip the lecture and get back to work on the book?"

Garrett's jaw dropped. "You don't get it, do you?"

"What?"

"You're history, man. You're out of here, you slick Hollywood cocksucking bullshit artist." He paused, breathing hard. "What do you think of that?"

"Well, I guess we're down to it now, aren't we?"

"I'd say so. I mean, I give you a chance to get in print. I devote *my time* to getting this—this piece of shit in shape. And you turn on me like this."

It's slipping away, Jack realized. *Almost gone now.* Garrett had just been waiting for something like this to jump all over. Now he was going to push Jack right to the limit, until maybe he slugged him or something, with Ernie as a bodyguard and witness.

"Let me ask you something, Garrett."

"Ask away, Jackie boy. Ask away."

"Who is the book about? Your dad, who made millions of people laugh, or you, who haven't done a single original thing—had an original thought—in your entire life."

"I'm sorry—the book? Did you say 'the book'? What book is that?"

"That book." Jack pointed at his manuscript lying on the table.

"*That* is not a book," Garrett said, pointing at the manuscript with a look of disgust on his face. "That is paper with typing on it. Did you really think you were going to get that thing published?"

"That's what Walt wanted. Walt. Remember your father? He hired me. That's why I'm here."

"Oh, that's why you're here. I wondered about that. Okay, now we found the problem. Let me straighten you out on something. That"—he pointed at the manuscript—"will never get published."

"And yet we have a publishing contract."

"So what? Let me show you something." Garrett unlocked another desk drawer. He took out a large stack of paper. Jack glanced at the cover page and saw it was another manuscript.

Jack couldn't stop himself. "What's that?"

"My father's autobiography. There were others before you, Jackie. You're not the only guy with a box of crayons and a little talent."

"But it wasn't published."

"My dad pulled it back at the last second—canceled the contract. And this, look at this!" He thumped another manuscript onto the tabletop. "Another guy with talent. Another contract. He thought he was going to have a book with his name on it alongside Walt Stuckey. Wrong! And this"—he took another manuscript out of the drawer—"another manuscript. Another writer. Another contract. No book. See a pattern here?"

Jack stared at the manuscripts in front of him. He felt the ground slipping out from under him. He felt he was clawing desperately at the earth sliding out from under him to stop from falling into some dark pit of nothingness. He saw spots and realized he had stopped breathing.

"But—" Jack began, wanting to say that this book was different. His words were the right ones that would bring Walt's life to life again.

Garrett devoured Jack's expression and fed on it. "But? But what, Jack? Whatsa matter? Out of words all of a sudden?"

Jack was falling now. His whole world in pieces around him, tumbling through space.

"Let me help you out. Walt didn't *want* a book in print. He was a lonely guy. He knew he could find some hack like you to—to jerk him off." Garrett exploded with laughter. "No. I'm sorry. Not jerk off. *Jack* off. That's what you were doing. Jacking each other off."

Garrett turned to Ernie. "Hey, Ernie. He was jacking himself off!"

Ernie exploded with laughter.

"Pow!" Garrett said, throwing pages from the manuscript into the air. "I just shot my wad!" Laughing hysterically, he threw more pages into the air, yelling "Pow!" each time. The pages fell around him like big white leaves. Garrett's braying laughter got into Jack's head and began to expand. He stepped around the desk. Garrett saw him coming and backed behind his chair. Ernie dropped his laugh and stepped forward, hands balling into fists.

"Oh. So what are you going to do now, Mr. Hollywood Hack? Punch me out?"

Yes, it's all gone, Jack realized. But he could still make things worse. He suddenly remembered the call he had taken for Walt, the woman in jail, the echoes of cell doors slamming in the background. Did he want to end up there? That would give Garrett a lot of pleasure. And pleasure was the last thing Jack wanted to give him.

"Come on, big man," Garrett said from behind Ernie's bulk. "Come on. I hope you're better with your fists than you are with your mouth."

Jack took another step forward and was pleased to see a flicker of fear in Ernie's dull eyes. Garrett's mouth was still moving, baiting him, but Jack's brain had short-circuited, and he could hear only static. Then the static faded, and he imagined the leg sweep that would bring Ernie down, the short, powerful two-knuckle punch to the bridge of Garrett's nose, bone and cartilage breaking with a satisfying *crack!* In the dojo he punched the dummy that way all the time. Come to think of it, hitting Garrett might not be that different.

But the sound of cell doors slamming was in Jack's ears, stopping him. He stepped back, thinking, *Not today, my friend. No, not today.* But after he got his things from the boathouse and before he reached his car, another voice answered. *Not today—but another day, real soon.*

———

When Sarah came home from work that evening and walked in the front door, Jack saw her face light up with surprise to see him there. He had arrived an hour earlier after the long drive back to Los Angeles after his fight with Garrett. Surprise, delight, and then concern cycled through her expressions. She stood by the front door, keys still in her hand, regarding Jack warily.

"I thought you were staying up there till the weekend."

"Ran into a little snag."

Her face fell. "They didn't fire you? Oh, please don't tell me they fired you."

"I'm trying to get Carolyn on the line now. She's a good agent. She'll get things patched up."

"They fired you. Oh god, Jack. Not again."

"What? I haven't been fired before."

"But you weren't hired, either. None of your freelance jobs ever lead anywhere."

"Sarah, come on. It'll be okay."

The phone rang.

"That's probably Carolyn. I'll explain in a second."

Jack picked up the portable phone and went into the bedroom, closing the door.

"Carolyn, listen. I ran into a—"

"I know what happened. Garrett called. And he called the publisher too. It doesn't look good."

"What's happening?"

"You're off the project."

Jack sat on the bed, feeling the walls coming in on him. Through the door he heard Chloe asking Sarah a question.

"But they can't use my material."

"You were a writer for hire. They've got the copyright." *A writer for hire. A hack.* Carolyn continued, "You have no right to the material you created."

"That's in the contract?"

"Yes. Don't you remember? I told you it would be all right as long as—"

"So the book's dead."

No answer. In the silence he heard the front door closing. Where were Sarah and Chloe going? The apartment became very still.

"It's dead, right? The book is dead."

"Not exactly. Garrett's going to finish it."

"Garrett?"

"That's what he told the publisher."

Jack thought of all the other manuscripts that Garrett had strewn around his office earlier that day. He thought of how Walt had always backed off before publication. Of course, that was only Garrett's side of the story. Maybe those books weren't any good. Regardless, that was when Walt was still in charge of his name. Now, with Walt enfeebled and mute, Garrett had power of attorney, control of his estate. He would pick and choose from what Jack had written and twist it into his own view of his father's legacy. The thought of being an accomplice to those jealous lies made Jack sick with rage.

"The publisher's going to let him do that?"

"They've got a lot invested in it. They can't walk away. Besides, if Walt recovers, they see this as a tie-in to the comeback show on CBS. They're just trying to leave every option open."

"Listen, Carolyn. I've got more invested than anyone."

"I know how you feel, Jack. But there'll be other books. You will be getting a final payment. Why not take a little trip, think about what you want to do next?"

———

Sarah and Chloe came back later that night. Jack was already in bed. In the morning Jack finally broke the news to Sarah. Outwardly her face was unchanged. Behind her features he could feel Sarah hardening against him, the happiness they had shared for the past few months evaporating without a trace. He'd thought he had more emotional credit in the bank than that.

Back into silence, Jack thought. *Back into anger and darkness.*

"There'll be other books," Jack told her. "Carolyn is working on something for me right now."

She gathered up her work things and started for the front door.

"Don't be like this," Jack pleaded. "It'll be all right. A couple of weeks from now, I'll be into something new. Okay?"

"I'm sorry, Jack. I have to go to work now," she said pointedly.

A terrible rage exploded in his system. He pictured himself picking her up and—But then he realized the rage he felt was really for someone else.

Jack followed her to the door, hoping she would turn and say something encouraging. Instead, she said, "Why couldn't you just work in a bank?"

Alone in the apartment again, Jack went to his office with the idea of starting something new. Then it came to him that he couldn't start anything new, because his current situation with Walt and Garrett and Mary was far from over. Every writer knew that you always worked from conflict to resolution.

That's exactly what he would do now.

TWELVE

As Jack stepped out of his car, hidden in the trees outside Walt's Pajaro Beach house, he realized the long drive had left him stiff and light-headed. He paused in the darkness of the trees, pulling himself together, performing a stretching routine he used to get ready for sparring sessions. When he was done, he felt limber and alert. Ready. He slid the revolver out of his pocket and opened the chamber. *Fully loaded*, he thought, seeing the silver casings gleaming dully in the weak light.

He put the gun back in his pocket and moved forward.

Jack looked through a picture window in the living room. No one was there, of course. The living room was not for living. Garrett's wife, Diane, was probably in the TV room, where she spent most of her time seeing how others lived. Hilda was in the kitchen.

Garrett and Ernie were in the office.

Jack skirted the house, working his way around to the rear entrance and the wheelchair ramp that led to Walt's room. He looked in the window and saw Walt was alone in the room, lying in bed, eyes closed. Through another window he saw a light in the nurse's room. He had checked with Mary to make sure that Leslie would be on duty when he came. After what she'd done to them, he hoped to hell this would ruin her nursing career.

Standing at the back door, he dug the key out of his pocket. *I'm passing the point of no return,* he thought, sliding the key into the lock and turning it, realizing that—*click!*—the locks hadn't been changed. The door opened, and he was inside now. Back on the inside, if only for a moment.

He pulled the door shut behind him. He crossed to the hall-way door and listened. Leslie had her TV tuned to the evening news. He closed and locked the door. When he turned back to the bed, Walt was staring at him, recognition in his eyes.

"Hey, Walt. It's me, Jack. You didn't think I was going to leave you here like this, did you?"

Walt's eyes were wide open, watching. Jack stood over him, hoping this wouldn't hurt him. The last thing he wanted to do was cause him more pain.

Jack pulled back the covers, exposing the old man's withered body. He slid his arms under Walt's legs and shoulders, lifting him like a child, like he had carried Chloe when she fell asleep downstairs and he had to take her up to bed. He felt that same protective feeling now with Walt in his arms. Here he was, pro-tecting another innocent, someone powerless to help himself.

Jack gently set Walt in the wheelchair next to the bed. He pulled the blanket off the bed and wrapped it around Walt. He took all the pill bottles from the top of the dresser and threw them onto the pile of clothes. He also took Walt's medical chart that showed the medications he was taking, the dosages, and the times. Then he opened the nearby bureau and piled clothes, underwear, and socks onto the top of the bed. When he finished, he lifted the corners of the sheet and created a huge hobo's bundle that he slung over his shoulder.

He was pushing Walt to the door when he remembered the note he had written earlier that day. Taking the paper from his pocket, he set it in the middle of the bed. They would see it when they came in to check on Walt.

Garrett: I have your father.
Since you won't tell his story, I will.
Since you won't help him, I will.

Since you can't love him, I will.
Yours truly,
Jack Dillon, author

He got a kick out of signing the letter, *Jack Dillon, author.* When he wrote the note, earlier that day, he had pictured Garrett reading it and scoffing, saying, *That hack's no author.* But the fact remained. He was a writer. A damn good writer. And Walt's story would be told whether Garrett liked it or not. Walt's legacy was at stake here.

Turning back to the wheelchair, Jack saw Walt was craning his neck, looking up at him, his eyes glittering, his mouth curling into a smile.

"No. No. No," Walt said.

Jack had decided he would respond to everything Walt said as if it were a clear statement.

"Where are we going? We're out of here. This place is history."

"Where the hell're we—?"

"We're off and running, pal. Just like you always said. Off and running."

Something like a laugh came from Walt. The wheelchair jerked forward. They were out the door and into the night, the chair gliding down the ramp then bumping and lurching on the soft earth.

"Don't worry, Walt," Jack said as they left the big house behind. "I'm gonna take good care of you. And Mary will help. She knows what she's doing. We're gonna help you get better."

"No. No. No."

"We're gonna finish your book. It'll be like a working vacation."

Walt turned in the chair, grinning as he said, "No. No. No. No-no-no."

"You hired me to write your damn book. I'm not going to desert you in the middle of it."

Walt laughed. "Hell, Jack, I—"

Jack waited for more. When nothing followed he said, "That's right, Walt. We're gonna have a hell of a time."

Walt was laughing—yes, laughing as they moved forward, sharing this moment with Jack, enjoying the absurdity of what they were doing. Jack was armed and dangerous. But no one would get hurt. He'd make sure of that.

They had reached the road now. No cars coming in either direction. Just the sound of the wind in the branches overhead and the surf in the distance. He rolled Walt across the pavement, then toward the dark shape of his Pathfinder tucked in among the trees. *Home free. Almost home free now*, Jack thought.

Ahead, Jack saw a smaller shape separate from the dark mass of the car. Someone was there waiting for him. *Shit!* The figure was coming at him now. The pale oval of a face turned up toward him.

"Jack?"

"Ernie?" The stocky man was still holding his plastic briefcase. Jack thought of the thermos and empty paper bag inside it. He thought of Ernie's blind devotion to whoever was in charge.

"I was getting in my car when I saw the lights," Ernie said. "I wondered what—"

"Yeah, it's me."

They stood facing each other in the darkness. Ernie glanced down at Walt.

Ernie said, "So what're you doing?"

"Leaving." Jack rolled the wheelchair around him and toward the car. "Sorry, Ernie. You're going to have to pretend you didn't see this." He opened the door and was about to lift Walt into the car.

"You're not taking him."

"Yes I am, Ernie. Just go home. I won't tell Garrett you saw me."

"I can't let you do that."

"Sure you can. Don't worry, I'll take good care of Walt." He patted Walt's shoulder.

Jack stooped to pick up Walt. He felt a hand on his shoulder. Jesus, Ernie had a strong grip.

"Jack, if Garrett ever found out that I saw you and didn't do anything—"

"I'm telling you he never will. Now—" He threw off Ernie's hand. "Go home and keep your mouth shut."

Jack turned away from Ernie. He was crouching over Walt when Ernie jumped on his back, shouting, "Stop! Stop! Garrett! Jack's taking Walt!"

Walt began yelling, "No! No! NOOOO!"

Jack straightened with Ernie still on his back. He spun around, staggered a few paces, and smashed Ernie back against the open door of the car.

OOF! Ernie let go. Jack dug the gun out of his pocket and pointed it at Ernie, sprawled on the ground.

"I'm going to make this easy on you, Ernie. This is a gun, see? The gun is loaded. Now stand back over there, or I'll shoot you."

Ernie slowly got to his feet, breathing hard, and backed away, watching him.

"Are you going to stand there now?"

Ernie nodded.

"I really don't want to shoot you. Okay?"

"Okay."

Jack turned back to Walt, ready to lift him into the car, gun still in his hand. His face was close to Walt's when he heard the old man say, "No!"

Jack turned and saw Ernie rushing him. Jack sidestepped. Ernie whirled, his arm lashing out. Jack blocked the blow and instinctively counterpunched. The revolver was still in his hand, and it smacked into Ernie's face with a mushy *crunch*. Ernie staggered back then crumpled.

"Shit, Ernie. Why'd you do that?"

The form on the ground was very still. Jack crouched next to the fallen man. He was still breathing. Blood leaked from a cut on his forehead.

"Go!"

Jack turned and saw Walt bouncing excitedly in his wheelchair. He rocked back and forth, humming and saying, "Go. Let's go, go, go..."

Taking Walt in his arms, Jack set him into the backseat of the Pathfinder. He slung the bundle of clothes in after him. He folded the wheelchair and put it in the back then circled the car and got in. As he backed out, his headlights shone on Ernie, still lying on the ground like he was dead. When he was on the paved road, he dropped the car in gear and accelerated away.

"That wasn't cool," Jack muttered as they picked up speed, leaving the house behind them.

"Cool," Walt said, laughing. "Cool."

"*Not* cool. I said *not* cool."

Jack looked down at the speedometer and saw the needle was creeping up. He forced himself to slow down. Darkness pushed in tight around the headlights of Jack's Pathfinder. From the backseat he could hear Walt's hoarse breathing and his humming mantra, a string of *no, no, no*s. The knowledge of what Jack had done was crashing down on him now, making him feel hot and panicky, hunched over the wheel, peering through the darkness ahead.

"Where?" Walt suddenly said. "Where? Where? Where?"

"We're gonna take good care of you, buddy," Jack said.

"Where?"

"I got a great place picked out. You're gonna be real comfortable."

Jack stared hard at the road. Christ, where was that turnoff? All he could see was a tunnel of trees stretching into the distance, branches waving as a storm moved in from the Pacific. Time to leave this place behind.

Walt slapped Jack on the back of his neck.

"Ow! What was that for?"

"*Where?*" Walt shouted.

"I told you," Jack said, turning. Walt was bouncing around in the backseat waving his arms. Jack checked his mirror. No one coming. He pulled over.

"There's a cabin about six hours from here. Mary and I have it all figured out. We've been planning this for the last week. Mary and I are going to take you there."

"Mary?"

"Yeah, Mary and I have this all planned out. I'm going to meet her now. We'll take her car, and we'll be in the cabin before dawn.

"Mary," Walt said, relaxing.

"Yeah, Mary. We both want you to get better, and we don't think you're getting the care you need now. Mary will take care of you while you and I finish the book. How's that sound?"

"Mary," Walt said again.

Headlights swung around the bend of the road ahead of them. Jack watched as the light played on Walt's face. He looked nervous but reassured by repeating Mary's name, as if holding onto a life preserver. Living in Walt's head after the stroke must be scary. And now he was being taken somewhere in the middle of the night. No wonder he was scared.

Jack took Walt's hand and squeezed it, feeling the smooth skin, as thin as tissue paper.

"Trust me," Jack said. "This is for you—and the book, our book."

No response.

"And for you and Mary," Jack added.

"Mary," Walt said, and Jack could feel his hand relax. He needed his hand for driving, so he slid his hand out of Walt's grasp, feeling the old man's bony fingers clutching at him. He turned back to the road and accelerated into the darkness.

THIRTEEN

The town center appeared in the headlights of Jack's Path-finder, a border of flowers around a rectangle of grass. The flowers were colorless and angry in his lights, tossing their blossoms in the wind. Now, where was Mary's car? The plan was for her to park at the square. Jack circled the block, searching, panic clutching his heart. He pulled into the public parking lot and crept along the rows of parked cars. Movement. A figure stepped out from between cars.

"There's Mary," Jack said to Walt, relief gushing through his system.

"Mary," Walt said, breathing out the name. "Mary."

A parking space was open next to her old Mercedes. Jack pulled in and cut the lights and engine. Mary's face appeared looking in the front window then the back. She opened the back door and slid in next to Walt.

"Hello, dear." She kissed Walt on the cheek.

Walt said, "Mary."

She clapped her hands. "Yes! Mary!" She looked at Jack, her eyes sparkling. "Jack! It's working already. That's the first time he's said my name since—"

"I sure hope it works. We're gonna need a healthy Walt to get me out of this jam."

"Oh, he'll get better. I know he will. Won't you, Walt?" She kissed his cheek.

"Mary," Walt said, a big goofy smile spreading across his face.

"Just keep saying it and saying it," she said, laying her head on his shoulder.

Jack watched them from the front seat. "Ah, guys, I think it's time we hit the road."

"Yes, of course," Mary said. "Let me get my things."

"Get your things? We're taking your car."

"I don't think that would be wise."

"Why not?"

"Well, I didn't have time to renew the registration."

"*Time?* You didn't have time?"

"Actually, it slipped my mind. The sticker's is going to expire in another week. So we better take your car."

"Jesus Christ, I told you—"

Walt frowned and said, "No."

"Jack, please." Mary signaled for him to step outside. They got out, and Jack felt the wind cold on his face.

"I really don't think we should argue in front of Walt. It might upset him."

"Yeah, that would be really awful if he got *upset*," Jack said half laughing, amazed. "Look, we've got a problem."

Her face clouded. "What happened?"

"When I went to get Walt, Ernie followed me out."

"Ernie? Who cares about him?"

"He tried to stop me. We had a fight. I hit him."

"Hard?"

"I knocked him out. I left him lying there in the woods. I didn't want to do that, but I did. And now we can't use your car. I mean, *Jesus*, couldn't you just have just gotten your car ready to go like I asked you to? Was that so hard?"

"Jack, I got it all ready and changed the oil and gassed it up. But I forgot about the registration. It's like one of those things that's really easy to overlook. So please don't get too stressed about this."

"You're damn right I'm stressed. It's my neck on the chopping block."

"No Jack. We're in this together."

"I broke into his house. I—I kidnapped Walt."

She reached out and squeezed his arm reassuringly. Jack saw that she was wearing jeans and a black leather jacket over a white top. The wind brought a whiff of her perfume to him. When he spoke again, his voice was controlled.

"I don't want to leave Ernie lying there. But as soon as we call the paramedics, the cops'll be onto us." He paused, running the options in his head. "Okay. Let's take my car. Drive for an hour, then call the cops. I just hope to Christ Ernie doesn't have brain damage or anything."

"How could anyone tell?" She waited for Jack to laugh. She playfully punched his arm. "Oh come on, Jack, that was funny."

"I'll laugh later. Come on, let's get going."

Jack slid in behind the wheel, thinking how Mary was taking this so lightly, like it was a practical joke or something. He thought back to the way she had ripped that nurse Leslie who had walked in on them when they snuck into Walt's room. It seemed like her whole personality had flipped from happy-go-lucky to hatchet woman. Jack couldn't help wondering how many other sides there were to Mary's personality.

Mary sat in the backseat and took Walt's hand.

"Where?" Walt asked Mary.

Mary stroked his face and kissed him. "We're going to a better place. A place where we're all going to be very, very happy."

Mary obviously meant the comment to be comforting. But as Jack began driving, it echoed in his head with a very different tone, one reserved for terminally ill patients or any lost soul beyond help.

PART THREE
MOUNT WHITNEY

FOURTEEN

"What makes you think Jack Dillon was on crack cocaine at the time of the abduction?" Pajaro Beach Police Chief Ullrich asked Ernie as a paramedic put a neck brace on him. Behind them, in Walt's office, cops were busy interviewing the house staff, talking on cell phones, taking pictures of the scene.

Chief Ullrich had a fringe of brown hair around a naked, freckled dome. His accent seemed to indicate Texas in the same way that airline pilots assumed a folksy drawl in the face of impending doom. Garrett wondered what the hell this hick was doing in Pajaro Beach, one of the richest towns in California. In the morning, he would go down to city hall and raise hell. But tonight, he was stuck with the bozo.

Before Ernie could answer the chief's question, Garrett jumped in. "Give me a break! Jack was coked to the gills. He had to be, to charge in here like a wild animal, grab my father, and pistol-whip my assistant."

"He didn't really pistol-whip me," Ernie said. Then he saw the look on Garrett's face. "But he hit me pretty hard."

The chief turned his lazy eyes to Garrett. "Mr. Stuckey, I'm going to ask you not to interrupt again. Let the witness respond. Ernie here's perfectly capable of that, aren't you?"

Ernie nodded dubiously.

Garrett cleared his throat and forced a patient expression. "Captain Ullrich, I—"

"Chief."

"Okay. I'm concerned about Dad's well-being. I mean, this psychopath has kidnapped Dad and—"

"It's not kidnapping yet."

"Of course it's kidnapping."

"California Penal Code 207-210 defines kidnapping as having to involve extortion or asportation."

"Aspor—what the hell are you talking about?"

"Taking the victim a certain distance. We don't know where they are."

Garrett was silent for a moment. Then continued quietly. "By extortion, do you mean like a ransom?"

"That would establish kidnapping. But you said you didn't find a note of any kind. Right?"

"Right," Garrett said, looking away evasively. His hand strayed to his pocket, fingering the note Leslie had found on Walt's empty bed, the one Jack had written. It was a lucky thing she had found it first. He told her not to tell anyone she had seen it. That way he had more options. Besides, he didn't much care for the tone of Jack's message. And he'd hate to have someone leak it to the media, turn Jack into some kind of a folk hero.

Garrett turned his back on the chief and began pacing. "This is so bizarre. He took my father at gunpoint, and you're telling me that's not kidnapping? I mean, come on. Where is the FBI? Where are the—gosh, I don't know—the tracking dogs."

A cop in the background stifled a laugh. Garrett whirled around but couldn't find the offender.

The phone began ringing. Garrett looked across the room at the cop who had the phone hooked up to a tape recorder. Garrett counted down *three, two, one* with his fingers—like they did on the set before a live show—and they both picked up the phone at the same time.

"Hello."

"Mr. Stuckey?" a woman's voice asked.

Garrett could hear lots of background noises, a police radio, people talking.

"This is Garrett Stuckey, yes."

"This is Trisha King from KNBC in Fresno. We got a tip that—"

"You *people*!" Garrett exploded. "I can't believe you! We are in a middle of a situation here! Doesn't that mean anything to you? Now good-bye—and don't call back!" He banged the phone down and rubbed his face.

"You go off like that on the media, and it only makes 'em want the story worse," the chief said. "Now, what we have here is a lot of rabbit trails, and we're gonna have to run down each one before we know what direction to go in. Fact of the matter is, this Dillon fellow might have just taken your dad out to a picture show, or out for a piece of pie."

"Pie? Get real."

"When an abduction takes place without the perpetrator leaving a ransom note, it's usually a sign that they're not real serious. Could be a hoax. Or it could be that he'll get cold feet and return your daddy."

"You don't know this Dillon." Garrett sneered. "He's obsessed with my father. People get like that around us. You wouldn't know the effect that fame has on people like Jack Dillon. He just wants to be someone."

"Then why didn't he leave a letter, a note, a message of some kind?"

"Good question," Garrett said, touching the note in his pocket again. It seemed like a bomb he hadn't yet figured out where to detonate.

A deputy appeared. "Chief Ullrich?"

"Yes, Dave."

"We checked Mary LeBeau's house. No one on the premises."

"You sure?"

"No one answered the door. No lights visible. No vehicles in the driveway."

"Any luck on the other suspect?"

"No. But we got this from the DMV. It's Dillon's plate number and VIN." He handed the chief a piece of paper.

"Thank you, Dave."

Garrett cleared his throat impatiently. The chief turned back to him.

"Let me clarify something, Captain."

"Chief."

"Okay. If a ransom request is found, then it would officially be kidnapping?"

"That is correct, sir."

"And the FBI would be called in?"

"Correct. But I got to warn you, I worked with those boys before. We can do every bit as good a job as they can."

"I'm sure you can, Chief Ullrich. I didn't mean to imply otherwise. I was merely speculating that the FBI might have more—more resources than the Pajaro Beach Police Department."

Like, a whole *lot* more resources, Garrett thought. This one-horse police department did everything back-assward. And he needed his father ASAP. Without him, the network might cancel the pilot of *The New Walt Stuckey Comedy Hour.* The execs had no way of knowing that Walt was in such rough shape. He had made sure they felt Walt was on the road to recovery. And once he inked a deal with the studio, Walt would either have recovered, or they would be in so deep they would go on with the show with just him.

Now, with the FBI involved, the kidnapping could turn this thing into a media circus that would make them *beg* him for the pilot. Garrett pictured the phone ringing, and the VP—no, the *president*—of programming saying, "Okay, Garrett, let's talk deal."

"The FBI has a whole lot of resources we don't have," the chief admitted, passing a hand over his baldpate, as if to smooth down hair that had once been there. "But let's see what we're dealing with here before we do anything rash."

"If you'll excuse me, I need to be with my family. They're very upset about this."

"Understandably."

Garrett stepped back, gesturing for the chief to continue questioning the injured Ernie. "You may continue with Ernie. And Ernie? Tell them everything, okay? For Dad."

Ernie looked suitably impressed by the gravity of the moment and his own role of importance in it. He nodded and turned back to the chief.

Garrett moved into the house. He passed the family room inside where a flicker of light showed on the walls. He looked and saw his wife, Diane, doing her nails and watching a rerun of *The Mary Tyler Moore Show.*

"Nothing yet," Garrett said, leaning in the doorway.

Diane looked up. "Huh?"

"They haven't found out anything yet."

"About what?"

"Oh for Christ's sake! About Dad."

"Well, I didn't know what you were talking about."

"I just assumed you would be—ya know, worried. But forget it. Just forget it."

Diane turned back to the TV, saw something, and laughed.

"Unbelievable," Garrett mumbled as he moved down the hallway. He looked into the nurse's room. Leslie was sitting there reading *People.* He stepped in and closed the door.

"There's something I need you to do for me," Garrett said, smiling as a plan began to unfold in his mind.

Leslie smiled back at him and stood up, unbuttoning her blouse. Garrett saw the black bra appearing underneath. He knew if it was fully revealed he was a goner.

"Not now!" he barked. "I mean, Jesus. Show a little respect."

"Well, it's what you usually want."

"Just siddown. I've got something you have to do for me."

Garrett took the note from Jack out of his pocket. He moved to a mission-style desk in the corner of the room. He switched on a Tiffany lamp and smoothed the note out flat on the surface of a desk, examining it.

"You must never, never tell anyone you found this. Okay?"

"Okay."

"Never."

"I already said okay. Okay?"

"Well, I just wanted to make sure."

He turned back to the note. In a desk drawer he found a lined yellow pad and a pencil. He began writing, checking Jack's note from time to time, trying to match the handwriting.

Finally, Garrett sat back, satisfied.

"I want you to drive to Salinas. There's a copy store there that's open all night. I want you to fax this here, to the house."

"Why?"

Rather than answer, he handed what he had written to Leslie.

She read it and looked up at him. "You're gonna get in trouble for this—big-time."

"Who's going to prove I did it?"

"The cops."

"You mean Andy of Mayberry out there?" he said, referring to Chief Ullrich. "The guy's a moron. Now move it."

She started for the door.

"Leslie."

"Now what?"

"There was a housekeeper who used to work here. Ernie told me she got caught ripping off some lady she worked for and went to jail."

"Sandy Blades. Yeah, I remember her."

"I heard she had a boyfriend who just got out of Soledad. He served eleven years for murder."

"Really? Who'd he kill?"

"How the hell should I know? I just want to know how to reach this Sandy Blades."

"Why do you want to talk to her?"

"I don't want to talk to her. I want to talk to this boyfriend."

"Why?"

Leslie waited for an answer, then put it together on her own. "You're gonna be in trouble—big-time."

"No," Garrett said. "Jack is."

FIFTEEN

Mary's soft, tired voice came from the backseat of the Pathfinder. "Jack?"

"Yeah?"

"Look. Over there. Sun's coming up," she said.

He turned and looked out his window, to the east. A faint line of mountains was silhouetted against the sky. Jack knew that somewhere, over those mountains and down miles of twisting road, was Death Valley. While it was still winter in the mountains, the temperatures only a hundred miles away could be soaring.

They were driving south on Highway 395, along the eastern wall of the Sierras, doing an even sixty-five miles per hour. Exactly the speed limit. Not a car on the road at this hour. Just an eighteen-wheeler passing them now and then, with a violent rush of air. Then the truck's taillights shrank in the rearview mirror until they disappeared.

Seeing the dawn stirred a new fear in Jack. The darkness, like a big warm blanket that they had been hiding under all night, was peeled off by the coming daylight. But he also knew that they were only a few minutes from Lone Pine, where hot coffee and food was waiting for them.

In the backseat, Walt slept with his head on Mary's shoulder. Through the night his damaged mind had thrown up frightening images, and they heard him fighting with phantoms from his past, shouting instructions to the cast and crew of *The Walt Stuckey Comedy Hour*, talking to his long dead father, or bickering with ex-wives and unseen devils. Through it all Mary calmed him, answered him, held his hand, and guided him through the horror show of memories his existence had become since the stroke.

Around three in the morning, Walt gave up the fight and fell into a peaceful sleep. He was still conked out now, a rumbling, contented snore filling the car like surf on a pebble beach. *Nothing like a road trip to bring peace to the soul*, Jack thought. It had always done the trick for him, hitchhiking across the country when college didn't make sense anymore, taking off with his buddies on spur-of-the-moment camping trips. And later, exploring the ghost towns of Death Valley with Sarah and Chloe. He loved that feeling of being out of reach; whenever he was on the road, he was happy. What the hell did that say about him?

Mary tapped him on the shoulder. "Look."

Her hand appeared on the edge of his vision, and Jack followed her finger, this time to the west. A ray of sunlight—the first of the day—illuminated the summit of Mount Whitney. It was a golden pool of light suspended high in a blue-black sky. As they watched, the light slid down from the summit and showed that a light coating of snow clung to the granite walls of the Sierra Nevadas.

"It's the most beautiful thing I've ever seen," Mary said. "It's a sign."

"Yeah," Jack agreed. Then added, "What's it mean?"

"Everything's going to be all right."

"I sure hope you're right." He rolled his head side to side, trying to work the kinks out of his neck.

"You must be exhausted."

He felt her cool hand on his neck, working the tired muscles. Her touch sent a tingle down his back. Just to be touched was heaven. It had been a long time.

"That better?" she asked.

"Just a little more."

"Greedy."

She pinched his cheek then withdrew her hand. His skin was suddenly cold.

He turned back to the Sierras. Seeing the sunlight made Jack think this stunt might actually work out. Maybe Walt would find his way out of the maze he was trapped in and would save Jack's ass, just as Jack was now trying to save his.

A sign appeared in the headlights: Lone Pine 5. A few minutes later, Jack slowed as they passed a cluster of buildings, a fast-food restaurant, a gas station, and a city park with slides and swing sets. And then a long street with restaurants, stores selling camping equipment and fishing tackle, and a few sad-looking motels looking like time had passed them by. A bank clock read 5:43.

A neon sign fought the coming dawn, flashing "Bonanza Café" in a cowboy's lariat. A pickup truck pulled up in front of the restaurant, and two ranchers climbed out wearing boots, jeans, and cowboy hats. Jack pulled in beside the pickup.

He left the engine running, afraid the sudden silence would wake Walt, then stepped out.

The air was cold and clean. While it was near freezing now, here in the Owens Valley, he knew that by noon it could be in the seventies. This area had wild temperature swings. Jack looked up and down the main street. The highway dividing the town was straight as an arrow. The air held the stillness of dawn, like it was waiting for something to happen. The neon sign above snapped and hummed like a huge bug zapper.

Jack pushed open the doors of the café and stepped into a wall of morning smells. Coffee, hash browns, toast, and bacon. His appetite roared to life. The ranchers were straddling stools at the counter, shooting the breeze with a beefy waitress in a brown cardigan.

"Sit anywhere," the waitress called to Jack.

"I want some breakfast to go," he said.

She pulled her order pad out of the pocket of her uniform. The ranchers turned sleepy faces to Jack then went back to their coffee. A TV above the end of the counter showed the hosts sitting on a couch drinking coffee, yakking about the news.

"What can I get you?" she asked, her pen poised above her pad.

Everything on the grill, Jack thought. But out loud he said, "I want three breakfasts."

"Three?" She looked around.

"My wife and kid are asleep in the car. I want scrambled eggs, hash browns, bacon, and sourdough toast. And I want two large coffees."

"Any milk?"

"Milk?"

"For your kid."

"Yeah, thanks," he said as if he had forgotten. "I been driving all night and—"

The waitress tore off the order slip, passed it through a window to the kitchen. Jack was glad to see the cook immediately pull it off the spindle. He heard the eggs hiss as they hit the griddle.

"Where're you driving from?"

Jack was about to say LA but stopped himself. "San Diego."

"Long drive. I'll get your coffees."

As she moved away Jack realized he needed to hit the men's room. He moved down along the counter and saw two doors: POINTERS and SETTERS. Very cute. He was staring at the two signs when he heard the announcer's voice.

"...Stuckey was the host of the highest-rated TV show in the late sixties. He has been living in seclusion ever since the show was abruptly canceled in 1973..."

Jack froze. Then he slowly looked up at the TV and saw a jumble of police and emergency vehicles pulled up outside Walt's Pajaro Beach house.

The newscaster continued: "Garrett Stuckey, the famous actor's son, told police the gunman broke in through a rear door and took his father out of his bed. When a family friend tried to intervene, the gunman pistol-whipped him, leaving him unconscious and bleeding. The suspect has been identified as Jack Dillon, a frustrated Los Angeles writer who had been working with Stuckey on his memoirs. Dillon was thought to be under the influence of drugs at the time of the abduction."

The face of Garrett, glaringly white in the bright lights, suddenly filled the screen. "I just want Dad home again. That's all that matters. I don't know what Jack Dillon has against him, but I just pray that he has the decency not hurt him. That's all I can say at this time."

The shot widened and showed Garrett turning away, his arm around his boy.

The two TV hosts, sitting on their ridiculous couch, returned with suitably grave expressions.

"And I understand, Jeff, that police have now confirmed that a ransom note *was* received, but the demands were not revealed."

A ransom note? Jack was so startled he wondered if he had said it out loud.

The woman host said, "We just got word that a photo of the suspect, Jack Dillon, will be released shortly. We'll bring that to you as soon as we get it. And I have to say that we'll certainly be keeping the Stuckey family in our thoughts as this drama unfolds." She paused, changing the mood, and then added, "Next up, what one family did to make sure the Y2K bug didn't catch them by surprise." Jack's feet felt as if they were bolted to the spot. The cafe was hyperquiet around him. He was afraid to turn around and see if the waitress and the ranchers and the cook were looking at him.

Just hit the john, he thought. *Just pretend you're just a regular guy going to take a leak. Nothing the least bit suspicious about that.*

But somehow, his legs wouldn't move. They were jittery and weak. He sat heavily on the nearest stool. Nearby, the two old ranchers were talking about the report.

"That's a hell of a thing," one observed.

"Sure is," the other agreed, then added, "I loved that show."

"Funnier'n hell."

Jack waited for more. Then he was startled by a new voice.

"That'll be $17.37."

Jack looked up as the waitress set the white Styrofoam containers in front of him. Out of the corner of his eye he saw the ranchers were staring at him. The cook's face appeared in the service window. *They're all staring at me!* Jack's mind screamed.

"Yes. Right. Okay." Jack pulled out his wallet. He watched his hands sorting through the bills and saw his fingers were shaking. He handed the waitress a twenty.

"Keep the change."

Jack picked up the food and the cardboard rack of drinks, and walked toward the door. The ranchers' eyes fell heavily on him.

Outside, the sun was up, and a few cars were moving along the street now. He opened the back door and set the food next to Mary and Walt. She looked up, saw his face, and said, "What?"

When he didn't answer, she asked more urgently, "Jack, what happened?"

"The bastard faked a ransom note."

"Garrett?"

"Yes, Garrett. You know what that means?"

"No."

"It means we've committed a federal offense. It means the FBI's gonna be on us."

"Oh, Jack. I think you're being a little melodramatic. What have we done wrong?"

She was about to continue when Jack slammed the door shut. As he moved around to the driver's door he glanced back toward the café. Through the front window he saw his picture appear on the TV screen. Seconds later, one of the ranchers swiveled on his stool and peered out at them.

SIXTEEN

They turned off the main road, following the signs for the Whitney Portal, and climbed up through dusty foothills lined by barbed wire fences holding back blowing tumbleweed. Jack spotted the worn plywood sign that said, Rainbow Lodge, 2 1/2. He turned onto a rutted dirt road and pulled up in front of a trailer with a wisp of smoke drifting out a stovepipe chimney. *Just like I remember it*, he thought. It had been two years since he'd stayed here with Sarah and Chloe, but it hadn't changed a bit.

Mary climbed out, and Jack watched her walk to the front door of the trailer and knock on the door.

In the backseat Walt's eyes suddenly blinked open.

"What?" he asked, looking around. "Where?"

"We're in Lone Pine," Jack said. "Look, there's Mount Whitney—our nation's highest mountain. Or at least, the highest in the lower forty-eight states."

"Where?" Walt said with greater urgency. "Mary? *Where?*"

"It's okay, Walt. She went to get the key for our cabin. This'll be our new home. Till we finish the book." *Or until I go to jail*, a voice in his head added.

The trailer door opened, and Mary appeared, waving and closing the door.

Opening the car door she said, "They wanted to see some of them."

"See what?"

"Your paintings. I told them you were an artist. That's why we're here on the off season. For the vistas, the snow on the peaks."

"Snow on the peaks." Jack smiled. "That was inspired."

"You *are* an artist—it wasn't a lie," Mary said, as if it mattered. She turned to Walt. "And you are an art collector, aren't you?"

"No," Walt said firmly and clamped his jaw shut. But then he got a startled look on his face, as if discovering something new and unexpected, and said, "What the hell'm I talking about? I love art."

Jack and Mary looked at each other. It was a real, honest-to-God complete sentence.

"Yes, you went to art school. Didn't you?" Mary asked, taking his hand.

"No. No. No—" and then the look again. As if something inside him was saying, *I can talk!* "Brooklyn College of Art. One semester, 1934."

He's talking! Jack thought. *He's really talking. And remembering too.* That thing about going to art school he had read in some of Walt's press clippings. He knew that Walt was a pretty good artist himself.

"Jack, let's get to the cabin," Mary said, a quiet urgency in her voice.

The trailer door was opening, and an old woman with a housecoat appeared.

"We're on our way," Mary said, waving to her. "On our way to cabin 5."

The road narrowed as it approached a wooden bridge over Rainbow Creek, the creek that gave this place its name. It tumbled down out of the Sierras, icy cold from melting snowfields and jumping with rainbow trout. Two months from now this place would be crammed with guys wearing funny hats and tying flies with names like hoola-poppers and woolly buggers. But now, the rows of cabins lined up at the foot of the mountains were empty and forgotten. Just the way they wanted them.

Jack had asked for cabin 5 because it was where he had stayed with Sarah and Chloe on a long-ago happy visit. They had sat on the front porch, on a crisp autumn morning, and admired the view of Mount Whitney. But he also recalled it was farthest from the road, hidden from the caretaker's trailer and anyone else who wandered up this road. Jack pulled the Pathfinder up beside the cabin with the screen porch and cut the engine. It was the first time the car had been turned off since he'd grabbed Walt last night, since he even let it idle while filling up outside Fresno, thinking they might have to leave in a hurry. Now, as the engine died, his energy dropped. He'd done what he had to do. Now he was whipped.

Mary saw Jack close his eyes and lower his forehead to the steering wheel.

"Let's get inside," she said. "We'll enjoy the wonderful breakfast I've been smelling. Then we'll all get some rest."

They carried their bags inside. When Jack came back out to the car, he found Walt sitting in a pool of sunshine, the morning light reddening his old face. He looked rested from sleeping all night. Walt inhaled and looked at the wall of mountains, a light dusting of snow on their granite cliffs. An expression of wonder and happiness spread across his face.

"How ya doin', Walt?"

Walt nodded emphatically. He looked like he was searching for words in his mind. He hummed then said, "No." His face clouded. "No, no, no."

Mary appeared and watched Walt's struggle. "Be patient, honey. The words will come." She gestured at Mount Whitney, rising above them. "Just let this inspire you."

Walt smiled and nodded. He seemed ready to try to speak again but just glanced away.

Jack lifted Walt out of the car and carried him inside. Mary had his wheelchair set up on the screen porch near the front door, and Jack eased him into it. The wheelchair rolled easily on the wide pine floorboards. They moved into the kitchen, which had glass-doored cabinets, Formica counters, a white enamel-topped table, and an ancient refrigerator with cooling fins on top. The two bedrooms each had a bureau and two cots, the beds neatly made up with red flannel blankets.

They ate their breakfast in the kitchen, not talking much, the food still surprisingly hot, the threads of steam snaking up into the sunlight like tiny beads of gold. When the eggs and potatoes hit Jack's stomach, they brought back his energy. He remembered that from a tough stint he did on the night police beat when he was just starting out. You could eat, or you could sleep. Either one gave you energy when you hit the wall.

"Now it's time for some rest," Mary said.

"Rest? Who needs rest? Right, Walt?"

Walt smiled and nodded.

"Don't be silly, Jack. You're exhausted."

"If I am, I don't know it."

She laughed. "I think that proves it."

"Actually, there's something we need to do right away."

"What's that?"

"Prove that Walt's in good hands. America loves Walt. And they're worried about him. Let's put their minds at ease. I hope you brought the video camera like I asked?"

"I did you one better—I bought a brand-new one." She lifted the small Sony out of a tote bag. She opened the foldout screen on the side that doubled as a viewfinder. "Convenient color screen for viewing your family pictures…a handy remote-control gizmo," she said, showing off the little remote-control wand. She opened the back of the camera and slid out a computer disk, hamming it up like a hand model in a convention booth. "And look, the wonders of the digital age! A storage disk and a tape with mucho megabytes of internal memory."

Serious again, she handed it to him. "Why did you want it?"

"Garrett told his side of the story. Now I'll tell mine."

Mary frowned and screwed up her forehead.

"Go ahead, turn it on and point it at me. Just make sure you don't get anything in the background that shows where we are." He looked around behind him at the old refrigerator and the glass-door cabinets of the kitchen. "This ought to be all right. Okay. Action!"

Mary folded out the viewfinder screen. Jack saw the red record light on the camera come to life and begin blinking. He took a breath and began.

"My name is Jack Dillon and I'm the host of *The New Walt Stuckey Hour Comedy Hour*. In a few minutes we'll be talking to my guests, Walt and Mary—"

Mary turned the camera off. "Jack, Jack, Jack. Wait now. Wait. That's all wrong. They'll think you're a wacko."

"I am a wacko. I must be to be doing this."

"But think how it will look on TV."

Jack shrugged. "I was just having some fun. Okay. Take two!"

The red record light started blinked again.

A few minutes later Mary shut off the camera. They viewed the message a couple of times, looking for clues that would reveal their whereabouts, and considering the impression it made. Jack read the instruction book and learned how to make backup copies on a separate disk so they had a record of everything.

"I think it's good," Mary said. "Walt looks healthy. And you seem rational."

"So I fooled everyone, then."

"Sorry. You *are* rational."

"Yeah, well, I hope it undoes the damage Garrett did—we have to keep public opinion on our side." He stood up. "Okay. Take that into Bishop and drop it at one of the news stations."

"But they'll ask who I am. Then the police will find us."

"Just hand it to the receptionist. Tell them the news director should see this ASAP. They can send it by satellite to San

Francisco or LA. Maybe it'll go national later today. And while you're gone, Walt and I will get down to work."

"Doing what?"

Jack took out his tape recorder and his notebook. "Working on the book. I have an idea. I'll let you know when you get back. You need to get moving." He hustled her out the door.

Jack watched her drive away. Then he turned back to Walt. He maneuvered the wheelchair so Walt could see out the window and look up at Mount Whitney.

"There it is, Walt, highest mountain in the lower forty-eight." He handed Walt the pad and pencil. Walt turned his eyes up to the mountain. The morning light blazing down on him, ignited his white hair, making him look like an Old Testament prophet. Walt turned the pencil in his fingers. Then he gripped it like a memory returning to him after many long years.

SEVENTEEN

Something about the tall tattooed man inspired terror in anyone who looked at him. Watching from his car, parked nearby, Garrett saw the hairless man striding through the park to the exercise area next to the playground. As he quickly covered the ground with angry pounding boot steps, mothers in the park instinctively checked on the whereabouts of their children.

And then he took off his shirt.

The man's scarred torso, covered with crude jailhouse tattoos, looked like someone welded it together from scrap iron. Thick cables of corded muscle crisscrossed his ribcage, his chest, and his shoulders, even though, judging from his lined face, he was not a young man. He was, in fact, in his sixties, but Garrett had been told that he had dedicated his life to being stronger, more alert—more ready to kill—than anyone around him. And that was how he had survived a childhood in the slums of Philadelphia, how he had survived two tours of duty in the jungles of Vietnam, how he had survived a bloody turf war between the Sicilians in Newark, New Jersey, and how he had survived eleven years in Soledad Prison for a double homicide he'd committed with his bare hands.

The hairless man stretched briefly, flexed his knotted fingers, then grasped the chin-up bar a foot above his head. He faced the gaping mothers in the park and, with a big smile on his face, began a set of thirty-five chin-ups. By the time he was done, a light sweat showed on his chest and shoulders. He then repeated the set by pulling himself up so the bar was behind his head.

Moving to a pair of hanging rings, he slowly pulled himself into an iron cross and held it for a ten count, the smile never leaving his lips, no sign of exertion showing in his expression.

"Good God," Garrett whispered, reaching for the door handle and stepping outside.

By the time the hairless man lowered himself to the ground, the playground was empty—minivans and SUVs in full flight.

The man lowered himself to a prone position and began doing a set of push-ups that looked like it would never end. At the count of sixty-seven, a pair of feet standing beside him drew his attention.

At the count of eighty-three, Garrett cleared his throat and said, "Excuse me—"

"No!" he barked.

He continued until he reached one hundred, then gave one great push and was on his feet, breathing hard through a hooked nose from which a crop of nostril hairs flared. His hawk-like eyes peered down at Garrett to see who had dared interrupt his holy ritual.

"Yeah?"

"Are you Slade?"

"I am Slade."

"I'm Garrett Stuckey, a friend of Sandy Blades. She told me I'd find you here."

"So what?"

"She said you might be able to help me."

"Why would I want to do that?"

"Well, for money."

"Okay," Slade said, with something approaching a distant smile stirring in his expression. "What've you got?"

"I need you to find someone."

Slade man snorted disgustedly. "Do I look like a detective?"

"No. I need someone who can track an individual and...and use force—if necessary."

This seemed to please Slade. The edge of his mouth curled upward slightly as he said, "Who are you using force against?"

"It's complicated," Garrett said. "My father's been kidnapped. You probably heard about that on TV."

"I don't have a TV."

"Okay, well." Garrett seemed to reconsider. He said, "My father is Walt Stuckey. He used to host a TV show called—"

"Hang on. You're not talking about *Walt* Stuckey?"

"Yes."

"Man, I loved that show! Funnier'n hell."

"Oh," he answered, shaking his head in surprise, then realizing he could use this against Jack. "Yeah, my dad's in trouble."

"He's been kidnapped?" the glistening face darkened.

"Yes."

"Someone would kidnap Walt Stuckey? What a sick-ass world we live in."

"Exactly my point," Garrett said, pleased that this new angle was working. "So here's the thing: I want you to find the monster who kidnapped him."

"And?"

"I want Dad back."

"And this sick asshole that kidnapped him—what do I do to him?"

Garrett paused, realizing he now had a terrible force at his disposal. All sorts of expressions passed over his face, hinting at the thoughts churning in his head.

"You look like a reasonable man," Garrett said absurdly. "I'll leave that up to you. But let me ask you something."

Slade waited.

"Do you think our court system is the place to seek justice?"

Slade snorted. Short violent blasts of air shot from his hooked nose. His eyes became dark. "I have a name for the courts. I call it the criminal *in-justice* system."

Garrett forced a laugh. "Good. Very clever. So let's just say that justice is yours."

"Meaning?"

"That the kidnapper's fate rests in your hands."

"Fair enough. So you know who did this to your dad?"

"I do indeed. His name is Jack Dillon."

"Jack Dillon," Slade said locking in on the name with the certainty of a homing missile.

"He's a big guy—your height—and he thinks he's really tough."

"He does, huh?"

"When Dillon grabbed my dad, he punched out my assistant, Ernie. He's just a little guy, never hurt anyone. And he punched him out just to show how tough he was. And I should tell you this too: Dillon is armed. Do you carry a firearm?"

"I'm on parole. Where the hell'm I gonna get a gun?"

"Maybe I can help you out with that. What else do you need?"

"I need wheels."

"Okay, I can loan you an old Explorer we loaned to one of our nurses. What else?"

"I need a scent to follow."

"Meet you back here tonight, at seven. I'll have everything for you. How's a thousand to get started?"

"Make it five. And ten when I deliver your dad."

"What about Dillon?"

"What about him?"

"How much for him?"

"I'll do him for free." Slade smiled.

Garrett started to extend his hand to seal the deal. But he looked at Slade's gnarled, sledgehammer fists and dropped his hand.

"Okay, then. See you back here tonight."

"Yeah. Get that stuff I asked for. And I'll get your dad. I loved his show. Funnier'n hell."

Saying this, Slade reached above his head and found the iron bar. The smile returned to his face as he lifted himself off the ground again.

EIGHTEEN

Pulling into the driveway at Walt's house, Garrett noticed a new car parked beside the Pajaro Beach Police cruisers. It was a white Ford Crown Victoria with US government license plates. Garrett could see through the office windows to a knot of men inside, clustered around a flickering TV screen.

Chief Ullrich turned as Garrett entered. With a look of annoyance he said, "You got your wish, Mr. Stuckey. The FBI just rode into town." Then turning, he said, "Gentlemen, this here's Walt Stuckey's son Garrett."

A tall, handsome man with an oddly high-pitched voice gave Garrett a noncommittal handshake and said, "Special Agent Watson." He indicated the woman at his side, late thirties, dark hair shot with gray. Fit and still attractive in a dark business suit, her hair cut at her shoulders and curled under. "This is Special Agent Boxell. We'll be coordinating a team that's on its way down from our field office in San Francisco."

"Now that's more like it," Garrett said. Out of the corner of his eye, he noticed Ullrich eyeing him coldly. "Has Dillon's car been spotted?"

"No," Ullrich said quickly then added, "But there is one development."

Garrett refused to look at the chief. Instead he addressed the FBI guy. "What's happened, Agent Watson?"

Special Agent Watson turned to Special Agent Boxell. "You took the call. Why don't you bring them up to speed?"

Special Agent Boxell tucked a strand of hair behind one ear. It seemed to be her way of triggering speech. "We received notification from a CBS news affiliate in Bishop that someone dropped off a disk containing a video file. They're turning the file over to us. But they also made a copy for broadcast."

"For broadcast?" Garrett asked. "Meaning *what* exactly?"

"Usually broadcast means they're gonna show it on the TV," Ullrich observed.

"You mean—? What's it say?"

"We don't know exactly. We understand it's this Jack Dillon. And he's—well, let's just catch the noon news and see."

Garrett whirled and found Ernie at his desk. "Ernie! I want to talk to this news director in Bishop. Get him on the line—now!"

"You're a little late for that, Mr. Stuckey," Chief Ullrich said, smiling. "I got twelve o'clock. Straight up."

As if in response to Ullrich's statement, the theme music of the news program blasted importantly into the room. They looked at the screen and saw 3-D logos and pictures of news anchors flying in from a map of the San Francisco Bay area. When the CBS logo flew into the picture, Garrett mumbled, "Hmmm, our network."

"What's that?" Ulrich demanded.

"CBS will be carrying the comeback show. Maybe we could get them to give us a plug."

Ullrich looked at him with contempt.

"It's a natural." Garrett shrugged.

Special Agent Watson folded his arms across his chest and frowned at the TV screen. "Maybe this footage will give us a better handle on just what this fellow wants."

"That'd be nice," Ullrich said. "That damned ransom note seemed a bit incoherent for a writer."

Garrett glanced sharply at the police chief, who suddenly turned his attention to the television.

"Special Agent Boxell here is handwriting expert," Watson said. "She'll want to take a look at that note."

A guy 'n' gal TV news team appeared on the screen. The news guy suddenly looked up from his paper shuffling, peering intensely into the camera.

"Welcome, and here's what's happening at the noon hour. Charges and countercharges in the Walt Stuckey kidnapping case. And we will be bringing you an exclusive statement from the kidnapper. Right after this message." Cut to commercial as some handsome jock lathered his scalp with dandruff shampoo.

Garrett suddenly wheeled on his minion. "Hey, Ernie, get this on tape. Come on! Quick as you can!"

Ernie was apparently used to these last-minute commands. He sprang from his chair like a mechanic in a pit crew, wheeling a large recording deck up behind the TV monitor, yanking and inserting cables. Checking digital gauges, he saw they were all at the appropriate audio and picture levels. Satisfied, he turned to his boss. "Got it."

"A remarkable development in the Walt Stuckey kidnapping," the anchor said. "We have footage of the kidnapper and an apparently happy and healthy Walt Stuckey. We take you to Bishop, California, for the story."

The picture cut to a reporter doing a standup in front of a brick building on a dusty side street, mountains in the background. Under the frame, it read, "Trisha King, KNBC Fresno."

"It was ten thirty this morning when a woman walked into this CBS affiliate in Bishop—"

"Mary LeBeau!" Garrett exclaimed.

The agents looked at him suspiciously. Garrett backed down quickly, muttering, "Well, it had to be. I mean…"

"Can we save our comments until the end?" Chief Ullrich muttered.

Back to the TV. "—the unidentified woman dropped a disk at the receptionist's desk saying only, 'Your news director will want to see this.' She then left before she could be questioned. The recorded video footage was sent to San Francisco by satellite, and we bring it to you now, exclusively."

The screen cut to the lower-quality video of a camcorder and echoing sound. The picture was at first washed out as the camera caught a bright light. Then the brightness control took over and focused on Jack, sitting in a wooden chair with pine paneling visible in the background.

"I'm Jack Dillon. I was hired by Walt Stuckey to help him write his autobiography. As you probably heard, he had a stroke two months ago. At first it seemed that Walt couldn't talk anymore. But then I found that he could talk only to me. I also discovered that Walt wasn't getting proper treatment from his son Garrett Stuckey. I decided to rescue Walt and bring him to a place where he could recover his faculties and finish his book. When he has recovered he can speak for himself about whether I have done the right thing. Walt is here with me now. Walt?" Jack gestured across the room.

The pictured washed out with light again, then panned across to what looked like a rustic kitchen, to find Walt sitting in his wheelchair.

"As you can see, he is in good health. He's not tied up or anything. I even think he's enjoying himself. He has been speaking in some complete sentences, and we expect to be recording some of his thoughts soon."

The shot flashed white again then panned back to Jack. "I want to tell everyone that I am not holding Walt Stuckey for ransom. I'm doing it for his health and so his book can be completed, and his story can be told. At one time, Walt gave America a wonderful gift—he made us all laugh. Now, I'm trying to help him, because he once helped me. So if you remember his shows, his jokes, the skits, call your local TV station and tell them you're rooting for Walt. Or get onto one of those Internet bulletin boards and post a message. Share your favorite bit from his show. And laugh all over again. This is the best way to keep Walt in your thoughts. And one more thing. I want to apologize to Ernie Loynes—I never meant to hurt you last night. Well, all I can say now is—" Jack imitated Walt's trademark phrase. "We're off and running."

The picture cut back to the shot of the studio anchors. They were silent, looking at the lingering shot of Jack on the screen. After a lengthening beat of silence, the newswoman turned to the camera and said, "Truly surprising developments in a case that can only be described as, well, bizarre."

The agents turned back to Garrett, whose face was a frightening shade of scarlet.

Chief Ullrich was the first to speak. "That's a hell of a thing," he said, shaking his head.

"Really," Special Agent Boxell said. "Why would he send a ransom note then say he hadn't sent it. Does he want money or not?"

"Of course he wants money," Garrett snarled. "Why else would he storm in here and kidnap my dad?"

"He just told you in that little deal on TV," Ullrich said. "He wants to finish the book."

Special Agent Watson looked at Ullrich. "You ever get any calls here?"

"Calls?" Ullrich responded flatly.

"If there was any grounds for Dillon's allegations, maybe you were called out—or heard something."

"Oh for Christ's sake!" Garrett said. "The guy's a maniac! Guys like Dillon always have elaborate rationales. But they all want the same thing—money and fame. You don't know how people get around us—around people like us who are famous. It does something to them. Now let's just forget this horseshit about abuse and get on with it. I want to know what your next move is."

Special Agent Watson let his words hang in the air for a moment. Then he turned to his colleague. "Special Agent Boxell will want to look at the ransom note. And we're going to have to analyze the disk when it gets here. We'll set up a command post and coordinate with all the municipalities in the Bishop area."

"But how are you going to find him?"

"Who?"

"This Dillon maniac. Why don't you just go up to Bishop and sweep the whole area?"

Special Agent Watson looked down at Garrett and used a snide tone. "And how do we go about sweeping the area?"

Before Garrett could continue, Ernie interrupted. "Garrett? I think you should see this."

They all looked back at the screen, where the TV anchor was talking to a technician with a headset.

"Amazing! So you're saying that many of the calls are actually supporting this Jack Dillon, the kidnapper?"

"They're saying that they want anything that will help Walt Stuckey recover. Everyone is talking about how much they loved the show."

The technician flipped through a pile of messages, skimming them and reading them aloud. "Here's a typical message: 'Loved the show—funnier than heck!' Here's another: 'Always made me laugh—even if I was depressed. Funniest show ever.'" He flipped through a few more. "'Loved Walt. Funny, funny, funny.'"

"And how many calls would you estimate we've received here at the station?"

The technician said, "It takes five calls on each of the ten lines to clog the switches. Once that happens, it's impossible to say how many calls are coming in."

"And how many of the lines are jammed?"

"All of them."

NINETEEN

Jack was watching Walt sketch on a pad of yellow notepaper. As Walt worked, he glanced up, looking through the window at the Sierras, the jagged rock pillars leading up to the summit of Whitney. It was midafternoon now, and the sun was behind the mountains, casting shadows toward them, the light turning the haze into bars of gold. It was quiet here in the cabin. Mary was in the other room, asleep. Jack was on the edge of sleep himself. Walt was intent on his drawing. The only sound was the scratching of his pencil across the page.

Jack might have dozed off. Time began jumping ahead, then slowing, like a tape recorder slipping its reels—now too fast, now too slow. A face appeared in Jack's mind, Chloe's face, and he awoke with a start.

"My little girl loves to draw," Jack said in a too-loud voice. He looked around and saw where he was, and his mind cleared. He slid his chair closer to Walt.

"You didn't know I had a daughter, did you, Walt? You never asked me anything about myself at all. Who is this person that you hired to tell your life story? Why didn't you ask before? Did you think I'd start mooching off you—try to get your money?"

Walt glanced nervously at Jack, then back at his drawing.

"My girl's name is Chloe, and she has very big eyes. Maybe that's why she loves to draw, because she sees so much. Didn't someone say that about artists? They see life more clearly than other people."

The pencil continued scratching. Jack wondered if the other kids in school had heard about the kidnapping on TV. They might tease Chloe, saying her father was crazy, or a criminal. Kids were cruel. He began wondering how Sarah was explaining all this to her. She'd probably say something like, "Daddy's having problems." Or maybe, "Dad is confused right now." He hoped she would say, "Your father is doing what he thinks is right." Yeah, that's what he hoped she was telling Chloe. And he imagined Chloe drinking it all in, her big eyes filling with tears, trying to look at it in the most positive way, saying something like, "Daddy always tries his best."

"It's funny," Jack said, clearing the emotion from his throat. "Chloe's really not a good artist. But she has absolutely no fear. She gets an idea for a picture, grabs her colored pencils, and just starts drawing. And she always likes the way her pictures look. She doesn't do all that second-guessing crap that grownups do— that I do. She draws it, she likes it, she draws another picture."

During that little speech, Walt had turned to Jack and begun listening. His milky eyes were intense, like sunlight through a gauzy curtain. The energy was still there, but it was distant.

"Are you like that, Walt? Do you always like your pictures?"

Walt's mouth opened. He took a breath. His lips trembled. "No," he said. But Jack heard the emotion and understanding in that simple word. It wasn't a filler word, like the other nos.

Jack waited.

"All my life," Walt began, "I felt I should do better. Even... even when the show was at the height of its...popularity. It wasn't enough. See—" Walt took another breath. He opened his mouth, and the words weren't there anymore.

Jack patted Walt's knee. "I know you're still in there, Walt."

Walt stared back at him, both frightened and angry.

"I know you're still in there, and I'm not going to give up on you. You just need time, and the words will come."

But time, Jack thought, *is the one thing we don't have much of.* "Go back to your drawing, Walt. Finish your drawing. And when you're done, tell yourself it's the best damn drawing you've ever done."

Walt looked up at him and smiled. He laughed at something in his head. Something he wanted to express, but couldn't. And then, beaming, he turned the drawing around so Jack could see it. "Look, Jack," Walt said, smiling, proud.

Jack looked at the drawing. He made himself study it and smile and nod as if admiring the composition, the details, the subtle touches. It was hard for Jack to do this, because on the page was nothing more than a series of scribbled lines that added up to absolutely nothing.

TWENTY

"Right there," Garrett said, pointing at the video monitor. "Back it up."

Ernie rewound the tape. It turned into a blur of images.

"Frame by frame, dammit!"

"You didn't say that."

"How the hell else am I gonna see anything? Jesus, Ernie. Do I have to spell everything out for you?"

They were in the editing room off the main office in Walt's house. Walt had the equipment installed last year when it looked like *The New Walt Stuckey Comedy Hour* was going to get the green light. The room had two editing decks and an Avid digital remastering console. Now they were examining the tape they had recorded from the noon news.

"I don't know," Ernie said. "I sure don't see anything."

"A picture is worth a thousand words," Garrett said. "And we've got thousands of pictures here. Come on, Ernie! Think! Think!"

The interview rolled again. Jack looked into the camera and said, "I'm Jack Dillon. I was hired by Walt Stuckey to help him write his autobiography. As you probably remember—"

"Kill the sound, Ernie. If I hear this moron's voice one more time, I'm gonna puke."

The interview moved forward silently. They froze it at different points, studying the background of the room where Jack and Walt were videotaped.

"Wait!" Garrett said. "Right there." It was the part where the camera panned over to Walt. There was a flash of light—both panning to Walt, and panning back to Jack.

"What's that flash right there?" Garrett asked, pointing.

"I guess it's light."

"I know it's light. Where's the light come from?"

"A window?"

"Yes. But there are no windows in the background. Right? But there is that—" He pointed at the screen, showing that there was a glass-doored kitchen cabinet in the background. Garrett's face was intense in the bluish video light, eyes searching the images held in an electronic netherworld.

"When they panned over to Dad, the light was reflected from that glass door behind them. Export that frame. We'll stick it in the Avid."

Ernie bent to the task. His hands moved quickly over the knobs and switches. A few minutes later the washed-out frames appeared on a monitor.

"Isolate just the reflection."

Ernie used a mouse to move the cursor. He circled the lighted area then moved it to another file. He clicked on an arrow that blew up the image. What had looked like a single blast of light was now filled with dark and light areas. But it still didn't look like much of anything. Kind of like clouds in the sky.

"Now enhance it."

"How?"

"How? Use the—the 'sharpen' doohickey," Garrett said, his breath hissing through his teeth.

Ernie clicked. The cloudy, amorphous image took on definition. But it still didn't look like anything recognizable.

"Sharpen it again…" Garrett said.

A picture was emerging. It looked like—like a jagged horizon.

"Sharpen it again. Then goose the contrast."

Ernie worked the controls. "There!"

"Yeah, there it is all right!" Ernie said, caught up in the spirit of things. But then he added, "What is it?"

"It's...well, it's obvious. It's mountains, I guess."

"So Jack took your dad someplace up in mountains," Ernie said, as if that was a big discovery. "But which mountains?"

"Those mountains," Garrett said irritably, pointing at the screen. "That's a reflection of whatever's outside the window where they're holding Dad. Does it look familiar to you?"

"No. You?"

"No," Garrett admitted.

"Hey, maybe you can give this to those FBI agents. I bet they have a file of mountains. They can take this reflection and compare it to—"

"'A file of mountains?' Oh Jesus, Ernie, sometimes I can't believe the stuff that comes out of your mouth. That's the stupidest thing I've ever heard. I mean, how the hell could they take a reflection of—" Garrett heard what he had said and stopped, his mouth still open. "Ernie! This is a reflection of the mountains. That means it's backward."

Ernie had begun pouting. But he stopped, amazed.

"You can reverse it, can't you?" Garrett said softly.

"Yes I can."

"Then do so, Ernie, old boy."

Ernie clicked a button. The image disappeared. They waited. The hard drive churned. The new image reappeared. They stared at the result.

"Now that looks familiar," Garrett said.

"It sure does," Ernie agreed out of sheer reflex. But then he was forced to add, "So where is it?"

"How the hell should I know? But it is familiar." Garrett leaned back, rubbing his eyes. "Oh crap."

"You want me to make a print of it? You can give it to Agent Watson."

"Why should I do that? He couldn't find his ass with both hands. Ullrich's even worse. No Ernie. We're going to move on this ourselves. And I don't want you saying anything about this to—"

A knock on the door. A muffled voice strained through the wood. "Mr. Stuckey? Can we have a word with you out here?"

"Just a minute!" Then: "Yeah, make me a coupla prints, Ernie."

Garrett stepped out of the dark room. The two FBI agents stood there with Chief Ullrich. In the background, other agents and detectives came and went. Out the window Garrett saw the ranks of the media had grown substantially. They strained against a length of rope, yelling requests at three uniformed cops.

Special Agent Boxell handed Garrett a piece of paper with a list of names on it. She threaded a lock of hair behind her ear and then, of course, spoke. "Is this a complete list of your household staff? Cook, gardener, nurses, and all other personnel."

Garrett barely looked at it. "Yeah. Fine." He handed it back.

"Which nurse was on duty the night your father was kidnapped?" Chief Ullrich asked.

"Huh? Oh, ah, Leslie Lustbader."

Watson checked the list. "Her name's not on here."

"You said the list was complete," Ullrich said.

Garrett grabbed the list from Watson's hands, scribbled her name, and then handed it back.

"Well, now it is," Garrett said, looking like he wanted to be somewhere else.

"You said the list was complete, and now you added a key witness," Watson said. "So why don't you check the list again? And really check it this time."

Garrett sighed heavily and took the list. As he reviewed it, Special Agent Boxell said, "They've been asking if you are going to make another statement."

"Who?"

"The media. They want you to address the charges Dillon made in his statement."

"Why should I react to anything that psycho said?"

"There's no evidence he's ever had psychiatric problems," Ullrich said calmly.

"Nothing except that he broke in here with a gun and took my father," Garrett said, his face reddening.

"Even sane people can be driven to extreme actions."

Garrett heard the accusation. "Exactly what does that mean?"

Boxell jumped in. "Sir, we think you should make a statement."

"You do? Why? Are you siding with this madman Dillon? You think he was justified in what he did?"

"We're not siding with anyone," Watson said.

"Well then, speculate," Garrett demanded.

"We don't speculate, we gather evidence."

"Oh, come on," Garrett said. "You're telling me that you two don't run scenarios? I know how you work."

Special Agent Boxell remained silent for a moment, gathering herself. Then she said, "Making a statement would help the investigation."

"How?"

"In two ways," Boxell said. "One, we need public support for our investigation. If people believe this Dillon is doing the right thing, they may not come forward with information that could lead us to your father. Two, it keeps the media guys busy. If not, they'll try to get anything they can. They have telephoto lenses, parabolic mikes. They'll pick up our conversations, use anything they get. We already caught them going through your trash."

"My trash?"

"Yes."

Garrett looked like he didn't want to ask. But he did anyway. "What did they find?"

"We have no way of knowing. But we think you should make a statement." She looked to Special Agent Watson for support. "Right?"

"Right," Watson said.

"Okay. I'll make a statement."

"When?"

"I don't know. At…let's say—" he looked at the clock on the wall.

And that's when he saw it. He froze, staring up toward the clock. Seconds passed, and he was still silent.

"Sir?" Boxell prodded. "What time should I tell them to expect a statement?"

Garrett's eyes were staring at the photograph next to the clock.

"At…at five o'clock."

"Very good."

The FBI agents turned away. Pajaro Beach Police Chief Ullrich remained behind, watching Garrett with hard old cop eyes. The police chief followed Garrett's eyes to the clock on the wall, searching for the cause of his amazement.

"See something?" Ullrich asked softly, confidentially.

"Huh?"

"You look like you saw something—like a light bulb went off."

"Just thinking what I'd say to the media. Gosh, I hope Dad's okay."

"We all do," Ullrich said, dryly.

After Garrett turned away, disappearing back into the editing room, Ullrich remained standing there, looking at the clock on the wall and the nearby picture, and wondering why Garrett had been so fascinated by something he had probably seen many times before: a framed photograph by Ansel Adams, showing the distant, jagged summit of Mount Whitney.

TWENTY-ONE

Jack was standing behind their cabin in the late afternoon stillness, watching the sun outlining the mountains with an edge of molten light, rays of sunlight descending from the heavens like in a religious painting, with only one thought in his mind: What the hell have I done?

Maybe I'll just walk up into the sunlight, he thought, realizing how exhausted he was and yet how much had to happen before he could ever sleep—really sleep—again. It was so still now, so peaceful here, and yet he knew a storm was brewing over the mountains somewhere and bearing down on him at this very moment. *Time's a-wasting, Jackie boy*, he heard a voice say, the familiar voice of failure that always came to him disguised as a friend. Here he had staked his life on Walt's recovery, and now he saw how scrambled Walt's mind really was. The few fragments of speech that had enticed him into this scheme had been little more than a tease, a false promise of something that didn't exist. Or if it did exist, it was hopelessly lost, like a radio signal bouncing aimlessly through distant constellations.

A door opened behind him, and he heard Mary's voice call out for him.

"I'm in back," he answered.

A moment later Mary came around the edge of the cabin and hurried toward him. She had on that big woolly sweater he liked and, feeling the cooling air, she pulled it tight around her. As she came toward him, Jack saw her face was still lined with creases from her nap. But she had combed her short blond hair neatly and put on fresh lipstick.

"Is Walt okay?" Jack asked, trying to interpret her urgency.

"He's sleeping," she said. Then she suddenly held out a portable radio and commanded, "Listen."

Over the tinny little speaker, Jack heard the resonant voice of talk-show host Larry King, whose show was nationally syndicated in hundreds of markets.

"You're absolutely right about that," King was telling a caller. "It wasn't about jokes. It wasn't about punch lines. It was about the characters Stuckey created. Like Stanley Laurel, Buster Keaton, or any of the great comics, Stuckey knew the underdog got the laughs."

"You won't find a better example of that than the janitor sketch," the caller said. "That was an absolute crack-up, the way he—" Laughter poured out of the radio.

"'It's not my job!'" Larry said, imitating the sketch's signature line.

"And meanwhile, poor Walt is up to his ankles in water, and the damn thing just won't stop. It's sooo perfect."

Standing there behind the cabins, with the sun setting behind the mountains, they listened to laughter along with millions of listeners from coast to coast. Mary watched Jack's expression, seeing the enthusiasm return.

Larry King finally contained his laughter and said, "Hey, if this Jack Dillon character is trying to get Walt's story on paper—and get some credit for the poor guy—more power to him. I never met Walt's son, but I know how dysfunctional show business families can be. I mean, look at my own, right? When my teenager wants to tell me he loves me he yells, 'You suck!'" More laughter in the studio.

"I just hope Jack gets what he needs before the cops find him," the caller said. "After that, he's gone."

Gone, Jack thought, the word sinking in.

"Sad, but true," Larry King said. "Get us that story, Jack! And take good care of Walt."

"Hear that, Jack?" Mary said. "You're all over the radio—every station. They love you!" She hugged him. "You're a hero."

Here I was getting ready to walk away, Jack thought. *Now I'm a damn hero. That's the way my life has gone. Zero to hero.*

"And while you're at it, I hope this Jack Dillon tells us why Bill Paley and CBS gave Walt the boot back in '73," Larry King was saying.

"There's an interesting rumor about that," the caller said. "Being in the entertainment business, I hear things, you know, and—"

"I bet you do!" Larry said. "But we're going to have to leave that topic for another visit, Sheldon. We're right up against the five o'clock news hour. Sheldon Kaufman, the great director, thank you for being my guest. And now they're telling me Walt Stuckey's son is going to make a statement from Pajaro Beach."

Mary frowned. Jack felt his gut tightening.

"It's five o'clock, and this is the news," an anonymous radio voice said. Click, background noises, then a young boy's voice said, "I want Grampie back."

A news announcer took over. "Those were the words of young Benjamin Stuckey, grandson of kidnap victim Walter Stuckey, who is being held by a biography writer, allegedly for ransom. We take you to the family's home in Pajaro Beach for more."

A female radio reporter took over. "Garrett Stuckey met with the media today to counter implications of elder abuse. But instead of speaking directly, he let his young son do the talking." The child's voice issued from the radio again. "I miss my grampie. Why won't the bad man let him come home?"

The announcer continued, "With his four-year-old son sobbing beside him, Garrett Stuckey, who appeared drawn and exhausted, had this to say."

"Yes, absolutely, I'm guilty of abuse. If you call dropping my own career and devoting myself to helping my father recover, then, gosh, I am guilty. I mean, I had around-the-clock nursing, a speech therapist, a complete medical staff. And none of them decided I was abusing my father. But if a writer says I'm abusing my father then, heck, I guess he would know best. I just feel a little confused, because my dad gave Jack Dillon the break of his life. And this is how he repays him? Taking him away from the medical care he needs? It's very confusing."

"Meanwhile," the announcer added, "FBI Agent Tina Boxell said the ransom note is being examined for authenticity, and the household staff has been interviewed. Boxell would not say if there are any leads in Stuckey's whereabouts. Earlier, public opinion tipped briefly in favor of the kidnapper, thirty-four-year-old Jack Dillon after his videotaped message to the nation. Now, everyone is wondering what he will say in his sequel. I'm Julie Cooley in Pajaro Beach, California."

Mary turned off the radio and said, "Well?"

"Well what?"

"What are you going to say in your sequel?" She laughed.

"My sequel. Yeah, right. That's just media bullshit."

"People love media bullshit. That's the game we're playing right now."

"I only made that earlier message because I wanted to tell everyone Walt was okay. And we weren't complete flakes. I mean, you're a nurse, so he's getting his medicine. He's being cared for."

Mary's mouth fell open as if she couldn't believe how dense he was.

"Let's walk a little," she finally said, taking his arm and leading him down the dirt road. "Let me think how to put this," she said as they walked. Jack could feel her warmth through the sweater, her hand on his arm.

"You were a newspaper man, right?" she said.

"You know I was."

"Say you break a big story. Is it over with one big article?"

"Depends on the story."

"I don't think so. Newspapers milk every story to death. Follow-up after follow-up. TV and radio do the same thing."

They were walking along behind the row of cabins, glancing up at the mountains and down the slope toward Lone Pine, exposed and vulnerable on the flat, hard valley floor. Ahead of them was the main lodge and a restaurant, closed now in the off-season. When they reached the narrow wooden bridge they saw the stream flowed right under the lodge itself. Jack stared into the moving water, thinking about what Mary said. It rubbed him the wrong way.

"Okay, I get your point," he said. "But I want to make something clear. I'm not out to manipulate the media, to turn into some sort of marketable commodity. I'm just a kid from Jersey who's in way over his head. I'm here, I'm doing this so I can finish the first half-decent thing I've ever written. I really got my teeth into that book. And it got into me. And I want to finish it. Man, do I want to finish it."

Mary was impressed by his outpouring. She looked at him with new eyes.

"I guess I sold you short, Jack. Anyone else would just grab the spotlight for their own celebrity. But you really do want to finish Walt's book. That's really beautiful. But maybe you've underestimated yourself in a way, too. You can provide a follow-up—an honest one. Did Walt say anything while he was sketching?"

"A sentence here and there. Nothing I could use. Why?"

"'A sentence here and there's a hell of a lot more than he ever said back at home."

Staring into the water, Jack saw that the bottom of the stream had begun moving. Then he realized he was looking at brown trout darting through the current. He turned back to Mary.

"In a week or two I might get something out of him. But we don't have that kind of time."

"You're a journalist, and you deal with facts. I get that. But now you have to grow up a little, Jack. You have to do what any real writer would do."

"What's that?"

She bit her lip, unsure whether to say it. "Speculate. Extrapolate. Whatever you want to call it."

"Fabricate?"

She moved so that she stood in front of him. Her face upturned, the short blond hair falling back, the clean line of her jaw, and her intelligent, full mouth.

"Jack, millions and millions of people have seen *The Walt Stuckey Comedy Hour.* Of those untold millions, you are the only person on earth chosen to write his autobiography."

"Not exactly," Jack said bitterly. "You probably didn't know this, but Garrett showed me earlier manuscripts. Walt just didn't really want to publish his biography. He always got cold feet and—"

She cut him off with a short laugh. "Sure, I knew about those *books.* Did you read them?"

"No."

"They were terrible."

"But he had contracts from publishing houses."

"Jack, Walt's a big name. Of course they wanted to publish anything with his name on it. But those manuscripts weren't any good, and Walt knew it. Your book was good, and Walt knew that. He felt it in his gut."

Jack felt an enormous weight lifted from his shoulders.

Mary saw his relief and continued. "Jack, you, of all people, know Walt best. You are in the best possible position to finish his book."

"Even if he doesn't say a word?"

"It's just you, me, and Walt. Who's to say he didn't tell you all the wonderful things you're going to put into the book?"

Jack laughed, feeling the energy coming back into this adventure.

"What's so funny?"

"I was just thinking of what we used to say at the newspaper."

"What?"

"Never let the facts get in the way of a good story."

TWENTY-TWO

"Chief Ullrich?"

It was Special Agent Boxell, motioning him toward a spare bedroom at the back of Walt Stuckey's house. The FBI had been conducting interviews here all day and using it as a meeting room. Now an agent was posted outside the house, in the backyard, to make sure no overzealous media types tried to spy from the rear. Just to be sure, Special Agent Watson pulled the shades, blocking the last rays of light straining through the pine trees.

Chief Ullrich entered the room.

Special Agent Boxell was holding the faxed ransom note in a plastic sleeve. "Jack Dillon didn't write this," she said.

"Okay," Ullrich said.

Special Agent Watson raised his eyebrows. "You don't sound surprised."

"Nothing about this case would surprise me," Ullrich told them.

"Why?"

"You know how it is. Usually we're looking at crimes of passion, revenge, greed. But here, I mean, shoot, you might as well throw the book away."

Special Agent Boxell waved the ransom note again. "You mean, if this is fake, then Dillon isn't after money."

"Correct."

"Then what is he after?"

Ullrich shrugged. "You've got his statement on tape. Why not consider the possibility that he's telling the truth?"

"The truth," Boxell echoed, as if uttering the word for the first time. "Two problems with that. One, if he's not after money, what's he get out of it? And two, kidnapping someone at gunpoint just to finish a book seems an extreme overreaction."

Ullrich ignored the redundancy of the phrase *extreme over-reaction*, even though he was usually a defender of the English language. "Let me answer number two first," he said, picking up on her speech pattern. "Garrett Stuckey could drive the most reasonable man to extreme measures."

Special Agent Watson jumped in. "So now you're suggesting Dillon was seeking revenge."

Special Agent Boxell ran that scenario in her mind. "Dillon kidnaps Garrett's father to get back at him? No, I just don't see it."

"Neither do I," Ullrich said.

Special Agent Boxell sat on the edge of a mission-style desk in the corner of the room. A matching Tiffany-style lamp sat on the desktop. Chief Ullrich noticed that Special Agent Boxell's navy blue skirt had hiked up, revealing a little thigh. He had long ago accepted the fact that he was a dirty old man, and he enjoyed the cheap thrill like an unexpected gift.

"Let's get back to this," Boxell said, still holding the ransom note. "If Dillon isn't the author, then who is?"

"You did the interviews," Ullrich said. "Who stinks?"

Special Agent Watson emitted a high, nasal, unattractive laugh. "Besides Garrett Stuckey?"

They all laughed a little.

"Yeah, this house is a regular snake pit," Ullrich said. "What is it about rich families that makes them all so nutty?"

"You would think all that money would make them happy," Boxell said, revealing an unexpected naiveté. Ullrich pretended to be studying his nails, when his eyes were actually looking at Boxell's thigh again. She was wearing dark stockings. Dark stockings made him crazy.

"You hear anything from your local sources about Garrett?" Special Agent Watson asked.

There was something about the way he had said *local* that Ullrich didn't like. He held Watson's eyes as he pretended to review his mental notes. He had, in fact, heard that Garrett was shacking up with one of the nurses, Leslie Lustbader. And she was the one Garrett had "forgotten" to put on the list. But he didn't really want to share this with Watson. Maybe he could catch Boxell alone and give her the lead. She was a lot easier to deal with than that stiff, Watson. And she was easy on the eyes too, in kind of an official businesswoman way. Or maybe he would just run down this little rabbit trail himself. He surely would love to catch Garrett in something real dirty and use it against the arrogant little prick.

"Special Agent Boxell, did you determine where the ransom note was faxed from?" Ullrich asked.

"It was faxed from a copy store in Salinas."

"Nice work. How did you determine that?"

"It has the sender's number at the top of the fax."

"I see," he said, trying to save face. "You've probably already had an agent over there."

"Of course." Watson sneered.

"Anyone remember seeing who faxed it?"

"No."

"Maybe I'll pay a follow-up visit to them," Ullrich said, moving toward the door. "Sometimes these locals are hesitant to speak candidly to a federal agent."

As he opened the door, Ullrich thought how he had been unable to stop himself from hitting the word *locals* with a little extra emphasis. And he was also thinking how Leslie Lustbader's apartment was conveniently located on the way to Salinas—his alleged destination.

Chief Ullrich left the room, walked down the silent hallways, crossed through the office, and stopped outside. He saw the TV camera lights blaze to life. As he ducked under the yellow tape, the reporters converged on him, barking questions.

"Chief, is there a break in the case?" someone shouted.

"No breaks, but I'm going to take one anyway," he drawled good-naturedly. It was a manner he used to deflect further questions. "Just headin' back to my office for routine business. I still got a department to run, you know. You want anything on this deal, you'll have to get it from Special Agent Watson. He's in charge."

"Come on! We need something for the ten o'clock," a voice behind the lights pleaded.

Ullrich paused. He pretended to be thinking. Actually, he was watching movement over near the garage. Garrett Stuckey had seen the media swarming Ullrich and emerged from the side door. Now he was hightailing it to his car. Maybe Ullrich should give him a little cover. If Garrett ran off on one of his little *errands*, and Ullrich had him tailed, he might turn up something he could use.

"I've just met with agents from the FBI, and they may have an announcement soon concerning the ransom note," Ullrich said, thinking, *Shoot, what could it hurt?*

A volley of questions greeted this revelation.

"Are the terms of the ransom being met?"

"Where will the drop take place?"

"Has Dillon threatened to harm Stuckey if he doesn't get the money?"

Ullrich watched Garrett's black Suburban pull out unnoticed. *How about that?* Ullrich thought, making a mental note of the vanity plate that read OFFNRNN2. *The guy had been waiting for a distraction so he could slip away.*

"You want my opinion of Jack Dillon?" Ullrich said to the reporters.

"Yes, Chief. Are you profiling him now?"

"I am. I'm profiling him using an advanced law-enforcement technique. It's called intuition. My gut tells me that Jack Dillon has no intention of harming anyone. Now I think you should all go home, let this deal blow over, and let everybody go back to acting civilized again."

Ullrich heard someone mutter, "Shit, thanks a lot."

TV lights clicked off.

"Now, if you'll excuse me." Chief Ullrich moved to his car and climbed in. Before he was out of the driveway, he keyed the mike on his radio.

"Chief Ullrich to dispatch."

"Dispatch."

"Go to computer."

"Acknowledge."

Now a half mile from the media pack, Ullrich pulled over and typed on the computer terminal in his car. You couldn't be too careful these days. Reporters were always listening to police scanners. All kinds of people had them. The computer was more secure. He typed, "Units in the vicinity of El Cajon Road, look for a black Suburban, CA License OFFNRNN2."

Ullrich began driving again. A short time later a message flashed on his screen: "Unit 37: Vehicle spotted NB Hwy. 50, mile 10. Pursue?"

Ullrich picked up the radio. "Car 1 to Unit 37. Stay with the vehicle until further word."

"Acknowledge."

Ullrich put the radio mike back in the cradle. And he put the pedal to the metal. It was damn considerate of Garrett to be heading toward Salinas. Either he was going to visit Ms. Lustbader (whom Ullrich planned to interview, too), or he was going to drop another ransom note on the world.

TWENTY-THREE

The park near downtown Salinas was dark now. The fountain had been shut off. There were no children on the playground equipment. No mothers holding lattes and cell phones. No joggers or bikers or Rollerbladers. Just the permanent occupants of the park: the prostitutes, the homeless, and the drug dependent.

Slade sat in the exercise area on a wooden bench used for leg lifts. His head turned now and then, watching cars pass in the street. Tonight, a navy skullcap covered his hairless head. He wore a dark windbreaker over a T-shirt, jeans, and running shoes. A small duffel bag rested on the ground near his feet.

Out of the shadows, four punks in baggy pants and loose plaid shirts ambled toward him. They spotted Slade and abruptly stopped, watching him with narrowed eyes. They huddled, exchanged words, then advanced. Two of the punks stood in front of him while two slid around behind. All of this registered in Slade's mind, even though he didn't move a muscle, didn't turn his head. His eyes took it all in, his eyeballs moving alertly in their sockets.

The ringleader stood before Slade, sizing up this old man alone in the park. Distant lights shone dully on the kid's oiled hair. When the kid smiled his teeth were very white and even, as if filed to a specific length.

"Hey, bro, got a smoke?" the lead punk asked in a lazy voice.

Slade just sat there, smiling at him.

"I said, 'You got a smoke?'"

"I heard you," Slade growled.

"Do you got one? Or don't you?"

"I only *got* one thing for you, shitbird."

The punk flashed his teeth. "What's that, old man?"

"Why don't you come and get it?"

The kid got a lazy look on his face, which might have been meant to distract Slade. But Slade wasn't watching his face. He was watching the kid's hands, seeing his right hand reach around behind his back. But the hand never had a chance to grasp what it was after.

Slade came off the bench and took down the first kid. Swept his legs right out from under him so he hit hard with a sudden *ugh!* The second punk, charging, fell over his friend.

Slade whirled, hearing footsteps. The two were coming in fast, swarming him, steel flashing in their hands. He sidestepped the first, then dropped him with an elbow behind his ear. The second stopped and faced him, doubt showing on his face in the dim light.

Back to the fallen punk. Slade knew he'd be going for his weapon. And there it was, a nasty little *filero*, its sharpened point flashing in the weak light. His first kick launched the shank across the park. The second kick took the wind out of the punk. When he hunched over like a dog, puking, Slade put his foot on his ass and shoved him down into his own filth.

"Vamos!" he barked at three of the kids, now reduced to frightened teenagers. They ran for it. He waited for the one under his shoe to get his wind back. Then he rolled him over and hauled him to his feet.

"Listen to me."

The kid spit in his face. Slade hit him again, doubling him over. He made retching noises. When he recovered, Slade jerked him up straight.

"Ready to listen?"

The kid nodded, crying.

"You think you're so damn tough. But guess what? There's always gonna be someone tougher than you. Always. Got that? Now get your punk ass home." He gave the kid a shove. The kid turned and spit in Slade's direction. *Still trying to act tough,*

Slade thought. He considered taking him down again. But what was the point? Instead, Slade fake-lunged at him, and the kid scrambled away in terror. Slade's laughter followed the kid into the darkness.

Settling back on the bench, Slade saw a man had been watching all of this. He came out of the shadows and said, "Wow."

Slade waited.

"That was…something," Garrett said.

"You get what I asked for?"

"Uh, yeah. I have it right here." He held out a backpack. Slade took it and opened it. He sorted through the contents: an envelope of money, a wooden-handled, Western-style Colt .45 revolver, a box of ammo, and several maps.

"Okay," Slade said. "Now—you get me a car?"

"Yes. It's a friend's. But she's going to let you use it. I'll drive you to pick it up."

Slade stood up.

"Before we go," Garrett said, nervously looking up at Slade, who loomed above him. "There's been a new development."

"Yeah?"

"I know where they're hiding. Roughly."

"Roughly. What's that mean?"

Garrett smiled, stalling. "Ever hear of Mount Whitney? It's the highest mountain in America."

"No it ain't," Slade corrected him. "Mount McKinley's higher."

"Uh, yeah. I meant, Whitney is the highest in the lower forty-eight. And the thing about Whitney is, it's only a six-hour drive away. And its profile is very recognizable."

"What the hell are you babbling about?"

Garrett held out a folder. Slade opened it and saw it held photographs. But it was too dark to see them.

"That is the view from the cabin where my dad's being held. When you get to Lone Pine tomorrow, find the view that matches that, and you'll find my dad."

"Then what?"

"Don't do anything. Just call me." He handed him a cell phone. Slade put everything in the backpack.

"All right, then. Let's book."

A few minutes later, when Ullrich saw the tall man with the navy skullcap get out of the black Suburban and climb into the White Ford Explorer parked outside of Leslie Lustbader's apartment, he had a decision to make. Whom should he tail?

He had seen Garrett drive to the park, and he had seen him talk to the tough old guy in the knit hat who tangled with the punks. His gut had been right. Garrett knew more than he was letting on. Basically, he was taking the law into his own hands. Or trying to, by hiring what looked like some ex-con bounty-hunter type. He radioed the man's physical description to his office and told them to begin checking the files for parolees living in Salinas who might fit that description.

Watching the Suburban pull away, Ullrich thought, *Old Garrett's probably heading back to the hacienda. But this other fella's ready for action. He looks like he's going on a damn mission. It's a no-brainer, really—take the ex-con in the Explorer. He's the one to tail.*

The Explorer's engine cranked up. The lights flashed on. It pulled out slowly.

Ullrich pulled out too, following the Explorer at a distance. As he drove, he communicated with the dispatcher again, telling her he would be out of service until he phoned in. Then he took his wallet out of his back pocket and set it on the seat beside him. If he sat on his wallet too long, it made his back ache. And it looked like he was in for a long drive.

TWENTY-FOUR

Mary stood at the door to Jack's room, watching him sleep. He had been lying on the bed reading press clippings from Walt's scrapbooks and reviewing notes on his tape recorder. But exhaustion finally took him out, and he had dropped right on top of his work. Now he was breathing deeply, like he had just finished a long race. His face was peaceful in the light of the lamp on the side table, his curly hair spilling onto the pages of the book.

It was almost midnight, Mary saw, looking at the old electric clock that buzzed and hummed on the kitchen wall, sweeping away the seconds and minutes and hours.

Her bare feet padding on the broad pine floorboards, Mary walked to the side of the bed. She took away the clippings and tape recorder before turning off the light. Jack murmured something and turned over. She pulled a flannel blanket over him.

Mary left the light on in the kitchen and went into her room, where Walt was already asleep on one of the twin beds. She removed her clothes in the dim light, standing naked for a moment as she groped for her nightgown in her bag. She turned with it in her hand and found Walt staring at her with an urgent look on his face. He was trying to rise, shaking, straining forward to reach for her. She turned to him so he could see her body. He extended his hand, as if he wanted to touch her. She crouched beside the bed, still naked, now in range of his hand.

Walt could have touched her breasts. He might have reached lower and touched her more intimately. But he didn't. His hand went to her face. She closed her eyes and yielded to his touch. His fingers felt their way across her cheeks; he ran his forefinger down the length of her nose. He stroked her soft cheek and held her clean jaw in his hand.

When his hand stopped moving, she opened her eyes. Tears were pouring from his old milky eyes. She knew that stroke victims sometimes got cross wired. A happy person began crying; an angry person began laughing. So here was Walt, crying. What did that mean? Was he sad because he could only make love to her face?

"No," he said, urgently. "No, no, no."

"I'm here, Walt." She kissed his mouth as it struggled to speak. "I'm here, and I'm going to stay here. Don't worry."

"Jack," Walt managed to say.

"Jack," Mary echoed wistfully. "Jack, Jack, Jack."

"You—" Walt stammered.

"What do I do?"

"You—" he repeated. Then he said, "Jack."

"Me and Jack?" She repeated, surprised. "What about me and Jack?"

"You...love...Jack."

Mary felt Walt watching her face as she reacted to what he said. Now it was her turn to stammer.

"I—of course I—well, I don't *love* him. It's you and me."

"No. You...and...Jack." He pointed at the other room. "Go."

"*No.*" She stood up and pulled the nightie over her head.

"Go," he said, pointing again.

She went into the kitchen and killed the light. As her eyes adjusted to the darkness, she glanced out the window and saw a crescent moon had risen over the valley. A square of weak moonlight fell on the floor of their cabin. Now that her eyes adjusted to the dark, she found she could see quite well. She stood at the entrance of Jack's door and looked in at him, one arm thrown out to the side, sleeping so deeply. She found herself thinking how it would feel to be in the arms of a young man again.

Mary moved back into her room and lay down alone on her bed. It took her a long time to get to sleep.

TWENTY-FIVE

"Walt Stuckey has something he'd like to say to everyone out there," Jack said into the video camera early the next morning. "He heard how everyone was calling in to talk radio shows, and getting online and talking about the skits and routines he did over the years. He even heard how Jay Leno did a tribute to him on his show."

Jack turned to Walt who was seated across from him, drawing on his pad of paper, his head bent intently over the page. "Isn't that right? Walt?"

"After my show got canceled I was kinda sore at everyone," Walt said, still looking down, his head backlit by strong light pouring through the window. "I felt like people forgot about me. I mean, I felt like I had given everything I had to America, and then everyone forgot about me. But I found out how wrong I was."

Walt suddenly looked up from his page. Walt's words kept filling the room, even though his mouth wasn't moving anymore. That's because his voice was actually coming out of Jack's tape recorder. This had been tape recorded months earlier—before the stroke. But it wouldn't look that way when this interview was shown on the news later that day.

"Stop," Jack said to Mary. "Stop it and back it up."

Mary rewound the camcorder and looked through the viewfinder, trying to find the best place to begin recording again. She pressed record and Jack saw the red light appear. When they put this all together, it would look like Walt had recovered and could speak again. And public support would be behind Jack again. If they could convince the public of their cause, the police and the FBI would tread lightly, Jack hoped.

"I'm here to work with Walt on his book," Jack continued. "Now he's here telling me all about his life. I discovered a weird thing—as long as Walt is drawing, he's able to talk. But his hand has to be in motion. Don't ask me why this works. But it does."

Mary panned to Walt, who was back at work, his pencil moving with purpose. Jack quickly put another tape in the recorder and pressed play.

"Lotta people don't know it, but art was my first love," Walt said. "I even had this crazy idea I'd go to art school. But when they saw what kinda talent I had—*forgetaboutit!* So I went into entertainment. I already had what I needed—a big mouth and a knack for making a jerk out of myself."

The camera moved back to Jack, enjoying what Walt had said.

"Walt spent yesterday listening to the radio," Jack said. "He listened to people calling into radio stations saying they still remembered him."

Back to Walt. Jack pressed the tape recorder again, and Walt's voice said, "First time I cracked a joke, the first time people laughed at something I did, it was like they were telling me, 'We understand'—but without words. Right then I was hooked. Hooked on laughter. And I never got over it."

When Mary panned back to Jack, he blinked rapidly, thinking how good it would be to have Walt here with him, really here—not this trick existence he was selling to America.

Jack's voice was husky when he said, "So you can rest assured that Walt is doing fine. And I hope you understand why I had to resort to extreme measures to help him. Yes, I broke the law, but I'm not dangerous." Jack smiled at the camera. "And now he's filling me in on all the details of his life. He's even promised to tell me why his show was canceled suddenly in 1973. He hasn't told me the whole story yet, but—Any final words, Walt?"

Mary panned back to Walt. He looked up from his drawing and into the camera. And he looked like he understood everything that was happening. He really did. His eyes were clear, and his mouth moved, trying to form words. But nothing came out. So Jack pressed play on his tape recorder and gave Walt the taped words.

"Ladies and gentlemen, we're *off and running.*"

Mary shut off the recorder. "That was *wonderful!*" She threw her arms around Walt's neck and kissed him.

Walt's eyes were angry when he looked up at her and said, "No."

"No what, dear?"

"No," he repeated.

"Until you start talking again, Jack and I are going to talk for you. And we're going to do the best we can."

Jack crouched in front of Walt, looking into the old man's eyes. "Hey, anytime you want to correct us, Walt, jump right in."

"Look, I'm tellin' you—" Walt blurted out.

They waited. But they had been teased like this before. And nothing had followed.

Jack stood up and turned to Mary. "Better get the disk to Bishop."

Mary put on her coat, took the tape, and headed for the door. "What are you two going to do?"

Jack looked down at Walt. He seemed to be following their conversation.

"We're going to write the end of his book. I think it's time America knew the deep dark secrets of why the show was canceled."

"I can't wait to read that," she said. She kissed Walt then faced Jack. He waited. She touched his arm then headed out.

"That's quite a lady you've got there," Jack said to Walt.

"Mary," Walt said.

"Mary. Right. She's really something."

Jack took a blanket and laid it across Walt's lap. "Let's get you wrapped up. We're going to go out and see the scenery. Let it inspire us while we—"

As he put the blanket around Walt's legs he knocked the sketch pad on the floor. It fell face down. Jack picked it up and, as he turned it, he prepared himself to see more incomprehensible scribbling.

Instead, he saw it was a sketch of his own face. Not realistic, but oddly, a good likeness. Almost like a caricature. The drawing was framed, and over it Walt had begun drawing in the word "TIME." He had put Jack on the cover of *TIME* magazine.

"Walt," Jack said, stunned. "This is good."

"Good," Walt nodded.

"I mean, yeah, thanks for putting me on the cover of *TIME*. But your drawing's really good."

Jack crouched in front of Walt, and they faced each other at eye level.

"Walt, buddy, you comin' back to us?"

Walt opened his mouth to speak but then just nodded up and down. Yes.

TWENTY-SIX

"Hey," Slade said when he heard a voice on the other end of the line.

"Be right with you, *Ernie*," Garrett said, trying to fool someone who must have been standing nearby. Slade heard bumping sounds and cut-off voices as Garrett cupped the receiver and moved to someplace where he could talk.

While Slade waited for Garrett to come back on the line, he saw the waitress bring his breakfast and set it down at the booth across the restaurant. She stood there, hands on hips, looking around for him. She saw him on the pay phone and nodded. The morning sun slanted in the front window of the Bonanza Café, catching the steam rising off the food. He felt like hanging up, eating his food while it was hot, calling the jerk-off later. He knew cops used scanners to monitor cell phone calls and could find him by triangulating the signal. He didn't want to run that risk. Not when he didn't have to. So he had used the pay phone.

"Okay, I'm back," Garrett said, breathing hard. It was quiet in the background now. "FBI's all over the place."

Slade said nothing.

"So where are you?"

"Lone Pine."

"Find out anything?"

"I just got here." His tone said, *Want to make something of it?*

Pause. Garrett said, "Okay. Good. So what's your next move?"

"Get some sleep. I drove all night. Then I'll find him."

"I hope so."

"If he's here, I'll find him. I'll wait till the sun's at the same angle in that photo you gave me. I'll match the coordinates, run him down."

"When you find him, call me. Okay?"

"What're you gonna do? Grab him yourself?"

"No. But—you never know. Something might change."

"Like what?"

"How should I know? I'm just saying, *call me*, okay?"

"I'll think about it."

"Now hold on a second—"

Slade turned down the volume of his voice but turned up the intensity. His words hissed through yellow teeth. "No, you hold on, you little twinkie-shit motherfucker. I'm the guy in the field. I call the shots. You get your father back. That's all we agreed on."

"Okay. Right. Fair enough."

Slade hung up before Garrett could say anything more. He walked back to his booth and slid in behind a plate of steaming food. Eggs, toast, bacon, hash browns, and salsa on the side. He breathed the smells up into his hawk-like nose. Then he lowered his head and went to work. Moments later he looked up from the empty plate and saw the waitress, a fleshy woman, standing there, hands on hips.

"Wow," she said. "I thought the plate might disappear too. Just get pulled in in the suction."

Slade eyed her. "If I had time, I'd eat two more of those."

"What's your hurry?"

"Looking for a buddy of mine. He's staying up there somewhere, in that lodge. What's the name of it?"

"The foothills are full of little places. You're gonna have to be more specific."

"This one's got a view of Whitney. Nothing between it and the top of that mountain."

"Could be the Chinook. Or the Olivas Ranch, Lazy J. Maybe even the Rainbow Lodge. Just drive up the Portal Road and follow the signs."

"I'll do that."

Slade slid out of the booth and straightened. She watched as he reached his full height. "My God," she said, looking up. "I could break my neck looking up at you."

"I wouldn't want that, now," he said softly. His feet were light on the floorboards as he left the restaurant. He moved quietly for a big man.

A couple of blocks down the street, Slade found the Dow Villa. It was an old hotel with a frontier facade. A plaque on the front wall said that actors from the early Westerns used to stay in the hotel while they were filming in the nearby Alabama Hills. It said John Wayne always took Room 223.

Inside, a young Hispanic woman watched Slade approach the desk.

"May I help you?"

"Need a room for a couple of nights."

He filled out a card, writing a fictitious name and address, and paid in advance.

Moments later he climbed the creaking stairs and found his room at one end of a long carpeted hallway. Above each door was a transom, like in the old movies. The doors were still locked with keys, not computer cards.

Slade found his room and opened the door, stepping into the quiet, neat room. A double bed with a knotty pine headboard was against the wall. An old porcelain sink was contained in an alcove. A tiled bathroom was off to one side. Two windows faced the street. Over the tops of the buildings across the street, Slade could see the front range of the Sierras. Mount Whitney loomed above it all. The west face was sheared off flat. The south ridge was a row of craggy teeth. The rising sun was just touching the summit with gold.

Slade pulled his chair over to the window and sat admiring the view, thinking, *No wonder the Duke liked this room.* And he also thought, *It's appropriate that it's exactly the view I need for my own mission.*

———

Later that morning, Slade stood beside his car parked along the Whitney Portal Road.

In one hand he held the photograph Garrett had given him. He had located the tall pillar of sandstone, and he was using it as a landmark. In the photo, the shadow cast by the pillar stretched toward his current location. If he waited until the pillar in front of him cast a similar shadow, it would point him on the same line as the kidnappers were located. But the sun wouldn't reach that position for maybe another hour.

Slade tucked the photo under his arm and pulled out the topo map he had bought in an outfitter's store in town. He found his place on the map—about five miles up the Whitney Portal Road, a quarter of a mile in front of the gates to the Inyo National Forest. On the map he saw the honeycomb of dirt roads and trails through the rocky foothills, the tiny black squares indicating houses or cabins or maybe even abandoned mining shacks. *They could be hiding in any one of these places*, Slade reasoned. *Or they could have moved on by now. Only one way to find out.*

He folded up the map and tucked it in the leg pocket of his fatigues. The sun was well up in the sky now, and it warmed his shoulders as he waited. It felt good to be here, good to be away from Salinas and that shit job slinging cases of pop in a convenience-store cooler. His parole agent found him that job. And he had stuck with it for a couple of months, arriving five minutes early each day, leaving five minutes late each night, to earn himself the freedom to make such a move as this. When he called in sick yesterday, the owner wasn't the least bit suspicious.

If all went well, he'd be back for work tomorrow morning, with a pocketful of bills to show for his work.

Looking up, he saw the sun had advanced to a position behind the rock pillar, where it was throwing the shadow toward him. He looked at his watch. It was 10:30 a.m. He took the topo map and aligned it with the angle of the shadow. He drew a line across the map extending in both directions from his current location. The line crossed several roads.

He climbed back in the car and started driving again. He found the fork in the road he had seen on the map. A hand-painted wooden sign told him it was Olivas Ranch Road. He bumped the Explorer down onto the dirt road and began threading his way between sand-colored boulders looming as big as houses. In the rearview mirror he saw a plume of dust rise behind him. He tasted the grit between his teeth, reminding him of distant lands, of other causes, of moments in his life scattered now in a past that was becoming increasingly dreamlike. Instinctively, he reduced his speed until he crept forward without creating the high plume of dust behind him that would be a visible sign of his progress to anyone watching for a pursuer.

The road rose to a broad, flat plain strewn with boulders. He stopped the car and stepped out onto the dirt road. Looking down, he saw tire tracks in the soft dust. Going which way? The turning tires were erased by the following wheels. That meant the car had been heading toward him, going to town. Garrett had told him Dillon was driving a Pathfinder. The width of the wheelbase stamped in the dirt matched an SUV.

Now where was his landmark, that pillar? As he was reaching for his binoculars, he heard a rushing sound, like a volcanic eruption, echoing off the rock walls around him. He looked up. Over the ridge, two F-16 fighter jets flashed into view, cutting the sky in two with a pair of vapor trails. He watched the fighters pull an arching turn and disappear to the south, probably heading back to Edwards Air Force Base or China Lake.

He raised the binoculars and swept the front range. The rock pillar appeared in his view, the shadow elongated now, pointing to his left. He lowered the binos and saw that the road was splitting again, another wood sign appeared: RAINBOW LODGE. The road leading up there was narrower still. It stopped in front of a trailer then disappeared over the rise.

Looks good. I'll give it a shot, he thought.

It was a good day. And he needed to stretch his legs. He'd skirt the trailer and do his recon the old-fashioned way—on foot.

TWENTY-SEVEN

I t was noon in the FBI's command center in the office of Walt's Pajaro Beach house. Silence had fallen over the agents, the police officers, Ernie and, of course, Garrett, as they watched the latest message from the kidnappers on the noon news. But as Jack Dillon spoke about Walt's miraculous recovery, the attention of everyone in the room was slowly drawn by a force they didn't understand, until they were all looking at Garrett. His face was swollen with blood, his eyes wild and staring, his fists clenched at his sides.

Garrett had been bracing for this message since they got word from the Bishop TV station that a new interview would be broadcast. He had promised himself he'd stay cool—show no reaction. But at the first sight of that slick son of a bitch Dillon with that shit-eating grin on his face, Garrett forgot where he was and surrendered to the delicious fury growing inside him. The rage spread through his system like a hungry fire. The more incensed he became, the more anger he unconsciously sought, like an addict desiring the drug that would eventually kill him. At first, the anger kept Garrett from viewing the message critically. But as it progressed he began to feel something was wrong. There were those awkward jump cuts in the tape (allowable because it was obviously shot with a cheesy camcorder). But the sound levels were staggered too; Jack's audio didn't match Walt's. And, come on, could Walt recover this quickly? He not only spoke in complete sentences, but he put together rational, philosophical observations on his career.

Still, Garrett had to wonder how the hell Walt was talking. Was there some chance they had tried a new drug? Or were they stimulating him in some way (other than this sketching nonsense) that he didn't know about? It didn't really matter because, with a delicious sense of anticipation, Garrett knew a terrible force was moving toward Jack to exact justice. At this very moment, the lethal Slade was working his way through the small town of Lone Pine, stalking Jack with all the certainty of the Grim Reaper.

When Garrett had Walt safely back home, he'd get on the horn pronto to some studio honcho and let them know he had outmaneuvered the kidnappers. Everyone would want to hear his story. And by the way, Walt was talking again. That would mean green-lighting their show would be a slam dunk. They'd have to be brain-dead not to run the show after all this free publicity.

When the news segment finished, and the local anchors had done their oh-so-obvious response to this latest "revelation," Special Agent Watson turned to Garrett and said, "So, what's your take on that?"

"I don't believe it for a second," Garrett said slowly, still seething.

Special Agent Boxell said, "What exactly don't you believe?"

"First of all, I can't believe any of this is happening. I mean, I can't believe you can't find him based on these tapes. And I can't believe my father is really talking. Of course I want him to, but I can't believe he really is."

Special Agent Watson didn't seem to be the least bit intimidated by Garrett's accusations. He casually responded, "Not talking? I thought we just heard him talk."

Garrett said, "When you've spent a life in film production like I have, you realize there's always a way to get the shot you want."

"You're saying he faked your father's speech?" Watson said.

"I'm saying this whole thing is a fucking fiasco."

"Okay, then," Watson said, looking at Ernie, still hovering over the recording deck. "Back up the tape, and we'll watch it again."

"You watch it again. I've had a belly full of that guy. If you don't find him soon, I'm going to take steps. Understand? Steps."

"Are you threatening us?" Watson said slowly. He had been smiling constantly since Garrett had used the word fiasco. Apparently the word had connected with something he was thinking.

"I'm saying I'm ready to do whatever it takes to get my father back. Ernie, you've been here the whole time. You've heard what I've gone through, how patient I've been. When it all comes out, you'll be my witness."

Garrett let it sink in, looking from Special Agent Watson to Special Agent Boxell, to the cops standing around enjoying this little pissing match. Then, when he was sure it had grown to a dramatic pause, he stamped out the door—

—and right into a blazing wall of TV lights and shouted questions.

"Why do you think your father started talking again?"

"Do you know why Walt's show was canceled?"

And finally, "What's your reaction to the kidnapper's message?"

The energy from the camera crews' lights seemed to flow into Garrett's brain, to infuse him with a sudden giddy sense of power. They were all looking at him, waiting for his thoughts and reactions. And it wasn't just these yapping media monkeys with their questions, but it was the news station directors and producers behind them and—most important of all—the millions of viewers being fed by each reporter and news station. Now this was power! His father once had it and fed the TV hunger with jokes and novelty acts. Now it was his turn. His time had come.

"My reaction to this message," he said, savoring the moment. "First of all, gosh, I'm just so relieved and happy my father seems to be talking again. And that there is progress on the manuscript." He was careful not to say book. Hell, the thing wasn't published yet. Probably never would be. "And that he seems to have recovered his faculties."

"I'm sure you can all imagine that this has been a very difficult time for myself and my family." He let his voice get heavy and added, "It—it was like seeing my dad come back to life. That's the only way I can describe what it was like to watch that clip."

"Does this mean you'll drop the charges against the kidnappers?" a hatchet-faced reporter with sharp teeth asked.

Garrett coughed, covering his reaction. His gorge rose when he thought of Jack Dillon walking. No, that couldn't happen. He pushed the thought away and focused on the image of his own face on a TV screen, rational, articulate—even understanding—in the face of this tragedy.

Garrett looked at the reporter and recognized him from hours of vegging in front of the tube, waiting for calls from the studio about different projects that he had pitched and, more recently, the call to green-light the father-and-son reunion show. "Dave, come on, you know I can't drop the charges, even if I wanted to. But let me say this—if my dad really is talking again, why doesn't Mr. Dillon bring him home? They can finish the… the manuscript here."

"You're in favor of this book project?"

"You bet I am, Trisha," Garrett said, recognizing another face in the pack, an Asian woman, a real babe. Young, eager. An up-and-comer. She had joined the pack after breaking the story about the first interview tape dropped in Bishop.

"As you know, Trisha, my dad and I have teamed up for *The New Walt Stuckey Comedy Hour.* Now that my dad is recovering, there is every indication the show will go forward."

"Is that definite?" someone in the back shouted.

"I'm talking with the network now," Garrett said, thinking of how to shape his response so the network execs wouldn't think it was an outright lie. "They've been monitoring this situation. I think they're encouraged by what they've seen. That's all I can say at this time."

"When will it air?" another reporter asked.

"We're in talks," Garrett repeated. "That's all I can say now."

Trisha stepped forward and said, "Garrett, if you could say anything to your father right now, what would you tell him?"

She held her mike out for him, and Garrett saw that she had just tossed him a big fat pitch right down the center of the plate. It was hanging up there in the air—and he would knock it outta the park.

"The best thing that's come out of this is the public support people have shown for my dad. So I guess I'd like to tell him— just like I used to when I was a kid and he was ready to go on the air. I'd say, 'Dad, your fans are waiting. Go out there and knock 'em dead.'"

From his acting background, he knew how important it was to be in the moment. And the moment had overwhelmed him, making it hard for him to get out the words "knock 'em dead." His voice cracked, and he had to blink to hold back the tears. Call it shameless if you want—he knew it made good TV.

Garrett concluded by saying, "I'm sorry, I have to go. Ernie?" He signaled to his assistant, and together they hurried to his Suburban, pursued by the pack of reporters. As he was about to pull away, the reporter named Trisha jumped out of the pack and waved something at him. He slowed just enough to allow her to shove her business card in through a crack in the window. After he was out of sight of the horde, he picked up her card from the floor of the Suburban and tucked it into his wallet. You never knew when you'd have an exclusive you'd need to give to the right reporter.

A hour or so down the road, with Ernie dozing beside him, his mind returned to the problem at hand. He began to see, very clearly, that Jack couldn't survive this situation. If he did, it would be Garrett's undoing. The media would glorify him, the way they do with serial killers. But if Jack was exposed as the opportunist he was—and was a casualty of this drama—then the limelight would return to its proper place: to Garrett. So, how could he make sure of the outcome?

As he left Pajaro Beach behind and headed inland toward the Sierras, a new strategy began to form. As he elaborated and built on a central idea, he was able to include most of the prime players. It would focus on Jack's demise, of course, and make full use Slade's ruthlessness. It might even have a guest appearance by the wily Chief Ullrich if he pursued them, as Garrett suspected he would. The old chief was turning out to be less of a country bumpkin than he first thought. He saw that when the FBI arrived on the scene and began crowding his territory.

The ending of this episode he was crafting was still a bit sketchy, but Garrett was beginning to see that it might culminate in a bungled late-night raid on the kidnapper's cabin with a burst of unscripted gunplay.

TWENTY-EIGHT

Jack rolled Walt down the dirt road in his wheelchair, waiting for Mary to get back from dropping the latest message in Bishop. As he walked, he could feel the thick wad of manuscript pages in the pocket of his cargo pants—the pages he hoped would unlock Walt's memory.

The road circled behind the cabins then climbed gradually, narrowing to a rutted track, the crown of which just fit the wheels of Walt's chair. As they moved forward, the wheels crunching in the dirt, Jack looked down on Walt's head, the baldpate looking almost like marble. Walt's head turned as he looked at the mountains. He hummed, nodded, and pointed at what he saw.

The road doubled back, and Jack saw that they were now approaching an old mining camp, a collection of dilapidated shacks, the walls busted open or leaning at crazy angles, pine boards baked black in the sun. Tin cans were strewn around, peppered with buckshot and .22-caliber bullet holes. Jack set the brake on Walt's chair and sat on a stack of railroad ties. The smell of creosote was sharp in the pure mountain air. A crow circled above, bitching at them in a nasty screech.

Sitting there in the sunny stillness, Jack thought of Mary dropping the tape off. He imagined the message being broadcast, the air filled with urgent radio and TV signals. And he thought how weird it was that the eye of this media hurricane, Walt Stuckey, was sitting in front of him. The answers to so many questions, including Jack's fate, were still locked somewhere inside that pink, freckled dome. Everything Jack needed was still there behind those fierce, faded eyes, the angry, betrayed expression. The answers were just a breath away, just words away.

Jack took out Walt's sketchbook and handed it to him. "Here you go, buddy. Make me a masterpiece."

Walt took the pad and began sketching, his left hand hooked around, glancing up at the view, then back at the page. The crow fell silent and flew away. Soon, the only sound left was the scratching of Walt's pencil.

"Walt, I'm going to finish your book—with or without your help," Jack said, tearing open the Velcro strip on his cargo pants and taking out the wad of papers. But he'd reached into the wrong pocket and come out with his topo map of Lone Pine and Death Valley. He tucked the map away and pulled out his manuscript pages. "I constructed most of what I need from the press books you gave me. And the interviews. But there's still a big hole in it."

Walt stopped drawing and looked up. His eyes looked startled.

"In 1973 you had the highest rated show on TV. Then in mid-season, they canceled you. Why?"

Walt held his eyes then looked away. Was he confused and trying to understand? No, he was thinking about it.

"Why was your show canceled?" Jack repeated, his voice with an edge of impatience.

Walt went back to his sketching. He was drawing one of the dilapidated mining shacks. An old truck was parked inside, and the roof had collapsed on top of it.

"Here's what I've got so far," Jack said, smoothing the pages on his leg. He began reading from the unfinished book:

I was rehearsing the cast for a special we were doing for New Year's Eve, when the stage manager came over to me and said, "He wants to see you—in the tower."

"In the tower!" My heart almost stopped. When you got a call from Bill Paley, who was then the head of the

network, they called it "going to the tower." And I knew directors, producers, entertainers who went to the tower didn't come back. They hit the streets and were never heard from again."

Jack stopped reading and looked at Walt. He guessed Walt's question and heard it in his head: *Where the hell did you get this stuff from?*

"I read this in the press clippings, that you were called up to the tower to meet with Paley," Jack said. "But there's no mention of what Paley said to you. Can you fill me in?"

No answer. Just that startled, angry look.

"Okay, so here's what I came up with." Jack began reading again.

I took the elevator up to the sixty-seventh floor of the CBS building. You had to change elevators on twenty-five, check in with the receptionist, and then take the special elevator. The elevator opened right inside Paley's office.

Jack paused and looked at Walt. He had stopped sketching and was staring off into space. "So far so good, right, Walt?"

"No," Walt muttered. "No."

I got on the elevator searching my memory, trying to think what in the name of God was going on here. I mean, usually I found out pretty fast when I was in trouble. But this was Friday afternoon, and we had a new show slotted for Sunday. So whatever it was had been brewing for some time. That wasn't a good sign.

Jack saw that Walt was slowly looking up at him, waiting for him to continue.

The elevator opened, and I stepped out into a hushed silence. It was a huge room with a glass ceiling and what was probably the best view of Manhattan I'd ever seen. Across the room was Bill Paley. He was standing looking out, south toward the Empire State Building and across the harbor to the Statue of Liberty. I remember it was a clear day, and out of reflex I guess, I looked over toward Jersey, where I was raised.

"Mr. Paley," I said. "You wanted to see me?"

He turned slowly, and I could see a look of pain on his face.

"Have a seat, Walter," he said, gesturing at a chair nearby. "This is very painful for me. You know what a big fan I am of your show. But I gotta cancel it."

"What?" I actually shouted it at him. It was the last thing I expected to hear him say. "Why?"

He looked at me a long time, like he was debating whether or not to say anything. Finally he said—

Jack stopped reading and looked at Walt.

Walt nodded a few times, apparently recalling the incident. Then, he opened his mouth.

Jack waited. But he heard only the silence of the mountains.

"You went up into the tower, Walt, and Paley said he was canceling your show. *Your show!* The thing you'd worked so hard on all your life. It was gone in a...in a heartbeat. Paley dropped the ax on it. Why? You know why! Now tell me!"

Jack heard his own words echoed from the foothills. He found he had risen to his feet and was standing over Walt, shaking the pages at him. He crouched beside the wheelchair and looked up into Walt's eyes. The old eyes had been peering back through the years. Then he turned to Jack, and words formed on his lips.

"Why?" Jack whispered, gripping Walt's legs.

Walt's lips trembled. He breathed in and then slowly said two words: "Bebe Rebozo."

"What?"

"Bebe Rebozo."

"That—that friend of President Nixon's?"

Walt nodded.

"What did he have to do with anything?"

"No," Walt said, staring down.

Jack waited. But he could feel the doors in Walt's mind closing, locking, the pathways to information disappearing. He waited for several minutes, asking again and again for more information.

Finally, Jack stood up. "Bebe Rebozo..." His mind began whirling, his imagination in overdrive, searching for what he would put into the book. An idea began to grow in his imagination. It was so bizarre, so unbelievable; it could be good, very good. He looked back at Walt and said, "Okay. Bebe Rebozo. Sure. Why not?"

TWENTY-NINE

"Look, are they going to get Walt back or not?" asked the voice on the other end of the phone. "What the hell is going on up there?"

"I'll let you know tomorrow for sure," Garrett said into his cell phone as they rumbled along in the big black Suburban, Ernie at the wheel, driving them along the front range of the Sierras.

"That's what you said yesterday. Now listen, the tower is getting very nervous. And when the tower is nervous, I'm nervous. The network is at a go-no-go point with your show. So you've got to get me an answer."

"I'm doing my best, believe me," Garrett said, pointing at a highway sign at a junction. He nudged Ernie. "Turn here! Here!"

Ernie cranked the wheel, and the Suburban rolled into the curve.

"Jesus, Ernie, take it easy." Then into the phone, "Sorry about that, we're on our way right now. We might have a meeting with the kidnappers tonight."

"So that means you'll have an answer for us tonight?"

"It means I expect some resolution. Soon. I'll call you as soon as I know anything." Garrett took a deep breath, trying to keep the anxiety out of his voice. "Did you get an answer for me on the other thing? You said you'd have an answer."

"Regarding?"

"Regarding my role."

"As?"

"Cohost. You said you'd ask next time you talked to the tower."

Long pause and a troubled sigh. "I talked to the tower."

"And?"

"It's not looking good."

"Not looking good? Why? The network was very positive about the whole father-and-son concept. You said so yourself."

"Yes. But they said they were, ah, disappointed."

"Disappointed? About what?"

"Your tests."

"My tests? Okay. What about my tests?"

"The tower was disappointed."

"I gathered that. Can you be any more specific?"

"They said they would never have known you were Walt Stuckey's son. Basically, they said there were no sparks in your scenes."

Garrett felt he was being strangled. He was hot and panicky and trapped, hearing those words he'd always suspected, the words he'd seen in reviews of his early TV parts as an actor. He covered the phone and savagely turned on Ernie.

"Would you step on it? You're driving like an old lady! They'll probably kill Dad before we get there." Then into the phone he said, "Well, tell the tower that's not the only bit I can do. I've got lots of characters. My dad and I, we used to try different gags out on each other, tried to top each other. People would get hysterical watching us."

"I'm sure they did. But the fact remains, they were disappointed."

"Tell them I'll test again. I'll give 'em what they want. But I am going to be cohost of the show."

"That's for the tower to decide."

"That's not for the tower to decide, dammit. There are some things that are bigger than the tower. The Stuckey name is one of them. If I don't cohost, you don't get Walt Stuckey back. It's as simple as that. Now you go tell whoever-the-fuck up in the tower that that's the way this is gonna be."

Garrett cut the connection then instantly wondered if he had done the right thing, going off like that. He turned to Ernie. "Look, if I have to talk to you one more time about your driving, you're gonna be on your ass by the side of the road. Stay in our lane! You're all over the goddamned road."

"You said to go faster."

"But I want to get there alive. So slow the hell down."

They saw the first sign for Lone Pine a few minutes later. Ernie backed off on the gas, and they rolled down the main street. Before they knew it, they had driven out the other side of the little town.

"Where the hell's the Holiday Inn?" Garrett said. "Every town's gotta have a Holiday Inn."

Ernie pulled a U-turn, and they cruised north on the main strip again. "What's up with this place? No Burger King, no Holiday Inn." Then pointing, he said, "This place'll have to do. Pull in here. Here, Ernie! Right here!"

Ernie nosed the Suburban into the parking lot of a place called the Dow Villa, an old two-story western-style hotel. They parked and entered the lobby, where they were immediately met by a cheerful singsong voice.

"Welcome to the Dow Villa! My name is Sylvia. How can I help you?"

"Get me your biggest room," Garrett snarled, looking everywhere but at her. "And make sure it's near the Jacuzzi."

"Smoking or nonsmoking?"

"Do I look like a smoker? Nonsmoking, of course."

"Is two double beds all right?" she asked, looking at Ernie.

"Huh? No! He gets his own room. I just want—" He stopped, staring into the adjoining room, a big, pine-paneled sitting room with a fireplace. A row of mission-style chairs faced a big-screen TV. On the screen Garrett saw his own face, talking to reporters earlier that day. It had been reedited, Garrett noticed, and they had moved one of his sound bites up to the top of the segment. He was the focus of attention. All eyes were on him, waiting for his words, his insights, his reactions. It was TV at its most dramatic. And those bozos in the tower said he was disappointing.

But it wasn't his face on TV that had stopped Garrett in his tracks. It was the sight of a familiar figure sitting in one of the mission-style chairs. Garrett walked over to the man and stood beside him. He took his time looking up, as if he had been waiting there for him.

"Well, well. What brings you to town?" said Chief Ullrich.

"Same thing you're after," Garrett said icily.

"I told you I'd get in touch with you when I had any news," the chief drawled easily. "There's no need for you to be here. Had you told me where to go, I wouldn't have to chase all over creation on my own."

"I told you everything I knew."

"Well now, that's not exactly true, is it? Who is he?"

"Who?"

"That ex-con you hired? I followed him here."

"I have no idea what you're talking about."

"Look Mr. Stuckey, I can tell the FBI and have them break you down, or you and me can work together on this thing." He produced a business card as if it were an ace pulled out of his sleeve. "Call my cell phone before you do anything stupid. You could get yourself shot. Could even get old Ernie boy here killed."

Ernie jumped as if touched by an electric shock.

"We wouldn't want that now, would we?" The chief continued. "You tracked Dillon down. That's fine. Now I'll take it from here."

Ullrich stood up slowly. He seemed to have grown taller and towered threateningly over Garrett. Ullrich turned and strode across the lobby, walking tall in snakeskin cowboy boots with two-inch heels. His boots clomped with authority as he strode across the lobby, pausing to admire an oil painting of the Duke cradling a Winchester in his arms. He mounted the steps to his room and disappeared.

Garrett stood nailed to the spot for a full minute, his head spinning with possibilities. Then he slowly smiled, thinking how this was all going his way, how all the loose ends—including the old chief—would be wrapped up in one final scene. Then the media exposure he'd get would make him a household name. Him, not his dad. Then the tower would take him without his dad. Yes, sir, the phone would ring one fine day, and the network would say, "Anything you want, you got it, baby. Just sign on the bottom line."

THIRTY

"You did it again, Jack."

Mary was standing in the doorway of his room, holding the radio, looking down at him as he lay on the bed, the press clippings strewn around him like autumn leaves. Her eyes glinted in the dim light of his reading lamp. Her short blond hair was rumpled from lying down, but she smoothed it back in place with a quick pass of her hand. She wore jeans and a black V-neck sweater with—Jack suspected—nothing underneath it. Her breasts were round and free. Her throat was exposed, and her skin glowed a healthy red.

She padded barefoot across the pine floor and sat on the bed next to him. Her eyes glinted with excitement.

"What's up?" Jack asked.

"I can hear TV stations on this radio."

"Yeah?" Jack's stomach tightened, knowing he was about to get another bulletin from the outside world.

"You're on the CBS nightly news. They teased it and then went to a commercial. Listen—" she held the radio out. Her eyes locked on his face. She bit her lip with anticipation.

Over the tinny radio he heard the moronic jingle for a kitchen cleanser. The ad ended, and there was a beat of dead air, during which Jack was aware of Mary's expectant breathing.

"We're off and running." It was Walt's voice, lifted from the tape they made that morning. Then they heard anchor Katie Couric say, "The voice of Walt Stuckey—who entertained a nation with jokes and wisecracks for more than two decades—silenced six months ago by a stroke, is silent no more, at least according to his kidnappers. In a case that becomes more bizarre each day, Jack Dillon, who abducted Stuckey from his home two days ago, released a tape of the former TV icon talking about his life. Dillon has said he kidnapped Stuckey so they could finish his autobiography. But Stuckey's son Garrett charged that the tape is a fake."

"First of all, gosh, I'm just so relieved and happy my father seems to be talking again," they heard Garrett tell the interviewer. "But let me say this—if my dad really is talking again, why doesn't Mr. Dillon bring him back home? They're welcome to finish the…the manuscript here."

"Yeah, right," Jack heard himself say. Garrett's voice brought all the hatred bubbling back up again.

The news continued. "For more about alleged kidnapper Jack Dillon, we go to correspondent Heidi Muntz in Hollywood."

Pause, then a woman's voice: "Little is known about thirty-four-year-old kidnap suspect Jack Dillon, who until recently lived outside Los Angeles in this San Fernando Valley apartment with his wife, Sarah, and a young daughter."

"Chloe. Poor Chloe," Jack said. Then, a moment later he added, "And Sarah too. I've put her through so much."

Mary touched his arm. "They'll be okay, Jack." Her hand lingered, rubbing his muscle, then withdrawing.

The reporter continued, "Dillon wrote several scripts for Universal Television. Before that he was a newspaper reporter at the Phoenix Sun writing feature stories. He was described this way by Sun veteran columnist Bernie Spirko. 'Jack's a real writer, ya know? Not a hack, but someone who's gonna go the distance someday—write a damn good book. He wouldn't hurt Walt Stuckey in a million years. My money's on Jack.' Neighbors and friends described Dillon as friendly but private, rarely speaking to others. A month ago, Dillon separated from his wife and daughter and came to this small apartment to live alone and—who knows?—plot to kidnap TV icon Walt Stuckey and capture his fifteen minutes of fame. Katie?"

A pause, then it was Couric's voice again. "Meanwhile, the FBI named Dillon's accomplice in the crime as Mary LeBeau, a thirty-nine-year-old executive secretary for the Pajaro Beach Community Hospital and Walt Stuckey's longtime friend."

At the mention of her name, Mary jumped. Her hands jumped to her throat. Her expression began as fear and surprise and then blossomed into exhilaration. She turned to Jack. "They know it's me. They said my name on the national news."

"Yeah, sorry about that," Jack said.

She looked at him, horrified. "Sorry? Why?"

"They could throw you in prison for this. Unless you—"

"Unless I what?"

"Unless you get a good lawyer."

"That wasn't what you were going to say."

Jack smiled. "I can't fool you, can I?"

"Say what you were going to say."

"They'll lock you up—unless you turn me in."

She hugged him, rocking him in her arms. She murmured, "Oh Jack. Jack, Jack, Jack. They can't split us up."

She pulled back, studying his face.

"You don't know how the cops work," Jack said.

"I've seen 'em at work in the ER. I...used to date a cop." She thought back to that time and added, "Until I found out what a sick son of a bitch he was."

"Exactly. They know how to get to you. If they turn us against each other—we're done."

"Have faith, Jack." She hugged him impulsively. He felt her breasts pressing into him. "Will you do that? Just have a little faith in our relationship."

"I can't help it. I'm a cynic."

She laughed. "You, a cynic? Jack, you don't know yourself at all, do you? Have you even read your own book?"

"What book?"

"Your book about Walt! It's full of this great feeling of"—she groped for words—"of humanity! It wasn't written by a cynic. That's why it's so wonderful. Walt was like a child—and he made other people feel like that too. They could be silly and laugh and forget their problems. He didn't have a sophisticated, cynical sense of humor. If he did, no one would remember his name. Whether you know it or not, you're like that too."

No one had ever talked that way to Jack. Hell, no one had ever looked deeper into his writing than the headline and the second paragraph.

"Thanks. But look, this can't last forever. The TV guys'll get sick of this story and turn on us."

"They'll stay interested as long as we have Walt. And now you know why his show was canceled. That's news."

"He said, 'Bebe Rebozo.' That's all he said. What the hell does that mean?"

"How should I know?" Her forehead creased with irritation. "You're the writer, make it up."

Her outburst startled him. He looked at her, wondering what this said about her.

"I'm working on it, believe me," he said after a long silence. He waved at the press clippings, his tape recorder, and notes. "All I know is that the Bebe Rebozo sketch Walt did was a repeating gag, like a 'Who's on First?' kind of thing. Someone would ask Walt what his name was and he'd say, 'Bebe Rebozo.' Then they'd say, 'Rebe Bebozo?' And it went on like this, getting screwed up in all different ways until Walt got so mad he starting stuttering and couldn't say his own name."

"I remember that!" Mary said. "It was hilarious. But I brought it up once with Walt, and he got upset. I never mentioned it again."

"Well, I wish I knew what the hell it was all about. I've got to come up with another bombshell soon. I figure I've got one more chance."

"What do you mean?"

"How long do you think this can go on? The second something more newsworthy comes along, this little drama is history. So I figure I've got one more shot."

She thought it over and had no answer, so Jack continued. "Besides, what if Walt really does start talking again, and the first thing he says is"—Jack did his Walt Stuckey imitation—"Jack, where the hell'd this garbage come from?' Or even, 'Why'd you grab me and drive me all over hell like that?'"

She laughed and play-slapped him. "You're terrible. You sound just like him."

"Imitations. My hidden talent."

Her eyes were sparkling again. "Jack, you don't seem to know how big this is. When this is over, we can have anything we want."

"Anything who wants?"

"You and me." She saw his expression and nodded. "That's right, you and me. Your writing career is going through the roof. And I'm going with you. I can do research for you—read your first drafts. Maybe I can help with publicity. You're so shy about your work. I'll tell everyone how brilliant you are. Everything's gonna open up for us."

"You're saying 'us' like we're, we're…I don't know. Something."

"Yes, we are something, Jack." She saw him doubting it and used her little voice, the voice with the lisp, the voice that always melted him. "You and me, Jack. Who did you think I meant?"

He waited, reading her upturned face, her blond hair falling back off her face, her face so completely open to him that he felt something melt inside. "Don't you mean things will open up for you and Walt?"

She looked toward the room where Walt lay sleeping. She got up and closed Jack's door. She turned and smiled at him, and he felt his system filling with a dull, insistent lust, like a drumbeat. But along with the lust came so many other thoughts and feelings. Sarah's face rose in his mind, but he easily pushed her aside.

But then he saw Chloe, her pure, innocent face, and he realized how important it was for a child to have someone to believe in.

Mary padded back across the room and sat down next to Jack, closer this time, her thigh warm against his leg. When she spoke, her voice was low and whispery. "I was going to tell you this before but…" She was breathing hard, her chest rising and falling under the soft sweater. She looked so alive. Man, she was alive. "Last night, I was getting ready for bed. Taking off my clothes. Walt motioned for me to come to him. I thought he wanted to touch me. I waited for Walt to touch me, but he didn't. Then he said, very slowly, 'You…and Jack.' I said, 'What?' He said—I swear, Jack, this is what he said—'You love Jack.'"

She watched Jack's face as he took it in. Then her voice was small again. Small and vulnerable. Pleading and inviting too. "Isn't that bizarre? I mean, I know Walt likes you. But it was like he was saying it's all right with him if—"

"If what?" Jack realized he was touching her hair. He didn't mean to. It just happened. She tilted her head to him, like a cat being stroked. She pressed into his hand.

"You know…" She caught his hand and pressed it to her cheek. Mary searched his eyes, trying to read his expression. "I'm older than you. Does that scare you?"

"Walt's older than you."

"That's different."

"Why?"

"Women age faster. I'll be all withered while you're still— still a young buck." She laughed, squeezing his arm.

He laughed. "I've never thought of myself that way."

Their laughter died and left a big hole of silence between them.

"You looked disturbed," she said, stroking his arm.

"This isn't easy, you know. I'm separated but still legally married. Sarah cut me off long ago—first physically, then emotionally."

"I'd never do that to you, Jack. I mean, look where we are. I went all in for you."

They were moving toward each other now, and he touched her face, his fingers in her smooth, soft hair. He pressed his nose into her hair, breathing her smell. They kissed, and Jack felt her lips on his, touching lightly, lightly, then finding the right place and wanting it harder, pressing harder, moving slowly and just right. His arms were around her, his hands sliding up her back and thinking how long it had been since he had held an eager, willing woman.

They were into it now, falling down into a tangled dark place that was warm and inviting. It was a place Jack knew he shouldn't go now, but it was the place everything led to. His hands worked their way up under her sweater and found that, yes, there was nothing underneath it except wonderfully soft wool against her wonderfully soft, bare skin. His hands were moving up toward her muscular shoulders now, and he worked her sweater upward, waiting for her to stop him. Instead she wriggled so the sweater worked free and slid over her head and off. And now, in the warm yellow light of the room she was naked from the waist up, and he thought again, as he had so many times before, *What a woman.*

She hooked her fingers in the opening of Jack's western-style denim shirt, popped it open down the front, and peeled it back, exposing him. He pressed his chest against her, and they worked against each other. Their flesh was hungry. His ears were filled with the crush of blood and their rasping breath. She fell back, and he was on her, working his knee up between her legs as she willingly opened them and sighed, moving against his thigh. The seconds stretched to minutes—the minutes exploded and spun the room around him.

But then the voices started, the voices in Jack's life that always circled around him. The voice simply said, *It's not the right time.* It sent a cold current through his system, and she tasted it on his lips.

"What is it?" she whispered urgently.

"Don't you feel it?"

She stroked the side of his face. "I felt you pulling away. You were there, really there, then you were gone."

"I've been mad at everything for so long I've forgotten how to—to be like this. It's like I need time to melt all the stuff that's wrong inside me."

"We don't have a whole hell of a lot of time, Jack."

"You can't speed up some things. If this is going to work, we—"

He stopped, listening. A bump came from Walt's room. Then another. Was Walt turning over in bed? Coughing? Trying to get their attention in his wordless way?

Jack lay back beside Mary, his passion or lust or whatever it was still at full throttle. She raised up and looked down at him, her breasts pendulant. He was reaching for her when he heard it again.

He was on his feet. "Did you hear that?"

"What, Jack?" She looked pissed. What'd he expect for leaving her hanging like that?

He tore open the door and stepped into the kitchen. It was strangely cold and the smell of the outdoors hung in the room. How could this be? He charged into Walt's room and hit the light. The covers were turned back.

And Walt was gone.

Jack felt the sheets. Still warm. He ran back through the cold kitchen knowing now that someone had come in while they were together in the other room. Someone had opened the door, the door he was now throwing wide on the black rectangle of night that was so complete, complete except for two red taillights from a car that was speeding away. The brake lights blazed then rounded a corner and vanished.

Watching the blackness fill in again, Jack realized this would have never happened if he hadn't been groping Mary in the other room. And then another thought hit him. Whoever grabbed Walt must have been watching them. When he saw them going over the edge, he made his move.

There's still one chance, Jack thought. He ran to the Pathfinder, ready to jump in and chase them. But there wasn't much point to that—the hood was open, and the distributor cap rested on the air filter. He changed course and ran for the high ground behind the cabin. From there he could see across the slope and down toward Lone Pine. He stood in the dark, shirtless, watching the Whitney Portal road, waiting for the headlights to reappear. Finally, a car's lights came out from behind a rocky hogback. And then it did something strange. Instead of turning right, toward Lone Pine and the rest of the outside world, it turned left up the box canyon road. The road that led to only one place: Mount Whitney.

THIRTY-ONE

When Slade got to the trailer, he leaned in the car door and was about to pick up Walt Stuckey when he saw the look on the old man's face. Terror. Wild, animal terror. He'd seen the same look on the faces of people he had killed, one last snapshot of emotion before he snuffed out their life.

"What's the matter with you?" he demanded.

Walt whimpered and shrank away from him.

"Hey, if I was gonna do it, you'd be dead now." He grabbed Walt's shirt and hauled him closer to the car door, then he threaded one hand under his legs and another under his arms. He straightened. The old man weighed about as much as one of those cases of pop he was throwing around in the cooler back in Pajaro Beach. He turned and moved toward the dim shape that was the trailer. He slid his feet forward so he wouldn't trip on the loose soil, rocks, and tree roots. His hawk nose gulped the thin air that carried the clean smell of pines.

Shit, why was he so winded? The altitude, of course. It was over eight thousand feet here. He paused with Walt still in his arms, one knee up on the trailer steps, the cold seeping into his bones. Down the mountain, through the V of the canyon, he saw the scattering of lights around Lone Pine. One of those lights was the cabin where he'd grabbed Stuckey. Instinctively his eyes searched for headlights coming up the portal road. Nothing moved.

Looking up the slope, he saw the dark outline of the Sierras under a half moon and barely made out the summit of Mount

Whitney. He remembered a map on the wall of one of the foster homes he'd been in as a boy in Philly. He couldn't sleep, so he'd read Westerns with a flashlight under the covers. Then, when the batteries ran out, he stared at the map, illuminated by a street-light out front, dreaming of the states with mysterious names like Wyoming, Montana, California. Finally falling asleep, those names swirled like smoke and wove themselves into adventures in which he was always fighting for law and order. Yet in his adult life, he rarely fought on the side of justice. As he faced the end of his years, this bothered him. A creeping, insistent urge overtook him, making him reject his primal desire to blindly conquer, dominate, and kill.

With the old guy still in his arms he popped the latch on the trailer door and moved into the tight, stuffy interior, the smell of bacon still hanging in the air from his dinner earlier that night. Moving by touch, he threaded his way between the fold-up table and the bench and found the bed at the end of the trailer. He set Walt down, and feeling his way along the wall, clicked on the light. The weak bulb threw a yellow light on the dirty interior. The waitress at the Bonanza charged him two hundred bucks to rent this place for a week. It was her brother's hunting camp for deer season, so he wouldn't be using it for another six months, she told him.

"Comfortable?" he barked, looking down at Stuckey, lying there still looking terrified.

No answer.

"I said, 'Are you comfortable?'" He reached toward Stuckey who cowered like a dog about to be smacked.

"No," the old guy said, a glint of defiance in his eyes.

For some reason, hearing him speak like that made Slade laugh. "No," he said, laughing. Then, "Remember that bit you used to do on your show?" He imitated Walt's pained voice: 'It's not my problem!' Hey, can you say that now?"

The request brought a flicker of recognition and perhaps an urge to comply, but all he said was, "No."

"No?" Slade said. "What if I give you one of these?" He held up his hand, ready to backhand him, his customary response to resistance from anyone. "Then would you do it for me? Huh?"

Terror and defiance vied in the old man's eyes. Slade's anger melted and left him feeling ashamed. He dropped his hand.

"Sorry," Slade muttered, taking out the cell phone Garrett had given him. At this altitude he got a good signal. He dialed. Garrett's recorded voice immediately came on the other end, telling callers to leave their name, number, time of the call, and all sorts of other bullshit. *The guy was so anxious to get his dad back*, Slade thought, *now he's not even answering his goddamned phone.* Where the hell was he?

"I've got him," Slade said into the little phone. "You want him, come and get him. I'm in the trailer at the end of the portal road."

Slade cut the connection and tossed the thing aside. He popped open a beer, pulled a campstool over, and sat next to Walt. They stared at each other for a long time. Finally he said, "Cold?"

Walt said, "No."

"You look cold."

He reached down to the foot of the bed where the ratty old blanket had been pushed into a heap by their feet that afternoon as he wrestled around with that waitress from the Bonanza. Man, she was one live mama. He pulled the blanket up to Walt's chin. He felt a strange dislocation to be looking at a face he'd only seen on television. Flashes of scenes from his life jumped into his consciousness as if he were watching a newsreel of his life. Some of the scenes jabbed him, giving him a quick snort of laughter. The more he looked at the old man's face, the more these things came rushing back at him as if his whole life was accelerating toward this moment. He let these images wash over them and settle until one rose to the surface, and he had to deal with it.

Finally, in the stillness of the trailer, he heard his voice speaking and listened to it with surprise as if it was the voice of some stranger who knew his secrets.

"I used to tell you stuff," he said finally, searching Walt's face for a reaction. Then, trying to explain it, he continued, "See, I never had a home, no father. I got in trouble a lot—for fighting, mainly. I was angry all the time. They put me in reform school. They had a TV, and they let us watch your show. Me and all these thrown-away kids, laughin' our asses off. Then I'd go to bed, and I heard myself talking to you, 'cause I didn't have anyone I could tell stuff to. But you were like my friend."

Slade stopped, feeling an odd sensation. Embarrassment. For the first time in his life, he cared what someone else was thinking. But the fact that Stuckey wasn't saying anything, just blinking at him occasionally, made it easier. Those old eyes were taking it all in, and Slade felt it connecting with other things and making sense.

"So later, I'm in the Special Forces, right? In Cambodia. They grabbed me and threw me in this cage, like some animal. And I'm thinking, this is it. I'm done. I'm just gonna give up. Because out there, you give up, you're done. You know? Then I see that the guy that was in there before me, in this cage, he's scratched something into the wall. It says, 'Your body's here, but your mind is off and running.' Off and running—get it? From your show? 'And now ladies and gentlemen, we're off and running.' And I heard your voice saying it, and I remembered all us kids laughing."

"I realized there are two ways to die. They could kill your body—I was ready for that—or they could break your spirit. But when I saw that message that someone wrote on the wall, I thought back to reform school and remembered all those thrown-away kids, laughin' our asses off. And I started laughing.

And then I knew I was going to make it. Two years in that shit hole. But I made it."

He searched Walt's face to see what this meant to him. And he saw the understanding in the eyes, and he relaxed, feeling light-headed and clear inside, like he finally got something important off his chest.

"I knew that if I ever had a chance to meet you, I'd tell you about that. So there you are. You see? So I guess I owe you. So what do you want to do about this deal? You want to go home to that pissant son of yours or—"

He stopped. His head snapped up, his senses alive. He moved to the window and looked out, watching a light flicker as it moved behind the trees.

THIRTY-TWO

The road in front of Jack's headlights was a tunnel of trees, tossing their branches in the angry wind. They came around a corner, and the road opened up onto a high prairie with an ocean of rocks, pickup truck-size boulders, and tumbleweed ricocheting among them. Jack felt the Pathfinder start struggling up the slope, dropped it into third, and felt the engine dig in with a growl.

"The good news is, whoever grabbed Walt turned left here," Jack said. "They went up the Portal Road toward the Mount Whitney trailhead. That means it wasn't Garrett, or the cops, or the FBI."

"How do you know?"

"If it was the cops, they wouldn't sneak in and grab him. They'd have surrounded us with a SWAT team, and we'd be hog-tied on the floor right now. But it wasn't Garrett either."

"Why?"

"Garrett doesn't really give a rat's ass about his dad. He wants revenge. He'd storm in here with some goon and try to beat the hell out of me."

"So who was it then?"

"I don't know. But we're gonna find out soon."

The road snaked right, then rose steeper, clinging to the side of the sheer rock wall, bright patches of snow visible among the trees. Jack could feel the temperature dropping as they climbed higher. He flicked the heater on high and squinted through the windshield. Ahead, the road disappeared around a hairpin turn.

He cut the wheel, and when they swung around the corner, a wall of white came rushing at them.

"Jack!"

Mary braced herself against the dash. He hit the brakes and heard a crunch as his front end plowed into a snowbank blocking the road. He backed up, training his lights on the drift. It was dirty and glazed from freezing and refreezing, encroaching farther into the road. He stepped out. Jack clicked on his flashlight.

When he returned he said, "Someone just came through here. I could see their tire tracks."

He shifted the transfer case into four-wheel drive. Gears crunched. He rammed the stick into first and, moving forward, he felt the tires bite all around. They lurched forward, slower now. They came to another sharp hairpin, and he made the turn slower this time. Another huge snowdrift loomed ahead. Jack steered around it, feeling his right tires crunching on the gravel shoulder. Mary looked out the side window. Then she quickly turned away.

"We're very close to the edge, Jack," she whispered.

"How do you mean that?"

She gave a quick nervous laugh as she understood the double meaning. Then they were silent again. His eyes focused on the road, and he forced his mind to focus too. He didn't want to think back to the sight of Walt's empty bed, the darkness outside, and the retreating brake lights. Then he felt he was dead in the water. Now that he was back on the trail, he had the chance of making it right again. He had a mission. And as dangerous as this new player might be, it was a hell of a lot better than having the cops or the FBI to deal with.

He shifted down to second and began crawling forward, weaving between drifts frozen solid into looming icebergs. The road turned hard right and began climbing steeper. He clicked on the dome light and handed the topo map to Mary.

"We're almost to the first turnoff. It'll be up here on the right."

She scanned the map then looked up through the windshield. She killed the dome light and pointed. "There. What's that?"

He flashed the high beams, and a weak spark of light winked back at him. It was a reflector, coated with a layer of dust from the winter storms.

He headed for the reflector, turned in, then hit the brakes. No one was going down this road. A chain was strung between two steel posts and a foot of snow with no tire tracks covered the road.

"One down and five to go," he said. Then he muttered, "I hope they're not all like this."

The next road came up in a quarter mile. It was heavily wooded on one side, a sheer drop on the other. He turned in and saw deep ruts cut in the snow. He yanked on the handbrake and got out, crouching over the tracks with his flashlight. He came back to the car, blowing on his hands.

"No one's been down there for weeks. Let's keep going."

Backing out, he found the next side road and turned the Pathfinder in. He quickly killed the headlights.

"What?" Mary asked.

"I saw a reflection. A window maybe. I don't want them to know I'm coming."

He climbed out, and she saw him checking the tracks again. He came back to the car and opened the door. "I think this is it." He reached over and touched her hand. She wanted to say something but decided against it.

"Turn the car around and wait here," he said. "Leave the motor running. We'll be leaving in a hurry."

He pulled back, but she squeezed his hand, hanging on for a moment, searching his face before she slowly let go.

Jack started out on foot down a steep grade. The tire tracks looked fresh, and they were the same ones he'd seen lower down the mountain. This was it. This had to be it.

It feels good to be alone now, Jack thought, moving by feel, the bite of the wind keeping him sharp. The pines were sparse, and the moon threw shadows on the ground that was patched with snow. Once his eyes adjusted, he saw there was enough light to work with; he could make out shapes through the trees and pick his way on bare ground. He cradled the flashlight in his left hand, the beam turned off. He touched the gun butt in his belt, the .38 Smith & Wesson with the bobbed-off hammer. The gun he used to hit Ernie with two nights ago. Was it only two nights ago? It seemed like he'd been on the run for months.

He reached a fork and saw the road circled a clearing. Beyond the trees he saw a log cabin, plywood across the windows. Moving closer he saw a thick hasp and padlock across the door. No one in there.

Edging forward, he saw a humped shape, moonlight glinting off its surface. Closer now, he saw it was an Airstream trailer, the shape of a Quonset hut with gleaming aluminum siding. Another light-colored shape appeared behind the trailer and, moving forward, he saw it was the hood of one of those monster SUVs, a big GMC or Chevy. He circled the trailer, expecting to find some old junker shot full of holes with a spider-webbed windshield. But no. His pulse quickened as he saw a new Ford Explorer.

Jack heard the sharp *tink* of cooling steel. He broke into a tight smile as he realized the sound came from the Explorer's engine, contracting in the freezing, high-altitude air. That meant the car had been driven recently. This was the car he was looking for. It had to be. And this was the trailer where Walt was being held.

A fist crashed into Jack's gut, and as he fell to the ground he thought, *And this is the guy who grabbed Walt.* The wind shot from his lungs, and he dropped to his knees. He hit the ground and rolled, knowing there would be a follow-up blow, wanting to get out of range. He rolled again and found his feet, partly straightened, and looked up at the still form towering above him.

At first, Jack was relieved to see the big man in the navy skullcap wasn't holding a gun on him. Then he realized that the fact that this guy didn't need a gun was actually a very bad sign.

THIRTY-THREE

T he scary part was that he had to follow Dillon's vehicle with his headlights off. Driving up the winding mountain road, Chief Ullrich had to hang back a good half mile, using nothing more than the moonlight to navigate with.

As he drove, he speculated that Dillon had two hideouts. One was down in the cabin in the foothills, the one Garrett told him his man had discovered. Then there was this other hideout they were headed to. Maybe Dillon had Stuckey stashed in one location, and his base of operations was in the other cabin.

It was a surprise that Garrett had come around like that, phoning him in his hotel room and telling him that Dillon would make his move tonight. It seemed out of character, but Ullrich decided to play along, go down another little rabbit trail, and see where it led him. Sure enough, as he took up a position to keep Dillon's cabin under surveillance, he saw a pair of headlights blink on, and the Pathfinder started moving.

Ullrich knew he'd get some answers soon—that was if he could just keep the big old Crown Vic on the road. More than once he felt his tires going over the side of the mountain and had to hit the brakes hard, hoping the cruiser wouldn't slide over the edge and down into the canyon. It'd be months before they found him down there.

Driving like this reminded him of when he was a wild-ass kid, drinking with his buddies on the back roads near Cut and Shoot, Texas. They'd be barreling down some country road, drunk as skunks, when old Reggie Boman would just reach over and kill the lights. For a second or two it was like free-falling. There'd be yellin' and cussin' and scrambling for the lights. Someone would yank the headlights back on again, and with a quick jerk of the wheel he'd pull the car out of a ditch. He got that same feeling now. Only the lights didn't come back on, and he had to keep going anyway.

Peering through the darkness up ahead, he saw Dillon's parked vehicle. Ullrich parked his cruiser a hundred yards down the slope, got out, and worked his way up the road on foot. He was about to give the Pathfinder a walk around when the dome light clicked on, and he saw someone was still inside. A female, bent over a map. Okay, so they split up. Dillon was on foot, and the woman waited with the car. For a quick getaway maybe?

Ullrich gave the Pathfinder a wide birth and picked his way through the trees. The patches of snow made walking treacherous. He had to pick his way between the piles of frozen snow, grabbing tree trunks to keep his footing, his hands coming away sticky with pine pitch. He could see Dillon's flashlight click on once or twice, the beam partly shielded by his hand, and he got the impression that Dillon was himself stalking someone.

The road circled a clearing, and Ullrich saw several cabins, dark and boarded up. At one end of the cul-de-sac was a trailer, and Dillon was giving it a good looking over. Why? The chief changed positions, moving out from behind a huge rock, and the reason became clear. A vehicle was parked by the trailer, a big old white four-wheel-drive job. Wait a second now. He'd seen that car before. But where? The answer would come in a minute. He ducked back behind a rock and pulled the heavy flashlight out of his belt. He touched his .38 Police Special. He wouldn't draw just yet. He needed a free hand to navigate the unsteady terrain.

As he tried to thumb off the snap on his holster, he noticed his fingers were slick on the leather. Here he was, freezing his ass off, but his fingers were sweaty. That's because it had been a long time since he'd been in the hunt like this, a long time since he'd made a big collar. He'd spent too many years behind a desk all the time, getting old and soft. If he brought in Dillon, he'd make headlines. Hell, this was national news. And he would be the arresting officer—the Pajaro Beach Police Chief, not the FBI.

But this might be a little trickier than he thought, Ullrich realized as he moved forward, because the trailer door was opening silently, and a new player was appearing. It was the tall man, the ex-con whom Garrett had hired, sliding into view and sneaking up on Dillon. No, the old chief concluded, this wouldn't be cut-and-dried at all. But there was no turning back now. He was here. And he'd have to make his move. Ullrich drew the .38 Police Special, feeling his fingers, slippery with an ice-cold sweat, closing around the knurled butt of the revolver.

THIRTY-FOUR

J ack really hated it when he got the wind knocked out of him. Not only did it give him that *I'm-gonna-die!* feeling, but it meant he had nothing to work with. Someone could wade in and do with you as they pleased while you made weird gasping noises trying to get air back in your lungs.

Working out at the dojo had prepared him for just this kind of thing. He knew the crashing blow to his solar plexus had a follow-up punch attached to it. So as he fell, he turned, landing on his side and rolling, using the slope to carry him out of range. He heard a whoosh as the big guy's foot whistled past his ear. That would have turned the lights out, he knew, so he rolled once more and came up with the Smith & Wesson. Problem was, he didn't have the breath to shout, "Back off! I've got a gun!" So he squeezed off a round and saw the guy pause a second then charge, shoulder down, arms in tight, looking for an opening. Jack let him come like that and found himself thinking this guy was a pro, like a commando or something. He sidestepped then kicked his legs out from under him. But this guy, this old commando, knew all the tricks. He landed easy and got back to his knees, ready to get up fast. Jack was ready for him, shoved him sideways, and put the gun in his ear.

"Enough," Jack hissed, his breath still short. "Where is he?"

"You want him, you're gonna have to go through me first," the commando growled. He batted the gun away, and Jack fired into the dirt. In the muzzle flash he saw the man moving again, moving opposite to what he'd anticipated, and half rising. Jack kicked, missed, and felt himself tipped up as the commando caught his boot and lifted. And now he was falling backward, thinking, *If I go down again, I'm finished.*

He hopped backward, off balance, sensing the hood of the Explorer behind him, using it like a fighter bouncing off the ropes to stay on his feet, swinging the gun and feeling the heavy barrel glance off the guy's skull. He shuddered but regrouped instantly and kept coming. But it gave Jack a second to get his stance, aim the gun, and say, "Hold it now! Just hold it a second! Okay?"

The guy was breathing hard, winded at this altitude. But he recovered fast and began sliding sideways, crouched low, looking for his opening.

"You're working for Garrett, right?" Jack asked, gasping for air.

The commando processed Jack's words, and his lips twisted in a snarl of rejection. "I work for no one but myself."

"Then why'd you take Walt?"

"Why'd you grab him in the first place?"

"To help him."

The commando laughed. "Goin' after a big ransom's gonna help him?"

"I never asked for anything. I just want to write his book."

"His book?"

"I'm a writer. Garrett didn't tell you that, did he? Walt hired me, then he had a stroke, and now I'm dealing with his dipshit son."

The commando stopped his stalking and gave a short snort. "Why should I believe that?"

"Well, for one thing," Jack said, "I've got the gun."

Those were fightin' words, and the old soldier began stalking again, looking for an opening. Jack didn't really want to shoot the guy. And he wasn't dying to go another round with him.

"Would you cut that out?" Jack said, standing easy, dropping the fighting stance. From a short stint as a bouncer in a nightclub, he knew that if you put your fists up, guys wanted to fight you. You stood there talking, it disabled the fighting instinct. Besides, everyone had a story to tell. You get them talking about themselves, you were halfway to making a deal.

"You're from Philly, aren't you?" Jack guessed, hearing the accent in the guy's speech.

"What if I am?"

"I'm from Jersey."

"You think I give a shit?"

"No. But I understand the problem."

"What's that, smartass?"

"Guys from Philly would rather die fighting than admit they're wrong."

The guy stopped his stalking again. "You sayin' I'm wrong?"

"I'm saying Garrett sold you a bill of goods, and you fell for it."

The commando lowered into his fighting stance again. "Okay, asshole. You're gonna pay for that."

"Think about it," Jack said, lowering the gun and folding his arms across his chest. Nonthreatening but ready, in case the guy made another charge. "Garrett's got his own agenda."

"I already got that figured out."

"So why are you throwing your muscle on his side?"

"I'm not turning Stuckey over to that little brat."

"Good, so I'll just take him then and—"

From behind them came the voice of authority, a loud, drawling voice. "Police! Get your hands up! And drop the gun!"

Jack dropped it.

A light blazed from across the clearing. They jumped back, startled, as the voice yelled, "I said get 'em up! Now!"

Jack slowly obeyed, remembering not to look right into the light so that when he looked away he wouldn't be blinded. Behind the light, he saw a pair of cowboy boots and a hand extending a revolver. The disembodied figure advanced on them.

"I want you boys to listen carefully," the voice said. He was ten feet away now, too far to put a face with the voice behind the light. "Walk to yonder car and reach for the hood."

Jack sensed the fear in the disembodied voice, like a teacher trying to control too many students. It triggered the rebelliousness of his high school days, and he thought, *No way I'm gonna lie down now. Not now. I've got another shot here. At least one more.*

He looked at the old commando and saw he was still game. He winked at him, partners in crime now, and said, "Count of three, you go left, and I'll go right."

"Hey you! Dillon—if that's your name—shut up! Reach for the hood, and spread your legs."

"One..." Jack whispered.

"Shut! Up! Now grab that car! Grab it, I said!"

"Two," Jack counted.

"Don't do that, sir! Dillon—whatever your name is. I said don't—"

"Three!"

Jack dove left, then crouching low, moved in behind the back end of the Explorer. He heard a gunshot and felt something heavy pluck at the air as it zipped past his head. He paused, getting his bearings, panting and trying to see where to go. Where were those shots coming from? They sounded farther away. They sounded like a rifle, not the short blast of a handgun. Who the hell was trying to shoot him?

The light found him, and a heartbeat later he heard another gunshot and *zing!* It was close—way too close. He heard shouts and the sound of running footsteps and another shot. Bam! The bullet splintered bark on the tree next to him. Time to hit the ground. Jack dropped low, and the light followed him.

The sound of footsteps moving off in the darkness. Jack looked out under the car, planning an escape route, a way to get out of the line of fire, and a way to keep that damned light off him.

"Police officer! Hold your fire!" The guy in the clearing, the cop that tried to arrest them, was yelling off into the trees. "Hold your fire!"

Who was he shouting at? Then Jack realized what was happening. The shots were coming from someone out in the woods, someone even the cop didn't know. The FBI? That wasn't their style. If it wasn't them, that left only one other person who might be trying to pick him off from a distance.

Jack peered out from under the Explorer and saw a pair of cowboy boots moving toward him. Coming at him around the back end of the Explorer. Time to make a move before the cowboy cop got him. He took off, back out into the opening, and—

—*Zip!* The bullet punched a hole in the side of the trailer.

Man, if I stay out here, I'll get myself shot! Jack thought. He saw the trailer door was still open and, looking for cover, he ducked in, into the darkness inside.

But it wasn't completely dark. A weak bulb on the wall lit the dirty interior. He looked around breathing hard. Dishes in the sink. Beer cans strewn around. A dirty blanket on a bare mattress. And then he saw a withered hand reaching out of the tangled mess of blankets.

"No..." The voice was pitifully weak.

"No..." The thin voice came to Jack again, and this time he connected the voice with the hand and saw Walt practically right in front of him, reaching out, speaking the only word he could: no.

"Walt—buddy. I'm here," Jack said, feeling the relief flooding his system. He grabbed the old, cool hand and squeezed it, feeling the connection restored.

Bam! A bullet came through the wall and hit a cabinet door opposite. The slug lost velocity and fell to the floor where it rolled around like a marble.

There was the sound of a scuffle outside. More shouting. Shots.

"We gotta get out of here," Jack said. He sat Walt up in bed. Walt flopped against him as Jack wrapped him up in the dirty blanket. He scooped him up and felt like he was carrying a child, the way he'd carry Chloe up to bed when she had fallen asleep watching TV. He heard Walt say *Jack* in a terrified voice, a voice that depended on him. And hearing his name, it melted his heart.

It was one of those times when Jack had to shut off all his thoughts. All he knew was that he had to rush out, carrying this man whom everyone was after, and reach the trees…and then the Pathfinder. He knew if he hesitated, he wouldn't do it, so he charged out—

—and ran smack into the cowboy cop. Jack felt the lawman's firm hand on his arm, the gun barrel rammed up into the soft flesh under Jack's chin, lifting him off his feet. This guy meant business.

"End of the trail," the cop said, grinning.

But then there was a shot, the cop went *unh!* And a corsage of blood exploded on his jacket. The smile faded, and he stumbled forward, held onto Jack for a second, then dropped to the ground. Jack saw blood shining on his back—the bullet had passed right through him.

With his human shield gone, Jack felt exposed, back in the line of fire from the sniper, from whoever the hell was firing from the trees. He moved left as another bullet slammed into the trailer, and he broke into a run with Walt still in his arms.

"Go!" Walt said.

Jack didn't need the encouragement. He was flying through the dark, legs pumping hard, feet slipping in the gravel, off balance and falling, then back up and moving forward with Walt clutched to his chest.

And then, just as suddenly, they were in the trees. Safe and in the trees. Out of the line of fire at last. He didn't need to run anymore. But he was all hopped up with adrenaline, and he still wanted to sprint—wanted to fly—back to the Pathfinder and

Mary. Because there was just the chance that they could get away before the sniper got to his car.

All of a sudden Jack hit the wall, oxygen draining from his leg muscles. He stood there in the night, hyperventilating like he'd just run for his life, which he pretty much had. He looked over his shoulder. There were lights in the clearing, figures moving. The cop's body lay by the trailer door. Now two figures stepped into the trailer, and flashlights shone through the windows as they searched for something inside. *For something?* Jack thought. *No, they're looking for the man that I'm holding in my arms.*

The man he had liberated for the second time that week.

THIRTY-FIVE

Slade was crouched beside the fallen cop when Garrett walked into the clearing carrying the hunting rifle. Garrett looked down at the still form, the dark stain in the dirt widening as they spoke. The cop's revolver lay several feet from his outstretched hand.

"Wow," Garrett said.

"You shoot a cop and all you can say is 'wow'?" Slade growled, standing up and advancing on Garrett.

"I never actually thought I'd hit him," Garrett said. "I mean, one minute I was aiming at Dillon, then it got all crazy, and I just got into it—you know, like in the Westerns. I guess Dillon got in the way."

"Like in the Westerns," Slade echoed then spit. "You're sick, you know that? Why'd you start shooting?"

"Listen," Garrett said, waving the rifle wildly. "I told you to kill Dillon. When I saw he was going to be arrested, it wasn't like I was about to let that happen."

"I think you were trying to set me up," Slade snatched the gun from Garrett's hands. "Shoot Dillon, then blame it on me. But you got the cop instead. Nice move."

Slade jerked the bolt back and looked in the rifle's chamber. It was empty. He ducked inside the trailer, and Garrett followed. He saw Slade toss the rifle onto his bed and begin rummaging in a duffel bag. When he stood up he held the Colt .45. They faced each other in the small space.

"All right, asshole," Slade said. "You gotta understand one thing. You shoot a cop, you go away forever. Understand?"

"I told you. It was his fault. I wanted to shoot Dillon but—"

Slade threw a haymaker, turning his hips and really getting into the punch. It caught Garrett on the point of his jaw, lifted him up, and dumped him back onto the bed. When Garrett opened his mouth to speak, Slade inserted the barrel of the .45 and cocked the hammer.

From the look on Garrett's face, Slade had his complete attention.

"Here's the plan, asshole. You take this gun, and go out and finish the cop. Then we drag him out into the woods and bury him. Then we find Dillon and the broad he's runnin' with, and we take 'em both out. Then, maybe, we can keep our asses out of prison."

Slade slid the gun out, and as soon as he did, Garrett's mouth started yappin' again.

"I like that last part, about killing Dillon. But not the cop. I'm not killing a cop."

"You're finishing the cop, and you're gonna do it right now."

Garrett tried to muscle past him and head for the door. Slade grabbed his shoulder, spun him around, and gave him a back-hand across the face. Garrett's head banged off the wall, and he sagged back. Red splotches formed where Slade had nailed him.

"Okay! I'll do it!"

Slade stepped back, releasing him. Garrett stood up, and Slade handed him the rifle, barrel pointed away from him.

"Load it."

Garrett pulled a box of cartridges from his coat pocket. He opened the box, spilling shells on the floor. His fingers were shaking pitifully but he managed to get a bullet in the chamber.

Slade turned Garrett around and shoved him toward the door, keeping the .45 on him. They moved outside, and he pointed the flashlight down at the cop. Or at the place where the cop had fallen. But the cop wasn't there. A dark stain on the dirt showed where he'd been lying.

"Holy shit, he's gone," Garrett said, a huge grin splitting his face as he exhaled.

Slade swept the ground with the beam. He crouched, looking closely at the dirt. He saw drag marks leading around the corner of the trailer.

"He couldn't have gone far," Slade said. "Let's go get him."

They followed the drag marks to the edge of the trailer. They saw a trail of shiny blood spatters on leaves and pine needles. Then they lost the trail, and Slade turned the beam up at the forest. The light illuminated nothing but a slope of rocks and trees and branches waving in the night wind.

THIRTY-SIX

Lying behind a rock, Chief Ullrich looked down the slope toward the trailer and saw Garrett talking with the ex-con. Garrett had a flashlight, and they were looking at the dirt, at the place he'd been lying five minutes ago. Then they began moving upslope toward him, looking at the ground, following his trail.

It was for just this kind of situation that he had always carried a backup weapon in his boot. It wasn't a real stopper, like his .38, but it could drop the con if he hit him clean. Not in the chest—the bullet could hit bone, and the small slug would bounce around. But if he hit him in a vital spot, the head or the neck, he'd be dead. If he could take out the con, it would be easy to deal with Garrett. Garrett was the kind of man who backed down from authority, who had some respect—or at least fear—of the law. The con, he knew, would die fighting.

Ullrich was sick about losing his .38. It had been his daddy's gun, and he'd worn it with pride all his life. His daddy had been a Texas Ranger and had taught him just about everything he knew about justice. At times, his father still came to him, stern and frightening, but always speaking the truth. Not the easy truth. But the truth he couldn't avoid. As a kid, growing up in a tough neighborhood near the stockyards in Fort Worth, he'd come crying to his father after losing a fight. The old lawman sent him back outside to deal with his problems on his own. Standing up for himself hadn't come easy, but his daddy saw to it that he learned the important lessons the hard way.

Ullrich knew he had to get to the .25 lady-stinger in his boot, but it might as well have been two miles away. Every time he leaned down to get the little pistol, a red wave of pain surged up from the bullet wound in his shoulder and washed over him. So he had to reach for the gun, then back off and fight the pain, then reach a little farther.

It felt like the bullet had gone through his left shoulder cleanly. Luckily for the chief, it wasn't a soft-nosed bullet. The ammo was probably used for target shooting, not hunting. Still, he knew that he'd lost some blood and he might black out. It'd be a damn shame if he was lying here unconscious when they found him.

His hand was on his right pants leg, and he worked his way down, spiderlike, grasping the material and pulling on it, lifting it up above the boot. Pull, stretch, hold for the pain. Pull, stretch, pain. Then he'd check on the twosome tracking him. They were veering off toward the road now, assuming he'd head back to the cruiser. He thought they'd think that. That's why he'd scrambled up between these rocks. It was harder to track him up here, as long he could keep from bleeding too bad. And he could get the drop on them if they did find him.

Pull, stretch, pain. He looked down the slope to see if they were coming. They were still focused on the ground, looking for his trail. But they were close, real close now. Close enough to see the flashlight reflected on their faces. Close enough to hear what they were saying.

"He couldn't have gone far, huh?" Garrett was saying. "We're wasting time chasing a dying cop while Dillon's escaping with my father."

The con whirled on him, shoving the flashlight and gun in his face. "First thing that cop's gonna do is get to his radio. He does that, we're done. This mountain will be crawling with cops."

"You dumb bastard. He never even saw who shot him. It could have been Dillon. That's why I was shooting. So Dillon would take the blame for all of this."

The con's flashlight caught something in the dirt. He crouched and looked closely. Then he stood up and swept the area above him with his beam. Ullrich tried to draw back, out of the light. The light lingered on the cluster of rocks. Had they seen him?

The voices were quiet now, and the light stayed close. Ullrich's hand was on his knee, almost to the top of his boot. The light was moving, sweeping the other rocks. It disappeared, then came back again. Still no voices.

"What the hell kinda lawman are you?" Ullrich heard his daddy say. "You gonna lie here and let 'em gun you down? Get your backup weapon out and finish the job."

The face of his father hovered in front of him, riding the night wind. Ullrich saw his daddy's big chin, heard his gravelly voice, smelled the whiskey that was always on his breath.

"I said finish the job, boy! What kinda candy-assed sissy boy are you?"

Ullrich strained for the gun, his hand moving down into his boot. He felt something reassuring in his hand now: the lady-stinger. But it was too late. The beam was on him like God's light of reckoning. But it was the voice of evil that spoke to him, the voice of that big con, the killer he knew would show no mercy.

"What have got here?" the con said. "A cop without a gun."

"Well now," Ullrich said. "That's not entirely true." He raised the lady-stinger and squeezed the trigger. The shot was like the snap of a cap pistol. But the slug was well placed. It smacked into the ex-con's forehead with enough force to penetrate his thick skull and bore its way into his criminal brain. The con's eyes rolled up. He struggled to raise his own gun to return fire, lost the struggle, and crashed backward down the slope, taking the light of reckoning with him.

PART FOUR
DEATH VALLEY

THIRTY-SEVEN

They were halfway to Death Valley when Walt started talking again.

Mary was asleep in the back, Jack at the wheel, and Walt was wide awake, staring through the windshield at the narrow, twisting two-lane road that snaked down into the immense valley. It was dawn, and the sun was just coming up, sharpening the silhouette of the mountains to the east. Every mile they drove they dropped hundreds of feet in elevation, turning winter into spring and eventually summer. Their headlights still picked out reflectors on the sides of the road. But beyond the reflectors, beyond the narrow shoulder with no guard rail, it was a sheer drop to the desert floor far below.

Walt was agitated, breathing hard, humming, shifting in his seat. Finally, he took a deep breath, cleared his throat, and said, "That was a close scrape."

Jack turned toward Walt and found the old man looking straight at him, his eyes bright, amazed he had spoken. Jack almost forgot he was driving, checked the road, glanced back in time to see Walt open his mouth and say, "At the trailer—all that shooting—we almost bought the farm."

"You're talking," Jack said, amazed.

"Talking," Walt said, nodding. "Yes, I'm talking."

Goosebumps ran up Jack's arms and across the back of his neck, prickling his scalp. It was like a ghost had just spoken to him, like his friend had returned from the dead.

"Walt, buddy, you're talking."

"Yes! Talking, talking, talking."

"How much do you remember of what's happened?" Jack asked.

Walt rocked back and forth, hummed lightly to get started, then said, "Mmm…All of it. All. Everything. But, but, but—it comes and goes. Comes and goes."

"What?"

"The pictures. They come and go." A coughing fit stopped him. "The heater…turn it up. I'm fr—fr—freezing my—my, my ass."

Jack laughed. Same old cranky Walt. God, it was great to hear his voice again. He leaned across and put his arm around the old man's shoulders.

"Are we gonna make it? Walt, buddy?"

"We'll make it, Jack."

"I'm in a helluva jam here, ya know. You gotta help me."

Walt shivered. "Need some heat. Heat."

"You got it, Walt. Anything you want. Maximum heat it is."

Jack worked the climate controls and felt the hot air coming out of the vent.

"Better?"

"Better. Better. Better. Yes, better."

They took a tight corner and then, in front of them, the whole valley opened up. They could see a hundred miles all at once. White patches of alkali that bubbled up from the ground looked almost like water from a distance. And to see the huge awesome valley at this great, great moment made Jack feel physically light, floating with relief. He had been right! He thought Walt was still within reach, and he took a chance to save him. Now here they were, connected again. He gambled and won. He was right, dammit! Right! He leaned over and slapped Walt's leg.

"I never thought we'd talk again like this."

"Old times again. Like old times." Then smoother, his voice changing, sounding different, younger: "Just you and me, kid. Thanks for everything you've done, Reilly."

Startled, Jack looked at Walt, who was staring at the road ahead, rocking and humming, hugging himself with his arms. Jack felt an icy blast of doubt, his good mood suddenly punctured.

"Walt?"

"Huh?"

"Walt, buddy. My name's Jack."

"I know that."

"You called me Reilly."

No answer. Just humming and rocking.

Confused, Jack turned back to the road. They were down on the valley floor now, skirting a mountain of black volcanic rock that flowed down to a suddenly smooth alluvial fan of dirt washed out of the mountains over millions of years. Jack drove in silence, his tired mind rearranging the pieces, trying to understand what this would mean. He swung around a long sweeping curve, feeling the engine freewheel as they passed a sign that read SEA LEVEL. Then another sign: FURNACE CREEK, 47. Furnace Creek was the only real town in Death Valley. And there wasn't much to it—a golf course, a motel court with cabins for rent, a general store, and an airstrip.

"Heater working?"

Jack felt the vents. "I can turn it up if you want. But it's getting hotter out all the time."

Suddenly, the quality of Walt's voice changed. It had a hollow ring, and the cadence smoothed out. He sounded much younger as he said, "The studio."

"Studio?"

"Yeah, and use the back entrance. The guard there knows me. He's a nice kid. Gratziano's his name. He's nuts about the show."

A chill went through Jack's system. "Walt?"

"Yeah?"

"How ya feelin'?"

"Like whipped shit in a Dixie cup. Can we get some rest soon?"

"You bet."

"Where're we going, anyway?" His voice sounded stronger now. *Maybe he's just tired. Maybe all he needed was some rest,* Jack thought. *After all, he's been through a lot in the last couple of days.*

"We're going to Death Valley."

Walt jumped. "Death Valley! Why?"

"There aren't a lot of places left for us to hide. When the sun comes up, I'm tellin' you, I want to be out of sight."

It was great to hear Walt talking again. But Jack had to know what he was dealing with. He was afraid to ask, because he was afraid of what the answer would be. But he had to know.

"Walt, do you know who I am?"

"Of course I do. You're Jack."

Jack felt a burst of relief. "Yeah. Right. I'm Jack." But then another thought hit him, and a question formed that he didn't want to ask. But he had to. He had to know what he was dealing with.

"Jack who? What's my last name?"

"You've been with me since the show started. I guess I should know your last name. You're Jack Reilly."

THIRTY-EIGHT

Special Agent Watson had to raise his voice over the roar of the chopper blades as he said, "It's a poor statement on the moral fiber of law enforcement when we have to electronically monitor another department to get our leads. It's a good thing Oldham and Beck picked up their trail and followed them here."

"Yeah, those guys are sharp," said Special Agent Boxell. "But why's Chief Ullrich holding out on us?" She leaned forward, scanning the landscape below that was as dry and barren as the surface of the moon. She had changed into a pair of jeans for the trip, and Watson noticed that they outlined the swell of her hips nicely. Her hair was pulled back, and she sported a navy windbreaker with yellow letters stenciled across the back: FBI.

"Some of these locals play it close to the vest," Watson said. "It's the territorial imperative. The FBI is just so intimidating to old guys like Ullrich. They feel they'll be shoved aside, and we'll grab the glory."

"We'd never do that."

"No. Nothing could be further from the truth."

Their eyes met, and they exchanged a look. As they looked away, they each smiled.

It was early morning, and they were flying south, parallel to California Highway 395, the front range of the Sierras on their right. Watson touched Boxell's shoulder and pointed to the glowing mountaintop. "Mount Whitney—highest point in the United States." Boxell turned to him, about to correct him, when he added, "Highest in the contiguous United States, anyway."

She nodded. Pointing east, toward low, dirty hills, she said, "The lowest point in the United States is over there somewhere, in Death Valley—Badwater, 237 feet below sea level. Oddly enough, the high and the low are only separated by 170 miles."

Watson was scanning the horizon with a pair of binos. He said, "You really know your California geography."

"Lowell Elementary School, Long Beach, California. Miss Parker, fourth grade. I did this report called, 'Our Nation's Highs and Lows.'"

"You're from Long Beach? I didn't know that. I'm from—" He suddenly located whatever he was looking for. He spoke into a radio, received an answer. He touched the pilot's shoulder and indicated the flare was sending up a swirling ribbon of smoke that flapped in the wind.

Moments later, they stepped from the chopper that had set down on the mountain road. They were greeted by a short solid agent with thick black hair just beginning to turn gray. The butt of a huge black handgun protruded from a worn leather holster on his hip. He led them to a clearing near an Airstream trailer and several deserted cabins. He showed them where the first officers on the scene had found a .38 caliber Police Special revolver lying on the ground, fully loaded. Then they followed yellow evidence markers, indicating blood droplets, to the rocky outcropping where the discovery had been made earlier that morning.

At this altitude Watson and Boxell were breathing hard when they reached the body. But they continued breathing hard long after they recovered from the climb. The corpse was lying on its back, the face downslope, causing it to fill with blood and become hideously discolored and bloated. The lips curled back on yellow teeth, some missing, exposing a ferocious animal snarl. The eyes were milky and clouding. The bullet crater, dead center in the forehead, was as symmetrical and innocent as a star on a car's windshield from a flying rock. Only in this case, the bullet had drilled a neat cavity through the skull and into the dead man's brain. Ants had discovered the wound and had industriously set up a heavily traveled trail leading into, and out of, his head.

Watson crouched beside the body and peered intently at the wound. "Small caliber weapon." He straightened up, feeling dizzy in the high altitude as he did so.

"A .25 automatic maybe—Saturday night special," Boxell said.

"Smaller," Watson said. "A .22 caliber maybe. And no shell casing was ejected so it was probably single-shot. Maybe one of those little hideaway guns—a lady-stinger."

The short solid agent said, "Buddy of mine, worked homicide at Oakland PD, carried a fountain pen that fired one round. Lotta old-timers carry a trick piece like that. In case they lose their service weapon."

The agent's words connected with something Watson was thinking. He said, "Old-timers, huh?" and smiled at Boxell.

"The .38 revolver you found—you run the serial number yet? You know who it belonged to?"

"We called it in—haven't got a match yet. Looks like a service revolver, police issue."

Boxell nodded, smiling. Almost absentmindedly she said, "Our chief—Ullrich."

"Ullrich?" The solid agent looked from one face to the other. "Who's that?"

Boxell and Watson remained silent, staring at the corpse at their feet.

"You two know something I don't?"

"Nothing solid," Boxell said finally.

The solid agent waited for more.

"A case like this comes along every once in a long while," Watson said in that high, nasal tone of his. He shrugged. "Locals get all hot and bothered, and now it looks like we could have a renegade cop on our hands."

"Great," Boxell said. "Let's put him on the list of all the other people we're tracking."

THIRTY-NINE

"Wake up. I've got a surprise for you," Jack said, talking to Mary, who was still asleep in the backseat.

Mary's eyelids fluttered, then opened. She looked around, disoriented, as if trying to figure out where they were. Looking up out of the car window she saw nothing but blue sky. As she sat up she saw the stunted, wind-blown mesquite bushes and the sand dunes. Miles of empty sand dunes. But no ocean. Then she remembered that they had been headed to Death Valley. Yes, that's where they must be. Her mind was clearing now, and her eyes focused on Walt, who was turned around and looking at her over the back of the front seat. The look on his face was different. Knowing. Something had changed.

Walt smiled at her and said, "Lady Mary."

"Walt?" She turned to Jack, startled. "Jack, is he talking? Really talking now?"

"Yes," Walt nodded. "Talking. I'm really talking."

She threw her arms around his neck. "Oh my God! It's a miracle!" She pulled back and stared at him, tears streaking her cheeks.

She turned to Jack and said, "See? I told you everything was going to turn out all right." She hugged him again, laughing and crying.

Jack shifted and looked around uncomfortably. He suddenly opened the door and stepped out. "I, uh, I'm going to go to the bathroom." He started walking toward a blue port-a-potty on the edge of the parking lot. The National Park Service had posted plaques to give visitors information before they hiked into the dunes. But the parking lot was empty now. It was dawn, and it was absolutely still here in the desert. The feeling of a hot day hung in the air. Crows were fighting around an overflowing garbage can, cawing and pecking each other over scraps of rotting food.

———

Back in the car, Mary was saying, "It's horrible to say this, but I never thought I'd talk to you again. It was like you were dead." She hugged him again. "I have so much to tell you. We've been through hell, Walt."

"I know. I know."

"You—you do? So you know what happened?"

"I saw it all."

"All of it?"

He nodded. The meaning of that statement hung uncertainly in the air.

"So all that time you were mentally, you know, lucid, like they said?"

Walt frowned then nodded. She studied his face, sensing disapproval. She glanced across the parking lot and saw Jack approaching the car, walking slowly, not wanting to interrupt them.

Mary patted Walt on the arm. "Excuse me, Walt dear, I have to use the restroom." She stepped out, and when she reached Jack she whispered, "How much does he know?"

"How much does he know about what?"

"About us."

It was very still around them, the crows temporarily quiet. The silence of the desert magnified the question.

"Why are you worried? You said it was what he wanted."

"That was before."

"Before what?"

"Before I knew he'd be all right."

"Wait a second—did he or didn't he give us the okay?"

"Well, yes, he did. But—"

From the car they heard Walt's voice: "Let's go. We're going to be late."

They looked at each other.

"Late?" Mary asked.

"I want to do a run-through before the taping."

"What taping is that, Walt?"

Before he could answer, the sound of a car's engine broke the stillness. They turned and saw a green sedan approaching. A National Park Service patrol car with a ranger at the wheel. The car rolled slowly across the parking lot, tires crunching on the loose gravel, and stopped near the overflowing trash can.

"Jack…" Mary said softly. "I think we better get going."

"That might look just a little suspicious. Why don't you go ahead and use the luxury accommodations as if nothing was wrong. I'll get the video camera."

"What? Why?"

"We're tourists, shooting the beautiful desert sunrise—that's what tourist like us do. And I need to shoot some pictures of Walt talking." He dropped his voice and whispered, "Besides, we have to let his fans know he's recovered."

Jack casually walked back to the car. He opened the door and began rummaging for the camera. Walt was watching, so he asked, "You and Mary have a nice chat?"

"Yeah, but I couldn't forget what she did," Walt said, his voice faltering.

Jack found the camera and was about to start playing tourist for the ranger's benefit. Then Walt's comment hit him. The tone in his voice was different, connected. Maybe this was real. He had to learn to differentiate.

"What'd she do, Walt?" he said, still searching for the camera.

"Aw, she's just like all the rest of 'em."

"In what way?"

"Right after the stroke—she'd come in my room." He breathed, paused, struggling to find the words. "When no one was around. She always said the same thing."

"What?"

"She'd say, 'Promise me'"—he paused, searching again—"'promise me he won't get a penny.'"

The words hit him hard. They seemed like they were going to connect with other suspicions he'd had. But there was no time to think about it now. He was watching the park ranger, who was speaking into the radio mike.

"She doesn't think Garrett deserves to get your money," Jack said, trying to pass it off. "Neither do I."

"Not Garrett," Walt said impatiently. "NOT!"

Jack got a strange empty feeling in his stomach. And he didn't know why. "Then who was she talking about?"

Mary called across the parking lot to Jack, "Honey, can you get a shot of the sunrise? It's so pretty."

"Just a second," Jack yelled back. "Who was she talking about?" Jack asked Walt.

The old man was staring out the windshield at the nothingness of the desert. But Jack realized he was actually seeing something else. Again his voice was smoother, but hollow, coming from the past. "I'm pooped. But I thought the show went well. What'd you think, Reilly?"

"Walt," Jack said, desperately. "Don't leave me now. Who was Mary talking about?"

In the same distant voice Walt said, "Take me over to the club. I want a steam bath and a rubdown. Then I could go for a big steak at Hugo's. Call ahead for a reservation, would ya?"

Across the parking lot, Jack heard Mary talking to the ranger. She cheerfully said, "Feels like it's going to be a hot one."

"Sure does," the ranger said. "Where're you folks from?"

FORTY

It was sometime after nine in the morning when the maid jiggled the doorknob of room 235 at the Dow Villa in Lone Pine and called, "Housekeeping!" When she didn't hear an answer, she put the master key in the door and opened it up.

The enraged face of Garrett Stuckey filled the doorway, sleep-glazed eyes turning to fire, lips pulling back in a snarl. He was standing there in boxer shorts and a rumpled T-shirt, his hair wild, arms flailing, kicking a long dark object back out of sight under the bed.

"You people!" he roared. "Did it ever occur to you to knock?"

"Sorry, Señor," the woman said, backing out the door.

"You should be fired! "Despedir! Comprende?"

"I'm very sorry, Señor. Please—"

Garrett slammed the door. He threw himself back in bed and lay there, knowing he needed more sleep but realizing that it was unlikely, now that he'd blown his stack like that. *Stupid bitch. I mean—these people!* He just hoped she didn't see the rifle before he shoved it under the bed. God knows whom she might tell about it. He twisted among the sheets in a state of anxiety and agitation, alternately flashing on the events of last night and planning what he should do next.

Everything had started out so smoothly. Ernie let him know that Ullrich was on the move. They tailed the cop and watched as he reached Dillon's cabin. Then they tailed him as he climbed the winding mountain road to the trailer, hot on Dillon's trail. Garrett left Ernie in the car, took the hunting rifle, and found a spot that was perfect. All he needed was a clear shot at Jack, and this whole mess would be wrapped up. Slade was armed. Jack was armed. And so was Ullrich. One shot from Garrett, and they'd all start blasting. With all those guns they'd never be able to figure out who shot Dillon.

But then everything fell apart. It was hard to see in the dark. And that stupid cop got in the way. Then Dillon escaped, carrying his father. Jesus. To top it off, the wounded cop plugged Slade. (Actually, maybe that had an upside to it; Slade was getting a little hard to control.) But seeing Slade gunned down, Garrett lost his nerve. And he ran for it. When he got back to Ernie, he realized that the cop might pull through. And that left a very messy loose end.

Garrett reached over and hit the power button on the remote. The ancient TV—Christ, what he wouldn't give to be in a Holiday Inn right now—struggled to life. He surfed until he found a news channel and let the images flicker before him, the sound off.

There had to be a way to flush Dillon out. Or maybe a way to get rid of him for good. He hated the idea that Dillon might come out looking like a hero. The reports that Dillon had cured his father really fried his ass. He wished Dillon was the one lying on his back in the woods instead of Slade. That's where he belonged.

Images on the TV screen caught his eye. What the hell was this? He cued the sound.

A woman announcer was saying, "Events took a deadly turn early this morning with the discovery of a body near a mountain trailer where they think the TV legend was held captive."

Video footage appeared of a coroner's van and a body wrapped in a yellow plastic sheet. Then the picture cut to a woman reporter doing a stand-up. She looked familiar.

"The body of an unidentified man, shot to death, was found in a rocky area behind the trailer. The FBI, who is on the scene, is saying little about who the man was or how he was involved. However, we have learned that the killing is connected to the kidnapping of Walt Stuckey, who was taken from his home earlier this week by author Jack Dillon."

"He's no author," Garrett growled at the TV set. "He's a dime-a-dozen hack, that's what he is."

"Thanks to our Trisha King for that live report from the scene," said an anchor woman, a dolled-up blonde who squared up her papers, wrapping up the report. "Meanwhile, the eighty-one-year-old TV legend remains missing. We'll be bringing you updates of this highly unusual case as details become available."

If they only knew what I know, Garrett thought. *Then they'd have a real story, not this half-assed puff piece. Pets, tits, and tots. That's all TV news is. And they keep treating Dillon like he's some kind of folk hero—the stupid whores. Reporters are just a bunch of whores who'll do anything to get a story.* Like that reporter who shoved her card in his car window. She was young and hungry, stuck at some boondock station in Fresno, looking for a big break. A big break like an exclusive interview with a kidnapped TV icon. Or his son.

Garrett lay there, feeling a variety of urges and emotions. Then suddenly, these feelings all wove themselves into one overwhelming desire and provided one answer for his next move. He fumbled excitedly in his wallet for the reporter's business card, picked up the phone, and dialed.

———

"Did anyone try to follow you?" Garrett said, shutting the door behind her.

"Who would follow me?"

"Other reporters. Cops. I don't know."

"I drove back to my station in Fresno to clear this assignment with my editor. Then I drove up here on 395. There wasn't another car behind me for miles. There's no way I'm being followed."

"Okay, fine. Good. The point is, you're here. Have a seat, have a seat."

Garrett indicated the chair near the knotty pine desk, but Trisha King remained standing, her arms folded across her chest, the strap of her purse still looped over her shoulder. Garrett noticed that she was shorter than she appeared on TV. The rest of her didn't disappoint, though. Her white silky blouse pulled tight across her assertive chest, and he saw a hint of lace underneath. And she was hungry. Very, very hungry. That much was written all over her face.

"You have something for me?" Trisha asked.

"I do indeed."

"What is it?"

"Not so fast. I need something from you first."

"Oh?" She arched an eyebrow at him. "What do you need?"

"Ah, well, let's just call them assurances."

"Assurances. Okay. What can I assure you about?"

He indicated the chair again. "Please. Please. Sit down. I know how it feels to be on my feet all the time. I was a reporter once."

"Really? Where?"

"It was a long time ago. An intern kind of thing in college. Can I get you a drink? I have some wine. I'd order room service, but this hotel—man, what a pit."

"Just water."

She slowly sat down, setting her purse on the floor beside her chair. She took out a thin reporter's notebook and clicked a pen. Slowly, she wrote what looked to him like the date. Then she looked up, her black hair falling back to reveal her sharp, intelligent features and her wide, full mouth. She was nervous but determined, wanting to seem more seasoned, in control. But Garrett sensed her raw ambition. And identified with it.

Garrett turned his back on her, stripping the lead from the neck of a bottle of chardonnay. He plunged the point of the cork-screw deep into the soft cork.

"I was there last night," he said offhandedly.

"Beg your pardon?"

"I was there last night. At the death scene." He reminded himself to use short, punchy sentences. You had to actually write the story for these people. He poured two glasses of wine and handed her one.

"I said water."

"It was very upsetting," he said as if he hadn't heard her. "I've never seen a man gunned down execution style before."

She took a healthy swallow of the wine and, setting it down too quickly, sloshed a little on the tabletop. She eagerly began taking notes.

"We're talking about the shooting up near the Whitney Portal?"

"Yes."

"You have an ID on the victim?"

Garrett was standing above her now, swirling the wine in his glass. He nodded in response to her question.

"Yes I do."

"Who was he?"

"Trisha, that's one of the things I need assurance about."

She set her pen down, apparently realizing that the flow of facts had been stanched, and negotiations were about to begin. She took out a pack of cigarettes and lit one up. She didn't handle the cigarette and matches very expertly, and Garrett wondered if smoking was a recent affectation to make her seem older and tougher.

"Do you mind?" Garrett said. "I'm allergic to smoke."

She took a deep drag, blew out a plume of smoke, then stubbed out the butt. As she bent to reach her wineglass, Garrett was afforded a nice view of her ample cleavage. *A premeditated move on her part*, he thought. *Whores. I was right. They're all a bunch of whores.*

Straightening, she said, "What exactly do you have for me?"

He sat on the bed across from her. It was a small room, and their faces were close.

"Trisha, let me put it this way: I have everything you want."

"Everything?"

"That's right. You've had a nice run with this story. You get there first, you break the story. You're resourceful, and your delivery is exceptional. You deserve to work in a much larger market—San Francisco. Or LA, maybe. Eventually to New York. That's why I called you."

"Okay," she said cautiously, waiting.

"What I have will make your career—overnight. Tomorrow, everyone will know your name."

"What have you got?"

"I'll get you the exclusive, inside story on Dillon's arrest, his background."

"When's he going to be arrested?"

"I don't know, but I'll be there when it happens and—"

"Why will you be there?"

"I'm...well, I'm not leaving things up to the so-called authorities. I'm working this case myself."

"How?"

"I'm not at liberty to tell you that now," he said then quickly added, "The thing that gets me about Dillon is he pretends to be this Robin Hood character, helping my father. But he's actually a low-life killer."

"He shot the guy up at the trailer near Mount Whitney?"

"I saw the whole thing. I can tell you who pulled the trigger—everything. But I'll also get you an exclusive interview with me and my father. I'll have him back soon, and you'll be the first to interview him about his ordeal. And I'll cut off information to anyone else in the media."

"Why're you giving this to me?"

"I need a source in the media I can work with. I want this story handled, well, responsibly. Because there's an awful lot that hasn't come out yet."

She took a sip of her wine. He watched her throat work as she took it down. Her tongue flicked out and ran over her lips, making them glisten. *That's a buying signal*, he thought. She was buying his offer. And she was ready. Garrett shifted on the bed, stabbing a hand into his pocket briefly, rearranging his stuff. Then he hunched closer.

"Okay, Garrett," she said, her voice husky. "I'll bite." A reflexive look of anticipated pain spread across his face. She saw his expression, understood it, and rephrased her answer. "I want what you've got."

Suddenly he had an odd thought. He felt like she was talking to the camera. Only, he was the camera. It made him feel big and powerful. He was big and powerful. He'd show her just how powerful he was. He stood up and moved in on her. "You want it so bad, come and get it." The meaning of his words was clear.

"Wait a second. I want the story first."

"Sorry. Payment in advance." He unbuckled his belt and unzipped his fly. He'd let her do the rest.

She looked up at him, and he saw something happen in her eyes. *The decision to do it*, he thought. She took a belt of wine, then peeled his pants down. She opened her beautiful, ripe mouth and started working on him. He was right. She was a real whore. She knew where his every nerve and muscle were and how to set him throbbing with a flick of her tongue or a long pull with those full lips. His body was begging to explode. She worked him almost to the point of no return then suddenly detached.

"There's my down payment," she said, panting, suddenly sounding much older and savvier. "Now, who's the stiff up in the mountains? And who the hell killed him?"

His dripping member felt cold and exposed, waving around in the cold air of the dingy room. He whimpered in agony, wanting to explode, yet wanting to prolong the ecstasy. But above all, he wanted to be back in her wet warmth.

"Later," he gasped. "Finish me. Please finish me."

"All right, you little bastard," she said, standing up and yanking up hard on his briefs, crushing his nuts. "Fun's over until you deliver. It's time to tell me exactly what happened last night. And you're gonna have to name names."

He whimpered some more. Then he gave her what she thought she wanted.

FORTY-ONE

They drove in silence for a few miles, heading east toward Furnace Creek, Jack checking the rearview mirror every few seconds for the ranger's patrol car. So far—nothing. But Jack had a gut feeling about cops, and his gut was telling him the ranger would run their tags and check up on them.

They drove along a two-lane road running across the north end of Death Valley. To the southwest, in the hazy blue sunlight, he saw Telescope Peak, dusted with snow. To the east were the Funeral Mountains, black and hulking, striped with layers of multicolored rocks. The valley floor was pocked with dirty-white salt crystals and dotted with sage, creosote, and mesquite bushes. The expanse was so vast, so unexpected—and yet it filled Jack with a bittersweet gnawing loneliness he couldn't explain.

Jack came here five years ago on a camping trip by himself, following another failed writing assignment. Sarah had suggested the trip, hoping the emptiness of the desert would clear his head, show him what to do next with his life. He spent much of the time exploring the back roads of Death Valley. One day, with only a quart of water, he struck out on a hike, heading for the mountains in the distance. It was the middle of winter but here, on the desert floor, below sea level, the temperature soared. After four hours of walking on the tricky footing, the salt crystals crumbling underfoot, he seemed no nearer his destination. The hills still shimmered in the distance, remote and unattainable, like his dreams. He stumbled back to his car hours later, dehydrated and exhausted. It gave him a respect for this place that never left him.

"I think this has gone on long enough," Mary said as they drove, rubbing Walt's neck and shooting nervous glances behind them. "It's time to go to the police. Now that Walt's better, he can clear all this up."

"Is that what you want, Walt?" Jack asked.

Walt's eyes were drooping. They snapped open again. "Huh?"

"You ready to go home again, Walt?" Jack asked. "You can go home and Garrett will take care of you again. Would you like that?"

Mention of Garrett's name sent a ripple of pain through the old man's system, and he winced at the thought. His face froze in a stubborn frown. "No." Then it came rapid fire: "No, no, no, no, NO!"

Mary said, "That's not fair, Jack. Can't you see Walt's exhausted? We need to get him to a doctor."

"No doctors," Walt said.

Jack saw a road sign coming up: FURNACE CREEK 2. He backed off on the gas. They had to make a decision fast.

"Jack, look at it this way," she said. "You go to the police now, you'll be on the cover of every magazine in America," she said.

"I told you, that's not what this is all about!"

"Then what the hell is it about?"

"Dammit!" Walt shouted, bouncing up and down in his seat. "Dammit it all! Hell! Dammit! SHIT!"

Jack and Mary looked at each other, amazed. Walt had picked up on their anger, their frustration.

"We better cool it," Jack said. "Sorry, Walt. Sorry, Mary. I'm really sorry. We're all tired, that's all. And things have gotten a little complicated."

Mary laughed at the understatement.

"Let me put it this way," Jack said. "Now that Walt's talking again, we have to finish the book. We're really close. But we can do it."

"Jack," Mary said. "This is bigger than the book."

"Exactly," he said. "It's about Walt's legacy. But the book will establish his legacy. I mean, fame comes and goes. But Walt's legacy will last forever."

It was suddenly quiet in the car. Mary looked at Walt. He frowned, thinking. Then began to nod—slowly at first, then emphatically.

"Finish," he said, still nodding. "Let's finish."

Jack caught a sudden movement in his side mirror. A plane was coming in low behind them. He looked again. It wasn't a plane—it was a helicopter. Then another. And another. Three helicopters. And they were getting larger by the second, coming straight at them. He felt exposed, with nowhere to hide, like a mouse with a hawk circling above.

Jack worked the gas pedal. The Pathfinder shot forward.

"What is it?" Mary asked, hearing the noise now and looking around.

Jack was watching the road and keeping one eye on the mirror. The helicopters were banking now. He could see lettering on the side of the fuselages. Probably the police. Or the FBI? It was someone looking for them, that was for sure.

The helicopters leveled out and came for them. He looked around for cover. A sign up ahead said, DEATH VALLEY GOLF COURSE, 1/4 MILE. *Where there are golf courses, there are trees to hide under,* Jack thought. The road straightened out, and he saw the turnoff at a grove of date trees. Almost there…One helicopter was so close he could see lettering on its belly. Sunlight flickered as they shot into the trees. Jack hit the brakes and jumped out as the helicopter roared past, low enough so he could read the letters on the side: CHANNEL 9, KCAL.

The media was gathering.

FORTY-TWO

"**S**ometimes it's like Walt's not all there," Mary said softly. She was whispering, even though she didn't have to. Walt was asleep in the car, and they were sitting at a picnic table nearby in the grove of date trees, many of which were dead or dying, the graying fronds sagging to the dusty ground and baking in the blast-furnace sun. It seemed impossible that, only hours ago, they were in the frigid cold of the mountains. Then, they were at high altitude. Now, they were below sea level. She looked around, disoriented. This place had the feel of a forgotten tourist attraction, some backwater area suddenly abandoned and going to seed. The thinning date trees barely provided enough cover from the blazing sun and the helicopters circling above.

"And then sometimes he is there," Jack said. "Just as good as ever. The problem is, you never know for sure what you're dealing with. He seems to think I'm someone named Reilly."

"Reilly?"

"Yeah. He keeps calling me Jack Reilly. Ever hear him mention someone by that name?"

She thought it over. "Sounds vaguely familiar." She squinted, peering into the past. Then she shook her head and said, "But I can't place it. Maybe it'll come to me."

Jack studied her face. He wondered how could she be so tired and still so beautiful. Then he realized it was because her beauty didn't come from her looks at all; it was who she was. Some women were like that. Beauty was shining from their entire being. Jack thought back to last night, in the cabin, when they kissed. It was dangerous and wrong, but it started a desire he couldn't stop. Here he was, caught in this shit storm and having all kinds of doubts about Mary's real motives, but he kept thinking of the feeling of her skin under his fingers.

He reached out and touched her shoulder. It wasn't something he wanted to do, but he did it anyway, acting on the urge before he could block it. His hand rested on her shoulder, and she looked up into his eyes then nervously glanced at the parked car—a telltale movement as if to say, *I hope Walt doesn't see us.*

"Things have changed, haven't they?" Jack said. "It was going to be me and you. But now it's you and Walt again. Right?"

"I never thought this would happen. I figured, if he did come back, he wouldn't really be himself. But he is."

"From the waist up," Jack said then wished he hadn't.

Her voice was soft, her lisp whispering at the edge of her words. "That's not always the case with stroke victims. Besides, that really isn't the most important thing for me right now."

Jack took his hand off her shoulder.

"I'm tired of running and hiding," Mary said, her voice wavering. "God, I'm tired. I can't think straight, I'm hungry, and I want to go home."

"Maybe we're closer to home than you think." Jack stood up. He'd been working something out in his head.

"What do you mean?"

"I've got a brilliant idea," he said, smiling with what he hoped looked like easy confidence. He expected her to argue, to protest. But she didn't. She waited, her face upturned. There were worry lines in her forehead, creases around her mouth, dark circles under her eyes. Jack knew all these flaws were there, but he didn't care. Besides, how did he look to her?

She returned his smile. And her look melted something inside him. "What's your brilliant idea?"

Jack pointed through the trees. "There's a road through the golf course that leads into Furnace Creek. There's not much there—just a restaurant, a general store, and a bunch of cabins for rent. I want you to check into one of the cabins under a fake name—your middle name maybe." Then he realized he didn't know what her middle name was; he realized he didn't know a lot of things about her. "I don't even know your middle name."

"Chandler."

"Nice name. You can be…lemme see…Ann Chandler. What do you think?"

"Ann Chandler," she said. "I like it. When you write your novel about this, that can be my character's name."

"Who said I was writing a novel?"

"Come on, Jack. I can see it now—based on a true story—you'd sell that in a second. Who will your character be?"

"Nick Downs," he answered quickly.

She laughed. "Where did that come from?"

"He was the coolest kid in my school. I always wanted to be like him."

"Nick and Ann," she said, trying it out. "You have to write that book."

"Yeah, well, there's only one book I'm worried about now: Walt's biography."

"Think about it."

"Sure." He nodded. "Anyway, get a room, scope the place out. If it looks safe, then tonight, after dark, I'll bring Walt to you. We'll get a good night's sleep, and it will give us time to see if the other half of my plan works."

"Oh yes, the brilliant plan. I thought that was it."

"There's more. I'm going to do another interview with Walt—make one last tape, to prove he's really better, that he can talk. If I can get it on the air, maybe people will get back on my side. And the cops will go easy on me. That's where you come in. You have to set up a meeting with a reporter."

"How am I going to do that?"

"Call KCAL. Their chopper's the one that dive-bombed us. Or maybe call one of the other stations—call that reporter who broke the first story in Bishop."

"Trisha King."

"Yeah, her. Tell her I'll be at the starter's shack at the golf course at dusk. Tell her to meet us there, and we'll give her an exclusive interview with Walt Stuckey."

"But what if he's in one of his untalkative cycles?"

"We'll have to risk that. Besides, at least it will prove that he's physically healthy and we're doing everything we can to make him comfortable. And make sure you tell her it's an exclusive."

She nodded, smiling. "Ann Chandler can handle it." She seemed energized now.

"You won't fall asleep and forget about us?"

She laughed. But the laughter was hollow, tired. "I won't let you down, Jack." She stepped in close. "Jack, I don't know what's going to happen. And I don't know what's right. But I want to hold you now."

She hugged him, and he felt her pressing against him, felt his body come alive, all the overtaxed neurons firing for all they were worth, his desire stretched as tight as piano wire.

They walked back to the car together. Walt was still asleep, head tilted to one side, features relaxed.

"Where will you and Walt be?" Mary asked.

Jack tore open the Velcro fastener on his pants and took out his map. He spread it out on the hood of the car. She was standing next to him, her arm brushing his.

"There's a jeep trail here. It climbs up into Wild Rose Canyon. It's in pretty bad shape, no guard rails or anything. When we get here"—the broken double line on the map forked—"we'll take this cutoff. It's not marked on the map, but it goes to this town called Beveridge. It's a ghost town—completely deserted—with houses, barns, even saloons. We can hang out there until the coast is clear."

"A ghost town," she echoed, her hand squeezing his arm casually, as if she wasn't even aware of what she was doing. She was natural again, the earlier friction melting.

"Yeah, we'll be in the ghost town."

He turned to her, and she clung to him.

"Set your alarm," Jack said. "Don't leave us hanging."

"I told you—I won't let you down," she said and kissed him lightly, easily. Did she want to be his friend or his lover? With Mary, he never really knew. There were just a whole lot of things that he didn't know about her. And that's probably why he was feeling all these wild emotions for her.

"Dusk at the starter's shack."

She smiled, waved, and began walking. He watched her go, feeling the emotions churning inside. In a few moments she had disappeared into the trees.

FORTY-THREE

From where he was parked, Chief Ullrich could just barely see the Pathfinder through the grove of date trees. Jack Dillon and a woman were standing beside the car talking, but it looked like they were going to start moving again soon. And when they started to move, he'd be right behind them. Only problem was, that would mean he'd have to find the strength to turn the key in the ignition. And put the shift lever in gear. Those things required more strength than he had right now.

His shoulder was stiffening up. And he had lost some blood. There was blood on the steering wheel and the mike of the two-way radio. Good thing he had a liter-bottle of water with him. And the first aid kit with gauze and disinfectant and painkillers. He must have taken about a dozen Tylenols, and his shoulder still hurt like hell.

He was still pleased with the way he'd picked up their trail again after the shooting last night. Fortunate, but not miraculous. Nothing more than good old-fashioned police work, really. After he made it back to the cruiser last night and got some emergency first aid in Lone Pine, he headed south on California 395 trying to think like Jack Dillon. North to Bishop, Tahoe, and Reno were too populated. Going south there were two choices—the Los Angeles area (too populated) or Death Valley. Just before the turnoff to Death Valley, there was one service station and a big sign saying, No Gas for 137 miles. Anyone heading into Death Valley would gas up. And according to the attendant, that's just what Dillon did: a red Nissan Pathfinder had stopped there an hour before him.

From time to time Ullrich picked up the radio, and they patched him through to Deputies Moon and Gallegos, who were driving toward him from Pajaro Beach in the department's Dodge Durango 4x4. Of course, he didn't tell them he was nursing a through-and-through to his shoulder. But he did give them updates on his location so they could find him in case he passed out. When his backup arrived, they would move in and arrest Dillon. But right now, he wasn't feeling up to much more than just keeping Dillon in view and maybe tailing him again if he ran.

Once they arrested Dillon, they would move in on Garrett Stuckey and book him for attempted murder of a police officer. Yeah, it had to have been Garrett out there in the woods last night, banging away with a hunting rifle, trying to take out Dillon. Ullrich realized he'd been set up. He saw that plainly now. It was going to be a genuine pleasure to bring Garrett Stuckey down.

One of Ullrich's problems was that he didn't have great cover. He pulled the squad car behind a maintenance shed near the golf course. Dillon couldn't see him from here, but it left him roasting in the sun. Even with the windows down, it was probably a hundred degrees in the big ole Crown Vic. Not a breath of air was moving. Damn flies all over the blood.

"Tell you what you need to do," he heard a familiar voice say. He looked over and saw the vision of his father sitting next to him, dressed in the tan-and-green uniform of the Texas Rangers. His Stetson rested on the seat between them.

"Daddy, you're here," Ullrich said, knowing it was just a vision, but unable to keep himself from responding.

"That's a fact. And I don't like what I see."

"What's that, Daddy?"

"I see my little candy-ass, cryin' his eyes out as usual."

"But I been shot."

"Did I ask you to talk?"

"No, sir."

"You always were a quitter. Couldn't even do the simplest thing, like arrest that old boy out there."

"I can't take a prisoner now. I can hardly stand up."

"Are you blind, son? Do you not see the star on your chest? That means you're gonna bring that man to justice. Ain't no one else gonna do it for you. Got that?"

He looked at his father for a long time, remembering the last time he'd seen him. He'd been sitting on the front-porch swing of their house in Cut and Shoot when he was about twelve. It was a hot summer night, too hot to be indoors, and as darkness fell, the cicadas began to sing. His father came out of the house, already sweating through the dark shirt. He sat next to his son, his aftershave mingling with the whiskey on his breath. It was a sour, ambiguous smell, but since it was familiar, it held a degree of comfort.

His father left him that evening, heading out on a manhunt down to Brownsville, near the Mexican border. They found his body next to the Ford squad car along a barren stretch of Texas Highway 83, a bullet hole behind his left ear. He never did get his man. And he never came back to his son—until now.

Why is it, Ullrich wondered, *that fathers always expect their sons to do the very thing that they failed at?* Maybe this was the essence of what kept life moving forward, what kept one generation wanting another one to succeed where they had failed, to do what they couldn't do. This was what made life worth living. The chance to finally get things right.

"Have I made myself clear?" his father asked, his gray eyes steady.

"Yes, sir."

"Now it looks like that old boy is getting in his car. So you're gonna have to run him down. You hear?"

"Yes, sir."

"Okay, then. I'll be seeing you."

"So long, Daddy."

With difficulty, Chief Irwin Ullrich reached for the ignition key and fired up the Crown Victoria equipped with the police interceptor package that had those stiff shocks and that big old 4.6 liter V8. He moved the shift lever into gear as the red, late model Pathfinder bumped down the dirt road toward the highway. He gave the Pathfinder a half mile's head start and pulled out, the big old muscle car's V8 barely purring. It was easy to tail someone here—could see them across the valley, a red dot moving against the mountains.

As the SUV came around a turn, the sun caught the Pathfinder, silhouetting the driver—obviously Dillon—and the hunched figure of Walt Stuckey. But where was the woman? What the hell was going on here?

The turn signal flashed on the back of the Pathfinder. Ullrich backed off on the gas, giving him time to make his move. He saw them clearly now. Where the hell was the woman? The red SUV lumbered across the shoulder, leaning hard as it hit the jeep trail leading up into the mountains. Couldn't follow them up there. Not in the Crown Vic. He'd have to wait for backup. Moon and Gallegos were still a couple of hours away. That'd give him time to have a doctor take a look at the shoulder.

He turned in the driver's seat, feeling flames of pain in the shoulder as it stiffened, looking back and seeing Dillon's Pathfinder kicking up a long tail of dust as it moved toward a row of black mountains, shimmering in the heat. And Ullrich felt the sickening separation, the empty cutoff feeling in his gut. He just hoped the good agents of the Federal Bureau of Incompetence didn't get there first. Walt Stuckey had been taken from his jurisdiction—that meant Dillon was his man. Like his daddy said, it was his sworn duty to bring him to justice.

FORTY-FOUR

The jeep trail came up on the right, like a fading scar across the desert floor, and climbed into Wild Rose Canyon. It was so easy to miss. In fact, Jack hoped everyone else would miss it. No other cars were in sight, except an old Ford, half a mile back. For a moment he ran the car though his memory, trying to think if he'd seen it before. But his exhausted brain quickly rejected the assignment.

He slowed for the turn, eased the Pathfinder over the highway's shoulder, and lurched down onto the sandy dirt track. Walt snorted and coughed but slept on. Jack worked the stick into 4WD low and feathered the clutch for a smooth launch. He wanted Walt to get as much rest as possible so he might rally and deliver a compelling interview for the reporter. Often, with seasoned performers, they came alive when the audience arrived and the lights blazed. He desperately needed Walt to give a stellar performance so maybe, just maybe, Jack could start that long trip home.

Did he even have a home anymore? He knew that Sarah was dying of humiliation with all the publicity he'd focused on her, so going back to her was out of the question. But had Sarah turned Chloe against him? Thinking of his daughter made him remember what it was like when she was a baby, to hold her against his chest and breathe in the smell of her head. Would he ever do that again? By the time he was out of prison, she would be grown and gone. Unless…Unless he didn't go to prison at all. Unless he could put a plan together that gave him freedom and a jackpot ending.

His sleep-starved brain flashed hot and cold, crashing him to the depths of despair, then sketching a happy ending to this caper. Which would it be? Life in the slammer? Or a slap on the wrist from a smiling judge and a million-dollar book contract? It reminded him of when he pitched a story concept in Hollywood. Producers would always listen until they got the gist of it then impatiently demand: Does this yarn have a happy ending? Does the hero get the money and the girl?

Now he wondered if he would get the money and the girl. Or make that the rights to the book and the girl. What would it take to pull this off? He needed a statement from Walt to show he hadn't been harmed, to prove that he had been abused at home, and to prove that the extreme measures Jack had taken had actually benefited the book. To do that he needed an ending to the book's final question: Why was the show canceled? Would Walt answer that question? He didn't even seem to know who Jack was. Actually, he thought Jack was some other Jack, a guy named Jack Reilly, whoever the hell that was.

"The name sounds familiar," Mary had said. Funny, it sounded familiar to Jack too. But he couldn't say why. Maybe he'd find the answer in his notes, some reference to Jack Reilly. If he had his laptop, he could search for the name. But all he had were printouts of his interviews.

Ahead, Jack saw the road climb over a rise, twist to the right, and then disappear between the walls of Wild Rose Canyon. The road was eroded, almost washed out in sections, and they were creeping along barely faster than someone could walk, the transmission whining, the suspension pounding underneath. He eased the windows down, and the cross breeze cooled the sweat on his forehead. It was a lot cooler now that they were climbing up into the canyon. Still, he was feeling thirsty. Lucky thing they filled their water bottles before they left the cabin last night.

His right front tire hit a football-size rock, and the car lurched, tossing Walt to one side. He moaned and said, "No."

They were halfway up the canyon now, climbing hard. The Pathfinder was like an oversized burro, struggling stubbornly up the slope, picking its way between rocks. As they crept around the corner of the canyon, the first shack came into sight. It was a shed above a mine shaft, the sun-blackened beams of a hoist still standing ready to lift buckets of ore from the ground. Below the shaft was a plume of yellow mine tailings streaming down the canyon wall, the sandy soil sifted for gold a century ago.

Now Jack could see the main street of the little town once called Beveridge. The wooden sidewalks, the corrals, the houses and, on the outskirts, the cemetery surrounded by the wrought-iron fence that guarded the headstones from nothing but time and the desert wind. More headstones were scattered on the hillside outside the boundaries of the fence. He read somewhere that only respectable townspeople were buried inside the proper cemetery; buried outside were the prostitutes and gunfighters.

As he looked at the graves, an odd question hit him, something he'd never thought of before: Where would he be buried? Thinking this, his mind flashed on those gruesome autopsy photos he'd seen as a police reporter—only the corpse lying on the coroner's slab was his, eyes empty, face white, expression slack. He tried to push the image out of his mind, but it hovered in his consciousness and reappeared again and again.

He had never found Beveridge listed in any books about Death Valley ghost towns. It must have been a strike a few miners made that looked good but quickly went bust. Jack had stumbled on it purely by accident. And he found that the cluster of houses was untouched—plates still on the table, cans on the shelves—as if the people would come home soon.

Jack eased the Pathfinder into a barn on one end of town. The shingles had blown off long ago, and sunlight shone through gaps in the roof. He cut the engine, and a stuffy, hot blanket of silence dropped over them. He thought the sudden silence might wake Walt. He waited, but Walt slept on. *Let him sleep for another half hour,* Jack thought. He'd grab a quick nap himself. He leaned the driver's seat back and opened his door for ventilation.

And let go.

———

Jack woke suddenly, sweating, disoriented. At first he couldn't remember where he was, what the hell he was doing here. He looked around and saw Walt sleeping beside him, saw the old barn and the sunlight slanting through, now on a sharper angle. Late afternoon. He had to wake Walt. But first, there was something else he had to do. He stepped out of the car and, dopey from his nap, rummaged in the back until he found his notes, a thick sheaf of papers held together with a binder clip. Somewhere in here he'd find who Jack Reilly was.

The transcriptions were interviews he had done with Walt six months ago in his house in the Hollywood Hills. For each anecdote he had a bold-faced heading so he could locate the information later. Most of the information was about the stars who appeared on his show, or the writers or directors. Had Jack Reilly been a comedian? A musician maybe? Or what about a network executive?

Reading through his notes was like going back in time. When Jack first heard these stories he was on the upside of the project, dreaming of hitting a literary home run, winning the publishing lottery. Now there was something very different at stake—he was fighting for his freedom. He sat on a wooden crate in the barn and, with Walt still snoring away in the car, began scanning the pages, which felt dry and brittle in the desert air. Bars of sunlight moved across the dirt floor as he flipped the pages, feeling at times that Jack Reilly was lurking behind the scenes of the news items he read, ready to reveal his identity. But then his presence receded into the darkness of lost years again. He had to find Jack Reilly. His life depended on it. The more he looked, the more he felt it was exactly what he needed to understand Walt's state of mind and release the secrets he needed to finish the book.

But he was running out of time. The patches of sunlight had moved across the empty barn and were climbing the walls now. A lonely wind kicked up dust and moaned sadly through the deserted buildings.

An idea tickled the edge of his consciousness, teasing him. A concept took shape as he remembered Walt describing how he tested ideas for the show, taking a poll of ordinary people whom he ran across in everyday life. He told Jack that there was a guy that worked in the tollbooth on the way into Manhattan to record his show. Every week, the guy would give Walt a quick reaction to the last show. And Walt valued his opinion more than the writers', the director's, and the critics'.

"But there was one person whose opinion I valued more than anyone else's…" Jack remembered Walt saying that to him. "One person I could always count on for a gut response to a gag or a sketch. None of this fancy bullshit. Just yes or no, straight from the hip."

Jack began shuffling through the pages, looking for that section of his notes. He was sure that's where he read about Jack Reilly. He was turning the pages frantically, almost at the end of his notes, the light in the room fading, time running out. And then he saw the bold-faced name, Jack Reilly. And he read these words:

One guy I could always count on for an accurate reaction to the gags on the show was my driver, Jack. He was this kid from New Jersey who didn't mince words—kind of a meat-and-potatoes Irish guy who always spoke his mind. When I was driving into Manhattan, I'd run through some of the bits with him, and he let me know exactly how he felt. And lemme tell ya, he was tough. If a bit worked, he just belted out this no-holds-barred laugh and said,

"Walt, that was funnier'n hell." If he didn't like the joke, he let me know. "Forgetaboutit, Walt. That bit ain't funny." When he said that, I didn't argue—I just scrapped it on the spot.

Sitting here in this ghost town, where so many had come in search of a fortune, Jack felt that he had just struck gold. But it was the last lines, so innocent at the time, that really got Jack's heart pounding:

Over the years, I came to confide in Reilly about more than just the show. His judgment and support never let me down.

FORTY-FIVE

Mary drank the ice water, feeling the beautiful liquid coolness all the way down her throat and into her empty stomach. She was standing in the motel lobby in Furnace Creek, about to pour herself a second glass of ice water from the sweating pitcher on the counter, when she heard a TV news announcer's voice coming from the next room. She moved around to the edge of the counter and looked at the portable TV set in the inner office.

The shot showed a circle of cops standing around a body in a forest somewhere. The corpse's legs stuck out from between the standing men. On the back of one man's windbreaker were the letters FBI. The shot cut to a young Asian woman doing a stand-up with the mountains behind her in the distance. Mary recognized the view as being from Lone Pine. At the bottom of the screen it read, TRISHA KING, KNBC FRESNO.

"Initial reports said the killer's identity was unknown. But new information indicates there was a witness to the shooting. This witness was hidden during the gun battle and watched as Jack Dillon allegedly cornered and executed the victim with a single shot to the head. Dillon has presented himself as a sort of Robin Hood, kidnapping Walt Stuckey for his own good. But if these charges are true, it certainly casts new light on his motivations. Meanwhile, investigators in the case say Dillon was spotted in the Death Valley area early this morning by a park ranger. The manhunt for Dillon continues at this hour."

Stunned, Mary stood there, thinking, *Well, this changes everything.*

She didn't know how much longer she stood staring at the screen, rearranging the pieces in her mind, when she looked up and found the motel manager watching at her.

"Can I help you?" he asked, his smile probing, asking what the hell she was doing in his office, staring at the TV with her mouth hanging open. He was a young kid, brown hair, well put together, with a smile that seemed to be on the make. "Something wrong?" he asked.

"No. I—I just want to rent one of your cabins for tonight."

"How many people?"

"Just me. But I'm very sensitive to noise. Is there something away from the road?"

He pulled out a registration card and pen, then turned and checked keys hanging on cup hooks. "I have one that's right on the golf course."

"Great."

She wrote her name on the registration card as Ann Chandler, gave an address where she had lived once in Oakland, and wrote down her license plate, transposing the last two digits.

"Is there a pay phone nearby?" she asked.

"There're phones in the room. But there's a pay phone across the way outside the general store." He dangled a key out to her. "Here you go—cabin 7."

Mary paid in cash, took her key, and was about to leave. But she couldn't resist. She had to know. So she turned around. Sure enough, the clerk was watching her with that smile on his face. That smile that seemed to say, *I know who you are.*

———

The heat hit her in the face when she stepped out of the air-conditioned motel office. She crossed the dusty parking lot, the sun blistering the back of her neck, and found the phone on the wall by the general store. Thank God it was in the shade.

"I've got one hell of a story for you," Mary said when she had finally talked her way into having them connect her to Trisha King, the KNBC reporter. "It's about the Walt Stuckey kidnapping."

She kept one eye on the two-lane highway, looking for police cars. The road was clear. But in the distance she heard helicopter blades beating the air, landing at the airport behind the date grove and the golf course. News crews were arriving all the time, maybe sensing a showdown.

"Who's this?" Trisha asked.

"Someone very close to Walt Stuckey."

"How close?"

"Close enough to know you got it all wrong about last night."

"Are you Mary LeBeau?"

"I'll tell you who I am when we meet." She knew she should hang up, but she couldn't resist. "Who told you Jack Dillon shot that guy execution style. Come on, Jack would never do that."

"How do you know?"

"For one thing, he was with me."

"Is he with you now?"

"Not this minute. But I know where he is. And he was ready to turn himself in—until you did that hatchet job on him. There's no way he'll do that now."

"Look, I had a source for that information—someone who said he was at the scene."

"Let me guess—Garrett Stuckey?"

Silence.

"I thought so," Mary said, bluffing. "Well, that's not how it happened. Look, there's an awful lot going on here that you know nothing about."

Trisha was quiet, absorbing this new information. Mary let it sink in then said, "So do you want to set things straight? I can get you footage of a new interview with Walt Stuckey."

"What's he say?"

"You're going to have to find out for yourself. You're in Death Valley now, right?"

"Yes."

"Meet me at the snack shack at the golf course at dusk. You can't miss it—it's right by the airport. But you have to come alone. I'll give you a disk that has the interview of Walt Stuckey on it. You want it or not?"

"Of course I want it. But I want to know what I'm walking into, too."

"I'm not going to hurt you. I need you on our side."

"I don't take sides."

"I know, I know. But if you report this the way it has really happened, people will be on our side."

"We'll see."

"No. You'll see." Mary paused. "Believe me. You want what I have."

There was a sudden silence on the other end of the line.

"Hello?"

"I'm still here. It's just that—someone else used those same exact words recently."

"Really. Who?"

"It doesn't matter," she said then added, "Okay. I'll be at the snack shack at dusk."

Mary hung up and breathed out a long sigh. She leaned her head on the pay phone and felt the cool of the metal box seep into her overheated brain. When she stepped out of the phone booth, she saw that the shadows were slanting across the highway now. A glance at her watch showed it was 4:05. The sun set at about six o'clock. Time to get moving.

———◆———

Mary pushed the key into the door lock of cabin 7. From here she could see across the fairway to where the date grove began.

Behind that was the snack shack. She pushed the door in on a room that smelled like emptiness, the air conditioner humming, battling the heat outside. Two double beds were made up with Indian-patterned blankets. Looking at the beds, she desperately wanted to lie down. Just for a moment. Just a moment.

Yes, the beds were as soft as they looked. And the sheets smelled so nice when they were pulled up over her. She shut her eyes, and the drone of the air conditioner closed in around her. But she wouldn't let herself sleep. No, she couldn't let Walt and Jack down. Using every ounce of her willpower she opened her eyes. She found that her vision was scrolling up like a TV that was out of whack. She sat up on the edge of the bed. See? She could lie down for just a few minutes. And get up again. It wasn't as much of a problem as she had thought it would be. So it would be safe to do it again. After all, she would need to be rested for tonight.

As she drifted off (or, more accurately, plunged into the abyss) Jack's voice kept echoing in her head. What was he trying to tell her? Here it came again. And this time she heard it. *Don't forget to set the alarm.*

FORTY-SIX

Trisha snapped shut her cell phone and sat in the news van parked on a runway of the Death Valley Airport. She felt certain it was Walt Stuckey's girlfriend who had just called. Mary LeBeau. The cops had said she was in on the kidnapping with Jack Dillon.

Sitting there in the van, Trisha couldn't stop thinking about what she might get from this meeting at the golf course. But the other part of her mind was running scenarios about what this would do for her career. It would put it on a rocket to the top, that's what it would do. Maybe it was worth it after all, going down on that freak back in the hotel, even if he gave her a bad lead. Still, putting herself in the middle of the action meant that sources came to her with tips, not ABC or, God forbid, CNN.

"Who were you talking to?"

She turned toward the voice and found Garrett Stuckey watching her as she put her cell phone away. How long had he been there? She got out of the van and stretched, looking around for her camera crew. They were across the runway, talking to a crew from Fox News. They weren't even looking over here. Talk about clueless.

"I thought we had a deal—we'd share leads," Garrett said. "Or were you just giving me lip service when you said that?"

She ignored his stupid joke and the leering smile that followed. "It was just my station manager. He wanted to make sure the crew was here in case something popped."

"Okay," Garratt said, nodding and watching her carefully.

She shuddered for some reason she couldn't explain and then asked, "Talked to the FBI lately?"

"Yes." He smiled but said nothing more.

He wants me to beg for it, she thought. *Well, screw it, I'm not going to.* But then, looking at that smug smile, she felt insecure. "And?"

"Nothing new. Not much, anyway."

"Come on. What'd they say?"

"They know he's here."

"In Death Valley?"

"In the mountains somewhere. They're getting the air force to bring in that device they used in the Gulf War, that heat-detecting thing that finds people from their body temperature."

She remembered reports of how the infrared device was used to spot and kill Republican Guard fighters. They were just a glowing dot on the screen. Then a burst of machine-gun fire shredded them. It was so inhuman, so frightening, so unfair. She found herself hoping Dillon didn't meet a similar fate.

As if he read her thoughts, he said, "Jack Dillon isn't going to win. He put up a nice fight, but he's going down. My father will come back to where he belongs, with his family. And I'm head of the family now."

Garrett let that sink in, then continued. "In twenty-four hours, this whole thing will be wrapped up. My father will be back. And if he's really talking, he'll have one hell of a story to tell." Trisha thought that over then shook her head as if to clear thoughts she didn't like.

"Look, Garrett, I have to run into town for cigarettes."

"Great. Let's go."

"No I—I need to think things over. We'll talk when I get back."

"Oh, so that's where you're meeting your source?"

"Give up. Okay? Just give up." She climbed into the van and closed the door.

She fired up the van and was reaching for the gearshift lever when he leaned into the cab and breathed into her ear. "Trisha, one lucky reporter is going to get an exclusive interview with my father. Who will it be?"

FORTY-SEVEN

Yeah, Jack thought, *this place will be perfect.*

He was standing in front of a deserted house on a side street of the ghost town that was once called Beveridge. It was a one-story clapboard bungalow with a faded stencil of a rose over a door that was falling off its hinges. A picket fence outlined the barren front yard where a flower garden might have once grown.

Stepping inside, Jack found himself in small living room, the pine floorboards warped under his feet. A scrap of rotting doily clung to a splintered side table and fluttered in the breeze. Four chairs surrounded a dining-room table, one of them fallen on its side, the cane seat broken out. The kitchen still had a woodburning stove with the pipe running up through the wall. And through a doorway he saw a bedroom with a mattress and box spring on it. *Yeah, I can hang out here with Walt*, Jack thought, *until Mary lets me know it's safe to turn myself in.*

Outside again, walking back to the Pathfinder, he found himself face-to-face with a coyote peering around the side of a shed, a rabbit in its mouth. The coyote stared back with dark eyes. Looking at him, Jack sensed a kindred spirit in the outlaw. Then he blinked, and the coyote was gone. Seconds later he spotted him loping across the hillside, his coat blending with the rocks and dirt. The animal disappeared in midstride.

———

A half hour later Jack sat on an old chair beside the bed, watching Walt sleep. He had carried him into the abandoned house and set him on top of the bed on a sleeping bag he'd brought.

"Walt." Jack shook his shoulder. He watched the old man's face for signs of reaction. "Hey, Walt." He shook him again.

From deep inside, consciousness slowly rose and spread over Walt's features. His eyes flickered then opened. He looked around, confused, then focused on Jack's face.

"Jack," Walt said, his eyes relaxing with relief as he saw a familiar face.

"Hey, Walt. How ya doin', buddy?" Jack said, letting his Jersey accent come through loud and clear. It was time to make his move. He had decided that, to get Walt to talk, he would have to become a different person. A different person with the same first name, but a different last name. He would have to be Jack Reilly, Walt's driver from years ago.

"So how ya feelin' there, Walt?"

"Lousy, Jack. Lousy. My brain's on the fritz. I'm all…confused." Walt spoke smoothly, no stuttering, but his voice was hollow, disconnected.

"That's bound to happen. After all you been through."

"What do you mean?"

"I heard you got called up to the tower."

Walt looked away.

Jack tried again. "I heard about the show."

"Yeah. That son of a bitch."

"I heard Bill Paley canceled the show. Why the hell'd he do that?"

Walt looked away. And Jack saw the tension, the anger, the bitterness, as if he had just received the news, as if the years between now and then had disappeared. Amazingly, he looked much younger. But this younger face was twisted in pain.

"Tell me what happened, Walt. You know I'll keep it under my hat."

"I know, Jack. I know. It's just so damn painful to talk about."

"So get it off your chest. You and me got no secrets."

Jack glanced across the room at the video camera he'd set up on the shelf. The red light was blinking. All of this was being recorded.

"So I heard you met with Paley this afternoon about that Bebe Rebozo sketch. What the hell was that all about?"

"Paley told me a friend from Washington had called. That's how he put it—'a friend'—but I guess we know what that means. This *friend* didn't like the bit I did about Bebe Rebozo. It reflected badly on the White House and all that horseshit. They wanted me to kill the whole sketch. I got hot—told Paley he couldn't tell me what to do on my show. Paley said he was sorry to hear that, because there would be consequences."

"Consequences?"

"This friend from Washington said"—Walt hesitated then added—"said they had a file."

"A file? Walt, maybe I'm a little dense, but you're gonna have to spell it out for me. What's Bebe Rebozo got to do with a file on you?"

Walt shook his head angrily. "It wasn't a file on me. If it was I wouldn't give a rat's ass."

"I'm lost, Walt. Who was the file on?"

Walt took a deep breath. Slowly, one word at a time, as if he was tearing the words out of his heart, Walt revealed the whole awful story. And Jack got it all on tape. When Walt was done, Jack sat there in silence, letting it all sink in. It was tragic, ironic, shocking. Jack felt angry and sad for Walt, his friend. But as Walt's biographer, he began to realize he was in possession of a damning secret implicating the actions of the highest level of government. This revelation began to work in Jack's mind, weaving its way into an explosive ending for his book.

Jack stood up and walked over to the camera. He turned it off and took it down from the shelf. He checked to make sure the file was saved on a disk and also in the camera's internal memory. He turned back to Walt and saw he was curled up in a ball, his face knotted by the pain that had lived inside him all this time. Retelling it had brought back the pain as if it had just happened.

Walt's face began to merge with all the newspaper photos Jack had seen of him at different stages through his life. The face that was once so famous, then so mysterious. The face that had made so many people laugh in sympathy at his predicaments had, himself, been caught in the worst dilemma of all time.

As these pictures of Walt scrolled through Jack's mind like flashbacks in a movie, Jack realized this interview wasn't over. He saw a way to pave his way home safely and also give Walt the farewell he never had.

"Walt, listen," Jack said, sitting beside the bed again. Walt was still in the past, so he stayed in character as Jack Reilly as he said, "Hell of a lot of people are gonna miss the show. Lotta people who were huge fans. They stuck with you. It would be nice to say good-bye to them. Let 'em know you're okay but that you won't be back."

Jack held up the video camera.

"I got this little camera, see, and I'll film anything you want. And I'll see that it gets on the air."

Walt digested all this with his sad, dark eyes. Finally, he nodded.

"And while you're at it, Walt, would ya say something nice about me? The press has criticized me, ya know. Said I didn't take such good care of you. But you know me, I was just trying to protect you. Maybe you can set the record straight on that."

"You got it, Jack."

Jack turned on the camera and looked through the viewfinder to make sure the time and date stamp was visible. He could see Walt's eyes focus on the blinking red light on the front of the camera. And then it happened. His face underwent a complete transformation from frail old man to an energetic performer ready to send an audience into tidal waves of laughter. It was like handing a baseball to a hall-of-fame pitcher and seeing his gnarled fingers find the stitching and hold the ball just right. Although Walt's face had aged, his comedic instincts—his dramatic timing and sense of absurdity—returned, and every trace of the anger and frustration that had preceded this moment washed from his face when the blinking red light told Walt he was on.

Walt straightened up, composed himself, and said, "Hello, folks. You've all been sensational fans of my show, so I can't leave without saying good-bye. That's right. I've gotta go soon, and we can't share any more time together. It kills me to do this, 'cause I loved every minute of the show. But this is the way it has to be. So before I go, I got a coupla things I gotta say.

"Wherever I go, people tell me, 'You made me laugh—thank you.' But I always want to say, I'm the one that got the biggest gift—'cause I got your laughter. When I heard you laugh, it was like you were tellin' me, 'We get it…we understand…we share this moment.'"

Jack found he was hardly breathing, soaking in each word, and feeling pinpricks of emotion dancing across his neck and tightening his chest.

"I haven't been a good father, and God knows I was a lousy husband to all of my wives, but everything I gave to you, my audiences, it came straight from here"—he thumped his chest—"from my heart. I want to thank everyone who has ever listened to my show, and while I'm at it, I'll thank anyone who's ever laughed at my jokes. One last thing I gotta say, then I'll shut up."

Jack held his breath, waiting.

"A while ago, a nice kid came to work for me. A kid named Jack. He's the salt of the earth—a guy who doesn't have a dishonest bone in his body. So when it comes time to judge him, I want you to think of him as someone who always did what he thought was best for me. All I can say is, you should all be so lucky to have a friend like Jack."

Walt paused and took a deep breath as a wave of relief and joy swept over Jack. Everything he had felt for Walt was suddenly returned to him, along with plenty of interest. Jack imagined that anyone who heard Walt say this would look differently at this person who the media had called a kidnapper and a dangerous criminal.

Jack knew that Walt wasn't quite done. He waited for more and watched as a look of sadness passed through Walt's eyes. Maybe, like so many people, Walt had trouble saying good-bye.

"That's everything then. We've had a lot of good times together. But the show's over. I hope you won't forget me. So now I'll be one who's off and running."

Jack waited, watching the emotion move across Walt's face. Then he turned off the camera. "Beautiful, Walt, beautiful."

They sat there in silence, the tears running down Jack's cheeks. He tried to envision people who would soon be hearing Walt's speech played back. It was a long-delayed farewell. But at last he had finally got a chance to say good-bye.

Jack stared at Walt as the energy that had come alive for his last performance drained, and his tired face sagged. Walt himself must have sensed it happening because, before the destruction was complete, he turned to the wall, ashamed. Then he lay back down. Jack put his hand on Walt's shoulder, but there was no response. Time to get moving. He looked at his watch and made sure Walt had blankets, food, and water within reach. Then he picked up the camera and left.

When Jack stopped halfway out the door and looked back, Walt was picking up his drawing pad, and his hand was beginning to move across the blank page. At the time, Jack had other things on his mind. But much later he realized why this seemed odd. It was because Walt wasn't drawing, sweeping his hand back and forth for shading, or carefully adding detail. No, he was writing something.

FORTY-EIGHT

Jack was on foot, moving through the date grove, the outline of tree trunks barely visible under the half moon, feeling the powdery sand under his boots, tripping over fallen palm fronds. He illuminated the dial on his watch. He was late for his meeting to deliver the disk to the reporter. Four-wheeling down the mountain from the ghost town had taken longer than he expected.

He had left the Pathfinder parked behind the general store, then cut through the date grove on foot. He hit a path, ducked through an opening in the cottonwood trees, and saw a sign for the golf course. A small wooden footbridge led across an irrigation ditch that gurgled faintly in the stillness. The dark clubhouse appeared in front of him. The snack shack was beyond it. He hung back, straining to see if anyone was there waiting there for him.

Jack stood still, listening. It was quiet, except for the irrigation ditch and the moan of the wind. In the distance, probably at the airport, he heard a car starting. He saw a pair of headlights moving along the road from the airport to the highway, the lights flickering as they moved behind the tree trunks in the date grove. At the airport, the blades of a helicopter began turning, picking up speed, whining as it accelerated and then lifted off. Someone looking for him, no doubt.

The snack shack was a wood-paneled building with a window on the side where golfers could pull up and buy drinks before the round or when they made the turn and started the back nine. The roof jutted forward, creating a pool of darkness. As he approached, a figure separated from the shadow and stepped toward him.

"Jack Dillon?" The woman had a husky voice, a professional TV announcer's voice, with a slight quaver of nervousness.

"Yes."

"Trisha King, KNBC news." She studied him a moment. "Everyone's looking for you, Jack."

"Yeah. And here I am talking to you."

"I'm glad you contacted me. Who was it that called me?"

"A friend."

She nodded, understanding, not wanting to push things right now. She dug in her purse and, seconds later, a lighter flared as she lit a cigarette. In the flame Jack saw a small, intense, and pretty face. Ivory skin, raven hair—a combination that would look great on camera. Her tight white shirt, open at the throat, defined her figure.

She blew out smoke and said, "Your friend said you had something for me."

"I do but—where is she? The woman that called you?"

Trisha shrugged. "I assumed she'd be here. Haven't seen her."

Jack felt a knot of anxiety forming in his stomach. What happened to Mary? He focused on Trisha again.

"I have a disk with an interview on it—an interview with Walt Stuckey."

Jack stepped toward her as he reached into his pocket. She involuntarily flinched and raised a hand to ward him off.

"I'm not going to hurt you."

"I'm glad to hear that but—" She stopped herself.

"But you never really know what you're dealing with," Jack finished for her. He took a deep breath and tried to relax. "I should thank you for coming here, alone and everything. I know it must seem pretty desperate, what I've done."

She laughed nervously. "Yeah. Just a little."

"I just want you to know, I'm not going to hurt anyone. That's not what this is about."

"What about the guy shot dead up in the mountains?"

In the mountains? Maybe she was talking about the old cop, the one who grabbed Jack as he was leaving the trailer in the mountains. Remembering this, Jack could feel the cop's strong grip on his arm, the slug hitting him, the blood on his shirtfront, the way he dropped at his feet. Had he died?

"I didn't shoot anyone," he said carefully. "I know it's only my word against theirs. But you gotta believe me. I didn't shoot anyone."

She nodded, smoking, arms folded across the white shirt, one hand up with the cigarette, watching him closely.

He continued. "See, I'm writing this book with Walt—Walt Stuckey. And he had a stroke. His son took over the project— took over everything—and I found out he was abusing Walt."

"Elder abuse. I did a series on it."

"Then you know that abuse takes a lotta different forms. Garrett wasn't, like, beating his father or anything like that. But Walt wasn't getting the care he needed."

"So you felt you had to kidnap him. You didn't want to go to the authorities?"

"And tell them what? He was isolated, marginalized—that Garrett was effectively holding him prisoner? Who would believe that?"

"But you didn't even try that route."

"I, well—yeah. It's hard to explain, but it seemed like the only way to help. And Walt agrees. He says so on this—"

He pulled the disk out of his pocket. She started to reach for it. But he wasn't ready to hand it over.

"Here's the deal." His voice was intense again.

"Oh God. Not another deal."

"Another?"

"Nothing. Go on, what's your deal?"

"You're gonna like this. I've got two interviews that no one's ever seen. One's of Walt revealing why the show was canceled. That's big, really big. If you want it, you have to air this first."

"What is it?"

"It's a farewell message to his fans. When his show was canceled, he dropped out of sight and never spoke in public again. For the first time, he says good-bye." He let that sink in. "It's very moving."

"I don't get it. Why do I have to show that first?"

"Walt talks about me—he says I didn't do anything wrong. I'll be straight with you, I'm hoping it'll clear me. Or at least make them go easy on me."

Trisha laughed doubtfully. "That's a tall order. You've broken a lot of laws."

"I have a daughter," Jack blurted out. "She's only nine and…I want to see her grow up."

"You should have thought of that before you did this."

"Listen." Jack was trying to calm down, to remain coherent. But he heard his voice cracking with emotion and weighed with desperation. "I know you're a journalist, and you have to be objective and all that. But try to remember how you felt when you were nine—what the world looked like. Then imagine just for one second what Chloe—that's my little girl—what this is doing to her."

Trisha was silent.

"Just give me a fair shake for…" He couldn't finish.

"For Chloe?"

"For Chloe. But also because it's the right thing to do, as a newsperson."

"Not that you're putting any pressure on me or anything."

Jack laughed, acknowledging her point. "A fair shake. That's all I'm asking."

She sighed. "Okay, Jack."

She held out her hand. He pressed the disk into her palm. She cocked her head and smiled as if suddenly understanding. "You actually like Walt Stuckey, don't you?"

"He gave me a break when I needed one. You don't forget someone who does that for you." Jack looked at his watch. "Look, you're gonna want to move on this. It's hot."

She threw down the cigarette and ground it out. She turned to go.

"Trisha." She turned, waiting. "Tell people I'm not crazy. Things got way out of control. But all I ever wanted was to tell Walt's story. There was a time when America loved the guy."

"I'll look at what you've got here." She held up the disk. "If it's good, I'll get it on the air. Then, call me. I want that other tape."

She was retreating into the darkness now, heading toward the road to the airport, disappearing among the trees. Her voice was weak and getting weaker. But then she unexpectedly added, "Stay safe, Jack."

And then she was gone.

FORTY-NINE

Mary lay on the bed, the sheet covering her naked and sweating body, trying to figure out what woke her up. She turned and looked at the glow-in-the-dark alarm clock on the cabin's side table and saw that the alarm hadn't yet gone off. She lay back, her heart racing, her ears straining for any sounds, and listened to the night. Did someone knock on the window? Did a bright light somehow penetrate her closed eyelids? Her mind was gradually clearing, her heartbeat slowing.

Mary climbed out of bed and padded into the shower, still wondering what had yanked her from the depths of a sleep. The shower revived her, and moments later she was dressed and ready to meet Jack near the golf course. She clicked off the overhead light, opened the door but remained inside the cabin, looking out and along the dirt road near the date grove. She could see parked cars, a few cabin lights, and then only darkness and vague shapes. She pushed the screen door open and stepped out.

There was a quick rustle and the scrape of a shoe. Then arms were around her, one pinning her arms, one over her mouth so she couldn't breathe. She fought, panicking, but it was obvious her attacker knew how to immobilize a victim. She went limp and waited.

"Where's Jack?" Garrett's voice hissed in her ear.

She could see Garrett's face was leaning in to her, whispering as someone else held her. She was running out of air and had that horrible suffocating feeling. She tore at the fingers over her mouth.

"Ernie, let her speak," Garrett said. "But if you try to scream, Ernie will choke the life out of you."

The hand over her mouth relaxed, and she hysterically gulped in cool night air.

"I asked you where Jack is."

Mary's mind was a jumble of terrified images. But somewhere in the panicked mess, she found the scrap of a plan.

"He's meeting with a reporter," she said. "He's giving her proof that you were abusing Walt."

"Really." Garrett sounded amused. "He's giving *her* proof that I was abusing my father. Now we're getting somewhere. So what exactly did Jack give to that little slut Trisha King? I knew she was up to something."

"I didn't say who it was," Mary said, backpedaling. "But it's proof. It's Walt's own statement. He's talking again—he's coherent. And he told Jack everything. So you better let me go."

Garrett was silent for a moment, and Mary hoped he took her threat seriously.

"Well, Mary, there's not very much for my father to tell," Garrett said, sounding confident again. "But let's just find out what the deranged Jack Dillon is saying about me. Ernie, escort Mary to our car."

Mary felt herself picked up off her feet and hauled toward the waiting Suburban. He slammed her against the side of the SUV as he groped for the door handle.

"Easy, Ernie, easy," Garrett said. "Just get her in the backseat all tied up and keep her out of trouble."

Mary felt herself being stuffed through the open back door.

"Hands," Ernie demanded.

She weakly held her hands out in front of her, and Ernie wrapped them in duct tape. As he was reaching for her ankles, Garrett's face appeared and leaned into her.

"And where was this alleged meeting between Jack and Ms. King going to take place?"

"Why? What are you going to do?"

"I'll tell my side of the story. Any good journalist would be fine with that. I'll tell her what it was really like to be raised by the oh-so-lovable Walt Stuckey."

Feeling the tape tightening around her, Mary had a horrible sense of claustrophobia, as if she was being snuffed out. She began shaking uncontrollably.

"Are you going to tell me where to find Jack?" Garrett asked. "Or do I have to have let Ernie do a little convincing?"

"Near the airport," Mary said, stalling, hoping to think of something to help herself.

"Near the airport. Okay, *where* near the airport?"

"I'll show you," Mary said, hoping she could somehow calm down and think of something.

Garrett waited, thinking. Finally, he opened the driver's door and climbed in.

"Okay, Lady Mary. Lead the way. But if we aren't there in ten minutes, things will become very unpleasant."

Garrett started the Suburban and the big SUV lumbered forward. He pulled a U-turn, passed the general store, and rolled out onto the main road. Turning left, he picked up speed.

"Okay, Mary. Tell me where to turn," Garrett said.

"It's still up ahead," Mary said. She was hoping to navigate him into the airport where the reporters were gathered. If he kept going far enough, maybe someone would see them, or the police would stop him. It was all she could think of.

"I'm not turning into the airport road, if that's what you've got in mind," Garrett said coming around a bend and seeing the road open up in front of them. The airport was another half mile on the left. Garrett let the Suburban coast and lose speed.

"If Trisha left the airport on foot, she was meeting Jack nearby," Garrett said, peering through the windshield. "That means she must..." He left his sentence unfinished as he spotted a white dot in the distance. As they glided closer, Mary saw it was a young woman in a white blouse walking along the shoulder of the road.

"Ernie, do you see what I see?" Garrett said, accelerating again.

"Yeah. Do you want me to get the disk from her?" Ernie offered eagerly.

"Good idea," Garrett said, accelerating harder.

"Pull over and I'll—hey!"

The huge SUV was hurtling toward the woman, closing fast.

"What are you doing?" Ernie shouted.

"No, Garrett!" Mary screamed.

Ernie instinctively braced against the dashboard.

The woman's white blouse flared in the headlights. An instant before the impact, Mary saw her head turn and the flash of her terrified face. Then with a deep thud, the body flew up over the hood and glanced off the windshield before it disappeared. Garrett slammed on the brakes and pulled onto the shoulder. The Suburban came to a stop, the engine idling quietly, as if everything were normal. In the silence, Mary heard herself sobbing.

Garrett turned to look back, and Mary saw his face and heard his short excited snatches of breath.

"Now go get the disk," Garrett said to Ernie in an oddly even tone of voice.

Ernie was still frozen in a braced position, staring at Garrett.

"Get the disk, Ernie!" Garrett roared. "And just remember. You're in this up to your neck. So don't get cold feet on me now."

Ernie slowly stepped out of the car and Mary could hear his footsteps crunching in the gravel as he jogged back to the body.

Garrett turned his eyes to Mary and looked at her a long time. He seemed to feel her terror and feed on it.

"I think you realize now that I'm serious," he said quietly. "So I'll ask you one more time: Where's Jack?"

FIFTY

"Can you connect me with Ann Chandler?" Jack asked when the motel clerk answered the phone. It was the name he had given Mary earlier that day and, sure enough, she had registered under the alias. But now the phone was ringing in her room. Ringing and ringing without being answered. Where the hell was she? She didn't show up when he met with the reporter on the golf course. And she wasn't in her cabin.

Finally, the clerk came back on the line. "Would you like to leave a message?"

"Yeah. Tell her that"—he remembered the name he had chosen for himself—"tell her that Nick Downs called. I'll call again."

Jack hung up the pay phone and stepped out into the parking lot next to the general store in Furnace Creek. Mary had set up the meeting as he'd asked her. But then maybe she had fallen asleep and slept through the ringing phone. The cabins where Mary was staying were nearby. But which one was she in? Were the police watching it, hoping he'd show up? He'd better not risk going there. Besides, he needed to get back to Walt. He'd just have to come back in the morning to find Mary.

He climbed into the Pathfinder and fired it up, pulling a U-turn in the parking lot. His tires crunched on the gravel then hit the smooth asphalt, and he worked up through the gears. On the one hand, he felt relieved that he had connected with the reporter. Once Walt's statement aired, and his words cleared him, then it would be safe for Jack to turn himself in to the police. Walt would go home, and maybe Mary would care for him. Or maybe one of Walt's other children from another marriage would look after him. After the kidnapping, they had begun to assemble in the Pajaro Beach area but kept their distance, letting Garrett take the lead. *But at least this adventure is coming to a head now,* Jack thought, realizing how incredibly tired he was. If he could only find out where Mary was or what happened to her. That was the only loose end at this point.

The turnoff for the golf course was coming up on his left. Maybe he should swing by once more and see if she was there. Maybe she had just been late. He slowed for the turn. Then stopped.

Ahead of him were lights. Headlights from a dozen cars. And flashing lights too. The cars were circled around something lying on the ground. Silhouetted figures, crouching over a still form, moved frantically across the backdrop of lights.

Jack heard the whine of a siren and saw blue lights sparking in the distance. A paramedic van was coming down the highway toward him. He pulled onto the shoulder, and the ambulance flew past him. He watched it join the circle of lights.

He stared at the accident scene for a very long time, watching the figures moving, stooping, lifting, kneeling beside the thing on the ground. He watched, hoping he'd see something that would show him that this accident was completely unconnected to him, just one of those random things you see and irrationally attach to your own life. *Everyone does that,* he thought. *And we're usually wrong.*

But then the rescue workers stepped aside, and he saw the small shape lying crumpled on the ground, at the center of the activity: coal-black hair, a white shirt. It was the reporter, Trisha King. And Jack felt everything inside collapse.

FIFTY-ONE

Through the windshield Mary could see only the black desert night. She was being tossed from side to side as they climbed a jeep trail into the mountains, slumped in the backseat of Garrett's Suburban, her wrists and ankles duct-taped, Ernie's powerful hand on her arm.

"You sure this is the right road?" Garrett said, picking his way up the steep canyon road.

"Why? What are you going to do?" Mary's voice was shaking like she was freezing in a meat locker. She hated showing fear to Garrett. *He's in complete control,* she thought, *and he loves it.*

"I just want to talk with him," Garrett said reasonably.

"Like you were going to talk with that reporter?"

"That was an accident," Garrett said. "She should have known better than to walk along a dark road at night. So do you think Jack is there now—in this ghost town you told me about?"

"He was supposed to meet me." Mary tried to steady herself by taking deep breaths, by blocking thoughts of what Garrett would do, by blocking all her thoughts. "I have no idea what he'll do when I don't show up."

"He'll come back up here, that's what he'll do," Garrett said. "And then we'll all talk—resolve this situation."

Garrett slowed to a stop, squinting at the road in front of the headlights. Mary shifted in the backseat, trying to see the road, trying to figure out where they were. It was hard to do with her wrists taped together. And with Ernie's death grip on her arm.

The hardest thoughts for Mary to block were the feeling of the impact of the body that shuddered through the Suburban. The only sign they hit the reporter was that horrible smear across the windshield. Thank goodness, Garrett had used the windshield washer, but you could still see some of it. And Garrett had forced Ernie to go and inspect the front headlight and grille. He shouted back that one headlight was broken. Mary watched, sickened, as Ernie picked things out of the front end of the SUV and threw them to the side of the road. When he got back into the Suburban, he kept wiping his hands on his jeans.

Mary tried to shake off those images as she strained her eyes to look through the windshield for a light, a landmark of any kind. The SUV's big engine was working hard, climbing. The single headlight illuminated only a sandy washboard road and a few boulders to mark the way. Besides that, it was just a vast pool of blackness. Moments later, her ears crackled and then popped from the altitude.

Garrett slowed to a stop, looking at something to his left. He rolled down the window and studied what looked like a turnoff that led down to the left.

"Ernie, step out for a second. Let's take a look."

Garrett set the brake, and he and Ernie climbed out. Mary watched them walk into the headlight beam and look around, talking, pointing, looking down over the edge of the canyon. He said something to Ernie, and he nodded, looking over the drop-off. Their body language told Mary it was a long way down. Then Garrett swung around and looked back at the car, looking straight at Mary. When Garrett got back into the Suburban, a cold blast of air followed him in.

"If you do anything to Jack, you'll never find Walt," Mary said. "He's up there now, Garrett—your father. Alone. He needs you."

"I'll get to him. Don't worry. Ernie, get out and help me back up. I can't see a damn thing back there. I'd hate to back off a cliff or something." He chuckled as he dropped the car into reverse.

Ernie released Mary's arm and jumped out. Garrett watched in the wing mirror and slowly backed in so the Suburban was on the inside of the curve, on the backside of a blind turn.

Suddenly, Ernie was running for the car. He yanked opened the door. "He's coming!" he shouted, his face contorted with excitement as he jumped back into the SUV. "I saw his lights! He's coming."

Ernie buckled his seat belt and braced himself against the door frame.

"Garrett, what are you going to do?" Mary pleaded.

Garrett's answer was more of a snarl. "You'll see."

"Garrett, stop—you don't have to do this."

Garrett laughed. "As if I would ever take your advice. Hang on, Mary. You're going for the ride of your life."

Mary tried to speak, to reason with Garrett, but her voice was a horse groan. "Please, no" was all she could say.

But then, Mary realized Ernie hadn't put his gorilla paw back on her arm again after he got in. He was too busy buckling up, getting ready to save his own ass. He didn't seem to care if she was buckled in or not. She'd better protect herself.

A beam of light from behind bounced across the SUV's interior. Mary slid low in the seat, bracing herself by putting her knees up on the seat back behind Garrett's head. Her taped ankles moved as one unit. But then, twisted into this position, Mary saw her feet were near Garrett's face, turned to watch the approaching headlights. Maybe there was something she could do after all. Maybe Garrett wasn't really in complete control.

Headlights were coming up the steep grade now, bouncing on the rocky jeep trail. Long slices of light danced on the canyon walls around them. Garrett dropped the shift lever into drive. The transmission engaged with a powerful *clunk*. The throaty V8 idled, ready.

"Come on, you bastard..." Garrett said. "A little closer... Come on..."

And then she knew what Garrett was planning to do to Jack, and she felt sick.

Hunched low in the backseat, Mary strained to see over the edge of the door. The headlights were coming close now, bucking on the rough road. She heard the engine of the Pathfinder working up the grade and imagined Jack at the wheel. Suddenly, she felt all kinds of unexpected emotions. She thought how vulnerable he was, driving into this trap, how trusting he had been to her, how much he had struggled to help Walt to finish the book. Mary wanted to protect Jack, to be with him again, to hear his low voice that was strong and understanding but always had a laugh in it somewhere.

"Just a little more..." Garrett hissed, one hand on the headlight switch, one on the steering wheel. The Pathfinder was coming around the corner now, moving slowly, nearly in front of them.

Mary drew her knees up to her chest, coiled and ready.

"Now!" Garrett yanked on the headlights.

But before he could hit the gas, Mary arched her back and lashed out with her legs, kicking at Garrett's head with all her strength. She didn't really expect to hurt him much. She only hoped she could stop him from ramming Jack's jeep, knocking him off the side of the cliff on the hairpin turn. Mary's feet connected, and Garrett's head shot forward as he screamed in pain and surprise.

Garrett recovered quickly, but Jack's car had passed and was climbing the steep road away from them. Jack must have seen the light come on behind him and begun accelerating. With a roar the Suburban shot forward, the four-wheel drive biting into the loose gravel and hurtling them toward the taillights of the Pathfinder. One of the last things Mary remembered, before the impact, was seeing Jack's eyes in his rearview mirror, a look of defiance and determination giving her a small ray of hope.

But that was just before they slammed into the back of Jack's car and she was thrown sideways, slamming her head into the door pillar. And as the darkness rose, and she was in and out of consciousness, she was vaguely aware that Jack's still form was thrown onto the seat beside her.

FIFTY-TWO

Jack felt as if he was hearing voices at the end of a long tunnel. Voices echoing and fading. Voices alternating with darkness. Comfortable, soothing darkness. Then lights flaring. The lights splintered into needles of pain that stabbed his eyeballs with each heartbeat. So Jack slid back down the tunnel into darkness and relief.

What seemed like a century later he heard more voices. He knew he had to return to that world. There was something he desperately needed to do—even though it was just out of reach in the clouds of his mind. He opened his eyes and saw it was still night. It was agony to open his eyes, but he forced himself to do it. He was cold and hot at the same time. His cheek was pressed into the dirt. And the dirt was as cold as night. He could see a figure silhouetted against blazing headlights.

"It's a shame, Jack," a voice said to him. It was Garrett. "It's a shame that you'll be blamed for my father's death. I mean, you're the only one who knows where he is. With you dead out here, they won't find him until it's too late. Your name and his together in history—an entertainment legend and the psycho who stalked and killed him."

An alarm went off somewhere deep in Jack's brain, telling him it was so important to speak that he had to endure the pain, no matter how great. But that meant he had to find the muscles to speak, air to breathe, words to form sentences. Those things had been shattered and lay in pieces in separate areas of his mind.

All the pieces of Jack's body were checking in now, and the news wasn't good. He felt he might not ever get back up off the ground—he might die here. And if that happened, he wanted to go alone, not drag Walt down too, leaving him stranded in the ghost town, miles from help.

"Beveridge," Jack was finally able to whisper. "Your father is in Beveridge."

"Never heard of it," Garrett replied.

"Dirt road...north of Highway 90. In a house with a rose over the door," Jack said.

"A rose?" Laughter. "Jack, I think the heat's got to you. I have no idea what you're talking about."

One more thing, he thought. *One more thing, and then you can go back to the darkness.*

"I planted evidence there—when they find your father, the evidence will finish you," Jack said.

There was a surprised silence. Then in a different tone of voice he said, "You're blowing smoke, Jack. The time for that has passed."

"I know why they canceled Walt's show."

"Give up, Jack."

"I know about the file."

"The what?"

"The file. The evidence is there...When it gets out, everyone will know what kind of a monster you really are."

Garrett began swearing and shouting, alternating curses with savage kicks to Jack's ribs, his legs. Someone else—was it Ernie?—was trying to stop him, but finally there was a solid thump to his head that shattered what remained of Jack's consciousness, and he was leaving them again, sliding backward. Back down the long tunnel to the comfort and protection of darkness.

———

Many hours later, when Jack regained consciousness and opened his eyes, he saw only two colors: the tan of the sandy desert floor and the pure blue of a cloudless sky.

He blinked a couple of times, and his vision began to clear. Now he could see the battered Pathfinder nearby, the front end smashed up against a huge boulder. Mary was inside. Motionless. Beyond the wreckage lay the black mountains. But they weren't the mountains where he had taken Walt. It wasn't the canyon he'd been climbing last night when he blacked out. These mountains were dark hulking heaps of volcanic rock, scorched for eons under the sun.

Jack ran his swollen tongue along his lips and felt grains of imbedded sand. He tried to swallow. Big mistake—it was like his throat was filled with broken glass. Arrows of pain shot up his neck and into his brain. He tried to move his head. Another mistake. The pain overwhelmed him again, and he heard himself groan, a strange, animal sound immediately swallowed up by the stillness of the vast space around him.

"Jack…" A hoarse voice came to him. "Jack…You're alive."

He rolled on his side and looked toward the car. Mary was leaning forward, looking at him out the open door. Why didn't she come out and help him? He looked again but couldn't see her face. Was it hidden in a shadow? He looked again, closer and saw that her face was covered in dried blood.

Rolling over, he pulled his knees up under him, checking for damage. So far, nothing broken. Lumps on the back of head. Cuts and bruises on his face and arms. Pain everywhere, each time he moved. He pushed himself to his knees then fell back again. He tried to rise again and slowly made it to his feet. Then, slowly, painfully, he straightened and stood unsteadily.

"Jack," her voice was weak. And getting weaker, as if she was leaving him.

He staggered over to the Pathfinder, leaned in. A gash had opened high on her scalp and blood poured down over one side of her face. The blood had congealed into a mask plastering her beautiful blond hair to her scalp. The wound still oozed, and flies had collected, picking at the edges of it.

She raised her arms weakly and draped them over his neck. He felt her moving spasmodically as she clutched at him. And then he realized she was sobbing.

"I thought you were dead. I was sitting here waiting to die. It was so lonely, looking at you lying out there, so still."

Jack pulled back and looked at Mary's face. Tears streaked through the blood mask. But in the desert, her teary eyes were an oasis of life. She stroked his hair and touched his face, crying all the time.

"What happened?" Jack asked.

She took a deep breath. "Garrett waited for you to ram you, to shove you off the road. I tried to stop him. I kicked him but... but he chased you and..."

It was coming back now. He remembered he had been driving up the jeep trail to Beveridge to see Walt. Then, a single headlight exploded behind him—gaining fast. *Where the hell did they come from?* He tried to outrun them, but the headlight kept coming. He swerved and tried to elude the other car, but the sound of the impact, breaking glass...He was tumbling around inside his car, tumbling into darkness and letting go.

"Your car rolled over and over, into a ditch, then back up on its wheels. Oh God, Jack, I was so afraid you were dead." Mary sobbed. "After they rammed you, you were unconscious. They thought you were dead. Ernie drove you here in your car— Garrett came in his, so they could dump us here. If anyone ever found us, it would look like we ran into that boulder."

"Do you know where we are?"

She looked like she would cry again. "I tried to pay attention. I knew I needed to. But I was so scared."

"How long did they drive? To get here?"

"An hour maybe. I don't know."

"Did they take dirt roads? Paved roads?"

"First, they went back to the main road. I know because it was smooth, asphalt, I guess. They turned right onto another dirt road—"

"Turned right," he echoed. "Okay, so that would be north. Okay. Then what?"

"Then they turned onto a dirt road…and drove forever."

"Forever? Come on, Mary. Please, you have to do better than that."

"*Forever*. It seemed like forever because I knew—I knew what they were going to do. When they stopped, they put me in your jeep, in the passenger side without the safety belt on. Ernie drove straight into the boulder, to make it look like an accident. I went flying into the windshield and—"

Jack saw the spider-webbed indentation in the glass. Strands of her blond hair hung down from the splintered glass. If she had gone through the windshield, he wouldn't be talking to her now.

Mary struggled to talk. The tears flowed again. "I played dead. So they would leave. It was so quiet I heard them talking out there in the darkness. Garrett had this big rock, and he wanted to—to make sure you were dead. But Ernie stopped him. He said you were dead already, and it should look like an accident. So they just left you lying there and drove off."

She pulled Jack's head to her, sobbing in his ear, her tears slick on his face.

"God, look at us, Jack." She laughed weakly. "We haven't got a chance, have we?"

Jack stood up and looked around. He summoned all his energy and stood up straight, rubbed his face and brushed the dirt from his clothes.

"Walt's up in the mountains alone," Jack said, feeling the beginnings of strength stirring. "We can't let him die there."

"But what can we do?"

Jack looked at the Pathfinder. The tires weren't flat. The hood was buckled but no water leaked from the radiator. He went to the driver's door—the keys were still in the ignition.

"After they smashed the car, I heard Garrett tell Ernie to leave it running," Mary said. "So the gas would be used up."

Sure enough, the ignition was on. He turned it off, hoping the battery wasn't drained, but if it had idled itself dry, what did it matter? He had to try it, of course. He had to. *Well, here goes.* He turned the key. The engine cranked. At least there was still juice in the battery.

"Come on, baby!" Jack whispered. "Come on."

No good. The engine wouldn't catch. The tank was dry.

"Dammit!" Jack stepped out of the Pathfinder and looked around.

Mary had been watching him hopefully. Now her spirits sagged. "So I guess we're finished."

"We have to make it out of here on foot."

"I can't."

"Then I'll go. And come back and get you."

"Right," she said, doubtfully. "Great plan."

This is the last thing I need now, he thought bitterly. But he couldn't let it drag him down. He couldn't afford to waste his energy reacting to her pessimism. He scanned the horizon looking for landmarks. The hard-packed dirt underfoot was chalk white and reflected the sun up into his eyes. Glare and heat enveloped him. And the sun was still rising higher. Everything at eye level danced in heat waves. But looking up, he saw mountains behind him and taller mountains to the west. The only thing he recognized for sure was Telescope Peak. Yesterday, in Furnace Creek, the mountain had been directly west—now it was far off to the southwest. That meant they were in the north end of Death Valley, north of the sand dunes. But he needed another landmark to know for sure.

Maybe if he stood on the roof of the car he could see better. He planted his foot on the bumper and was about to push up when he felt something binding in the leg pocket of his cargo pants. *His topo map!* It charted the Mount Whitney area. But maybe it had Death Valley too.

"Here's a lucky break," Jack said, pulling the map out. "I have a map of Death Valley."

"Wonderful," Mary said, looking away and dropping her face in her hands.

He sat inside the Pathfinder next to her. It was a relief to be out of the sun, even if it was still hot in the shade. He spread the map out against the steering wheel. "Mary, look. If Telescope Peak is here"—he pointed at the map—"then we're in this area." He drew a circle with his finger. "Last night, were they driving on a dirt road? Or was it just like this—no road at all?"

"Ernie picked this place. He told Garrett he used to come up here in his dune buggy. He said they used to go to a racetrack." She shrugged wearily. "I'm just telling you what he said. Why does it matter?"

Jack scanned the horizon again. "Is there any water left?" Jack asked her.

"I haven't looked." She sounded weaker each time she spoke.

He opened the tailgate and found their stuff in a jumbled mess on the floor. He rummaged among the grocery bags of food. There had been several liter-bottles of water. But they weren't there now. He stacked everything outside the Pathfinder and went through every bag. No water. But he did find a baseball hat. He pulled it on and felt it cut the glare.

He crouched and looked under the seats. Maybe their water bottles had been thrown under the seats during the accident. Leaning into the Pathfinder, he reached in and touched a cool plastic bottle. He pulled it out—a one-liter bottle of water. One beautiful liter of water, sloshing around and splitting the sun into a spectrum of colors. He wanted it to be a swimming pool so he could jump in and drink it up.

"We'll split this," Jack said. "Then I've got to start walking."

He held out the bottle, and she grabbed it and started drinking. He couldn't bear to watch the water disappear. Besides, he needed to plan his route. He climbed onto the hood of his car and then the roof. From there, he could see above the heat waves. He saw a rock outcropping about two miles away. Beyond that, he saw smoke trails snaking toward the sky. Would someone light a campfire in this heat? No, they were probably dust devils kicked up by swirling wind.

He climbed down off the roof and looked inside the Pathfinder. Mary had the bottle raised, and the water was disappearing down her throat.

"Hey!"

He grabbed for the bottle, and it slipped from their hands and fell on the floor. They dove for it, spilling it, and when Jack got it, it was a quarter full.

"Why'd you do that? I said we'd split it."

"I'm sorry, Jack. I'm so sorry." Her face seemed to break into pieces, and she began to sob.

"Half of that was for me!"

"I know, I know. But I couldn't make myself stop drinking."

"I needed that! I'm the one who's going to be walking out there."

She fell back against the seat. "My fault. All my fault."

Would a few swallows of water make any difference?

"Sorry," he said, still staring at the dust devils. "The sun's getting to me."

"I feel like I'm choking." Her voice was pathetically weak now. "If there was a breeze—anything—it wouldn't be so bad. But there's nothing."

No water, no shade, no wind, he thought, watching the dust devils scudding along the horizon. But then something hit him. Dust devils. How could there be dust devils without wind?

"Mary?"

"I'm still here." Her head flopped toward him.

"You said Ernie picked this spot because—what did you say?"

"He used to come here so he could go to the racetrack."

"A racetrack? Or *the* racetrack?"

"A—the—what does it matter?"

"It matters because if he meant *the* racetrack, then I know where we are."

"Where?" For the first time her voice held a sliver of hope.

"The racetrack is a dry lake bed, where the Indians used to race their ponies. It looks like it's only about five miles away. It's a big tourist attraction—there will be people there."

"Jack," she said. "I can't make it. I can't walk that far. I can't walk at all."

The tone of her voice, the apologetic look on her face, broke his heart.

"I didn't mean you," he said, carefully touching her face. "I'm going to walk there. If I can."

The map was where he had left it, spread against the steering wheel. He pinpointed their location. Then he traced a straight line toward where he had seen the dust devils. RACETRACK, the map said. He'd been there once before. It was a dry lake bed, perfectly flat and oval-shaped, with a ring of boulders around it like grandstands. That's how they got the name Racetrack. Between where they were right now and the area marked was only five miles.

Jack stepped out and looked again at the rising plumes of dust, the dust that he now knew was caused by ATVs and dirt bikes across the desert floor. The people driving those ATVs would have extra gas. And water. From here to there was only five miles. Under normal conditions he could walk five miles in two hours. Under *normal* conditions.

He turned to Mary. She was watching him.

"There are people over there."

She shrugged hopelessly, so he said, "I'll be back."

"Will you?"

"I will. I promise."

She reached out and took his hand. Her voice was a whisper. "About the water—I couldn't control myself."

He tried to smile. "Sorry I yelled at you." Then, "I'll be gone a couple of hours."

No contradictions this time. She just nodded sadly.

"Don't give up hope. I will be back."

"Sure, Jack." She looked away, her shoulders slumping.

He forced himself to step out into the sun, even though it fell across his shoulders like a bar of molten iron, searing his flesh. He took ten steps and felt exhausted. His own words came back to him, mocking him. *Don't give up hope.*

FIFTY-THREE

"Asshole at three o'clock," said Special Agent Boxell, watching the white Explorer come across the runway toward the motor home where the FBI had set up its command center at the Death Valley airport.

"He's got a new set of wheels," said Special Agent Watson putting down the piece of fried chicken he'd been gnawing. It was all they could get for lunch at the country store in Furnace Creek. "Yesterday he's driving a Suburban—today it's an Explorer. What's up with that?"

"When you've got his money, I guess it comes with the territory," Boxell said. Then, wiping her hands on a wet nap, enjoying the clean smell of the alcohol-soaked towelette, she added, "I wonder where he's been?"

"Even assholes need to sleep every once in a while," an Inyo County Sheriff's sergeant said, smiling at his remark.

Watson didn't acknowledge the comment. He hated it when officers from local law enforcement agencies joined in their conversations uninvited. He let the uncomfortable silence lengthen as his tongue probed his teeth, hunting for shreds of chicken.

The white Explorer stopped in front of the command headquarters. Garrett Stuckey climbed out of one door, Ernie out the other. The media guys, lurking nearby, saw them and scrambled for their gear. They rushed Garrett, lugging cameras and battery packs, shouting questions. But Garrett bulled through and climbed into the trailer without knocking.

Garrett stood in the artificial coolness, catching his breath, noting with disgust the tub of greasy chicken bones. His eyes were slung in puffy bags, like bloodshot eggs in fleshy hammocks. Looking around the trailer and taking in the FBI agents and the gathering of sheriff's deputies, he spoke with exaggerated reverence. "Any news about Trisha's condition?"

"Extremely critical," the Inyo Sheriff's sergeant said. "But she's still hangin' in there."

Garrett nodded solemnly. "What about the maniac that did it? You catch him?"

"No."

"But it's gotta be Dillon, right? I heard she phoned her news director. Said she had an exclusive interview with him."

Watson looked at Garrett suspiciously. "She regains consciousness, she might give a description. Right now, we haven't got much to go on."

Garrett turned to the window and saw a chunky C-130 parked at one end of the runway.

"That's it?"

"That's it."

"Why isn't it in the air?"

"The equipment doesn't work when it's this hot. They have to wait until it cools down. Then there's a difference between body temperature and the temperature of the rock around it."

"Then you can pick out a human being?"

"From five thousand feet."

"So they have to wait for nightfall?"

"Yes, sir."

Garrett banged his fist on the counter top and grimaced. "I just find it so damn frustrating."

"What's that, sir?"

"My father's out there somewhere. Who knows what kind of a hellhole Dillon has him trapped in? And everyone's just sitting around with thumbs up their asses."

Watson traded a look with Boxell.

The sergeant cleared his throat and said, "The Inyo County search and rescue team is all over the valley. We're chasing down every lead we have."

"What about the captain of the Pajaro Beach Police?" Garrett demanded. "What's his name?"

"Chief Ullrich," Boxell said.

"Yeah, him. Any word from him?"

Watson fixed him in a steady gaze, let the silence lengthen, then said, "Why do you ask?"

"He was all over the place in the beginning—now he's disappeared."

"Because he's not here now doesn't mean he's disappeared," Watson said. "We've been in touch with his department. Several of his deputies are in the area."

"Of course, of course. I'm just saying—we have to explore every option. I mean, it's just so damn hard to sit here and do nothing."

"Once again, sir, we're not doing nothing," the Inyo County sergeant said.

Watson really wished the sergeant would quit sucking up. He'd find out sooner or later what he was dealing with, and then he'd be sorry.

"What time do you expect to get that thing airborne?"

Watson spoke up before the sergeant had a chance to respond. "As soon as we can, Mr. Stuckey. That's all we can tell you at this time."

Garrett heard the tone in the agent's voice and regarded Watson coldly. "I should hope so, Agent Watson. Until then—" He turned to the Inyo County Sheriff's sergeant, "—can you tell me where the search is centered? I know I can't do much. But I have to do something."

"Understood," the sergeant said gravely. "They're in Skidoo right now. There's another group heading to Chloride City."

"I've heard of a place called Beveridge," Garrett said slowly. "Have they searched it yet?"

"They're sweeping the valley from south to north. They'll get there early tomorrow morning."

Garrett nodded. With an expression of resolve he set his jaw. "I'm joining the search."

Watson spun around. "You're doing what?"

"Sir, that's not necessary," the sergeant said.

"I know. I know. But I have to do *something*. Maybe you all can sit here eating chicken while a man is dying out there. But I have to do *something*."

The sergeant nodded gravely. "Understood." He picked up a two-way radio. "I'll let them know you're coming."

Garrett threw the door open and stepped back into the heat. Ernie had been standing in the shade alongside the trailer, fending off questions from reporters. When Garrett appeared, they both marched to the Explorer and got inside.

As they slowly drove away, Garrett said, "We're joining the search, Ernie. We're going to help them look for Dad."

Ernie was puzzled. "But Jack told you where he was."

"You really believe that maniac?"

"Why would he lie?"

"It's too complicated to explain. Oh sure, I guess I'll have to go to this Beveridge place later. But for now, we're joining the search."

"I still don't understand why—"

"Ever heard of public relations, Ernie? The TV cameras are where the searchers are. They need footage of me looking for my father. Then everyone will see how concerned I am about Dad."

Ernie was still confused. But he knew better than to say anything.

Garrett added, "I'll go up to that Beveridge place later, alone. Then we'll see if Jack was blowing smoke—which he almost certainly was."

FIFTY-FOUR

Jack had been walking for two hours when he realized that he had almost stopped making progress. He was still picking up his feet, but they were just churning in the white salt crust. It reminded him of when he was a kid, walking on snow that almost held his weight but crashing through to powder underneath. It took three times the energy to walk in these conditions, and the constant pounding jarred his knees, his back, every joint in his body.

Everything around Jack shimmered in an angry, white-hot glare. As far as he could see, in all directions, there wasn't a scrap of shade. He found himself craving shade like it was water. But the only sliver of shade was cast by the visor of the hat across his face. He forced himself to look up to the horizon. The dust devils from the ATVs were still there. But they were miles away. And he was hitting the wall big-time.

Dark thoughts invaded his mind. He kept wondering if it would it end here in this vast empty space, on this scorched earth. Would he fall face first into the dust where he would cook and swell then burst open and give his moisture back to the soil? As he saw it all happening, he wondered what had happened to the hope he had asked Mary to hold for him.

But he wasn't finished until he was down. And he wasn't down yet. He was still on his feet, still moving. But grim determination wasn't going to save him. He had to change plans and use his last scraps of energy. Or…

He cupped his hands around his eyes, to cut the glare, and scanned the horizon, looking for an easier trail. But everything looked the same on this bubbling, crusted, white surface.

Except...

Nearby, he saw a pair of faint lines wandering in the general direction he was heading. A jeep had come through here at some point and broken the crusty surface. Maybe if he walked in the tire tracks...

He changed course, stumbling in the new direction. And that was when he felt the first cool flashes moving up his legs.

Heat stroke.

He had it once before and knew the warning signs, like someone opened the door to an air-conditioned room. Cool air was swirling around his legs. Cool air that was the beginning of death.

He stumbled and went down on one knee. He'd rest like this for a minute. Just a minute. Then he would continue on to the tire tracks. He had to do it. For himself. For Mary. And for Walt. He forced himself back up on his feet again. *Ten more steps. Count the steps, and it will block all the thoughts, all thoughts...*

One...two...three...four...five...six...

His feet hit a different surface, and he looked down. He was standing in the tire tracks. He made it! Sure enough, the jeep tires had packed down the white crust. His boots moved forward without resistance. It was easier now. He was almost to the top of the rise. From there he would see down into the area where the ATVs were. In another twenty steps, he would be to the top of the rise.

The landscape around him was changing now. Low sage bushes cropped up here and there. Sage and mesquite. The bushes cast a shadow about the size of his head. He wanted to lie down and put his head in the delicious shadow to regain his strength. But he knew if he did, he'd never get up again. So he kept stumbling forward, because he was almost there. Almost there...

He crested the rise and looked down onto the racetrack, a flat disk among surrounding boulders. He squinted into the glare and saw tiny specks, still miles away, darting along the dirt road nearby. Heat waves swam across the surface, shimmering in the heat like a huge lake. He could even hear the gnat-like droning as they accelerated, sliding across the hard-packed surface, insects scurrying in search of crumbs. But as he watched the distant vehicles, his spirits began to collapse because, one by one, they were disappearing over the horizon, the sound fading out as they vanished. In seconds, the fatal stillness had returned to the desert.

The last of his energy drained out like a spilled canteen of water. His legs, weak and shivery with cold chills, began convulsing.

All that remains is to find a comfortable place to die. It was a chilling voice coming from the primal depths of his mind. He'd reached the end. And here, at the end, were no profound thoughts, no summing up of his life, no sudden understanding of his struggles—just an animal desire to find a comfortable place to deposit this shell, this body he had dragged through life. He would leave it here in the desert and let nature take it back again.

He was walking in a trance, surrounded by a rim of large boulders casting inviting shadows. He would head for one of these places, curl up, and let go. He stumbled forward, his legs swinging pendulum-like, on the verge of collapse.

Now that his decision was made, a peacefulness took over. It was best this way. He had come a long way, but he had come up short. So he would pass into the next life, hopefully seeing the design to this existence that had seemed like chaos as he lived it.

He was almost to the shadows among the rocks now. Almost there. The cold he had felt earlier was quickly gathering around his ankles. It seemed to swirl around his legs and move its icy grip up his body. But it was no longer pleasant. It was so much colder now. It was too cold. Too cold.

And then the desert alkali fields around him seemed to turn to snow, and he was a boy again. It was winter, and he was playing in freshly fallen snow in his backyard. He was tired, and the sun was setting sending shadows across his yard as the cold fell. Night was coming, and his teeth chattered, and there was no feeling in his hands. But he wasn't worried, because he looked across the snowy yard and saw his back door. The lights were on inside, and he knew that when he reached the house, he would step inside, into the light and warmth. And he would be home again.

FIFTY-FIVE

Shadows slid across the valley floor as Garrett reached the turnoff to Wild Rose Canyon. The heat was starting to abate, so he rolled the windows down and smelled the dust as it swirled in through the window. He scanned the sky and saw helicopters far off, hovering over the horizon, still searching for his father to the south. Garrett had spent the afternoon out in the heat, searching for his father, shoulder to shoulder with the local search and rescue teams. They looked in tumbled-down prospector's shacks, in vacant mining buildings, down abandoned mine shafts. All the while they were dogged by TV reporters who stopped him for interviews, asking questions in respectful tones, trying not to unnecessarily abuse the feelings of the distraught next of kin. He had answered with resolve tinged with sadness. He wasn't giving up, he said bravely, stubbornly. His father was out there somewhere, and he was going to find him.

And now he would find his father. But the cameras and the search and rescue teams wouldn't be there when he found him because, unfortunately, he had to face his father alone. *It's sad that it has come to this*, Garrett thought, making the turn onto the dirt road. He really didn't want to do this at all. He had hoped that the problem would take care of itself, that his father would expire peacefully in a shack in the mountains somewhere, without him having to take steps. But he had to make sure he was finally free of him.

He had grown up expecting that he would not only be as famous as his father, but surpass him in some way. He felt that was the way it was supposed to happen—to surpass the previous generation. But when it didn't seem to be happening, a little voice inside began telling him he was inferior, he didn't have his father's talent, and finally, that he was worthless. *Not only that,* the voice whispered, *but you'll look pathetic in your attempts to create something unique, something that's your own.*

But all that changed this morning. He cut a deal with the studios to host a show with or without his father.

"The exposure you're getting is going to mean killer ratings in the fall lineup," the network executive purred. In the background Garrett heard a TV and a reporter's voice, a live report from the scene of the search for Walt Stuckey. First there was the news of the kidnapping. Then, the report of the murder on Mount Whitney. Now it was the hit and run of a broadcast reporter in Death Valley. Everyone in the country was glued to their sets, not knowing what would happen next. And behind the scenes, Garrett was pulling the strings like some powerful producer, creating a new reality that gripped the nation.

Thinking ahead, Garrett visualized the next big development in the story. Tomorrow morning sometime, the news would break that Walt Stuckey had been found in a shack in the mountains. There might be an hour or two of agonizing speculation, contradictory bulletins: Oh my God, was he alive or dead? The camera would be trained on Garrett's tense face as the world waited for an answer. Finally, the word would come: the great entertainer was dead. The pain, the sorrow, the tragedy! The drama! Garrett could see it all, feel it all as if he had become the recipient of a wave of sympathy pouring through the television set.

"Let me put it this way," the executive had said. "If Walt comes back, we'll do the show. If Walt is, uh, no longer available, we still want you."

We want you. Sweeter words were never spoken to him. They wanted Garrett. Just Garrett. And he didn't want anything screwing it up. Now that he had dealt with Jack Dillon and Mary, there was only one thing left to take care of. The evidence Jack said he had left with Walt. Garrett didn't want anything to come back to bite him, so he would do his damage control up front. He couldn't let any interviews reach the media—like that one he had found on the disk he had taken out of the reporter's purse. Good thing he cut that off at the source.

So Garrett knew he had until sunset to face this problem. He dropped Ernie off back at Furnace Creek and headed into the mountains alone in the Explorer. He wouldn't expect Ernie to understand what he was going to do. He would have to do this alone. It had been twenty-four hours since his father was abandoned up there. But Jack Dillon, being the Good Samaritan jerk-off that he was, had probably given him food and water and blankets to survive all this time. He had about a two-hour window to achieve his mission before the C-130 climbed into the air and searched the cooling surface of the earth for signs of life in this hostile environment.

Garrett shifted into four-wheel drive and began the climb into the canyon, retracing the steps he had taken last night just before he intercepted Jack. That made him think of Jack and Mary and where he had dumped them in the desert. How long had they lasted? He pictured them, exposed on the desert floor, dying in a blaze of sunlight, at least fifty miles from where the search parties were looking for Walt. While most people knew about Death Valley, they didn't realize that the national park extended nearly a hundred miles to the north and included many remote sections inaccessible by road. Within days, most signs of foul play—their cuts and bruises from the accident—would be unrecognizable. In a few weeks, the evidence would be completely gone. In a few months they would be just bones bleached by the sun.

The road reached the mouth of the canyon and began to climb. Garrett realized he was already feeling a sense of relief as he thought about the steps he decided to take. Soon he saw the first broken-down shacks of the ghost town. The houses cast jagged shadows as he rolled down the deserted main street. On the first pass he didn't see the house with the rose over the door. So he turned down a side street. And then another, his eyes darting from one house to the next. But then, at dusk, with the sun disappearing behind the mountains, there stood the house in front of him, the house with the faded stencil of a rose over the door.

He heard a helicopter buzzing in the distance so he parked the Explorer out of sight in a dilapidated shed. Far away, on the valley floor, he heard the drone of the C-130 taxiing on the airport runway. Heading for the house, he picked up his pace.

Garrett's feet boomed on the wooden floor of the old house as he passed through the dining room with the formal table and chairs and the doily on the side table fluttering in the breeze that had kicked up at twilight. He passed through the kitchen with the old woodstove and bottles tipped over on high shelves. Framed by the doorway, he saw the bed with the figure humped underneath the blankets that were pulled up over his father's face. He sat on a chair beside the bed and leaned in close.

"Dad?" he said softly. "Dad, it's Garrett."

His father was motionless. Maybe he was already gone. But no, Garrett could hear him breathing hoarsely. He looked around the room. There was food and water and a note pad with his father's writing on it. Maybe that was the evidence Jack had threatened him with. He'd take everything with him, once he was done. Then, when his father was found, it would look like he had been cruelly abandoned to starve to death by Jack Dillon.

Garrett leaned in close to his father's head covered by the blankets. "Dad, I know how, all along, you've wanted me to take your place. What you didn't know was that the one thing holding me back was you. You'll be gone soon, and your passing will give me the boost I need. You're making the ultimate sacrifice a father can make for his son."

Garrett was touched by his own words. Tears were welling in his eyes, and his throat tightened as he felt the significance of the drama he was playing out. "You have an amazing legacy. And as people mourn your passing, your legacy will be passed to me. It's my turn now. My turn to have real success—the success you knew all your life. It's my turn now."

A huge sob rose in Garrett's chest. And as the tears fell, he felt an unexpected sense of release. He would be free now, free for the first time in his life. It would be just him—no more of those hateful comparisons to his father. No more people befriending him to get to his father. No more people asking, "What was he really like—your father?" From here on in, he'd be running the show. He'd be the one in charge.

Lying at the foot of the bed was a bulky comforter. Garrett carefully folded it so there was a neat, flat surface, big enough to cover a man's face. He held it poised above his father's still figure. He wanted to make this quick and easy. The last thing he wanted was a messy struggle. He set the comforter down and gently peeled the blankets back to reveal his father's head.

But in the gloom he realized that something didn't make sense. His father's hair was not a gray fringe surrounding a bald head. The figure below had curly brown hair, and the head and shoulders were bigger than his father's frail old body. He hovered above the breathing figure, trying to make sense of what he saw: a man's back turned toward him, the elbow crooked and pointed upward. Then suddenly, that elbow swung up and caught him in the jaw, snapping his head sideways and knocking him back across the room.

As Garrett staggered back, shaking his head to clear his vision, the blanket flew aside. And Jack rose to his feet and stood in front of him.

FIFTY-SIX

That afternoon, as Jack stumbled forward, suffering from the final stages of heat exhaustion, hallucinating that he was walking through snow, he had been spotted by a father and son exploring the desert in their ATVs. They helped him to their camper and let him rest in the shade on a reclining lawn chair, draped with towels soaked in water.

As Jack's mind cleared, he explained that he had been exploring the desert the previous night with his girlfriend when they had an accident. They drove him back to where Mary was waiting in the Pathfinder. When she saw Jack returning, she hugged him, pressing her face against his, and whispered, "I never gave up hope. I knew you'd come back."

They poured gas into the Pathfinder, and it started right up. Jack assured his rescuers they could make it to safety on their own. They drove to a little town just over the border into Nevada, where they cleaned themselves up in a gas station bathroom. Then Mary, wearing a scarf and sunglasses, checked into a motel where they rested for the afternoon, getting rehydrated and bandaging their cuts and bruises. They slept and waited in an air-conditioned motel room, watching live TV coverage of the search for Walt Stuckey. Slowly, they pieced together what had happened. And began to plan their next move.

An hour before sunset, Jack and Mary headed back toward Beveridge. As Jack drove back toward the jagged, dark mountains surrounding Death Valley, he thought of that day in Pajaro Beach when Garrett had fired him. Jack could remember the look on Garrett's enraged face, hear his mocking voice, recall the insults. He remembered how his body tightened, ready to smash his fist in Garrett's laughing face. But he had held off for the sake of Walt's book.

But Jack also had to make sure Garrett was arrested along with the evidence to put him away. He stopped at a pay phone along the way and called the Pajaro Beach police dispatcher. He told the dispatcher to relay the location in Beveridge to the police chief, knowing he would arrive a half hour behind him.

With these things in motion, Jack sped back up the winding dirt road with Mary beside him, back up into the mountains, to the ghost town, to get there before Garrett. They had seen Garrett on TV, seen him leaving the police command center in late-afternoon, planning to join searchers looking for his father in Skidoo. So at least Garrett hadn't been to Beveridge yet. Jack figured he was probably waiting to go there after dark, hoping to be one step ahead of the search party.

When Jack and Mary got to the little house, Walt was mad as hell that they had left him alone so long. Jack carried Walt out of the house, feeling the frail old man in his arms, and put him in the Pathfinder, parked out of sight nearby. Mary climbed in with Walt, calming him, talking to him, telling him Jack still had something to do before they could head back to safety. Jack returned to the room where Walt had been and carefully set up the video camera on a high shelf. He kept the remote control in his hand.

At dusk, with the light fading and the desert air finally cooling, Jack heard the drone of an approaching car engine. Staying out of sight, he watched Garrett's white Explorer come down the abandoned street and park out front. He had a strange feeling as he watched from his hiding place, knowing that Garrett had no idea what he was walking into. Jack also had a wonderful feeling of anticipation. He felt his hands balling into fists, and he rubbed the calluses on his knuckles, calluses he had built up with years of bare-knuckled bag work at the gym. Then Jack turned on the video camera and lay down on the bed, pulling the covers up over his head. He remained motionless as Garrett walked into the room and hovered above, whispering into his ear, giving him the evidence he needed. When Garrett started to make his move, Jack hit him with an elbow and stood up.

Now Jack stood in front of Garrett. Ready.

"Jack!" Garrett's forehead knotted in confusion and then twisted into a look of defiance and rage. Jack just stood there, enjoying the show, enjoying being in control at last.

Finally, Garrett seemed to decide his best approach was anger. "Where the hell's my father?"

"Outside. In my car. Mary's taking care of him."

"I want to see him *now*."

"Sorry, Garrett, he doesn't want to see you."

"What are you talking about?" Garrett said, shifting to one side, moving quietly on the pine floorboards, looking for the best angle of attack. Jack anticipated that—he wanted that—but he knew he'd have to be careful to finish this quickly before the police got here and took Garrett away.

"Remember that day you fired me?" Jack asked. "You threw my manuscript all over the place—called me a hack writer and a whole lot of other stuff."

"Oh Jesus, why go into that now?"

"There was something I wanted to do then that I'm gonna do now."

"Yeah?" Garrett said, imitating the Jersey accent. "Whatcha gonna do?"

"You're about to find out. You ready?"

Garrett laughed. "Jack, buddy, you looked in the mirror lately? You're death warmed over, man." Garrett had his hands up now, gesturing, legs apart. Jack just stood there, balanced, waiting for him to come at him. But he didn't want it to start yet. There was something else that had to happen first. Something far more important than personal gratification.

"Remember how you said Walt's book would never get published?"

"Jack, you're beating a dead horse. No one wants your pathetic manuscript."

"Actually, as you're about to see, I now have something every publisher in New York is going to want."

"And what is that?"

"The reason Walt's show was canceled."

Jack pressed the remote. The camera on the shelf came to life, the viewfinder screen on the side folded out so they could see it clearly. Garrett's head spun toward the camera on the shelf beside him.

"The hell's this?" Garrett snarled.

"I recorded this yesterday. Here's what your father told me."

Using the remote, Jack pressed play. Walt's face filled the screen, and they heard his familiar voice. Then Jack's voice was asking, "Walt, I still don't get why these guys from Washington would kill your show. Was it just because you were taking shots at the president's friend?"

"Look, about five years before, I had them pull the file, thinking they'd destroy it, okay? Later, I do the bit about Bebe Rebozo, and it's a big hit. I start doing it every week. Those bastards, Nixon's dirty-tricks guys, they start to lean on me about pulling the routine. Nixon's ratings are tanking, and Rebozo is the punchline of all my jokes. Now other comics and columnists are following my lead. But I refuse to back off, okay? So Nixon's henchmen say, 'You pull the gag, or we'll make this file public.'"

Garrett stood frozen, gaping at the screen.

On the recording, Jack asked Walt, "So what the hell was in the file? Was it something you did?"

"Jack, believe me, if it was about me, I wouldn't have given a damn. They had a file on Garrett—my son Garrett."

"Garrett?"

"Yeah, he was a troubled kid."

Jack turned and looked at Garrett in the small room. He was breathing hoarsely, his face reddening, his eyes riveted on the screen. He seemed to know what was coming.

"So what was in this file?" Jack asked Walt on the recording.

"Everything. The police records, the hospital records—everything."

"Garrett was hurt?" Jack asked.

"Not Garrett's hospital record! The girl's. The girl that he— The file had every damn thing he did to her. I gave her family a fortune to keep 'em quiet. But the feds got the medical records, the police report. It's all in the damn file."

"You're sayin' they blackmailed you by trying to nail Garrett for—?"

"Yes! Hell yes. Rape, aggravated assault, the whole nine yards. The girl was only fourteen. You know what that means! Garrett was eighteen, so they'd try him as an adult. They would put him away. It'd ruin his life. So I told Bill Paley, the network, I told them all I was done. And walked out."

"You threw away the show for Garrett?" Jack asked.

"I had to keep my hope alive."

"Your hope for what?"

"See, Jack, I had all the success, all the accolades, all the money I could ever want. But as you get older, there's something that becomes more important. See, the real measure of a man is what he leaves behind for future generations. Usually, you pass this on to your son. I wanted to pass the baton to Garrett. How could I do that if he was destroyed by this thing? What can I say, Jack? I love him. He's my son, and I love him."

Using the remote, Jack stopped the camera. "I want you to hear that part again, Garrett." He backed it up and ran the final words over again. "What can I say, Jack? I love him. He's my son, and I love him."

Jack stopped the camera. Then, using the remote control, he pressed the record button. The red light began blinking, the blank lens staring down at them, waiting.

Jack turned to Garrett, who was still staring at the blank screen. His chest was heaving, and his hoarse breath rasped in his throat. Once again, Jack thought about their plan to make him so enraged his heart exploded. Maybe it would work after all.

Slowly, Garrett turned to Jack. His voice was very quiet.

"What do you plan to do with that tape?"

"Air the interview. Put it in the book."

"Why?"

"People should know what happened. Our government killed one of the greatest shows ever. And the greatest entertainer of our time killed his own show to protect his son."

Garrett was silent a long time. Finally, speaking very softly, he said, "That camera's not leaving this room."

Jack's response was to point to the camera. "You're on the record, Garrett. And that's your response?"

"My response? To what?"

"There's not gonna be a father-and-son show. No spin-offs or movie deals. No fans for you. No people begging you for autographs or whatever pathetic dream you had. You'll just be an embarrassing footnote to your father's brilliant career."

The room was filled with the hoarse sound of Garrett gulping air, his nostrils flaring, the color rising up his neck and into his face.

"You can't stop me. I made a deal. The executives want me." He pounded his chest. "They want me! Not my father!"

"You shot a cop, you hired a hit man, you ran down a TV reporter. I don't think the network's gonna want anything to do with you."

Garrett was ready to blow now, so Jack had to be ready. *Light on your feet*, he told himself. *Get light. And get ready.*

"I'd enjoy this a lot more if I didn't know how much it hurt your father. Your father was a selfish tyrant. He could be a real son of a bitch. But he was a genius. He gave this country something beautiful. And he did everything to see that you would pick up where he left off. But there was one problem, Garrett."

"Oh yeah? What's that?"

"You have no talent—not a single shred of original talent."

Jack's simple statement struck Garrett at some deep level of his subconscious. A low moan started in Garrett's chest and grew. It was the hideous sound of a man's dreams being crushed. The moaning grew like the high whining that releases into sobbing. But the release never came, and the whining grew without control, getting in Jack's head and expanding. He was completely unprepared for this primal, naked reaction. He stood flat-footed, reeling. And that's why he wasn't ready when Garrett charged, not attacking him but lunging wildly for the camera. Jack missed a beat, moving at the last instant as Garrett's body was outstretched, his hand almost to the camera on the high shelf. Jack threw himself sideways across the rushing form, like a crossbody block in football. Garrett dropped and crashed head first into the wall. But he was on his feet in a flash, hands balled into fists, trying to drive through Jack, to the camera.

Jack let Garrett come. Then he spun, throwing an elbow that caught Garrett behind his left ear. Jack felt the bone-on-bone crack of a pure hit. Garrett went down, shook it off, and was back up fast, so much faster than Jack expected. He drove again for the camera, but Jack stepped in and hit him with a right cross that turned him so Jack could take a half step back and launch a kick up and under his ribs. Garrett crashed into the wall, rolled, and stood up with a revolver in his hand, Jack's nickel-plated five-shot Smith & Wesson that he had dropped by the trailer in the mountains.

Jack felt the bullet rip past his cheek, slicing the air. He turned and saw the revolver coming up again, saw everything hyperclear in that weird slow motion of a fight. Garrett was pulling the trigger, the hammer rising...He dove in under the gun, catching Garrett low across the chest.

This shot exploded above his head. They were rolling across the floor. Jack had to keep Garrett's arms raised so he couldn't angle the gun down for a shot at him. Garrett shifted the gun, worked an arm free, and hammered down on Jack's head with the gun butt. Jack's world shuddered, his vision blurred. He released Garrett, rolled away, found his feet and—

Garrett was on one knee, coming up off the floor, the gun coming up, pointing at him. Jack saw the barrel gleaming dully, the black hole of the muzzle sucking him in. Then he heard a quiet voice, a voice from his years of training, for just one moment. *Always strike with your closest weapon.*

Jack saw Garrett's finger closing on the trigger. He flicked his left hand out and backhanded the gun barrel so it angled away as—

The muzzle spit fire.

Jack grabbed Garrett's gun hand, held him by the wrist, turned his arm to lock the joint, rolled his weight against it and—*crack!* The gun clattered to the floor. He released Garrett's wrist and heard him go down. He rose, turned, ready to crush Garrett's Adam's apple. But—

The room exploded in light. Lights angling at him from all directions, lights blinding him.

"Police! On the floor!"

Footsteps on the wood floor. Feet scraping, furniture falling. Lights crisscrossing, stabbing his eyes. More lights outside. The roar of a helicopter overhead.

Jack tried to see where Garrett had fallen. But he was gone. He frantically scanned the floor for the gun. He heard Garrett's footsteps, feet scrambling on pine boards, saw him picking up the gun with his left hand.

"Police! Don't move!"

Figures moved into the room, shining flashlights in Jack's eyes. He had a stroboscopic view of Garrett, gun in his hand, aiming and...pain exploded in Jack's thigh. Burning, *Jesus,* burning like he had aimed an acetylene torch at his leg. His muscles turned to mush, and he went down.

Flashes of light. Garrett aiming the gun at Jack's chest. But Jack couldn't move. Could only wait for the bullet to rip through his lungs. But—

Shots fired from different locations. Garrett spun, a black swath of blood sprayed across his white shirtfront. He staggered back and fell, back arching, mouth open, screaming in pain.

Moments later, a cop bent over Jack, the cop who had been shot in the mountains, the one he'd learned was Chief Ullrich. The cop's shoulder was bandaged, arm in a sling.

Ullrich shone the flashlight in Jack's face, leaned in close. "You the one who called me?"

Jack tried to answer.

"You couldn't have given me a little more time to get up here? But I guess you wanted to be a hero. Take him on your own?" the cop asked.

"Complicated—" was all Jack could say. "Can't explain."

"Where's Walt Stuckey?"

Jack spoke through grinding teeth. "Outside...in my car."

"And Mary LeBeau?"

"With him."

Ullrich nodded, as if he had guessed the answers to his questions. He turned his flashlight onto the gunshot wound on Jack's leg. He wadded up his jacket and handed it to Jack. "Hold this on it. And press like hell."

Ullrich turned to his deputy and barked. "He's been hit. Get him down the mountain. And get a tourniquet on him fast." Jack felt a powerful grip on his arm. He was suddenly on his feet, his weight on his good leg. A cop was lashing a belt around his thigh. He looked across the room at Garrett, writhing, his legs kicking him around in circles, the deputies standing above, guns still trained on him.

"What about him?" the deputy asked the chief, jerking a thumb at Garrett.

"Handcuff that piece of shit." Ullrich steadied Jack and started him toward the door.

"You gotta get the camera," Jack said.

"What?"

"The camera, there, on the shelf." Jack's words were oddly hollow. Why was he so light-headed? Jack was swaying, words echoing down a long tunnel. He had to do this fast. "On the camera, there's a statement from Walt Stuckey."

Ullrich took the camera down. Jack pressed the buttons to lock the files. Ullrich handed it to a deputy, who dropped it into an evidence bag. Seeing this, and knowing that it was safe, Jack felt he could finally let go.

The deputy threw Jack's arm across his shoulder and took his weight off the bad leg. They hobbled out into the dusty street and the dark night that was cooling fast.

"On the camera," Jack said, "is a message from Walt to his fans. Give it to the news. His fans have to see it." Jack was running out of energy.

"Where'd you say Walt Stuckey and Mary LeBeau are?" Ullrich asked.

"There," Jack said, pointing at a nearby barn.

It was the last thing he remembered for a while. Next thing he knew he was flying across the black desert, propped up in the backseat of a patrol car. And it suddenly felt very cold.

Ullrich turned and looked at Jack's face, and Jack hated the look he saw on the cop's face. Ullrich turned back to the deputy and said, "Dammit! Can't you drive any faster?"

Jack felt a hand touch him. He looked up and saw he was leaning up against Walt. The old man was holding him, smoothing his hair off his sweating forehead. And when Jack saw the fear in Walt's eyes, he knew how bad he must look. But before he left, he would have to tell Walt what had started all this. He would have to make sure that his old friend knew the story behind this story. He had to tell him now. And there wasn't much time.

"Hey, Walt."

"I'm here, Jack."

"Gotta tell you something."

"What's that, Jack?"

"When I was a kid. I'd sneak out of bed listen to your show. Just *listen*. Okay?"

"What do you mean?"

"My parents wouldn't let me watch—it too late. So I listened from upstairs, because I could hear him—my dad—downstairs. And he was laughing."

Walt waited for more. He looked puzzled.

"*It was the only time he ever laughed!*" Jack whispered desperately. "You made him laugh." He had to make Walt understand. Because that had been the point all along, the reason he had done this. He had to make Walt see what he had done for Jack's father—for everyone who watched his show.

"Lying there, listening to my dad laugh..." He was running out of breath now, out of time. The darkness of the desert gathered around him, suffocating him. But he had to finish. He had to.

"Walt, buddy."

"Still here, Jack."

"When I heard Dad laugh, it was like music to me. It made me feel that, maybe there was a chance...maybe life is good."

He was surprised by his own words. But he knew it was true: when you laughed you felt that life was good. *Life is good.* Those would be his last words, Jack realized, as he felt his consciousness shrinking to a single point of light, like an old TV going off, a point of light that was quickly fading, no bigger than an atom, yet filled with a lifetime of memories for a man whose life was built on such high hopes and great dreams, most of which were left unattained. It had been a life of struggle. Ending in chaos. But still, *life is good.*

If Jack had been able to hold on for a few more minutes, he would have been pleased to see what happened. The patrol car roared up to the Furnace Creek infirmary, and the media guys, who'd gotten wind of the shooting, caught him on videotape, his head resting on Walt's shoulder, tears pouring down the old entertainer's face, a face filled with every shade of comedy and tragedy. The sad old face, with the wounded younger man lying against him, appeared on the front page of every newspaper in the country the next morning.

FIFTY-SEVEN

Jack wrote "The End" after the last lines of his novel and set his pen down next to his notebook. He sat back in the steel chair in the Monterey County Jail library and stretched, feeling relieved that he'd finally gotten it all down on paper, just the way it had happened, including how he had almost died in the back of the patrol car. But luckily, Chief Ullrich got him to the infirmary in time for the doctors to stop the bleeding caused by the bullet wound in his thigh. It had all been worth it, though, because now he could give his novel that magical tag line: "Based on a true story."

Unfortunately, his fifteen minutes of fame turned out to be almost literally fifteen minutes. For a few days after his arrest he was in the headlines and on the evening news. But by the time he began turning in his opening chapters to his agent, Carolyn, the news of the world had moved on. The editors she showed his writing to were encouraging but said it either needed to stand on its own or get another push of publicity before a publisher would buy it. So he quickly went from media hero to just another desperate guy rotting away in jail.

As he flipped through the notebook, reading what he had written, he thought how it had been lucky, in a way, that he got a year's sentence for the aggravated assault on Ernie. With all the publicity, the DA didn't want a media circus and offered Jack a year of easy time in county jail for his guilty plea. It was enough time for Jack to get his novel written. And he still had two months left to serve. Maybe by the time they released him

Carolyn would have sold his novel, and he might have some money with which to rebuild his life. He would need it, because he had lost the rights to Walt Stuckey's biography. Garrett would be listed as the author on the cover of that book. He survived his gunshot wound and was doing hard time in Soledad on two counts of attempted murder—one for his father and one for the reporter he ran down. Being in prison didn't stop Garrett from using the family fortune to hire a slick entertainment lawyer and lock up the rights to his father's biography, *Off and Running*. Jack kept hoping that Walt would get well enough to step in and give Jack credit, or at least a percentage of the royalties. But so far, the courts deemed Walt "mentally compromised" and "unable to make rational decisions." So now, the presses were set to roll, and all the book chain stores were ready with big promotional campaigns.

When Jack thought of that book—his book—-with Garrett's name on it, his anger was so strong he could feel blood pounding in his head, and he looked around for something to punch or kick or throw across his jail cell. But eventually he channeled his anger into writing his own book, and the words poured out onto the page until he got it all down on paper just the way it happened.

"Hey, Shakespeare!" He turned and saw one of the guards with a mocking grin on his face. The guards watched him writing in the dayroom and taunted him, calling him just another jailhouse Shakespeare.

"Hey, Shakespeare!" the guard yelled again, turning away from a TV set where a cluster of guards were watching some breaking news story. "You got a visitor!"

It must be Carolyn, Jack thought, *coming to get the handwritten manuscript*. She would have it typed up, edited, and sent off to New York. Jack tried to imagine what Sarah would think if his novel was published. Actually, he wasn't as concerned about her since they were divorced now. But he was worried about Chloe, hoping his daughter could understand what it had all been about, why there were pictures of her father in prison clothes, appearing in court. He wanted her to know he had good reasons for what he had done, and how sometimes you had to go outside the law. They'd have a lot to talk about next time she visited. She had only come once, with Sarah, and they sat in the dayroom, Jack realizing how quickly she was growing up. And how much he wanted to be with her. But without money, or a job, how could he expect to share custody?

Jack walked into the visitor's lounge and saw a woman with her back turned to him, waiting, staring out the window at the hazy blue mountains east of Salinas. They were the same mountains that had inspired his favorite writer, John Steinbeck, and were described in the opening of his book *Of Mice and Men*. Jack thought of that often as he sat here on long afternoons writing his own book.

When the woman turned to face him, Jack saw he was wrong. It wasn't Carolyn. It was someone he hadn't seen for months, but who had been on his mind every second of every day since he was shot and arrested ten months ago.

"Hello, Jack," Mary said, smiling. Her hair was parted high on her forehead. Maybe she did that to hide the scar she got from being thrown into the windshield of the Pathfinder. Whatever. The point was, it made her look classy. She was dressed in that simple way that Jack liked, black pants that fit her just right, a tight white top. She looked good. Hell, she looked great.

She saw the notebook in his hand and smiled. "Your novel?"

"Yeah."

"How'd it turn out?"

"It was like taking dictation," Jack said.

"Am I in it?"

"Well, there is a character named Ann Chandler."

He saw her search for the name then remember it had been her alias when they were separated in Death Valley. She gave him a look, like he was messing with her. And maybe he was. He had a lot of anger for the way she'd left him stranded in prison, never bothering to visit him. And that was even after he fought with the D.A., claiming that the whole scheme was his idea and getting her a suspended sentence with no jail time.

"So, what brings you here?" he managed to ask.

"I thought it was time. Especially now, since—" She suddenly looked as if she might cry. But then she caught herself and added, "I'm just really sad about what's happened."

She waited to see how that sat with him. But he didn't give her much to work with, just nodded and waited for more. Prison had taught him to be patient.

"Last time I heard Walt on the news he sounded good," Jack said.

She nodded. "He had some very good days. Days when he seemed like his old self. And then he'd always say, 'Let's go see my buddy, Jack.' But the doctors didn't want him traveling. And I was so busy taking care of him. That's why I never visited. I hope you understand."

"Oh sure. I understand."

"But there were other days when he was so confused—terrified. It hurt me to see him suffering like that. It seemed so pointless. He had a good life, and there was no chance he'd recover."

She paused, and in the silence Jack thought how great it was to hear Mary's voice again, the lisp whispering around the edges of her words, the little flaw that made her seem vulnerable and always appealing. He'd almost forgotten that. And he had forgotten how she made him feel so special, so intimate. *It's you and me now, Jack,* she had said to him that night in the cabin. But then she had returned to Walt's side after Jack was arrested and began taking care of him, hiring nutritionists and specialists and speech therapists. So Jack had tried to forget she ever said that. As long as Walt was alive, Mary would stay with him. Loyalty, Jack rationalized, was a good thing.

"I wanted to tell you about something that happened that night," Mary suddenly said.

"That night?"

"The night you got shot, when they arrested Garrett. After they took you away, everyone left me there, in that ghost town. I was there alone before the crime lab guys arrived."

"Weren't you in the cruiser with me and Walt?"

"No. No. That's what I'm saying. See, I went back into that little house—back to the room where Walt had been. I don't know why I went back there. I wasn't looking for anything. But—"

"You weren't?" Jack wondered why he couldn't he accept anything she said at face value.

She looked hurt. "Why do you say it that way?"

"I'm just trying to understand," Jack said. "So what happened?"

She turned and looked out the window again. With her eyes turned away, Jack was able to look her over, at her shoulders and back, her hips and long legs. It had been a long ten months, locked up here, and he felt stirred up and restless. "I'm forty now, Jack," she said suddenly, disconnecting from the story she'd been telling.

"You came here to tell me that?"

"That's a tough age for a woman. A year and a half ago I thought I had it made, traveling around with Walt. Everything first class, the best hotels. The world was open in front of me. I thought it'd never end."

"Yeah, you told me that before."

"Oh. Right."

"Life moves on—I get that. I mean, it's moved on for me too. I'll be out soon—an ex-con, no job, no money. What kind of a life will I have?"

She started to speak. But then she got lost in the past, staring at the mountains that had kept him company all these months. In the silence, he remembered what it was like to hold her that night in the cabin in Lone Pine. *It's you and me now, Jack.* They had been so close to it that night. And they never got back there. Lying awake in his cell at night, Jack reviewed those moments many times. Now, here was the real woman, in front of him, close enough that he could smell her. Reality, memories, and fantasies blurred in his mind until he almost felt dizzy.

"Okay. So you went back into the room where Walt had been," Jack prompted.

"Yes."

"And you found something."

"Yes. I found Walt's drawing pad. I took it with me. I knew if they put it in evidence I'd never get it back. I flipped through it quickly. And then I put it somewhere and forgot about it."

"You forgot about it," Jack echoed.

"Yes. I did. And then last week I came across it again. And I found something I missed the first time. Something Walt had written." She took a single sheet of paper from her pocket and unfolded it. "I made a copy of it for you. Walt must have written it while he was up there alone."

Jack suddenly remembered how, as he was leaving to meet Mary on the last night, he had looked back and seen Walt bent over the drawing pad. He remembered thinking how he was writing—not drawing, like he usually did. But in the chaos that followed, he'd completely forgotten about that moment. And its possible significance.

"What did he write?" Jack couldn't be patient anymore. "What did Walt write?"

She struggled to speak, forehead knotted, lips quivering. Then she found her voice and finally said it as if it hurt her, but she was trying to be reasonable.

"Read it yourself."

She thrust the paper at Jack and turned away. It was an addendum to Walt's will, in his shaky handwriting. He read it quickly, a wave of relief sweeping across his body. It was obvious that Walt hadn't forgotten him, that Jack wasn't just another one of *those* people that were always after Walt and his money. They had shared a friendship and created something real.

Jack looked up and saw Mary was watching him.

"Is it going to stand up in court?" he asked her.

"I had a lawyer look at it. He said that with Garrett in jail, and all the publicity about what you did for Walt, it's possible. He said he thinks he can find a doctor, a specialist, who will testify that Walt lived in two worlds—the present and the past. And that this was written in the present. We've definitely got a good case."

"*We've* got a case?"

"Well, yes, Jack," she said, her eyes searching him, looking for reassurance. "I mean, Walt said it was what he wanted."

"When?"

"In the cabin that night. He said, 'It's you and Jack.'"

Jack let that slide for now. He reread the note. "It's very generous," he said at last. He realized he was having trouble talking.

"It's more than he left me. I'm not in the will at all."

Jack might have picked up on the bitterness in her tone, but he was still thinking about how this would change things for him.

"If this goes through, you could get a lot," Mary said. "You could be very rich."

Jack looked back down at the copy of the will. Something was nagging him. Something wasn't complete yet.

"But this is a copy," Jack finally said. "They'll never accept this unless I show them the real thing, in his handwriting, dated, signed."

"I have the original."

"Why didn't you bring it?"

"I'm keeping it safe for you."

And how do I get the original? He wanted to ask her, but he didn't have to. Because he knew the answer: she wanted part of everything. It wasn't like that was a bad thing. Because he wanted her. And it was okay, now that Sarah had cut him loose. And Chloe seemed to be doing okay. He was free to do what he wanted. Lying in his cell bunk at night, everything Mary had said came back to him with new meaning. And he saw them being together at some point, maybe after Walt was gone. But when would that be? How old would they be?

"You'll need to think about what you want to do about this," Mary said. "I really think you deserve what Walt is giving you." She indicated the will that Jack was still holding.

"You were there," Jack said. "We did it together. So you deserve something too."

Relief spread across her face. For the first time, she looked flustered. She blinked back tears and breathed deeply. "Thank you, Jack."

There. They had a deal. Now all that stood between them and being together was their mutual respect for their friend. But Walt was confused, Mary had said. He was suffering. Jack hated to think of that.

"Hey, Shakespeare!" the guard yelled. "Someone else here to see you. You know the rules—one visitor at a time."

This had to be Carolyn. Time to wrap this up. Mary started for the door.

"Mary?" Jack said. She turned. "Thank Walt for me. Okay?"

She looked at him oddly. "You know I can't do that."

"Why not? You said you're with him every day."

She studied his face and suddenly understood. "Oh my God, Jack. You haven't heard."

"Heard what?"

"It's all over the news. I assumed you knew. I was so torn up, I guess I just wanted to pretend it wasn't true." She paused, her eyes preparing him for the news. "Walt died this morning."

Her simple statement stopped the flow of all thought in Jack's mind. For the first time in his life, his mind was completely empty. He was aware of each passing second, of each sound in the jail around him, the slamming of doors, the coughs of prisoners in distant cells. But there were no thoughts around any of this, because he never saw it coming. And now that it was here, everything Mary had said, and the way she acted, fit in place.

Abruptly, the film strip of Jack's life started running again, and everything rushed at him at once.

"I thought you knew," Mary was saying. "That's why I'm here. That's why I showed you his will."

Jack's mind was racing to catch up, to rearrange the pieces and understand what the hell was really going on. But there were too many things lying under the surface that he didn't fully understand.

"I thought Walt was getting better," he said.

"He was, but he was so confused—terrified. I couldn't stand to see him like that." She paused, tears trickling down her cheeks. "At least he died peacefully."

Jack stood there staring at her, the feeling of loss hitting him. He'd always thought he'd see Walt after he got out of prison, see him one last time. He liked to picture himself talking to his friend again, like they did when they used to sit around the coffee table in the house in the Hollywood Hills, with the rain coming down outside. Sharing secrets and laughing. He wanted to turn back time and do that again. But Walt was gone. Then, another side of his mind took over as he realized how incredible the timing was. Here was his novel, almost ready for submission, and now Walt dies. His death would give his novel the push needed to sell it. He hated to think that way but…

Then something else occurred to him. "You were there? When he died?"

She nodded. "He died in my arms."

Mary's words echoed in his head. *Died in my arms.* What did that mean? Jack searched her eyes looking for the answer. He thought that, if he stared at her long enough, maybe he could look right into her heart, to see what was there. Because he wasn't finding any answers in her eyes. Her face always seemed to be in a shadow, her motives unclear.

Jack came out of his thoughts and found Mary reading his expression, watching him cycle through the thoughts she had explored many times.

"Are we okay, Jack?"

He found he was still holding the copy of the addendum to the will, written in Walt's uncertain handwriting, so he read it again: "To Jack Dillon, a true friend who risked everything to help me, I leave the advance money for my autobiography, *Off and Running.* I also leave Jack Dillon all rights to *Off and Running,* including all current and future television and movie rights. Additionally, the book will have the following credit: 'By Walt Stuckey with Jack Dillon.'"

"You're an author now, Jack," Mary said, smiling. "Isn't that what you wanted all along?"

Author. He let that word sink in. He wasn't just another jailhouse wannabe with a notebook full of scribbling. He was going to be a real published author. He pictured the printers tearing the plates off the presses for *Off and Running,* changing the name on the dust jacket cover, removing the name Garrett Stuckey and putting in Jack Dillon. He felt a huge weight of resentment and bitterness lifting. And he knew he should just accept all this and move on. But he had to know.

"You say Walt died this morning?"

"That's right."

"So when did you have time to take this will to a lawyer?"

"A few weeks ago. Why does it matter?"

"You get a thumbs up from the lawyer last week and, lo and behold, this week Walt dies."

"He was suffering terribly, Jack. I did the right thing. You have to trust me. Now it's up to you."

She stood there, her weight on one leg, arm up in the door frame, studying his face. Then, softly, she added: "It was always you and me, Jack. Since the very first time I saw you, I knew it would be you and me."

And then there were footsteps behind her, Carolyn's footsteps echoed in the hallway. She was coming, accompanied by a guard, calling, "Jack? Jack?"

Mary glanced over her shoulder. They couldn't finish this conversation now. Not now. So she just put on her little voice, the one with the lisp that was so damn appealing, and said, "I know you'll do the right thing, Jack."

And then she left. A few minutes later, Carolyn came in. She stood there in front of Jack with all kinds of news about the biography, about how there was a rumor of a secret will that gave him rights to the book, how, now that Walt was dead, there was tremendous interest in his novel, offers to buy the film rights and a publicity tour for him when he was released.

Listening to Carolyn, all Jack could think was, *Thank God I've got another two months to get my head together, to think through this clearly. Maybe by then I'll figure out the right thing to do.* But he already knew one thing for certain: for a guy in prison, he sure had some damn good options.

THE END

ACKNOWLEDGMENTS

I have a tendency to get stuck halfway through a book and let the uncompleted manuscript sit for a long time, making me feel guilty and irritable. With this book, I showed the first half to my friend and traveling companion Phil Lebherz, who read it and enthusiastically began throwing out ideas. His energy and suggestions led me out of the darkness and helped me find an ending. And for that I'm very grateful. But behind this book is really a team of people who supported this project and deserve thanks. Of course, my wonderful wife Vivian has always been an essential part of the process along with my two creative sons, Drew and Tony. The Mavericks writing group, in particular Martin J. Smith, Carroll Lachnit, and Richard Cheverton were all so helpful. I also want to mention my agent, John Hawkins, who passed away before seeing this book published, but who always encouraged me. And my current agent, Robert Wilson, has been a trusted advisor and a constant friend.

Finally, I want to give my sincere thanks and appreciation to Brash Books founders Lee Goldberg and Joel Goldman, as well as my editor Kristen Weber, and the other folks at this revolutionary publishing company. Lee and Joel are reinventing publishing and I'm proud to be a small part of their bold undertaking.

ABOUT THE AUTHOR

Philip Reed is a former police reporter who turned to writing mysteries, nonfiction books, plays, and screenplays. His first novel *Bird Dog* was nominated for the Edgar and Anthony awards and optioned by Hollywood seven times. His many other books include *Low Rider, Marquis de Fraud, Free Throw*, and *In Search of the Greatest Golf Swing*. He is currently at work writing a nonfiction account of a year spent playing blackjack in casinos across the country with a professional card counter. He lives in Long Beach, California, and is an editor at Edmunds.com.

44214569R00207

Made in the USA
Charleston, SC
17 July 2015